Secrets of the Moon Fox

I0612962

Moonlit Memories: Book One

H. J. Harding

This is a work of fiction. Any resemblance to real people or events is a coincidence. Some places are borrowed, but all were returned more or less intact. No Werefoxes, Faes, or Vampires were harmed in the making of this story. Some humans were annoyed however. If you actually read this, please email the author at hjhardingbooks@gmail.com and let me know.

Finally, Korvou spoke, "How many times have we tried to kill each other?" He probably knew the answer as well as she did. Skipping from topic to topic to keep the other person disoriented, it was a favorite technique of hers. Perhaps one of them had picked it up from the other.

"Between eight and ten depending on how you count attempts. I'm counting Berlin, but not Moscow or Oslo. I don't know if you count them or not. Why, here to increase the tally?" She didn't even have to think about it.

"What about Prague?"

"Prague doesn't count."

"I had a gun to the back of your head for over an hour."

"Exactly. We both knew you wouldn't shoot me. Not a bound opponent and not from behind."

"Did you know that then?"

"Why do you think I didn't try to escape? You were clearly playing a role." She still didn't know the details to that one, but she wasn't going to admit that under anything less than pain of death. "So, eight?"

"Fine. Eight." He waved his hand airily, speaking in that irritating tone of one humoring a small child. Liska fantasized pushing him off her balcony but didn't change her expression at all. The fantasies got more violent as she saw the small notebook in his hand.

Acknowledgements

No book is created alone. This particular book owes its birth to more people than I can list. Some of whom I may never know and would never have met without the magic of the internet. Thank you to the online critiques and those who cared enough to send them. To those who encouraged me enough to continue. Thank you to those who read my earliest drafts and thought I had potential. To Pandaseal who asked me to include a Wererabbit. To Ishling who faithfully encouraged me with every part. To InterNutter who was the first to critique me. To everyone who loved Liska as a character. Thank you to the Critters community for reading my later drafts and other works. Thank you to Petticoat Betty for proofreading this latest draft and being so encouraging. Thank you to the Marscon community for convincing me to take this step.

Thank you to my family for allowing me to spend the last ten years boring you with my ideas and making you re-read the story whenever I made changes. I'm afraid that won't change. Sorry.

Thank you to anyone who reads this book, buys this book, or tells anyone else to buy and read this book. If you've done all three, thank you thrice!

Last but certainly not least, thank you to my Lord and Savior. No accomplish can be made without You, and if it could, it would be meaningless. May this book honor You.

Chapter One

Creatures that stalk the night usually hunt alone. – The
Kikitsutai Book of Wisdom

The third time Anna found her eyes skipping over
words, she gave up on reading. She was simply too
restless to concentrate. It was sheer force of will that
kept her from pacing the tiny college dorm room. If
she thought pacing would help, she probably
wouldn't bother to contain herself. It wasn't like
anyone was here to see her, and she walked too
quietly to be heard in another room.

Anna cast a wistful look to her inline skates
by the door. She wanted to put them on and just
skate somewhere, maybe along the intracoastal,
until she couldn't skate any longer. But no, not right
now. It was late, almost eleven, and West Palm
Beach wasn't the safest place to be out at night. No
point in tempting fate. Not without a reason.

So Anna looked for a reason. Oh, look, she
was almost out of milk. More importantly, she was
running low on tea. The store would close soon, she
had better hurry. It was a lame excuse and she knew
it, she seldom used milk and wouldn't need any of
either before tomorrow, but desperate times...

That settled, she checked the index card she
had filled out that morning. Every morning, after
dressing, she filled out a card listing what she was
wearing to the best of her ability. If anything
happened to her, Ryoko-*Sensei* could check the
card. It was the only part of her identity box she kept

in her room, having given him the rest when she moved to the dorm.

Her identity box held all the information needed to identify her body should she die under mysterious circumstances, something she considered highly likely. In the box was a copy of her fingerprints, a lock of hair, a copy of her medical and dental records, and a list of identifying marks and scars. She knew where to find his identity box too.

Unlike her, he could keep the box in his house. Her dorm room, on the other hand, wasn't secure. Being a college dorm room, the Resident Advisors, the Resident Director, and others, had to be able to come in to inspect the room or in case of emergencies. If it wasn't for that, she would have changed the lock as soon as she moved in. But it meant that she had to be careful, not only about what was in plain sight, but what she had in her room period. Too bad the college required all unmarried students under twenty to live either with parents or on campus.

Her card was still accurate so she replaced it behind the mirror. After a brief debate, she decided not to skate to the store. It would be faster, but she didn't have her reflective gear unpacked yet. Besides, she wanted out of the room, why hurry that time?

As soon as the night wind hit her face, she could feel Liska pulling at the edges of the mask. The mask of Anna Andrews. Anna was a normal college student from Great Britain. She also didn't exist. Just an identity she used to attend college here. But Liska wasn't supposed to be here.

Certainly she couldn't afford to be seen by anyone on campus.

That was the problem with some personas, they took on minds of their own. Then again, Liska had always been much more real to her than Anna or any of her temporary 'harmless' personas. Sometimes she had to remind herself that Liska *was* just another persona and wasn't her. Not all of her, at least.

Perhaps she had been going about this the wrong way. She had tried being firmly 'Anna Andrews' at all times, even in her dorm room when no one was watching. Maybe that was why she was so keyed-up, even though by lunar phase, she should be at her calmest. Well, if suppressing that side of her wouldn't work, maybe she should let it out for a bit. Not, however, until she was off campus and less likely to run into someone who knew Anna.

It was two blocks from the campus before she decided it was safe and saw just what she was looking for. A van with a mirror just about eye level. Anna looked in, but it was Liska who walked away.

The transition would not fool anyone who knew her, or actually saw her change, or even someone who knew what clothes she was wearing. But the change of attitude was enough to make someone who didn't know her, or who saw her at a distance, question whether or not it was the same person.

Anna usually hunched inward, slumped slightly, not inviting notice or comment. Invisible. Shy. Liska strode with a casual prowl, shoulders up, head erect, eyes tracking every movement and shadow, an attitude of confident control. When she wanted to, she could part a crowd with attitude alone. Right now, she simply wanted to be left alone. Stalking the streets like she owned them usually worked. Usually.

She was about half-way to her destination that she felt eyes upon her. Not changing her gait, Liska reached into her pocket and fumbled a minute before 'accidentally' dropping her keys on the ground. As she stooped to pick them up, she carefully peered in the direction she believed her shadow to be. A slightly feral grin formed as she spotted him.

A kid, and a stupid one at that. Liska ignored the fact that he was, at most, only two years younger than her own eighteen years. In fact, he was likely a little older than her. Not that she cared.

Someone who thought he was dangerous and was going to prove it to a potential victim. He didn't seem to be looking for a real fight, probably thought he could get what he wanted from sheer intimidation alone. Nearly six and a half feet tall, built like an American football player, he might not need to be armed to be threatening. No gun, she would notice that. Maybe a knife. He was wearing a hooded sweatshirt in eighty-degree temperatures, likely to prevent identification. Doubtlessly, he saw her as an easy mark. A lot of people looked at her, five-two in shoes, one hundred pounds, and made that mistake. Few made it twice.

He was after money; she was almost certain that it wouldn't go beyond that. The prudent thing to do would be let Anna handle this. She would pretend to be scared and hand over her fake wallet, containing seven dollars and an expired coupon for a shampoo she didn't use. It cost her practically nothing, was inconspicuous and wouldn't draw attention.

Prudence can take a long walk off a short pier. Liska was out and she wanted to play. It had been too long. She pulled enough Anna to the forefront to seem more victim-like, as she straightened up into a casual slouch, keys in hand, grin gone. She didn't have a mirror to check herself, but it should be fine. A mirror wasn't necessary, just helpful.

Her deliberations were short, but he was still almost on top of her, pushing her to an alleyway, out of sight, before she was fully upright. Anna let herself stumble backwards a little as cover for moving back, giving herself room to work. The alley was a dead end, narrow and dark. The remains of a decayed wooden lean-to and thick layer of trash meant there was clearly little attention from the street, and made moving around difficult. Point for him, either he had some experience or was really lucky at picking confrontation spots. Of course, those factors could work both ways.

He dominated the only entrance, and drew a knife. Liska inwardly snorted. Even from a distance, the knife screamed of cheap materials and shoddy workmanship, wielded by one whose knife experience clearly came from the movies. Anna, less versed in such things, blinked at him in confusion, hands in her pockets as she positioned herself in the best spot.

He swaggered closer, oozing confidence, certain he was in control. His ego tickled her nose from fifteen feet away. This was going to be fun.

Arrogance can be deadly, so remain on guard. She let him make the first move.

"Hand it over." This demand was followed by several unflattering and a few obscene terms for women, and a few supposedly impressive knife flourishes. He really did need a lesson in manners. Perhaps a lesson in how to handle a knife too. Not that she was going to help him with that.

"Hand what over? My keys? Sorry, I need those. Besides, I doubt they'd do you any good." Her hands moved to behind her back. He didn't notice.

"No, moron, your money!" Hm, getting mad already? This might be easier than she thought.

"Oh, I'm sorry, but I need my money. Though if you need a few dollars for cab fare or something, I might be able to help. If you say please." The last part was just to make him angrier. Angry people are easy to manipulate, but furious people were dangerous. It was a precarious balance.

It was working. For a moment he sputtered, unable to talk, though he recovered quickly. "Hand over your money, or I'll take it. And maybe something else too." He leered at her, deliberately letting his eyes crawl up and down her frame.

Empty threat, but it still stiffened her spine. "I'm not handing over anything if you're going to be so *rude* about it. In fact, I'm in a bit of a hurry, so kindly move out of my way." Perfect.

He growled and charged at her, knife first. Anna gone, Liska smiled. It was not a nice smile. Anyone with the sense of a turnip would have fled immediately at the sight of it. He either hadn't the sense, hadn't seen the smile clearly, or both. Nor had he noticed that Liska had slipped on gloves while her hands were behind her back.

She held statue still until he was almost upon her. Then, darting to his right, she grabbed the knife hand, spinning it with her. A judicious squeeze to a pressure point caused him to lose his already-faltering grip on the knife which she caught with her left hand, as her right hand forced his arm up his back. Struggling with balance, he lost it completely as she kicked him in the back of his knee. He fell to his knees, arm still twisted behind his back as the knife came up to caress his throat. Liska brought a knee up into his back and leaned on it enough to give her the leverage to keep him from falling back on her or untwisting his arm. Unable to go forward or back, he was well and truly caught, all in a matter of seconds.

Liska smirked as the scent of his fear assaulted her nose, before pondering what to do next. This was an excellent holding position, but she couldn't stay there all night, and unless she slit his throat, the instant she let go, they'd be back where they started from, except she'd have the knife. He was probably bull-headed enough to try and take it back from her, too. If he did, then someone was going to get hurt. While he might be a stupid punk, that wasn't a good enough reason to kill him. So she'd just have to make sure that following her was the last thing on his mind.

Leaning close, she whispered into his ear. "Listen carefully because I don't like to repeat myself. I walk where I please and I don't get hassled. Do you understand?" Nothing. She leaned in harder, nicking him with the knife, drawing a droplet of blood. "I said, do you understand?"

A slew of panic babble that sounded vaguely affirmative answered her.

"Good." She resumed normal volume, sounding almost friendly. "You could, of course, try for revenge, but that would be folly in the extreme. First of all, I just showed you that I am more than capable of taking you on. You could tell your friends, if you have any, and get their help, but then you have to admit that you got beaten by a girl with your own weapon. I would love to hear you explain that one. Secondly, you might not catch me in such a good mood twice. Word of advice for you; just because someone looks like an easy target doesn't necessarily mean they are one. Do you understand?"

The affirmative panic babble came much faster this time.

"Excellent." With one fluid motion, she moved the knife as she shoved him into the lean-to. It collapsed with a crash, giving her time to throw the knife, pinning his sleeve to one of the boards. Poor craftsmanship meant she had to compensate for the lack of balance. "Don't touch the knife for two minutes after I leave. You do *not* want to run into me again." It probably wasn't the wisest idea in the world, but as she backed away, she did a partial change, so that her eyes glowed when she hit the light just right. Like...now. That always made a big impact.

This time was no exception. Her 'assaulter' passed out, but apparently not before losing control of at least one bodily function. Liska raised an eyebrow, before shrugging and walking away. She hadn't expected that, but hey, it made her life a little easier.

It wasn't until she was almost home that the excitement wore off enough for her to second-guess herself. After all, she was supposed to be in the area for a few years. The last thing she needed or wanted was to get noticed. *Oh well, done is done.*

The thought went out of her head as she got to her dorm and froze. Something was wrong.

Chapter Two

Good news is fleeting. Ill news takes up residence. – The
Kikitsutai Book of Wisdom

Liska paused, foot hovering over the first stair to the
second floor of her dorm. A quick glance around
revealed no signs of trouble. No one was nearby, no
trace of traps or anything else. Gingerly she put her
foot down, relaxing slightly when nothing happened.

What was wrong and where? The courtyard
seemed empty of people, though someone could be
in a car. No one was watching her though. She
would feel that. Nor was anyone behind the
stairwell, she would have noticed as she walked up.
So where was the problem?

Her room. Someone had gone in her room,
she was certain of it. The dorm was built like a
motel, leaving the rooms accessible to the street; the
dorm itself on the edge of campus. The closest street
lamp had gone out about a week ago and hadn't
been replaced yet, offering a degree of anonymity to
those coming and going. Anyone could have come,
picked or forced the sub-standard lock and waltzed
in.

Liska climbed the staircase, pausing again at the top to analyze her room. It was close to the stairwell, and in a shadowy corner, allowing her to get in and out quickly without drawing much attention. Someone else had taken advantage of those factors as well. There was no visible proof of her suspicions; the blinds were in place, the door was shut, but instinct, deep animal instinct warned her that her den had been invaded.

Who was there and were they looking for Liska or Anna? She needed to know so she knew who should greet them. It could be a thief, or someone trying to set up an ambush. If so, Liska should deal with it, though possibly subtly, pretending to be Anna. Perhaps it was the Resident Advisor, she had to do inspections sometimes. It might be maintenance or the bug exterminator she had been warned would come sometimes. Those would be 'Anna' visitors. Probably not at eleven o'clock at night, though. Or maybe it was a family member, to test her, or deliver a message, or both. They would be looking for Liska.

She ran through the possibilities, trying to calm and focus herself, preparing for any outcome. This might have been more successful if she cared more about who was there and why instead of simply being angry that someone had dared to enter her territory without her permission. No, anger solved nothing and could only hinder her. *Calm, focus, breathe.*

Reaching the door, she bent over to scoop up an imaginary coin. Liska inhaled deeply, analyzing the scents caught in her doormat. Mildew, dirt, lizards, bugs, sneakers, perfumes, moss, her own scent; all the usual odors, plus one group of scents that didn't belong. She knew that group. Strange leaves, mist, magic. *Korvou.*

To the best of her knowledge, he was supposed to be somewhere in Southeast Asia, not downtown West Palm Beach, Florida. What could have brought him here? Silly question, she did. Somehow.

Definitely a Liska visitor. She straightened, trying not to sigh. This wasn't a good time or place to deal with him. What did he want anyway? They had sworn years ago to kill each other, though it had been at least a year since either of them actually tried in earnest. In fact, left alone, they were more likely to work together, or at least give each other space. Conflicting loyalties meant they weren't always given that option. Though someone ought to have warned her if Korvou's chief put a price on her head or declared war on them.

Anyway, unless he was under orders, chances were he wouldn't attack her, and he scorned ambushes as dishonorable. So she could probably at least enter her room safely. Unless he was being controlled or possessed. Unlikely, but not impossible. If a fight was going to happen tonight, it almost certainly wouldn't be here. Neither could afford the attention.

Well, she had been restless all night. Perhaps a decent spar, verbal or physical, was just what she needed. At least she knew how he had gotten in, there was just no way to stop it.

Liska gripped the bag in her hand, ready to swing the carton of milk at anything that moved as she unlocked the door. Opening it, she felt her calm evaporate at the sight of her enemy-ally lying on her bed, reading one of her notebooks. True, it was one of her school notebooks, not anything private, but it was hers and he had no right to it.

He was ignoring her arrival, despite the fact he probably felt her approaching from three blocks away. Fine with her. Pretending he wasn't there, Liska surveyed the room, trying to see what damage he had done. Korvou hadn't exactly made a mess, but neither had he tried to hide his work, likely knowing that she would be even angrier about being 'lied' to.

The postcards and curios on her dresser were awry, the books on her desk were in the wrong order, while the books on the shelf had obviously been rummaged through and put back only semi-neatly. From the smell of it, he had left the dresser itself alone. No doubt very honorable on his part, but also a bit stupid. Dressers were often prime hiding spots, a place she always checked and sometimes used. All in all, Liska supposed she shouldn't get too mad. It was no more than she would do in his position. Possibly less. She still made a mental note to do something to annoy him later.

Since the pest on her bed was still ignoring her, Liska decided to put the milk away. That was why she went out in the first place, after all. To get to the 'kitchenette', she had to walk past the bed. As she did so, Liska snatched her math notebook out of Korvou's hands, pausing just long enough to smack him on the head with it. Without a glance, she tossed the book back on the desk with the rest, hearing it land with a dull plop. One sniff in the abbreviated hallway told her that Korvou hadn't left the main room. She wouldn't have to check the kitchenette or bathroom later. Of course, she would anyway, but that was more paranoia than anything else.

Milk safely away, she rejoined him. Korvou was sitting up now, feet on the floor, ready to move in a heartbeat. The only chair in the room was at the desk, so she turned it to face him, mirroring his position. His body language was casual and non-threatening but could move to offensive or defensive in a split-second. Neither was willing to move first as they sat, pretending nothing was wrong. It was all part of their dance.

Korvou broke the silence first, but not in the way she expected. Which she should have expected. "You have a very boring room."

"I do try, thank you." He had a point. Liska had put very little effort into personalizing the featureless room. Any belongings she truly cherished were left home to protect them. Besides, her interests generally weren't Anna's. She wasn't Anna and this room wasn't home. It was a shelter from the elements, a place to store things, and a modicum of privacy. What more did she need?

"Seriously, haven't you heard of magazines or TVs? There's nothing to entertain a visitor." Why was he using English? They had five languages in common, but English wasn't the first or second language of either of them.

"I don't have visitors and don't consider it my responsibility to entertain intruders. If you insist on coming and get bored, there's always my trusty math notebook. Go ahead and do the homework, while you're at it."

Korvou rolled his eyes. "I like the knick-knacks, but they don't seem like you at all." He lazily indicated her dresser, lightly peppered with mementos, the only objects, other than her personal books and a teddy bear, that held witness that an actual person lived here.

Unless she was far mistaken, Korvou's casualness was a front to seem in control. Then again, so was hers. Something huge had to have happened, be happening at that moment, or about to happen soon, but they were chatting. If he brought up the weather, she might have to throw something at him.

"The RA said it seemed strange to see a room so sterile. These seemed typical of a student my age." They also served as tell-tales. If they weren't exactly where she had left them, then clearly someone else had come in and moved them. Someone like Korvou.

"The postcard from Paris is written in my handwriting. I don't recall sending you a postcard; from Paris or anywhere else."

"You mean my forgery practices? Yes, they were fun. Good experience. Your handwriting is tough to forge, by the way. Too many loops."

He smirked at the quasi-insult. "You seem to have managed."

She wasn't quite satisfied with that one, as it could be detected by someone examining it closely, but felt no need to mention that. "Did you know I wouldn't have a roommate, or were you guessing?"

If someone else had seen his normal methods of entry, they could have had problems.

"You, share with a Day? Besides, there's no other auras." She nodded to concede the points. "How did you pull that off?"

Liska shrugged. "Signed note from a psychologist saying I needed somewhere private to retreat to for my mental health."

An almost laugh. "True, even. Impressive. Forged or bribed?"

"Family."

They lapsed into silence. As much as she wanted, needed to know what brought him here, she couldn't bring herself to ask. That would be a point for him. If he gave in and told her without her asking, it would be a point for her. He had been the one to come to her, which could be to her advantage, depending on why he came. Hopefully he needed her help. That was much preferable to his coming for her sake. Liska hated being indebted, especially to him, and whatever dragged him half-way around the world promised to be big.

Finally, Korvou spoke, "How many times have we tried to kill each other?" He probably knew the answer as well as she did. Skipping from topic to topic to keep the other person disoriented, it was a favorite technique of hers. Perhaps one of them had picked it up from the other.

"Between eight and ten depending on how you count attempts. I'm counting Berlin, but not Moscow or Oslo. I don't know if you count them or not. Why, here to increase the tally?" She didn't even have to think about it.

"What about Prague?"

"Prague doesn't count."

"I had a gun to the back of your head for over an hour."

"Exactly. We both knew you wouldn't shoot me. Not a bound opponent and not from behind."

"Did you know that then?"

"Why do you think I didn't try to escape? You were clearly playing a role." She still didn't know the details to that one, but she wasn't going to admit that under anything less than pain of death. "So, eight?"

"Fine. Eight." He waved his hand airily, speaking in that irritating tone of one humoring a small child. Liska fantasized pushing him off her balcony but didn't change her expression at all. The fantasies got more violent as she saw the small notebook in his hand. "It's hard to do an in-depth aura reading on you. Do you know how long it took to find something you had a significant emotional attachment to? I had to use your diary. It was that or your skates, and that wasn't quite what I needed."

"What makes you think that's my diary?" Her tone was the same as when she answered roll call in class.

"You hid it well. Duct taped box under the bed, very clever; besides, it's in some kind of code."

"Cipher. I replaced letters, not whole words."

He eyed it speculatively. "So, I could figure this out with time?"

"Highly unlikely, even if I gave you that time, instead of say, using it to beat you to death." Besides the cipher, one she had invented and shared with no one, the book required the reader to be tri-lingual, and she knew he didn't know at least one of those languages. Even if he did decipher it, he'd probably be disappointed. It was less of a diary and more of a work journal. Of course, she didn't want him knowing any of that either.

Korvou looked at least half-way tempted to take her response as a challenge but refrained. Something must be very wrong. "So it is your diary."

Liska shrugged. "Perhaps. How did your aura reading go?" She might not understand exactly what he did or how, but she had learned to respect it.

"All too well, I'm afraid."

"Too well? Does this have anything to do with why you came halfway around the world to irritate me?"

"Shall I tell you what I found?" He smirked, waiting for her to ask.

An iron lump of dread formed suddenly in her stomach. She did not want to know. This apprehension took her by surprise both by its suddenness and intensity, before she shoved it forcibly away in a mental box, jumping up and down on the lid. Fortunately, Korvou couldn't smell emotions like she could, and she doubted the feeling lasted long enough to affect her aura. Any fear of his answer would be more by how deep he might have gotten than what he found. She hoped. However, while she may not want him to know much about her, it was very much to her disadvantage not to know what he knew.

Korvou was a Pattern Seer as well as an Aura Reader, and a very good one at that. He was able to see, not exactly what would happen, but where, approximately when, and who was likely to be involved or affected. It would be foolish beyond measure to ignore it.

None of that meant she had to make things easy. "If you wish," Liska answered, casually rotating her neck. It had gotten a bit stiff.

"I don't have to tell you. I could just leave if you aren't interested." A bluff. He had come too far to tell her. She desperately needed to know. Yet they still couldn't stop the dance.

"You know where the door is."

One split-second his control slipped. For one heartbeat, he showed his shock. It was gone as quickly as it came, but Liska noticed and would remember. Point for her. Now he tried to call her bluff. "If you insist." He didn't move, though.

There was no sense prolonging things, and Liska wasn't really in the mood to spit into the wind. "You're just going to sit there until I listen, aren't you? Might as well get it over with, then. I do want to get some sleep tonight."

He smirked, seeing her statement for what it was, and probably awarded himself a mental point. Then he got serious again. "The wind is changing. Big things, life-altering things are about to happen."

"Aren't they always for someone?" She hated it when he got cryptic. Unfortunately, when sharing patterns, he always got cryptic. For that matter, how did he know what events would be big, and what wouldn't? He was always right, but how did he know?

"Not like this. Splash a rock in a pond and ripples spread. Several rocks have been tossed and more are coming. Events are in motion and coming to a head."

That was actually more straight-forward than usual, even if it told her absolutely nothing. "What kind of head? What events?" She made certain to sound bored, even if she was anything but.

"That, I do not know. What I do know is that you are at the center. All the main players are acting because of you. Things you have done in the past, or are likely to do soon." Korvou hesitated. "I hoped to warn you earlier, but you did something tonight that made a collision inevitable. Possibly something very foolish."

Liska arched an eyebrow. "Oh, what did I do?" So she had been stupid tonight. Wonderful.

"I don't know. Maybe you do, maybe you don't. The biggest events sometimes spring from the smallest causes."

There had to be something useful he could tell her. "Who are the other main players?"

"I cannot tell." His voice revealed the barest trace of his irritation at that, which meant he must be incredibly frustrated. "There are at least four, though one is in question. One is very close to you, geographically, but I don't recognize the aura. Blue and green, paint and waves." Liska shrugged. She couldn't read auras. They meant nothing to her. "One is still distant, though it is the most dangerous. Blood, anger, red and black, violence. The one in question has to make some more decisions before the role becomes clear, so his aura is muddy and hard to distinguish. There are others, but their roles haven't been defined yet. I can tell you this, succeed or fail, you will never be the same."

Ah, lovely. She had been thinking that the night just needed a pronouncement of doom to make things perfect. "What's my aura look like?"

Korvou smiled. "Yours is orange and silver, moonlit forests and twisty steel. It suits you."

She shook her head. "So why the warning?"

"I owe you for last time."

"Tibet? You already paid me back." If he was waiting for her to ask how he managed to persuade thirty people to declare her a goddess and try to talk others into joining their cult, he was in for a very long wait. Even if she was intensely curious why he had proclaimed her the goddess of Hokey Pokey and why not use one of the other dozens of more practical and inconspicuous solutions. Then someone started a website. Membership was about three hundred strong. Korvou, the git, had signed them both up as members. Was it her or were humans insane?

"So I did. Then I suppose you owe me now." Liska clamped down on her irritation. He planned that. Irritation melted into puzzlement as he stood and moved to her window, looking somewhere between worried and wistful as he continued. "I may be calling it in soon."

"I see. Was that all you wanted?" She gave him a slight nod. She'd listen if he wanted.

"So eager to get rid of me? I came from Malaysia to talk to you." He got it. Not this time.

"I don't care if you came from Mars; you aren't staying the night."

Korvou scoffed. "Wouldn't dream of it. So what did you do that was so dumb? Tonight, I mean."

"I found an annoying pest in my room, and didn't immediately kick him out." Like she was going to tell him.

"Funny, I didn't see anyone else here." Korvou made a show of looking around.

"Exactly. If you're quite finished, it's getting late here," Liska hinted broadly.

"Far be it from me to keep a lady from her rest, even if we both know you don't sleep this early." He was almost at the door before he turned back to her. "Liska, what are you running from?"

She bristled at the unexpected question. "I don't—"

"You run away all the time. Why else are you here?" Before she could think of a response, or at least throw something at him, he was gone, stepping through the still closed door.

"Show off," She muttered. "Irritating, pesky, meddling..." Liska let herself trail off. He wasn't around to hear, so what was the point? Prioritizing the conversation, she was further annoyed to realize that for all his warning, there wasn't enough information to do anything yet. All she knew was what she had done that night.

"There's nothing I can do about it now. Worrying won't change a thing." Talking to herself, like her fondness for stuffed animals and fairy tales, was something she wouldn't admit to under torture. She had a feeling that a few people knew, but they also knew not to mention it.

Suddenly she remembered why she had been in such a hurry to be back home by eleven-thirty. *Stupid girl, you aren't allowed to get distracted like that.* Liska rushed to the computer. He was still on.

MoonFox says: Sorry about that. I had unexpected company.

Dragonclaw says: Oh? Anyone I know?

MoonFox says: Yes, don't worry, it wasn't bad.

Dragonclaw says: No fighting?

MoonFox says: Not this time, although I did have a brief altercation with a spectacularly stupid mugger a little before.

Dragonclaw says: Anything I need to take care of? Translation: Do you need somewhere to dump a body, an alibi, and/or legal counsel?

MoonFox says: "I am completely insulted! I also happen to be completely innocent! Of that... This time...

Dragonclaw says: You're bolder in print.

MoonFox says: Not surprising, most people are. No, he's fine.

Dragonclaw says: How is school going? Classes? Are you adjusting to everything? Do you have any jobs lined up?

MoonFox says: School is fine. I'm doing okay in classes. It is an adjustment, but I think I'm managing. As for work, I'm trying to concentrate on my studies for now. Jobs are a distraction.

Dragonclaw says: I suppose you're right. That is why you went over. You don't have to stay, you know.

MoonFox says: I want to. I know you don't understand, but this is important to me.

Dragonclaw says: Very well, get it out of your system. Goodnight.

MoonFox says: Goodnight. "Goodnight, Father, but this isn't something I'm just getting out of my system."

It was after midnight by now. Liska wasn't tired, but she did have to get up in the morning. Before trying to sleep, she wanted her knick-knacks back in place. They did no good as tell tales if she didn't know where they were to begin with, and seeing them askew was vaguely alarming, if only because she knew where they were supposed to be, and they weren't. So, pulling out a ruler, she lined them back up to where they were supposed be by the measurements she had written down.

Nodding in satisfaction, Liska prepared for bed. Before finishing, she stopped to think. Despite letting herself play a little, it didn't feel like enough. The blinds were drawn, she didn't have a roommate, the RA wouldn't come in this late unless there was an emergency and would still knock first. It should be fine.

So, hoping for the best, Liska changed. Restlessness soothed temporarily, she curled up and went to sleep.

Chapter Three

When swords dance, the heart sings. –The Kikitsutai Book of Wisdom

Liska woke the next morning, as she did every morning, being very careful to give no signs of wakefulness. Eyes still closed, breathing still in sleep patterns, she tried to figure out what woke her, where she was, and what was around her. She was in a bed. Her bed. That was her teddy bear she was slightly lying on. There was no sound or smell of anyone else in the room, so she was almost certainly alone. Light was trying to stream into her eyes. It must be morning. She risked cracking an eyelid, which shut immediately at the brightness. Yes, morning had definitely broken. Another glance showed her alarm clock. Time to get up.

Yawning, she straightened up and stretched before jumping to the floor completely awake. Liska wasn't fond of mornings but was grateful that at least she didn't need artificial stimulants to wake up.

She looked at the clock again as she changed, wondering if she had time for a shower. Probably not. Tonight, then or maybe in the afternoon. Once she was dressed, she filled out a new card for her identity box, ripped up the old one, and she was out the door.

One brisk run by the waterway later, she was ready for the highlight of her morning. The Kendo class should be almost over by now. By the time she got there it was completely empty. Surprising, she had expected the instructor to be there. Still, it didn't bother her. Picking up the bamboo practice sword, she closed her eyes and began the first *kata*.

***

Todd Kensworth, the Kendo instructor, a junior at the university, stood in the doorway watching Anna practice. The enigmatic British woman had intrigued him since the moment she walked in the door. She seemed to want nothing more than to be ignored, which Todd found impossible. It wasn't just her appearance, though that was interesting enough; petite, red hair, and those amber eyes, not to mention the occasional clothes clash. But there was more to it. An air of poise, an odd feeling that there was something a bit mysterious about her, and her skill... He smiled, thinking briefly of the first time she had come by.

It was about a week after the club had started up. She had come after the class dismissed to look around. Todd was cleaning the dojo. Normally, for any martial discipline, part of the discipline for the students was to clean the dojo afterwards. But the first time he taught, over a year ago, he had forgotten to tell his students that, and everyone left him to straighten up. To his surprise, Todd discovered he actually liked putting everything away. It was relaxing and made the lesson feel complete. So he stuck with it.

Looking up from putting the padding in the closest, he had seen her standing at the doorway peering in. His first thought was, 'She's like me!', a thought he still hadn't forgotten or deciphered. He shook his head and smiled at her.

She seemed slightly timid, but perhaps the swords bothered her. He only allowed shinai, the bamboo practice swords, for sparring, with a few wooden swords for certain exercises, but he had real swords on the walls. That was enough to make some people uncomfortable.

Eight years of Kendo experience and three of studying psychology had left him good at reading people. Most of the time he could get at least a basic idea of a person on the first meeting if he tried. Anna, well, she wasn't that simple. First impression was that she was a bit timid and probably wouldn't stay long. If she did join, she would likely quit soon. Still, as instructor, he considered it his duty to introduce a potential member, no matter how unlikely, to the club. "Hi. Come on in, I'm just cleaning up. Interested in Kendo?"

His first hint that his initial reading might be off was when she bowed upon entering the room before removing her shoes. Yes, it was what one did when entering a dojo, and it wasn't terribly uncommon for even the uninitiated to know that, provided some knowledge or dubious martial arts movies. What surprised him was the ease at which she did it. Most of his students were still uncomfortable with it, and some had been taking classes for years. She gave a proper half bow to the room at large, followed with a slightly shallower bow to him, all without the slightest hint of self-

consciousness. Only after that, and the removal of her shoes did she offer the Western greeting, her name and a handshake. "Hello, I'm Anna Andrews. Are you the Sensei here?"

His brain stalled at the faint hint of violets, and the flash of a smile. "Huh? Oh, yes. I'm Todd. Todd Kensworth. I don't usually make anyone call me Sensei, though."

Feeling extremely sheepish, he tried to get over it by explaining all about the club, a mostly memorized speech so he didn't stumble or forget what he wanted to say. It didn't take long for him to notice that while she appeared to be listening politely, her eyes kept drifting to the swords that were still out. Considering it unlikely she'd accept, he offered to let her handle one of the bamboo swords. She did accept, and to his surprise, handled it well, knowing the proper grips and stances without him telling her. So her knowledge of etiquette wasn't just from the movies.

"You obviously know what you're doing. We could try a quick spar, only if you're comfortable with the—"

"I'd love to," *She cut him off, with a bigger smile than before.*

Huh, he hadn't thought she'd take him up on that. Now he had to find armor that would fit her. The gloves were big, but close enough to work; the helmet was huge; but she swam in the chest armor. Considering it was designed for someone six to eight inches taller than her, that wasn't surprising.

"I can't move properly in this. Can I go without the do?" *She started taking off the chest armor even before he answered.*

Todd frowned, thinking about it. "I don't know. I don't let anyone spar without the complete armor. It could be dangerous."

"What if I sign something, promising not to sue?"

She finally convinced him, but Todd was reluctant. Bamboo was less dangerous than steel, but it was still possible, especially with skill, to injure or even kill someone with a shinai. It was just harder to do it accidentally. Well, he'd just have to go easy on her, especially when aiming for the torso.

That idea lasted about five seconds. Long enough for her score on him before he could raise his first block. She scored her second point, winning the three-point match, about ten seconds later. That was when he realized that the nervous tension he saw wasn't anxiety, but excitement.

Pride shaken, he had demanded a rematch. This time he wasn't going to make the mistake of going easy on her. He did a lot better this time. It took her almost a minute to beat him instead of fifteen seconds. He didn't know how many times he asked for a rematch, but he didn't score on her once. To say he had been surprised was akin to saying that Jupiter was larger than a pebble. Accurate to the point of being misleading.

Todd didn't consider himself an overly proud man, so after a brief struggle he managed to push his humiliation to the side, catch his breath, and ask if she was interested in co-teaching the class. It was difficult but he managed. That's when she shocked him yet again. Was this a game for her?

"I couldn't possibly. In fact, I really can't even join your club. Plus, I would be very appreciative if you didn't mention to anyone that I was here, or that I know Kendo." She was serious. How could she be serious?

He could understand not wanting the responsibility of teaching, and there really wasn't anyone who could challenge her, but not wanting anyone to know she could do Kendo? "Why?"

Briefly he wondered if it had anything to do with her kiai. *The* kiai, *or spirit cry, was given at every strike. He had heard a lot of variety, but hers were the strangest. The more she got into a spar, the more she sounded like a bird or animal.*

"It's a bit of a long story. Complicated, too. Simplest answer is that Mother never considered it ladylike or a proper activity for a girl." She shrugged with a soft smile. "I don't know, it feels wrong to tell people. Sort of like my little secret." By then, Todd was pretty sure he could read her a little more accurately. This seemed to be the truth, but not the full truth. Though if it was a secret, then it was odd she would tell him. Perhaps she just saw him as a semi-kindred spirit.

Still, Anna seemed reluctant to leave, and Todd didn't think he was imagining the slightly wistful look she had as she put back her sword and bowed to it. So Todd decided to take a chance.

"You're really good, you know. But you'll only stay good if you practice."

"Is that a hint?" She asked, a wisp of amusement in her voice.

"I'm not near your level, we just proved that. But, I am willing to spar with you anytime. Then you don't have to tell anyone else."

"And you'll get better, by practicing with a steady opponent."

Yes, he had thought of that, but it paled compared to the benefit of seeing her on a regular or even semi-regular basis. Fortunately, he had enough sense and restraint not to mention that. "Something like that. If you come by after practices, I'll already be ready and warmed up. Think about it."

Anna watched him for a moment, as if trying to read something. "You promise you won't mention I come by, to anyone?"

"Not a soul."

She cocked her head, thinking about it, before answering. "I accept your offer."

The final and most intriguing piece of the puzzle that first meeting gave him was that just before leaving the room, Anna turned and gave him a full half bow. There was respect there. She had trounced him soundly but respected him more now than she had when she had no idea of his skills. Respected him and promised to come again.

She did come again. Todd didn't think he had a single student that was so regular. He was still trying to read her, but all he had learned was that she was harder to read than he thought. The only time she didn't seem to be hiding anything was when she sparred.

A few adjustments had been made. They had made torso hits 'light contact' and he went without the *do* as well. In keeping with his promise, he made certain all his students were gone within ten minutes of class ending so she could come without anyone noticing her. It was a good thing he cleaned the place himself. This had worked pretty well until today, when one of his students wanted to talk to him afterwards. Leading the student away from the gym had clearly given Anna the chance to arrive before him, something that had only happened once before. *It would be a shame not to take advantage of it.* He smirked.

Pulling himself from his thoughts, he picked up a *shinai*, before creeping over to the apparently oblivious woman. She had long ago made it clear that attempted ambushes were fair game. So far, 'attempted' was all he had managed. He crossed the room as silently as he could, swung the sword...

And was immediately blocked by her own. Her eyes were still closed and she was smiling lightly. Then her eyes opened. Someday, he was going to manage to draw that expression. He hadn't been successful yet, despite repeated attempts.

"How did you know?"

"I know everything." She raised an eyebrow. "Shall we start?"

Chapter Four

A blunt truth is more dangerous than a sharpened blade. –
The Kikitsutai Book of Wisdom

The dojo was technically just another room in the gym. At least three different classes were taught in the same room on a regular basis. Occasionally she attended the aerobics class that met in there in the evenings. Still, it would always be a dojo for her. As usual, Anna was only nominally in charge. Liska was there even if she had to hide behind an increasingly thinning mask. Sparring probably wasn't a very Anna thing to do, but the chance of a steady partner was just too tempting to give up.

Initially, she hadn't planned on letting on how much experience she had, considering it too dangerous. While she never fought any two people exactly the same way, there were enough similarities that someone who had seen her fight before could recognize the style. Considering she was supposed to be incognito, that would be very, very bad.

There shouldn't be anyone here that she had fought before, but she wanted to keep it that way. Besides, she had no desire to raise suspicions.

She couldn't remember any details of the first fight or any of the ones after that. The instant it started, nothing mattered but that fight. Even more dangerous, she lost most of her situational awareness. Some small tendril was aware, and would undoubtedly warn her if another threat appeared, but everything else was focused on the opponent in front of her. The rest of the room could have been surrounded by fog for all she noticed. Even her plan, to not let on the extent of her experience, dissolved like rice starch in hot water. When she won, she was almost as surprised as her opponent.

It was rare for her to get so engrossed in a fight, causing her to wonder why it happened this time. It wasn't a real fight, and quite frankly, Todd wasn't a major challenge. Oh, he was good, but she had several advantages over him. She had been studying Kendo for ten years, two more than his eight, even if she had only been sparing for six, had faster reflexes, and he held back, probably because she was a girl. It was subtle, and almost certainly unconscious, but it was there. He was getting better though and reacted faster than most humans.

Still, she wondered at the wisdom of coming, the first time, and every time after. Forget that. Forget Anna. Forget all the secrets and lies. There was only the dance of death, the only place she was truly alive...

Then it was over. Again. How many times had they sparred today? She mentally rewound. Five. She hadn't been paying attention, but they sparred five times. When they stopped to catch their breaths, she pretended to be more out of breath than she was. It gave her time to put Anna back in place and ask, "You were standing there a long time. Is everything alright?"

He looked at her in surprise. "You knew I was standing there? Man, no wonder I can never sneak up on you. No, nothing's wrong. I was just thinking."

"Ah." She could have asked, but doubted it mattered. He had been thinking about her. The way he was looking at her, the body language, it was obvious. He was growing attracted to her. That wasn't good. At all. Personally, she thought it was about as safe as roller-skating around the Grand Canyon in the rain. It could conceivably be done but certainly wasn't worth the risk. Still, as long as he didn't say anything, she could ignore it. It would fade as he found someone else. Crushes were an inevitable part of growing up. Even she... Anna forced her thoughts back to order.

Todd looked about to say something. Instinct suggested it would be best to leave. "I need to go if I'm going to eat before class."

"Oh, right. Okay, Anna. See you Wednesday?"

"More than likely."

***

Anna ate a quick breakfast, wrapped an apple in a napkin, tucked it in her pocket and hurried to math. Every time she ate a meal, if there was any left and she could get away with it, she tucked some in a napkin and took it with her. She never ate half of what she took, but she had it if she needed it. It was instinct. She could probably fight it if she tried but rarely saw the need.

Breakfast took longer than she planned, leaving her running late. Anna barely managed to slip into her seat as her name was called on roll.

That was the problem with using Andrews as a last name. Maybe she should have gone for something later in the alphabet.

Once her presence was recognized, she immediately tuned out the class. Not only had she studied this math, the teacher was *still* reviewing for college algebra. Maybe she should have taken something a little more advanced, but she hated math.

Her education would probably be odd to her classmates. Liska was no stranger to mathematics or most of the sciences, could use a little more work on world literature, was shaky on what her classmates believed to be true in world history, but had memorized her family tree to twelve generations, was fluent in seven languages and somewhat proficient in another nine, and had other training that would boggle 'normal' students.

Then again, that was why she was here. To find out what being normal was like. Liska gave a slight snort. She wouldn't recognize 'normal' if it walked up to her and offered to shake her hand. She'd be too busy looking for the catch.

"Ms. Andrews?"

Apparently her snort had caught the teacher's attention. Mentally rewinding the past minute, she realized the question. "The quadratic formula is B squared plus or minus the square root of negative B minus four A C all over two A."

"Very good, Ms. Andrews. Now, if you could just look like you're paying attention?"

"Yes, Sir." She ignored the small titters of laughter and again tuned everything out the instant the teacher's back was turned, though she tried to look a little more attentive. It must have worked. She wasn't called on again. There were only thirty people in the class, and the teacher loved picking on students who didn't seem to be listening.

Chemistry Lab was more fun than math. Anna was still considering a major in Chemistry. Knowledge of poisons, antidotes, and interactions were always useful. But that would mean more math. Besides, she already knew most of that.

They spent most of the class period getting extracts of various substances, disguised so they didn't know what they actually were, before using the analyzer to test the PH balance. If it was an acid, it would be blue, if a base, it would be red. Something that would be a lot easier for her if she actually could see in color. Liska sighed, looking over the samples she had gathered. To the best of her knowledge, she had done the project correctly, but all the vials had gray liquid to her. Just two different shades of gray, which made things a lot easier.

This experiment didn't require a lab partner, so she was stuck figuring it out on her own. The only time she had a lab partner was when it was required by the teacher. While the average person couldn't tell on a conscious level, most had this subconscious feeling that there was something odd about her, and avoided her, often without realizing it. Normally she didn't care and actually preferred to work on her own. Right now, it was inconvenient.

Since there were only two shades of gray, supposedly one of them was blue, and the other red. If she could figure out what one of them was, she should be able to figure out the rest.

Looking around, it seemed everyone was concentrating on their own work. No one noticed as she carefully leaned forward and inhaled. Yes, it was a bad idea to go around sniffing random chemicals, but she was certain the teacher would warn them if they used anything dangerous in this experiment. The smells were heavily mixed, but mentally separating them, she was sure she got a hint of lemon. It was subtle, even for her nose, so it had probably been diluted, so the students didn't know what they were working with.

Lemon was definitely an acid, so she just had to figure out whether it was a dark gray or a medium gray. Slowly picking up the vials one at a time, she stared at them, trying to hide the fact she was smelling them. It was her fourth vial, and a medium gray.

The difference between medium gray and dark gray was difficult at times to tell, but she hoped for the best as she wrote each down. Hopefully she had gotten them all right. Plus, no one seemed to notice her acting oddly. Cone monochromacy, full color-blindness, was far, far too rare to admit to having. Well, it wasn't exactly what she had, but the closest she could come up with to explain.

Sometimes Liska got tired of all the secrets. Having to hide, being unable to tell anyone the full truth, not trusting others; it was difficult. But where there are differences, there are those who fear them. So the secrets remained secret. If people found out everything she was hiding, well, she hoped she managed to remain at least one step ahead of the lynch mob.

Chapter Five

Even better than having a mask, is having a place it can be removed. –The Kikitsutai Book of Wisdom

Liska had spent over a month painstakingly inventing 'Anna Andrews' when she decided to use it as a long term disguise. It had to be similar enough to her own personality that she wasn't uncomfortable and could be convincing, but different enough that she never forgot that she was acting. That was one of the reasons Anna was British. She had learned English from her mother who was from England, so she naturally had a slight British accent, which she accentuated as Anna. Anna had the same hair as she did, so there was no need for a wig. She had firmly decided on certain details that she could recite backwards, while drugged and sleep deprived. She knew. She had tried, with the eager help of a few cousins. This included details like Anna's birthday, the names and birthdays of family members, all former addresses, childhood pets, previous schools, etc. Other details she could make up as necessary and add to the dossier she had memorized. All in all, Anna was a comfortable mask.

Still, no matter how much effort she put into making her disguise comfortable, it was a relief to be some place she didn't have to hide, didn't have to pretend. There were only a few places that was the case. One, of course, was her room. Currently, she was on her way to another.

When she knocked, Ryoko-*Sensei* let her in the house without speaking. Liska slipped off her shoes, replacing them with indoor slippers, while taking a quick check for unexpected visitors or anything out of order. Satisfied that all was as it should be, she turned and bowed to the older man who had been quietly waiting for her to finish her inspection. After all, he would do the same at her place.

He must have read that she was Liska today, as usual, so treated her that way. She could drop even that mask here but rarely did. "Ah, Liska, would you serve the tea?"

"Of course, *Sensei*."

She poured, feeling his eyes on her. Liska had no doubt that he reported information about her to her father. That was fine, she had a contract too.

"How was school?" He asked, after taking the first sip.

There wasn't much to say. She had long ago decided not to mention Todd's slight infatuation with her. Briefly, she considered mentioning Korvou's visit, but discarded the idea just as quickly, wondering if she was crazy. "It was fine."

"Just fine?" He probably knew she was hiding something. She always was.

"Pretty much."

He inhaled the steam gently. "Did you see that Kendo boy again today?" As if he couldn't tell.

She took a small sip. "Yes, we sparred today."

"Is he suspicious?"

A little. "He doesn't seem to be. I told him I had been studying two years longer than he has, and he accepts that as sufficient."

"Do you have an explanation as to why you learned?"

"Anna's parents are university professors. I assume she picked it up from a different professor. Perhaps one who specialized in Oriental Cultures."

The older man nodded slowly, apparently satisfied. "And if he wants more information?"

"He hasn't yet, but if he does, we have the fake website, and I can give him one of our numbers."

"Be careful."

"I try, *Sensei*."

"I know, child. I know. Have you finished your tea? Are you ready?"

Liska jumped to her feet. This was what she needed. For this, she could even ignore being called 'child'. They moved to the other room, an empty one, with no carpeting. Liska tossed off her jacket, slippers, and socks, and emptied her pockets. On the other side of the room, her great-uncle made similar preparations. Once they were ready, they stood facing each other and bowed.

Starting to circle, Liska pondered how to get him to throw the first move. The man was in his seventies, but he'd no doubt be around to teach her children. Underestimating him would be a serious mistake. An opening appeared. She ignored it. It had to be a feint. After a moment or two, he rubbed the area over his heart, as if troubled by it. She didn't react. His heart rate was normal and there were no signs of panic or pain. Another bluff. Giving up on that, he smiled slightly, congratulating her for not falling for his tricks. Again, she didn't respond. The smile turned a bit wry. She was not letting down her guard.

They had been circling for five minutes now. Ryoko-*Sensei* hadn't managed to trick her into presenting him an opening or taunt her into making the first move. That was what usually happened, she got impatient. No, this time he was going to make the first move.

Another five minutes passed, then another. They had never gone so long without starting. Finally, almost twenty minutes after they 'began' Ryoko- *Sensei* gave a sweeping kick, hoping she would lose her balance trying to avoid it.

Liska jumped over the kick and threw a high kick towards his head before he brought the foot back. He blocked, pushing her away to fall on the floor. She turned the fall to a roll and sprang to her feet, a huge grin on her face. This was more like it!

***

It was well over an hour later by the time they finished. Liska wasn't sure who 'won' and was even less sure she cared. Her smile was matched by Ryoko-*Sensei*'s, even as she tried to hide her labored breath and sore muscles. He was likely in the same condition as they did separate cool downs. After finishing, she joined her mentor in the living room, carefully not groaning, sighing, or wincing when she saw what he had pulled out.

Despite her lack of reaction, he clearly knew, as he chuckled at her. "Come now, it's not so bad. Perhaps it will work today?"

Considering they had encountered no success the previous 112 times they had tried, Liska was less than hopeful of a different result. Nevertheless, she obediently sat at the table and waited.

A deck of square cards in his hands, Ryoko-Sensei sat across from her. "What card am I about to put on the table?" He asked without looking at the card.

"A square?"

It was a circle. "Now?"

"Wavy lines?"

They ran through the entire deck twice. Her results were slightly lower than average, but not enough to be significant. Undaunted, Ryoko-Sensei shuffled the cards for a slightly different test. "What card am I looking at?"

Her results were better, but still within the laws of chance.

He placed a paperclip on the table and told her to move it without touching it. Slightly annoyed, Liska was tempted to blow on it, but refrained, deciding that was too immature. Staring at the clip did nothing. Glaring did nothing. Imagining it wearing a top hat, holding a cane and tap dancing made her smile, but did nothing to move the stubborn piece of stationery. Finally she shook her head.

"Try to change the temperature of the paperclip."

Last time she had tried to heat it, so this time she tried to cool it down. She stared at it as hard as she could while thinking cold thoughts. Snow. Ice cream. Ice caps. Penguins. Shivering slightly, Liska was entirely unsurprised to see that the temperature hadn't changed an iota.

"Try to change it to a different metal."

That was a new one. Oh well. Somewhere along the line, she had memorized the atomic formula for copper, so she imagined copper atoms crowding out the steel ones already present. After a bit, blinking to get rid of eyestrain, she admitted that unless she had invented a strain of copper indistinguishable from steel, it hadn't worked.

She almost sighed with relief when he took away the dratted paperclip. The feeling of gratitude fizzled and died as he held up a match and quirked an eyebrow. This test was as 'successful' as the previous ones, so they moved on to less eyestrain-inducing ones.

Ryoko-*Sensei* left the room before coming back with a sweater that he dropped in her lap. "Tell me as much as possible about the wearer."

"It's yours. It smells like you and dry-cleaning chemicals. I don't believe I've actually seen you wear it though." She handed it back to him.

"Have you had any strange dreams lately?" He sat back down.

"No stranger than normal."

"Thoughts or emotions that aren't yours?"

"I don't think so."

"How are your plants?"

"One's dying, but the other's okay." She really wasn't that good with plants.

"Communication with animals?"

"No more than usual."

"Luck finding lost objects?"

"If so, I wouldn't keep losing my pens."

"Unusual luck, good or bad?"

"I don't believe in luck." He gave her a measured look. "Not that I've noticed."

"Remote viewing?"

"Nothing." She was so tempted to say something about the remote batteries being dead, but he wouldn't be amused.

"Invisibility? Flying? Anything unusual?"

"*Che,* I wish. Sorry, *Sensei,* doesn't look like I have any cool powers today."

"You have ESP, I'm certain of it. Your mother has it, and it's genetic."

"My mother can also see in color, something neither of us can do." They both knew that Espers were more likely to have children with ESP, but there was no guarantee.

"I'm still certain, and we will find it."

"Well, I'll let you know if anything shows up. Pity that thing with Kira doesn't count."

"Neither of you can do that with anyone else, so it isn't ESP, just a bond between the two of you."

"I know, I know." Liska gathered her things together. "I better get going, the cafeteria closes in an hour." She sighed slightly once she was sure she was out of hearing range. Ryoko-*Sensei* was one of the relatives she was on the best terms with. She so hated disappointing him.

Chapter Six

Argue not with hypnotists, lest your mind be changed. –The
Kikitsutai Book of Wisdom

Six-thirty was later than Todd's normal
dinner time, but he had been delayed today. While
he was pretty hungry, he thought it was worth it. His
roommate, Jamal, on the other hand, was not shy in
sharing his disbelief. Not that this was anything
new.

"You don't honestly believe those stories, do
you, man?" Jamal asked for what felt like the
hundredth time today. This was an old argument,
and not a serious one at that. They had been friends
for too long to let this get in the way.

"There are too many accounts to be
coincidence, and some of them are from trustworthy
sources."

"The same could be said of UFO's," Jamal
pointed out.

"Well, you never know..." Todd trailed off,
playing devil's advocate.

Jamal threw a balled-up napkin at him before
nodding towards the cafeteria at large. "Hey, there's
that cute girl you deny having a crush on. Why don't
you invite her over and see what she says about your
crazy talk?"

Sure enough, Anna was wandering around, tray in hand, looking about. The cafeteria was pretty crowded because of some kind of 'special' dinner, and there weren't many open spots and no free tables. If she wasn't already sitting with friends, then she might be circling awhile. After a hiss that he did *not* have a crush on her, he waved to get her attention.

"Hey, Anna! Need a seat?" He indicated the empty booth on the other side of the table that Jamal's sister had vacated a few minutes ago.

She hesitated a moment before speaking. "Yes, actually, I do. You don't mind my joining you?"

"Not at all. Anna, this is Jamal, my roommate. Feel free to ignore him if he annoys you." There was no room to dodge the elbow to his stomach under the table. "Jamal, this is Anna." He paused, then left it at that, not sure how to explain how he knew her without breaking his promise.

Jamal gave them both a curious look before turning to Anna. "So, Anna, you're friends with Todd-man here?"

"I suppose one could say that," She answered dryly.

"He tell you about Cats-eye?" Jamal asked, leaning forward.

"I'm sorry?"

"C'mon, Jamal. I don't think she's interested." Todd tried to lead the conversation away.

Anna raised an eyebrow. "If he's going to react like that, I think I'm very interested."

Jamal grinned. "See, she's *very* interested. Start from the beginning, bro. Don't confuse her."

"Fine." Todd sighed, though he truly was curious what she'd think. "From the beginning. First of all, did you know I'm trying to learn to be a criminal profiler?"

There was an odd expression on her face for a nanosecond before going back to her usual neutral expression. "I can't say I did. I was under the impression you were an Art Major."

"Art Minor. I love art but doubt I could make a career of it. Besides, I've been addicted to mysteries for too long. Anyway, my uncle works as a police officer. He's the one I get most of the information from. Well, it appears there are these stories going around."

"Stories?"

"Yeah, they seem to start with criminals, but the police hear them as they pick up the criminals."

"I'm confused," Anna admitted.

"C'mon, tell it right. Get to the good stuff," Jamal cut in.

"Don't you have someplace to go?" Todd eyed his 'friend', knowing it was useless.

"Nope, just here," Jamal answered with a wide grin.

"Swell." Todd turned his attention back to Anna. "Okay, this is still fairly obscure, but as far as I can tell, the first story was in New York, about two years ago. Some creep lures a girl, about six, I think, into an alleyway. He starts to touch her, and she's crying, when all of a sudden, this woman shows up. She tosses him off the kid and literally holds a sword to the guy's throat before telling the girl to run and find a policeman. Kid does so, cop checks the alley and finds the guy restrained and shaking badly, no sign of the woman. Creep says that the woman's eyes glowed golden, like a cat. That's why I call her Cats-eye. Anyway, she talked to the creep; no one knows what she said because he ain't talking, but he's made absolutely no attempts to claim innocence or be paroled. In fact, he's refused deals, and confessed to more in order to stay in jail longer."

"I see. That's," she hesitated, "interesting; but it sounds like an urban legend to me."

"Except for a couple of factors. One, it doesn't have quite the same feel of an urban legend. Not to be sexist, but in most urban legends, women are either victims or..."

"Femme Fatales?" Anna volunteered.

"Exactly. You get occasional ghost stories, but it still isn't quite the same. Two, other stories have popped up. Similar stories with presumably the same person. The stories come from areas and people who aren't likely to communicate with each other. At least, not at first. I suspect that totally fake stories are starting to be made up as more people hear about her, but there are enough that can be at least partially proven, which leads to the third point. With urban legends, you can never find the original source. I've actually talked to the arresting officer in the first story. Through official police channels, not just someone anonymous on the internet. This guy will testify that yes, he arrested the man, and this is what the guy told him."

"Okay, so there's a case of vigilante justice in New York a few years ago. What's the interest now?"

"Like I said, she didn't disappear into the woodwork. There have been scattered reports of similar stories in other places. Chicago, D.C., New

Orleans, Seattle, etc. Yeah, some of the stories have to be fake, and even the real ones are probably exaggerated, but there has to be *some* truth to it. I've been interested since I heard about her. Do you know how hard it is to break in as a psychological profiler?"

"Not easy, I'd imagine."

"I'll say. Most of the time, the focus is on serial killers, so there are few, if any, witnesses and all evidence has to be gathered from the crime itself. But they do it. Cats-eye, as far as I know, hasn't killed anyone. There are witnesses. I've been studying her. If I can prove she exists, and figure out information about her, well, it would be a major help."

"I see." Anna steepled her fingers. "What do you have so far?"

"I'd know more if I didn't have to sift through so many exaggerations. I know for a fact that she's below average height, pretty sure she has red or reddish hair, though a few instances I think were her, she was said to have a different hair color. The one factor that all reliable and reliable-sounding stories have in common is that her eyes can glow like a cat. That should help narrow it down. After all, I can't go after all short red-haired women."

"Yeah, he'd have to go after you," Jamal pointed out. Todd laughed, though Anna's smile seemed strained.

"Should I be flattered or insulted that you think I could be a serial... what would you call her?"

"Vigilante, I guess. That is what she is, after all. Unless she has a badge to go around threatening miscreants at sword point. That's in more than a couple stories also, though not all. Sometimes she has a different weapon, or no visible weapon at all. Sometimes she seems to be an opportunistic 'hero', just happening to be around. Though there's one story with some proof to back it up about her approaching a particularly vicious gang. I think it was Chicago. Anyway, she told them to stop targeting civilians, or else. They called her 'Cherry' there. Well, they not only ignored her, but some tried to take her out. When one attempt seriously injured a near-by child, well, she got mad. Over twenty of them wound up in the hospital or jail. The leader may never walk again."

"My heart bleeds for them, I'm sure," Anna said, with a roll of her eyes. "Are you sure it's the same woman?"

"The worst offenders stopped calling her Cherry and started calling her Devil Woman because of glowing, golden eyes."

"Speaking of those eyes," Jamal cut in, "how do you explain it?"

"Too many reports to be a total fabrication. And they show up in the first version of the stories, before she morphs into some flying demon with glowing eyes and flaming hair that sometimes happens by the tenth or twelfth retelling. All I can assume is that somewhere around is a short reddish-haired woman with an acute sense of justice, an interest in swords, and a very rare eye condition."

Todd paused to observe his audience. Jamal had heard all this more than once, proofread his blog, and while he didn't believe a word of it, was at least kind enough to let his friend ramble about it.

He was also waiting for Todd to get to the best part. Anna hadn't lost that neutral expression, but seemed just slightly... troubled?

"I'm not scaring you, am I?"

"Should I be scared? Your Cats-eye is likely fictional, or if real, in another major city somewhere. Even if she was real, she doesn't seem to threaten innocent bystanders."

"You're partially wrong."

"Oh? She does attack innocent bystanders?" Anna asked, raising her glass of water.

"No, no. You were right about that. What I mean is that there's another Cats-eye account, last night. Less than half a mile from the school."

Todd realized it was a bit mean, but he was actually hoping Anna might have done a spit-take. Sometimes her poise unnerved him. However, Anna was as composed as ever, just swallowed silently, and patted her throat delicately a few times. "Here? Last night?"

"Yeah, it's not like most of the other stories, but this guy doesn't seem to have heard the rumors. Apparently, about midnight, a cop found some guy unconscious in an alleyway with a knife in his sleeve. No injuries, no alcohol, no drugs in his system. Seems this poor idiot actually tried to mug Cats-eye herself. Man, he's lucky no one got hurt or she would have chewed him up and spit him out. I'm hoping that I can get a chance to talk to him. I've talked to a few police but never gotten a true first-hand account."

"Better hurry. Unless this Cats-eye shows up to press charges, the police probably don't have anything to hold him on," Jamal pointed out.

"I know, but I'm hopeful. They said the guy's currently spooked enough that he's in no hurry to get out and risk meeting her again."

"But it happened near here?" Anna shook her head in disbelief.

Jamal grinned. "So, being a short woman with red hair, what's your alibi?"

Anna raised an eyebrow, before sighing. "It's a fair cop. I'm Cats-eye. Unfortunately, I must now kill you both to protect my identity. You really should have left it alone." Looking them both in the eyes, for one moment she looked so sincere that Todd found himself trying to sink through the back of the booth. His one consolation to acting like a total coward was that Jamal was doing the same. Then she smirked, and her eyes changed, and it was normal Anna again. "You boys are *sooooo* gullible."

"Your eyes..." Jamal started, before deciding it wasn't worth it. "You looked really serious." He was laughing though. So was Todd.

"Were my eyes gold? Did they glow?" Anna asked rhetorically. "Come on, do I really look like some dangerous vigilante?"

"Well, part of the problem is Cats-eye doesn't look dangerous either. Not that you're her!" Todd pointed out at her exasperated glare. "Just that there are a few similarities."

"I give up," Anna sighed. "Anyway, as to my *alibi*, I assure you that I was in my dorm room, probably trying to sleep." She looked at Jamal as if daring him to argue with her.

Jamal held up his hands. "Okay, okay. Anyway, I've got to go. Lots of studying to do." While that was probably true, Jamal was pre-med after all, Todd suspected he was using the chance to escape.

Unfortunately, once Jamal left, there was an awkward silence. To break it, Todd said the first thing that came to his mind, "What do you think of Cats-eye?"

"Do you truly want to know?" The look in her eyes was intense and haunting.

"Yes." His voice sounded distant, like listening through water.

Her eyes, burning amber, held his and didn't let go. "I think you are going on an empty chase. Cats-eye is probably nothing more than myth or legend. Don't waste your time. Find someone different to profile."

The more she talked, the more sense it made. Cats-eye had to be a myth. There were so many better ideas to study. He wanted to be taken seriously. This would make him look like a crackpot. No, she was right. He thought he even told her so, his voice sounding strange in his ears. Foggy and muffled. Then her eyes, holding him in place like laser beams, shifted and relaxed.

Todd blinked a few times. "I guess I should find a new project."

"I wish you the best of luck." She glanced at her watch. "Oh, is that the time? I really must be going."

"Oh, okay. I ought to go too. Bye, Anna." His original plan had been to visit the police station to try to talk to the mugger. But if Cats-eye was a myth, then there was no point. There was something wrong with that line of reasoning but he wasn't sure where it was yet. He'd figure it out later. For now, he should study. After all, there was a test coming up in Abnormal Psychology.

Chapter Seven

The indirect path is often clearest. –The Kikitsutai Book of
Wisdom

Once securely in her room and certain she was alone, the mask of Anna dropped instantly, and a multi-lingual tirade burst from the vocal cords of the woman, as she berated herself in every language she could think of. Finally, she stopped to catch her breath, when she realized she was starting to repeat herself.

Korvou was right, she had been stupid. Possibly beyond stupid. How had she missed this? How had the small legion of people whose job it was to find this kind of thing missed this? How many people knew of this 'Cats-eye', and did any of them know her in a different form? If Todd was interested in pursuing Cats-eye, then he probably wasn't the only one. Still, at the moment, he was the most dangerous in that he actually knew her to an extent. Well, the most dangerous she knew of anyway.

She had thrown him off temporarily, but it probably wouldn't stay that way for long. She wasn't a very skilled hypnotist, and this seemed to be a passion of his. To her advantage was the fact that he trusted her and certainly didn't seem resistant to hypnosis. However, she hadn't put him fully under, which was pretty much impossible on an unwilling subject, at least without drugs. It was hard to hypnotize someone into going too far out of character. If studying Cats-eye really was a passion of his, unless he got redirected, then she had probably done no more than delay him, and that only by a day or two. At least that should prevent him from talking to the mugger, the most immediate danger.

Hmm, as long as she could keep Todd from drawing the connection, then she might be able to use this Cats-eye legend. Fabricating a few more stories, emphasizing or adding parts that didn't seem possible, then it might rate the level of Bigfoot, or Nessie. Interesting, but almost universally considered fake. It was worth considering later.

In the meantime, what should she do about Todd? What were her options? One, she could admit what happened to Ryoko-*Sensei*. He was very skilled at hypnosis and could easily redirect Todd without changing his personality. Of course, it would mean admitting her carelessness, disappointing him, and letting Father know she had failed. Again. She winced at the thought. Aside from the pain of that, they would probably decide this whole 'school experiment' was a failure and order her back home. Not a preferred option.

Option two, she could transfer schools. Todd would lose track of her, and she could try again someplace else, making absolutely certain not to change anywhere there might be a witness. Problem with that was that she'd have to explain why she wanted to transfer not two months into her freshman year. That would lead to much the same results as her previous option. Besides, she liked this school and didn't particularly want to transfer.

Option three, she could find another subject for Todd to fixate on. Todd was focused, and college was a busy place that interfered with one's perception of time. If she could keep him distracted, then he might forget about Cats-eye, or at least be too busy to pursue the issue.

Option four, she could do absolutely nothing and watch to see how things played out. Todd didn't quite suspect her, not yet anyway. Neither did his roommate for all the jokes he made, though she really wished he hadn't made them. Once an idea enters the mind, it never truly dies. Todd was pretty smart, but the concept that the quiet, shy girl you sometimes hang out with is actually a sword-wielding vigilante with possible supernatural powers was a leap the brain hesitated to make. If she didn't do anything suspicious, there was a good chance he'd never catch on. Hopefully. He would be less likely to believe it if he didn't know that she knew Kendo, but if she stopped sparring with him now, he would only get suspicious.

There were a few other options that she didn't take seriously, like actually telling him the truth or completely avoiding him. She wasn't going to avoid him because that would simply cause him to get suspicious. That was the only reason. It had nothing to do with the fact that he was one of the very few people on campus who didn't unconsciously avoid her. She was not lonely.

'Cats-eye' really ought to be mentioned to the public information control team. But that would mean revealing just how stupid she had been. Father would be livid. Perhaps it would be best to keep it quiet for now.

Her best bet was probably a combination of three and four. Try to get him interested in something else, but don't try too hard, or he could get suspicious. Most of all, try to make sure the subject never got brought up in his roommate's presence again. That was all she could do for now.

***

"Hey, back from your interview already?" Jamal asked as Todd walked in.

"Oh, I didn't go. I was at the library studying. There's a test on paranoia in Ab. Psych. coming up."

Jamal swiveled in his chair to face him. "You didn't go? What do you mean, you didn't go?"

"Well, I decided that maybe I was wasting my time."

"T-man, are you okay?" Jamal sounded very serious and a little concerned.

"Yeah, why?" Well, he felt a bit foggy still, but that was probably from studying.

"You're acting strange. Cats-eye is like an obsession of yours or something. Now that you're closer to proof than ever, it suddenly doesn't matter?"

"Hey, you've been saying for over a year now that she's probably a myth." His voice sounded defensive even to him.

"But *you* haven't." Jamal kept eyeing him, like he was looking for something.

Todd rubbed his forehead; he was starting to get a headache. "I know, but..."

"I just can't believe you don't want to at least talk to this guy! I mean, what's the worst that could happen?"

The weird mental fog started to clear out as he shook his head. "You're right. I don't know what's wrong with me. Hey, you using the phone?"

"Go for it, bro." Jamal shot him an encouraging smile before going back to his books.

It only took a couple minutes. A couple minutes to discover that the guy had left an hour ago. "You were right. The police had nothing to hold him on, and the guy's gone."

Jamal spun to face him. "Lousy luck. Will they give you his contact info?"

"No, invasion of privacy or something like that."

"And you spent the night studying."

Todd dropped the backpack before slumping onto his bed. "Rub it in, why don't you? I better get a good grade on this test, at least."

Jamal looked at him, as if hesitating before speaking up. "So, what happened?"

"What do you mean?"

"I mean with you. You were all psyched to go talk to this guy, then you go to the library and decide it doesn't matter. This seems more your field than mine."

Todd studied the ceiling, thinking it over. "Well, Dr. Phillips would probably say something like a deep subconscious fear of failure caused me to back into denial until it was a moot point."

He could feel Jamal looking at him. "You think it was cold feet?" He asked skeptically.

"Don't know. That's the problem with subconscious drives; you don't necessarily know you have them. On one hand, I hope that's not the problem, because it could be difficult to solve and I'd hate to think that I have that big a problem with fear. On the other hand, it does seem logical, and it means I'm not crazy."

"Hey now, I always thought you were crazy." Jamal's voice was laced with laughter.

"Takes one to know one."

"So, now what?"

Todd sighed. "Don't know. I'm pretty much back to the point where I was this morning. Except that I have reason to believe there was a Cats-eye sighting only a few blocks from the school. Maybe Uncle John can get me transcripts of the questioning."

"That'd be good. You know, you could wander around the streets at night hoping to run into her."

"In downtown West Palm? Either you're crazy or you think I am." Besides, as far as he could tell, she didn't stay in one area long.

"Maybe Super Chick would show up and save your butt."

Todd frowned, resting his chin on his fist. "Hmm, get in trouble and get saved by a girl, or get in trouble and have my rear handed to me? Decisions, decisions."

Jamal laughed. "Well, if you aren't going to try to lure her out, you want to quiz me on the circulatory system? You aren't the only one with a test coming up."

"I'll quiz you on the circulatory system if you'll quiz me on paranoia and phobias." Wasn't quite the evening he had planned, but he would make the best of it.

***

It was Wednesday that Liska learned her hypnosis had already failed. Todd complained about being distracted and missing his chance, something Liska would have been more grateful for if it wasn't so obvious how upset he was about it. Still, it gave her a bit of breathing room. As long as she avoided trouble she should be fine. Much easier said than done.

Further research had revealed that Todd Kensworth had a website dedicated to studying Cats-eye. How no one had caught this yet, she didn't know. The website was not overly visited, his hit count was in the hundreds, but there was enough that attempting to erase or change the website might cause more attention that she wanted to avoid. Asking Todd to drop it would definitely raise suspicions. So she ignored it the best she could. Fortunately, even Todd wasn't completely accurate in his information. For example, he believed her to be in her early or mid-twenties and seemed to think she was closer to average height, probably because when she was intimidating someone, they automatically assumed she was taller than she was. Good, that made it less likely he would connect her to Cats-eye. In addition, she wasn't actually responsible for every incident. Most, but there were a few that couldn't possibly be her.

In the meantime, she tried to subtly focus him on his studies and art. It meant learning more about art techniques than she really cared about, but that was fine. She knew most of the psychology, even if she didn't know the terms. Then he made an unusual request.

"You want me to what?"

"I want you to model for me. For a painting."

"What *kind* of model?"

Todd blushed. "Not that kind! Just, um, well, I'm supposed to paint a few members of the Greek pantheon and well, you struck me as a good candidate?"

"For whom?"

His close scrutiny was starting to make her uncomfortable. "That's partially up to you. I promised Shahara, Jamal's sister, don't think you've met her, that she could be Aphrodite if she helped me; and Jamal wants to be Hermes, but other than that, I'm pretty open. You have any preferences?"

"Who would see this?"

"My art teacher and the rest of the class, that's about it. Why?"

"I don't like the idea of a painting of me around where strangers could see it."

Todd frowned at her, clearly wondering why, but decided against asking. "Well, it shouldn't be seen by anyone outside of class, but even still, I'd probably make some changes so it would be harder to recognize you."

"Such as?"

"Depends on who you want to be. Hmm." He examined her again. "How about Athena? Between the helmet and the armor, I doubt you'd look much like you. Maybe a wig. How long is your hair? I've only seen it tied up."

Wondering if she was being beyond foolish, Liska removed her hair ornament. Without the pin to hold it up, her hair quickly fell to about her waist instead of hovering around her neck. Despite the fact she felt a smidgen more vulnerable this way, she was amused by the surprise in Todd's eyes. Artemis might be a slightly more accurate choice, but Athena worked too.

"On second thought, you might not need a wig. Um, do you mind either curling your hair or having it curled?"

"I don't mind it being curled, but I'm not overly savvy on hair care."

Todd shrugged. "Shahara is studying as a beauty consultant. I'm sure she can curl your hair. So, will you?"

She shouldn't. It was dangerous and she knew it. There were so many people who would love to see her dead, and if Todd was as good at painting as he was at drawing, there was a chance the painting would be displayed somewhere. But he was her friend, kind of, sort of, in a weird way. Besides, it was something to focus on that wasn't Cats-eye.

"You would let me know if it will be displayed somewhere."

"Absolutely."

"And I get to see it when it's done?"

"Of course."

"Do you have a specific outfit you want me to wear?"

Todd smiled, excitement obvious. "I'm borrowing costumes from the drama department.

They did a play set in Ancient Greece last year. It's possible that nothing will fit you, but I got permission to alter the clothes a little. Or we could have you stand on something so you look taller."

Not a bad idea, really. "Then I guess I'm in."

"Great! You won't regret it!"

"Wonderful," Liska dead-panned. It was probably a really bad idea, but as long as no one saw it, she should be fine. Why did that feel so much like famous last words?

Chapter Eight

Knowledge of a person is power over them. Be careful who
you give that power to. – The Kikitsutai Book of Wisdom

She had only agreed to this stupid idea two days ago,
and Liska was already sorry she had heard of it. To
begin with, there were Todd's friends who had
promptly decided they were also Anna's friends,
especially Shahara. In all fairness, Shahara was a
nice girl, even if she had the same uncomfortable
sense of humor as her brother. Unfortunately, as an
image consultant in training, Shahara apparently
decided that Anna would make a lovely project. Oh,
she didn't come out and say that Anna had the
fashion sense of a dust bunny, but it was pretty
obvious that Shahara felt that Anna was...
stylistically challenged. While Liska couldn't argue
with that, it still wasn't something she wanted to
think about.

It would be easier to handle if it wasn't so
obvious that Shahara wasn't doing this to be mean-
spirited or obnoxious. She honestly liked Anna and
just felt that Anna needed a little help in the area of
fashion. It was hard to turn down someone who was
that determined to 'help'.

Jamal, fortunately, wasn't as interested in Cats-eye, so he didn't make many jokes about it. At the moment, he was pretty busy studying for some class. Liska vaguely thought it was anatomy. She was staying out of it though. He still thought it strange that she knew the entire nervous system by memory. She tried to brush it off but wasn't sure how successful she was. Someday, she was going to learn to keep her stupid mouth shut!

Finally, there was Todd. He was still attracted to her, and it was getting worse. Today she had actually tried to back out of posing, but he had seemed so disappointed she couldn't say no. There really was no way of getting out of this without being rude, was there?

Shahara was attempting to curl her hair. It was too long for her to curl easily herself, and she didn't have much experience with a curling iron. Apparently, her hair had a natural antipathy towards the device. By the time the left side was curled, the right would be coming loose. Shahara's solution to this was to use enough hairspray to stun a bloodhound, and it *still* only held a curl for about an hour and a half. Liska hated the hairspray, loathed having to cover her nose and mouth to keep from gagging, and despised the lingering stench following her the rest of the day. How did anyone actually use this gunk voluntarily?

"Okay, cover your neck." Shahara prompted.

Having Shahara mess with her hair was uncomfortable, and the hairspray was nasty, but she could tolerate that. She could not tolerate people touching her neck, something Shahara learned very quickly. The first time her hand absently touched the back of Liska's neck, Liska had grasped it, nails digging in, even before she realized she had moved, surprising them both.

After some apologies and discussing her reflexes, they came to an arrangement. Shahara would do everything in her power not to touch her neck, and Anna stood with hands clasped to slow down her reactions if it happened by accident. When curling the hair nearest her neck, Anna had her hands over her neck, protecting it. So far, they hadn't had any more mishaps.

"I don't know why we're bothering to do this now. Don't you have class in an hour?" Anna directed her question to Todd while moving her hands to follow Shahara's instructions. "By the time you get out of class, most of this will be gone."

"I know, but you're almost done, aren't you?"

She rolled her eyes. "Yeah, only another fifteen minutes or so."

"You have unusual hair," Shahara said.

It took everything in her not to react outwardly to that. "Oh?"

"Yeah, the texture isn't normal for, well, a white girl."

Not surprising, since Father was Japanese. "Oh, well, Mother is half-Vietnamese. It's probably from her," She lied easily.

"Oh? It's that recent? I could see a few Asian traits, but I thought it was further back. It's the eyes mostly. The color's wrong, but you have the slant. Some of the complexion. I suppose I should have been suspicious of a redhead without freckles."

Liska bore the scrutiny with as much grace as she could scrounge up but was very relieved when it ended and Shahara went back to her hair.

"So, why haven't you mentioned it?" Shahara asked as she took another thick strand.

Because I barely know you and it isn't your business. "It never came up. I don't talk about it much."

"Are you ashamed of your background?" There was an odd stress in her voice. Or perhaps not so odd. Shahara and Jamal were first-generation Jamaican-Americans and it hadn't taken more than five minutes to find out that Shahara was proud of her heritage.

"No, but it's not a big deal."

"Then why not mention it?"

"It's complicated." Liska pondered and decided it wasn't wise to annoy someone fixing your hair, so she elaborated. "My father's family is rather conservative, and insular. Then Father went and married my mother, a total outsider, without warning. I'm not sure they ever got over it. Unfortunately, we lived in the same area as his family. Father is one of them and a head of house, so he's accepted. Mother, they are civil to. Me?" She shrugged carefully. "I had to put up with the children who hear the things the adults say and don't have to be diplomatic about it."

"Ah." That Shahara understood, and fortunately, dropped the subject. That was actually a lot closer to the truth than she had planned. She would have to remember to add that to Anna's dossier.

Shahara finished her hair then, so Liska put on the helmet and took the pose Todd wanted. The helmet ruined about half of the curls that were there, and she was actually standing on cans to add some height. The 'armor' was cardboard, that Todd had designed for her earlier, but the shield was heavy. It wasn't a comfortable pose, but she managed for the thirty minutes they had until Todd realized he had to get to class.

"It was going so well too! Hey, Anna? Can you come back in about an hour?"

"Yes, I can make it."

"I'll be back too; you need me to do her hair." Shahara said.

"Might as well come too, if everyone else is." Jamal glanced up from his textbook.

"Great. Thanks, guys!" Todd grabbed his notebook and made a dash for the door.

***

Todd hated, absolutely hated, being drawn away from something he enjoyed when it was going well. He liked class, but he had been having trouble with his painting and now that he was in the zone, he didn't want any interruptions. He had come close to deciding to skip class today, but Behavioral Therapies was hard enough without missing classes.

Today, they were studying hypnotism. Todd wasn't sure that he believed in hypnotism, if he was honest with himself. It was so hard to separate the truth from the hype and even the scientific community was divided as to its' effectiveness. He was a little behind on the reading and tried to pay close attention to the teacher but his mind kept wandering as he sketched in the margins.

Then, there was a description of what it was like to be hypnotized. The voice of the hypnotizer was most important, and it only made sense to go along with them. Some people reported it was like being in a fog. Wasn't that how he felt when he thought about giving up on Cats-eye? Starting with talking to Anna about her?

No, it couldn't be. He had to be mistaken. Anna couldn't have hypnotized him. Could she? She wouldn't do that. Would she? Even if she was capable, wouldn't it take a lot of set up and time? He raised his hand.

"Dr. Keith? Is it true that it takes a lot of time to hypnotize someone?"

"No, but that is a common misconception. Actually, especially if the hypnotizer is experienced and/or has hypnotized that person before, the trance can be brought on in seconds. There's a sidebar about it in your textbook, page 417."

"Can a person be hypnotized without knowing it?"

"That one's still being debated."

Todd nodded in thanks, mind a million miles away. He had to talk to Anna.

***

The instant Liska saw Todd, before he was close enough to talk to her, before she could smell his emotions, she knew something was wrong. She had a feeling she knew what, too. *He knows.*

It made sense. Her hypnotism simply wasn't strong enough to last. Not that she planned to make this easy for him. No, she'd make him ask or perhaps accuse. Then she would claim ignorance and act offended. Then she would avoid him, possibly for the rest of the time here. Until then, she didn't know a thing. Besides, there was a chance she was wrong. A slim chance, but a chance nevertheless.

Jamal was with him but apparently didn't have a clue what was going on, because he looked confused and concerned, trying to figure out what was wrong. She had been walking along the intracoastal when she spotted them, across the street from the campus proper, and slightly away from the crowds of students going to and from classes.

Todd had finally seen her, and was heading straight towards her, the crowds moving out of his way, possibly without him noticing. Jamal, who wasn't as upset, had to work to get around them.

Todd finally got to her, clearly trying to control his facial expression. Hmm, a struggle between anger, confusion, and fear. She might be able to pull this off if she could confuse him. He didn't want to believe it, that was obvious.

"Anna? Could I talk to you for a minute? Privately?" The last was more to Jamal than to her.

She opened her mouth, though she had no idea what to say, when there was a sharp cry. A child's cry, female, probably between eight and twelve. Her present situation deemed temporarily irrelevant, Liska turned her head with an almost audible crack towards the sound.

On the sea wall was a young girl, poised to jump. Tide was high, the water was choppy. Liska realized this only after she was half-way to stopping her. Just as the girl's feet left ground, Liska caught her. "No, it's not safe!"

The girl struggled in her grip, causing Liska to have to readjust and pull her back. "No! Muffy!" Liska quickly scanned the water, dimly aware that Todd and Jamal had come up behind her, and a crowd was starting to gather.

'Muffy' appeared to be a floundering cocker spaniel puppy. The puppy wasn't going to make it much longer. "Stay here," Liska ordered, barely remembering to keep up her accent as she let go of the girl to get the dog herself.

She didn't like dogs. She really didn't like dogs. Dogs hated her at first scent. Most dogs that were large enough tried to rip her throat out. But she couldn't let the puppy drown.

Liska took two steps before she froze as suddenly and painfully as if she had walked into a brick wall. It was because the dog barked. The dog barked and she was half the world and almost fifteen years away.

She was being held by a woman who was running. The woman was scared and running fast. Far away were the shouts of voices and the baying of dogs. That made her scared too. They came to a small creek. Sometimes she would play in the creek. Not now. The woman jumped to the creek and over it. There was a tiny cave on the other side. Big enough for her, but only barely. The dogs were coming closer. The woman put her in the cave and told her to stay there and stay quiet until help came. No matter what. She nodded. She was a big girl, four years old already. She would listen, even if she was scared.

The woman nodded, hugged her, and moved the plants to cover the hole, before starting to run, back across the creek and further into the forest. The woman didn't get far. She could still see her through the hole when the dogs came. She watched, too scared to move, too scared to scream, too scared to breathe, and most of all, too scared to look away. The dogs ripped the woman apart. The woman was screaming so loudly, so horribly. Blood and pain, both smells she knew but never to this extent, filled her nose. Worst of all was the men. They laughed. The woman was in pain, and was dying, and they laughed. And she did nothing, knowing they would do the same to her if they found her.

Something in her died that day. Part of her innocence was lost forever. Not just because she saw death, not just because of the cruelty, but also because she learned what hate was that day. She learned just how deeply she could feel it.

The sound of splashing pulled her from her memories. A stranger was exiting the water, a shivering puppy in his arms. Part of her mind noticed that she was actually relieved the dog would be okay, and was surprised at that, but it wasn't her first priority. Her first priority was to stop shaking!

How long had she been shaking? How obvious was it that something was wrong with her? A hand landed lightly on her shoulder. Liska jumped, spun a one-eighty in the air and landed, hands up, ready to defend herself before realizing it was just Todd. Apparently, it was pretty obvious. On the bright side, he didn't look like he wanted to confront her anymore. No, he looked startled and concerned. Just peachy.

"S...Sorry." Idiot! Quit stuttering!

Todd just looked even more concerned. "Are you okay? You look awful."

"Gee, thanks." Fortunately, the crowd was thinning out. Even Jamal was discretely making himself scarce. She must look horrible.

Todd ignored her sarcasm and led her to a bench. Suddenly feeling completely drained, she let him. Her legs had somehow been replaced with Jelly, so perhaps sitting would be best. She didn't need him walking her through breathing techniques to relax, so she tuned him out and focused on making sure Anna was firmly in place.

She could just box the whole thing up and deal with it later, in private. It was tempting, very tempting. However, it would be worse when she did face it, and Todd would be highly suspicious. Most normal people don't recover that quickly from a bad shock. Might as well deal with as much as she could now.

Her breathing was steady again, and probably her color had returned, because Todd would not be put off any longer. "Are you alright?"

"Yes, I think so."

"What happened?"

She gave a laugh that sounded far too shaky in her ears. "Would you believe I just don't like dogs?"

"I don't like snakes. I've never had a panic attack at seeing one. Besides, I saw you. You were about to go in after it."

She could have said something about the intensity of phobias but decided against it. "Have you ever seen anyone killed by a snake?"

Liska wasn't looking at him, but she could smell his horror as he realized what she was leading up to. "No, I haven't." His voice was surprisingly steady. He'd make a good counselor.

"Everything was fine, then I heard the dog bark. I was back there, watching her die."

"Watching who die?"

She shook her head. "I don't know. No one in my immediate family. I think. I can't remember. I remember everything else, the sounds, the blood, everything. Everything but who she was or how we ended up in the situation in the first place." No crying. She was not going to cry. She was not!

"How old were you?" Todd asked in a quiet voice.

"Four."

"Four years old?" He squeaked this time. If she wasn't so upset, it might be humorous.

Liska nodded. "That's how I learned what death was."

"What a way to learn," He muttered. She probably wasn't supposed to hear it, and he might not have known it slipped out. "The one who died; was it another child, or an adult?"

"A woman. She was trying to protect me, she put me where the dogs couldn't get me."

"You saw everything." It wasn't a question. "Was this something you just remembered now?"

"No, I've always known."

"Your family doesn't talk about it?"

"Would you?"

"Right, dumb question. If I can ask, how did you react then? Do you remember?"

Oh, she remembered. She remembered perfectly. "I hid until my family found me. It must have been at least an hour. They had to pick me up and carry me away. I couldn't move. I didn't talk for at least a week."

"I'm sorry."

"You didn't do it." Liska was coming back to herself, but she was still too vulnerable. She had to get away. She had told him too much already and didn't want to tell him more.

"Still, I am sorry. I'm sorry you went through that. I'm sorry that woman died. I'm sorry you have a phobia of dogs, though that's a justified phobia if I've ever heard one." He paused. "Is there anything I can do?"

"No, thank you. I just... Well, actually, could you just walk me to my room? I really need some time right now."

"Of course."

"Thank you. For everything."

Todd brushed the thanks off, standing and offering his hand. He didn't let go either. Any other time, she'd stop him, but right now, the contact felt reassuring, warm. And he had completely forgotten about asking her about hypnotism. She certainly wasn't going to remind him.

***

Korvou had not gone back to Malaysia, though he was sure Liska hoped he had. No, at the moment, he was less than half a mile away, watching. He couldn't hear her, and wasn't certain what was going on. That was fine, he didn't need to know. Not exactly. What he did know was that he had found another one of the major players he had mentioned. Even as he watched, tendrils of fate were binding them closer together. Did Liska have any idea what kind of a dangerous game she was playing? Change was in the air indeed.

Chapter Nine

How one deals after conflict is as important as how one deals during conflict. – The Kikitsutai Book of Wisdom

One of Liska's favorite ways to calm down was to make tea. She had turned it into a type of meditation, if not an art form. Here, a few substitutions were necessary. Her room didn't have a stove, so she had to use an electric water heater instead of her preferred copper kettle. She had left her heirloom teacups in Japan, so she used cheap mugs. There were differences, but it was mostly minor cosmetic changes. The intent was the same. It might not be the Japanese Tea Ceremony, but in just ten minutes she usually felt a lot better. Today was not 'usually'. Then Korvou popped through the wall in front of her, literally.

She managed to swallow her scream and hoped he hadn't noticed her flinch. "You nearly ended up with tea in your face." Actually, she almost wished she had jumped enough for that. "Why are you here?"

"You aren't going to offer me tea? I'm hurt."

"Sure, I'll offer you tea. Just give me a minute to find a suitable condiment. Would you prefer arsenic or cyanide? I'm afraid I'm out of strychnine."

Korvou plopped down on her desk chair, snagging a tea biscuit as he sat.

Liska sat on the windowsill, the only other available seat beside the bed. "Sit down, help yourself."

"I will, thank you."

"Aren't you supposed to be over in Malaysia or Bangladesh or someplace like that?" She knew exactly where he had been, but by pretending she had forgotten, she could send a message that he simply wasn't important enough for her to keep track of his whereabouts.

"Malaysia, and I'm done there."

"Congratulations. Why don't you take a vacation to celebrate? I hear the Bermuda Triangle is lovely this time of year."

She managed not to growl as he took another biscuit. He had to know that stealing her food was a major irritation. "You're in a bad mood."

"As usual, your perception is exceeded only by your tact. Now isn't a good time."

"It's not going to get better."

Liska tried to discretely rub her temples without sighing. She was going to have such a headache before this was done, she just knew it. "Did the auras tell you that?"

"Who was the man who walked you to your room?"

"Why?" The word dripped with suspicion.

Korvou smirked and relaxed his body language. "I'm curious."

"I don't care."

"You're engaged."

"Betrothed. He still has to propose."

"He still wouldn't be happy about it."

"Yes, well he can go take a long walk off a short pier. Make my life a little easier. Besides, you aren't the blackmailing type." Which was fortunate for her.

"I have no intention of telling Yoshiro. I'm no fonder of him than you are. So, who is he? The one who walked you to your room. What's going on?"

The headache was getting worse. "Go away."

"Not until I find out what I need to know." He was serious, she could tell.

"The only thing you need to know is what I'll do if you don't get out." She was growling now and trying not to change involuntarily.

"Deep breaths. I'll wait."

She glared at him but took the offered time to force her emotions back. "I don't want to talk right now."

"Either you were faking it something fierce, or something was seriously wrong back there. Short story, I don't need all the details."

"You don't need *any* details."

"Maybe not. But I could probably understand better than the human." She didn't say anything. Korvou sighed and looked her in the eyes. "Word of honor, I walk out the door, this talk never happened unless you bring it up again."

He wouldn't go back on his word, she knew that, but there were still too many loopholes. "So you won't use the door."

Korvou shook his head. "Fine, once *I leave*, this talk didn't happen. It will probably help you."

"I'm fine. Why do you want to know who he is?"

"I'll tell you if you answer me."

Annoying git. He wouldn't drop it, either. "I had a flashback."

"Ouch! In public?" She nodded. "A bad one?"

"Ooooh, yes." The words were a long, drawn-out hiss.

"What did you tell him?"

"A semi-sanitized version of the truth. He walked me back afterwards. That's all."

"That flashback, anything I would know about?"

"I doubt it." She hadn't even met Korvou at that point and hadn't talked to anyone about it for over a decade.

Korvou nodded. "You don't want to explain it again, I'm guessing."

"Not particularly." Not a chance.

"Fine. That's not a problem.

"Speaking of problems, what are you doing here?"

"Remember I said another major player in the upcoming changes is nearby? I found him."

A cold finger of trepidation walked up her spine. Liska shoved the feeling away with violent force. She was just a little shaken by the flashback; that was it! Time to get over it. "Who?"

"I'm still trying to get you to tell me his name."

"You're wrong."

"Not about this. I'm never wrong about this kind of thing. I don't know what's going on, but he is becoming more and more involved. Part of it is you getting him involved."

"Get out."

"My leaving won't change the truth. Do you know what kind of game you're playing?"

"I said, leave!"

"He's getting far too close. What are you going to do when that happens? Will you kill him when you feel too threatened?"

"GET OUT!" The shout tore from her before she realized it, about the same time as her mug flew from her hand to the wall, inches from his head. Interestingly enough, her first thought was that it was a good thing it was just a cheap mug and not one of her special teacups.

Korvou simply looked from the wet spot on the wall and then back at her. "See, emotion is making you careless. Otherwise, you wouldn't miss."

Before she could decide if it was worth strangling him, there was a knock on the door. "Anna, it's Karen. Is everything okay?" Hearing the RA and knowing she had a key to get in if she didn't answer, Liska literally shoved the protesting Korvou in her closet, took a deep breath and did a quick check to make sure nothing looked suspicious. Certain that all the Resident Advisor would see was Anna, she opened the door.

"Hi. Yeah, everything's fine. Why?"

"I thought I heard a scream."

"I was watching a movie on my computer. I guess I had the volume too loud. I'm sorry. I'll turn it down." Karen knew she didn't have a TV, but she had no way of knowing that Liska seldom watched movies.

"Okay. You're sure you're alright?"

"Of course." She tried to sound like it was an obvious answer.

"Fine. See you in a few hours for room check."

"Bye." Anna smiled at her RA before shutting the door. Liska listened until convinced Karen was gone before turning back to the room. "Okay, get out of my closet."

"You did push me in there." Korvou retorted, moving a blouse from his head.

"You need to leave before she comes back."

"I'll leave but remember what I said. He's getting more and more involved and you need to figure out how you are going to deal with it. And how involved you intend to let him get."

Liska watched him fade to near invisibility before walking through the closed door. When in doubt, one turns to old remedies. This wasn't something she could fight, so she'd deal with it like she dealt with other difficult things she couldn't do anything about. She'd ignore it. Suppressing a growl, she grabbed her inline skates and headed out the door. If only they'd let her outrace her thoughts.

***

Todd walked back to the waterfront in a daze, not realizing where he was until Jamal's voice broke the fog. "Hey, you okay?" Todd nodded. "Are you going back to painting?"

"I don't think I can right now. Will your sister mind?"

"Nah, I'll just call and let her know." After a quick call on his cell, Jamal turned back to him. "It's all good. Shahara wants to go shopping with a friend and was about to try and call off anyway." Jamal paused before continuing, "So what happened? Is Anna okay? Are you?"

"I'm fine. I just..." Todd's voice trailed off. Anna was, without a doubt, one of the most private people he had ever met. He truly doubted she would appreciate him telling anyone what she had just told him. In fact, when she calmed down, she would probably be upset she had even told him. "Anna had a bad experience with dogs when she was a kid. This ended up reminding her of it."

"That's why you're wandering around looking like you're wearing mime make-up?"

Not a big surprise. "It was a *really* bad story."

"Must have been." Jamal shook his head before changing the subject. "So, what was going on earlier? You know, when people were stumbling over each other to get out of your way?"

He had forgotten about that. "Oh, yeah. I never did talk to Anna. Just as well, that was the last thing she needed right then. Ah, it's probably stupid anyway."

"What's stupid?" Jamal asked with the air of one hoping to hear how a friend made a fool of himself. Todd resigned himself to telling him. Jamal might not press him to tell someone else's story, but there was no way he would drop this.

"Remember how I ended up not talking to the guy who tried to mug Cats-eye? Because I was suddenly acting like it wasn't important?" Todd started walking towards their dorm, Jamal following.

"Yeah, and I get to hold that one over your head for years now."

"Swell." It was to be expected though. "Anyway, that happened after talking to Anna. She suggested I might be better off picking a different target."

"I've been telling you that forever. You never listen to me."

"*Precisely.* But I listened to Anna immediately? Plus, it felt kind of weird, the whole evening."

Jamal thought about that for a few minutes. "Okay, what's your theory?"

"We're doing a unit on hypnosis in Behavioral Therapies. Some of it sounds similar."

"You think she hypnotized you?" From the sounds of it, Jamal didn't agree.

Todd responded defensively. "I wanted to ask her about it."

Jamal stepped ahead to open the door. "Man, she never would have forgiven you for that." Which was probably true. "Okay, let's take a look at this. First of all, she would have to be able to hypnotize people, probably pretty good, right?"

"Yeah."

"Has she ever mentioned studying hypnosis?"

"No, but that doesn't mean she hasn't."

"True. She's how old?"

"Um, eighteen or nineteen, I think. About Shahara's age."

Jamal nodded. "Right, she's a freshman. How many people in that age group do you know who can do hypnosis?"

"Can't think of any off the top of my head."

"Neither can I. Doesn't mean there aren't any," Jamal continued quickly when Todd had been about to say something similar, "But they are probably rare. Next, she would have to be able to hypnotize you quickly, without being obvious, without special equipment, in a very crowded and noisy place. I imagine even the best hypnotists would have trouble with that."

"Probably." It certainly didn't sound like prime working conditions.

"And that's guys with years of experience, probably doing it for their jobs. Not dabblers with a hobby. Then, it had to be without you knowing you were being hypnotized. All I know of hypnosis is from movies and stuff. Is that possible?"

"Still being debated with most saying 'no'."

"See? Last of all, why in the world would she hypnotize you?"

"I don't know. The only thing I remember is her suggesting that I find someone else to study." Todd pulled out his keys to open the room door.

"Right, and unless she's your mysterious Cats-eye, which I really can't see, then there's no reason."

Todd laughed a bit at the idea. Boy, it would be ironic if he ended up explaining his Cats-eye study to Cats-eye without knowing it. "So, you don't think I was hypnotized?"

Jamal shook his head. "Nah. I think it was a much stronger power. The power of a pretty girl. Think about it. Anna's pretty, and if she'd actually listen to Shahara's advice, she'd be beautiful. Deny it all you like, but you *do* have a crush on her. She makes a suggestion, you listen. Maybe it just happened to coincide with your getting cold feet. That would explain it, right?"

Todd sat down, thinking about it. "Maybe. You're probably right. Thanks."

"No problem. You can thank me by buying pizza tonight." Jamal tossed over the list of local numbers.

"Oh, great." Todd made a face, even if he didn't mind too much.

"Come on, Dude. I probably saved your friendship with that girl. Do you think she would have given you the time of day if you asked her if she hypnotized you?"

"Probably not," Todd conceded. "Okay, I'll buy, but I'm picking the toppings."

"As long as you *do* get pepperoni and *don't* get anchovies, we're good."

Jamal's argument made a lot of sense. Even more sense than the possibility of Anna hypnotizing him. However, as he dialed the number, Todd couldn't help but wonder if he had been right after all.

***

Liska was beginning to wonder if there were grocery store deities and she had somehow offended them. Last time she went to the store, she had run into an attempted mugger. This time, he was in the store, following her. Clearly, he had been planning for another encounter.

He shadowed her, probably trying to be subtle. Liska considered it akin to an elephant tap-dancing to the 1812 overture, complete with artillery. Still, he didn't seem to realize she knew he was there and was leading him to where he would do the least damage.

The first time she had come to the store, she had memorized the layout, where the exits were, where the cameras were, where one was in plain view, and where one could disappear. For whatever reason, there were no security cameras in the produce section, perhaps because the restrooms were there. So she led the way there, grateful that the store was pretty empty this late at night.

Once she was sure that no one was already in the produce section, she continued on to the corridor where the WC's were, making sure that her stalker saw her go in the Ladies' room. Sure enough, it was empty. Good.

Liska waited, hoping he'd come in, trying to make an attack in private. Of course, he couldn't know she was waiting by the door. One minute passed. Another.

Not fair. He's dumb enough to trail me around the store, but has enough sense or delicacy not to follow me in here?

Perhaps he was waiting outside. Or maybe he realized she knew he was following her and left before she could call the police. So, what were her options? She could call the police on him, but Todd would definitely hear about that. She didn't bring her bag, so she didn't have enough supplies for a disguise, just some scarves and a cheap pair of sunglasses. Since he had seen her come in, it wouldn't be enough to fool him. No windows, so she couldn't leave. If she stayed here too long, someone else might come by, and she didn't want to risk anyone else's life.

Not much in the bathroom. There were two stalls, two sinks, a paper towel dispenser, a plunger in one of the stalls, a spray can of air freshener, and a large trash can. She had brought in a small hand basket with a box of tea bags, some packages of ramen, and a box of popsicles. Not a whole lot to work with, though she could think of at least eight ways to cause some major damage with just that.

While she hadn't been able to study him too closely, not wanting him to know she had seen him, he was clearly carrying a gun. She hadn't actually seen the gun, so she didn't know what kind it was, but he didn't seem quite comfortable with it. Still, if he was stupid enough to bring a concealed weapon (poorly concealed, but still concealed) into a public place, he might be stupid or anxious enough to be trigger-happy. Opening the door and immediately getting shot was not on her to-do list.

Then again, he might not have come down the corridor at all, waiting for her to come out. Liska bit down on a growl of frustration. There were too many variables. No, no there weren't. She could see shadows under the door. Someone was out there.

Stretching out as far as she could, Liska turned on the tap of the sink. After another moment of hesitation, the door started to creak open. In a split-second, Liska changed the plan, moving away from the door and behind it, and arranging it so she was visible in the mirror. It wouldn't fool a second glance, but it might fool a first one.

Sure enough, the mirror shattered with a loud crack and cascade of glass. She winced, hoping no one heard that. A moment later, he stepped inside, clearly furious at being tricked. Unfortunately, she wasn't in a good position to disarm him. "Naughty, naughty. You shouldn't be here."

He flushed, and spun, gun now aimed at her.

Liska didn't particularly like guns, considering them too loud and obvious. That didn't stop her from using them or learning to recognize the most common and best quality firearms. Therefore, she was quite confident in her two-second assessment that the gun aimed at her, complete with homemade silencer, was a piece of junk. "Where did you get that thing? The 'everything for a quarter' box at a yard sale?"

"Hey, I paid good money for this thing!"

Liska scoffed. "They should have paid you to take it off their hands. Speaking of hands, you'll be lucky if it doesn't explode in yours." Ignoring him, she waved at the automatic towel dispenser, getting a fresh towel to pretend to dry her hands. Then she took another towel.

"It'll fire, that's the main thing."

It was the main thing. She wasn't wearing a bullet proof vest today. He probably didn't have great aim, but at less than five feet, it was hard to miss. On auto-pilot, her mind ran through a list of what was around, evaluating and rejecting several plans. He wasn't going to be distracted much longer. If she was going to grab the element of surprise, it would have to be now.

With a quick wish that this crazy plan would work, she threw a wadded-up piece of paper towel. Not deeming it a threat, he batted it away. He hadn't expected her to follow it up by spraying him in the face with the air freshener.

Choking, he fell back. Liska side-kicked the trashcan, knocking it to the ground. Sure enough, he tripped on that a moment later, falling through the door of a stall, hitting his head on the toilet inside. He wasn't quite unconscious, but he was dazed enough that Liska was able to pin his gun hand to the ground by kneeling on his arm and cover his nose and mouth. It took several seconds before he recovered enough to fight her, and by then it was too late.

Once he went still, and she knew he wasn't faking it, Liska checked his heart rate and breathing. Both normal, for someone unconscious anyway. He should be fine. And if he wasn't, well, then he shouldn't have tried to kill her.

They had been there too long. She'd have to move quickly. The bullet wasn't too deeply embedded in the wall, and she was able to pry it out quickly. Taking more paper towels, Liska got some water and washed his face, before wiping down the spray can and the tap. True, the chances of her leaving any usable fingerprints were unlikely, but if they did check, she'd rather be safe than sorry.

Her would-be attacker was still unconscious, so she wiped the door handles before darting to the produce section and grabbing several plastic produce bags. One went over each hand, and one picked up the gun. She hid that in her basket along with the bullet. Now came the hard part. A quick glance showed her that no one was watching the corridor, so she dragged the man out of the restroom, into the hallway. She had hoped to pose him on the bench, but he was just too heavy for that. Okay, new plan.

She put on one of her hair scarves, took her basket and went looking for the nearest employee. There was an older teen in deli. Perfect. She walked up to him and spoke in her best Southern accent. "Excuse me, Darlin', but this man had some kind of fit. He's in the corridor by the powder rooms."

If the clerk was calmer, or better trained, he would have asked her a few more questions immediately or at least told her to wait there so someone could ask her more questions later. However, this kid simply didn't know what to do and panicked, just as she had anticipated. As the teen quickly ran past her to check, she threw away the gun in the nearby trash can. Then she threw away the paper towels she had used, particularly ones that she hadn't touched directly, making sure the gun was completely covered. She'd throw the bags away later, somewhere at least a few blocks from the store. The bullet would be discarded in a third location, a few blocks from either.

Liska smiled as she removed the scarf. Assuming at least five minutes for her attempted attacker to wake up, she should have a minimum of twenty minutes for the confusion to clear up enough for them to wonder about her. She was leaving in ten minutes, carefully showing only average interest in the ambulance driving up.

Chapter Ten

Suspicion, once born, never completely dies. – The Kikitsutai
Book of Wisdom

The phone kept ringing. Todd covered his ears and tried to ignore it. It was Saturday, for crying out loud! He could actually sleep in! Who on earth was calling now?

Something soft, with a lot of give to it, hit him in the head. Jamal's pillow. Must be his roommate's 'subtle' attempt to get him to answer his stupid phone. "Alright, alright already."

Todd stumbled out of bed and blindly maneuvered his way around the dump they called a room before picking up the cell phone half-way through its sixth ring. "Hello?"

"Todd?"

"Uncle John? What time is it?"

"Not yet seven-thirty, but you won't care in a moment."

"Is something wrong?" Uncle John wasn't fond of mornings either. Todd forced himself to try to wake up.

"Quite the opposite, my boy. Remember the guy who tried to mug your mysterious Cats-eye?"

"Yeah, I didn't get a chance to talk to him."

"I know. Well, you've got a second chance. He got picked up again. Better hurry, this story's better than the last one!"

Now he was awake. "Another Cats-eye sighting? Are you sure?"

"Come listen to the story. See what you think. If you hurry, you'll even get breakfast."

"I'm on my way!" Another pillow hit him. Jamal's way of reminding him that it was still before a reasonable hour on a Saturday and some people wanted sleep. Todd was in too good a mood to care.

***

To get training to become a profiler, Todd had done volunteer work at the police station for a few years. He knew the station, and the cops, and most of them knew him, and his interest in Cats-eye. The first officer he passed, Juan Velazquez recognized Todd and told him where his uncle was. "Another Cats-eye sighting?"

"I hope so. Even if not, this guy may know more about an earlier one.

Officer Velazquez nodded. "Oh yeah, that one. Kinda weird to pick up the same guy twice in a week. Well, you better get to it."

"Right. Bye, officer."

Uncle John was in the break room. "Ah, Toddy, there you are. Grab a doughnut."

Todd did, ignoring the disliked nickname that his uncle would never give up. "So, what's up?"

"Our perp, the mugger from last time, decides he wants revenge on your Cats-eye."

Todd winced. "Bad idea."

"I'll say. He said something about buying a gun, though he doesn't have a license for one, and carrying it around hoping to run into her. Sees her going into the local Food Mart and follows her. When he gets her alone, following her into the bathroom, actually, he confronts her. Now, here's the good part. He said she beat him with air freshener."

"Air freshener?"

"Yup, sprayed him directly in the face, then overpowers him while he's choking. Knocked him out, presumably by lack of air."

"He okay?"

"He'll live. Don't think there was any brain damage, though he is an idiot, so it's a little hard to tell."

Todd nodded. "Then what?"

"According to an employee in the deli section, a petite woman came up telling him about a man having a fit and being unconscious in the hallway where the restrooms were. He checked that the guy was truly unconscious then called an ambulance. When the perp regained consciousness saying about someone trying to kill him, we got called in. Things just got more confusing from there."

"Did the deli worker mention the woman's hair color?"

"I asked him, he didn't remember."

"Is Cats-eye in legal trouble?"

Uncle John laughed, and grabbed another doughnut, glazed with orange sprinkles. "We can't even prove she exists, not to mention our perp's testimony suggests he was trying to kill her first.

We're still trying to decide if we can hold him on carrying without a license and possibly firing in a public place. There's evidence to suggest at least one shot was fired in the bathroom. But the gun's in the wind. When our guy realized that, and that we don't have proof against him, he shut up. Now he's claiming he had a fit and passed out."

"Food Mart has security cameras, right?"

"Not in that area."

"Any chance we could get a look at it anyway?"

"You want to try to ID Cats-eye?"

"I'd like a look, at least."

"I checked, it's in black and white."

That was disappointing, but it was still a starting place. "I'd still like to see."

"I'll see what I can do. Anything else?"

"Any chance the guy would talk to me about Cats-eye?"

Uncle John shrugged. "Unlikely, but I'll ask him."

"Great!"

***

It took over an hour, and several rounds of paperwork before Todd was given permission to sit in the room while the technicians went over the footage, provided he stayed quiet. By then, he knew that the guy refused to talk to him, and the gun had been found. Unfortunately, it had been wiped, so there were no fingerprints. While it had been fired recently, there was no bullet to prove it was fired in that bathroom. So, the evidence was circumstantial at best. Clever Cats-eye.

Most of the footage was pretty boring, though Todd did recognize a few people. Since the store was only a few blocks from campus, a lot of students did their shopping there. In fact, Todd had been there two days ago. There was some guy from his English class. There was one of his Kendo students. Oh, there was Anna.

"Okay, here's our guy." The technician pointed out. Todd blinked. That was only a couple minutes after Anna went in. Maybe she had seen something. Wait, the guy was following Cats-eye and went in a few minutes after Anna.

Anna. Anna was a short, red-haired woman. Anna knew swords. Anna liked to walk by herself at night. No, it was impossible. She was too young. If Cats-eye had such a distinctive British accent, it would have been mentioned by now. Besides, it was Anna!

But Anna wanted him to stop investigating Cats-eye. Anna might have hypnotized him. Anna surrounded herself with secrets. No, it couldn't be. Anna was in England during most of Cats-eye's reign. At least, that's what she said. No, this was ridiculous. If he went on like this, he'd go crazy doubting everything. Facts. What did he know?

Fact: Anna matched at least a cursory description. Not all the specifics, but those specifics often contradicted.

Fact: Both Anna and Cats-eye had experience using swords.

Fact: No Cats-eye account said anything about an accent. Anna had a distinct British accent.

Fact: Cats-eye had been active for at least two years. Anna would have been about sixteen then. One would think someone would have said something if Cats-eye was that young.

Fact: Cats-eye had been active in various parts of the United States during those two years. Anna said that she had first come to the States this July. Maybe he could ask to see her passport.

Fact: Anna was definitely in the right spot for these last two Cats-eye sightings. In fact, the place where the mugger had been found last time was almost exactly halfway between the campus and the food store.

Fact: Anna showed very little interest in Cats-eye. Which could mean anything, really.

All of these facts were quite interesting, but it wasn't enough to prove anything one way or another. But there were two ways to get that proof. One, he could see her passport stamps, if she agreed to show him. If he could come up with a decent excuse for why he wanted to see it. Two, he could ask her about going to Food Mart. She might know something. If she denied being there, well, then he would know something was up.

The technicians were complaining about how hard it was to match descriptions with such grainy film and in black and white. It's very difficult to spot a redhead without color. Todd kept his mouth shut. He wanted to talk to Anna first.

***

"Was I where?" Anna ducked under the swing of the sword, almost catching him off balance after his attempt. Or at least it would have if he hadn't suspected she would do that. It wasn't easy holding a conversation in the middle of a Kendo match, but it could be done, if one didn't mind the interruptions.

"Food Mart, Friday night."

"Last Friday, or a different one?"

"Last Friday." Come on, Anna, just answer the question.

Anna aimed a swing for his shoulder that he had to sidestep. "Why?"

"I thought I saw you going that way. I called to you, but you must not have heard me." He winced, both at the lie and the blow she got on his arm. Todd was lousy at lying.

"What time?"

"Oh, about ten?"

"You know, I think I did go to Food Mart. Sorry, I guess I didn't hear you."

"Did anything strange happen there?"

"Well, there was an ambulance going in that direction as I was leaving, but I didn't see where it went or what that was about. Why do you ask?"

"I heard an ambulance went to the Food Mart. I was wondering if you knew anything."

She blinked a few times in surprise. "It was going to Food Mart? Oh dear, I hope no one was badly hurt. No, I don't know anything about it."

"Oh well, I was just wondering. Thanks anyway. So, you up to posing for a bit this afternoon?" They were about finished here. Anna won again. What a surprise.

"Only if I can do some studying while Shahara works on my hair."

"That's fine. Maybe someone will quiz you, if you want."

"That would be excellent. Very well, see you after lunch?"

"Sure. Two o'clock?" So that was that. Unless she was lying. 'You're getting paranoid, Kensworth. Get over it.' If she was lying, she was very good at it.

***

Liska was very good at detecting lies. Besides that, she generally went with the assumption that everyone was lying until proven otherwise. Added to that equation was the fact that Todd Kensworth was a rotten liar. So, Todd was suspicious, was he? Why? He had lied about thinking he saw her, but he knew she was at Food Mart. At least, he certainly seemed to know.

She had claimed the man passed out instead of saying he attacked her for a few reasons. One, she wanted no involvement with the matter. Two, she had hoped that the whole thing would be dealt with by the paramedics, not the police. However, it would seem that her hope might have been in vain. If the police were brought in, then Todd had probably heard about it.

So how did he know she was at the store? Did she match the description the guy gave? Possible. Or the cameras. While there were no cameras where their fight was, she would be shown going in or out. Todd wasn't quite ready to declare her Cats-eye, but he didn't seem to trust her as much anymore. So he hadn't written off the idea.

Unfortunately, this left her in a bit of trouble. She couldn't just ignore this anymore, nor was she arrogant enough to think she could deal with this alone. However, there were few people she could ask for help without having to admit that she had not only attracted notice, but that she had messed up and not admitted it. This could lead to any or all of the unpleasant possibilities that she had been tying to avoid when she hypnotized him in the first place.

Fortunately, she did have a few tricks up her sleeve. Todd didn't want to believe she was Cats-eye. That was her biggest asset. All she had to do was give him a way out and she knew just how to do that. It was time to call Kira.

Chapter Eleven

True friends are the greatest treasure. –The Kikitsutai Book of Wisdom

It was Wednesday after 'Food Mart Friday' as Todd called it in his head. There were no more leads. Cats-eye hadn't left any fingerprints that could conclusively be proven as hers, the semi-victim wouldn't talk and had been released because there was nothing to hold him on. No witnesses. Just video footage that Anna had been in the store. But she freely admitted to that while denying any involvement. He wanted to ask Jamal his opinion, but if he mentioned the incident to Jamal or Shahara, Anna would almost certainly find out that he had suspected her. Absolutely no good could come from that. So this incident wasn't even on his blog.

Fortunately, Anna didn't seem to realize that he had lied to her. Currently she was trying to get her costume right for his painting. Shahara eyed her critically. "It needs something. Hmm, I know! I have a silver necklace from my Grandmother. It would look perfect with this. You can borrow it for the painting. I think I read something about silver being precious to Athena."

Anna's eyes expanded then retracted to normal so quickly Todd wasn't even sure he saw it. "Thank you for the offer, but that's not a good idea. I have a contact allergy to silver and cannot wear it at all."

"Really? It's good quality silver, not cheap stuff."

"That would just make it worse. I can't wear it, even for a few minutes. It eats away at my skin."

Shahara went ashy, before continuing in a higher voice. "You know, you'd look better in gold anyway. Is gold alright?"

"Gold is fine."

Todd suppressed a shudder while focusing on sketching Jamal. No silver around Anna, check. Not that he had any anyway. Then his cell rang. He almost ignored it, but he had a weird feeling this could be important. He got those occasionally. "One minute, Jamal. Hello?"

"Hey, Todd."

"Uncle John?"

"Yup, it's me. Looks like your Cats-eye moved on."

Todd blinked. "Moved on?"

"That's right. Sighting in Miami."

"When?"

"Oh, about an hour ago. I'm still working on getting the details. Not my jurisdiction, so I probably won't get them all."

There was no possible way Anna could have been in Miami an hour ago. She had been here at least twenty minutes, and driving from Miami was a nightmare, especially this time of day. Even the Tri-rail took two hours. Anna really wasn't Cats-eye. Unless...

"You're sure it's a Cats-eye sighting?"

"Sounds like one. Short woman, red shoulder-length hair, wielding a sword, glowing eyes..."

"Yeah, that sounds right." Anna had waist-length hair. So, it was true. She wasn't Cats-eye. That was a relief. Wasn't it? "Thanks. Let me know what you find out?"

"What I can. See you."

"Bye."

He had an audience. "Another Cats-eye sighting?" Jamal tried not to move from his pose.

"Seems to be. In Miami, this time."

"So she's gone. Good. I know you had a better chance of finding her while she was here but knowing she might be around made me uneasy."

"Shahara, you believe me? I'm touched. These two cynics doubted me. But as long as you stand by my side, I can face the world." Todd brought his hand to his heart with a large flourish.

"How heartwarming. When you two go around the bend, we'll make sure they keep you in the same institution," Anna deadpanned.

"Adjoining rooms perhaps. Though, T-man, you had better treat my sister right, even if you are in a loony bin."

"I think they're planning on locking us up so they can escape on some great romantic adventure," Shahara stage-whispered to Todd.

"Oh, of course. I fell in love with your brother's singing voice and he loves my sense of whimsy." Jamal did not sing very often. Something that anyone who had heard him sing was grateful for. Also, Anna and 'whimsy' were two words that did not seem to belong together.

"Not to mention your openness and freedom to express your feelings. And you were impressed by my tact and diplomacy, right, Sweetie?"

"Absolutely, Schnookums."

Anna was the last one to start laughing, but apparently Jamal's being caught between laughter and horror at being called 'Schnookums' was enough to crack even her icy façade. Todd didn't get much painting done, but he couldn't bring himself to care.

***

Todd, for the twelfth time that night, made a mental note to get even with Jamal. Jamal, his 'wonderful best friend', had signed up to be a tour guide for the school's annual Halloween walking ghost tour. Which would have been fine except that he suddenly backed out at the last minute and had to all but beg Todd to fill in for him. Considering Jamal had known of Todd's long-time hatred of ghost stories, Todd was still trying to figure out if this was the plan all along.

It wasn't too hard a job. He had a map to follow, and there were just as many tour guides as there were tours, so no repeats were necessary. But none of that changed the fact that ghost stories spooked him, no pun intended. Jamal owed him big time for this. The question was how to collect without letting on that he had been truly scared.

The next stop was the auditorium annex, lit only by scattered white candles. At first, no one was visible, until Anna stepped forward. Todd blinked at surprise, seeing her. Anna would be one of the last people he would have expected to see. But here she was, smiling enigmatically, wearing a blue-green lightweight kimono, furry ears, and what appeared to be a fox tail. The kimono was set up to let the tail through. The accessories looked very realistic by candlelight. The ears twitched occasionally, while the tail would sway with no discernable pattern. Must be some nice animatronics. Todd hesitated to even ponder the cost.

"Good evening, all, and welcome." Her voice was smooth and strange, possibly borrowed from old vampire movies. But instead of sounding campy and lame, it sent shivers down his spine. Judging by the uneasy movement of his group, he wasn't the only one. "Tonight, you have heard and will hear many a story of ghosties and ghoulies and long-legged beasties, and things that go bump in the night. But I am here to tell you a different type of story. A tale of a creature of the night that walks beside you by day. Yes, children, I am here to tell you of the Were."

She eyed the crowd, smirking as some moved back under her gaze. "Werewolves are well known in Europe and in this country, to the point that many don't realize that other cultures have their own Were legends. Werecoyotes exist in the oldest legends of this country. Werejaguars are known in South America. Weretigers roam the streets of China and India. African grasslands may be stalked by

Werehyenas. And Werefoxes," She briefly indicated herself, "are revered in Japan."

Anna paused again, sizing up her audience, before lightly pacing through the shadows. "Why do I tell you this? You are here to be scared, not listen to tales of other lands." She paused in front of one person, probably at random. He quickly backpeddled. Todd thought he knew Anna pretty well, but this was unnerving.

"I tell you because there is a story. A story that took place here, possibly on this very campus. Of course, it was before this campus was built. Before the United States was a country. Before the English had settled in Florida. Before the Spanish had settled in Florida. This story begins many centuries ago. Listen carefully and I will tell you."

No one talked. No one moved. No one dared so much as breathe too loudly.

Anna nodded, half her face lit up by candlelight, the other half in the shadows. "Long, long ago, there was a war. A fierce and bloody war. But it was not men who fought. Oh, no. It was Weres. Werecoyotes battled Werejaguars over territory. This territory, to be exact. With the animal mindset, territory is fiercely important. Something worth killing and dying for. And they did. In large numbers. Very large numbers."

She stopped, tail twitching, and made eye contact at a few more people, Todd included. He found himself instinctively stepping back at the strange light in her eyes. He had never seen anything like it.

"They might have kept fighting there until they destroyed each other, but something strange happened. Strange and perhaps wonderful. A fox appeared. Not an ordinary fox, but a Werefox. How she got here is unknown, but here she was. Now, foxes and coyotes are natural enemies and jaguars aren't much friendlier to the foxes of South America. Weres tend to follow the prejudices of their animal equivalents. But she waved the signs of truce, and she was heavy with kits. Most Weres refuse to attack pregnant women or young children. So they let her be. The vixen discovered they were fighting over territory. Now territory wars are as common for Werefoxes as for any other type of Were, but for some reason known only to her, she decided to end that war. So she asked each leader what it would take to make them stop fighting. They both answered the same. They would only leave if driven away by someone stronger."

Anna paused, as if expecting them to ask questions or offer suggestions. No one did. "Foxes aren't known for strength, but for cunning, and Werefoxes are even more so. The vixen thought and thought and came up with a plan. She went to the leader of the Werecoyotes and told him that she had a plan that would allow him to defeat the enemy leader, but he had to follow her instructions exactly. She took him to a field and told him to camouflage himself with mud. Then she handed him a plant to eat that she said would give him victory."

"So she sided with the Werecoyotes?" Someone asked.

Anna raised an eyebrow. "Did she?" No one spoke.

She continued, "Once she was sure he was in place, she went to the leader of the Werejaguars and told him that she could guarantee his victory if he did as she said. She had him wear a pale cloth completely over himself, and she gave him the same plant she gave the Werecoyote leader. Then she led him to the field where the other leader was hiding. She then left. The leaders saw each other but didn't recognize each other for the plant she had given them was a hallucinogen. They saw each other and grew frightened and ran the other way. They took their armies and left rather than facing the 'monsters' of the area. The war was over."

"So everything worked out?" Someone else asked.

"Not exactly. You will remember that many, many died before this. They were not properly laid to rest. Many say that their spirits are restless and still walk about, possibly still engaged in a useless battle for a territory they cannot have. Also, eventually both leaders realized or guessed that the fox betrayed them and laid a curse on her. Legend has it she died giving birth to twins. Without their mother, the twins also died. And that she could not forgive. All accounts agree that she could not rest. Some say that she is looking for her kits. Some say she tries to watch out for others like her. Some say that she is looking for the Werecoyotes and Werejaguars for revenge."

Another meaningful glance to the audience. "You can walk out that door tonight and brush this off as just another story, but that doesn't explain everything. It doesn't explain how people in North America learned of a mythical creature from Japan when they had never heard of Japan or Japan of them. It doesn't explain how the story also circulates in certain circles of South America, with little change. And it doesn't explain why foxes can be seen around here far more often than anywhere else in this part of the state." She smiled a knowing smile at the group now huddled together.

Suddenly a noise behind them caused everyone to jump and turn around. Anna walked in the door, flipping on the light switch as she entered, a headband with cardboard ears in hand. She was wearing a cheap pink lightweight kimono, with an obviously fake tail tied to the back. "I am so sorry I'm late. I couldn't get the ears to work. What's the matter with you lot? You look like you've seen a ghost."

Todd spun around, vaguely aware everyone else was too. The bright lights revealed empty air, an open window, and what might have been a fox running off in the distance.

***

It seemed to be unanimous. Anna's story was the big hit of the night. Everyone was talking about it and no one had a clue how she had pulled it off. More than few were regretting that they couldn't see it twice.

She smiled at Todd as he came up to her while she was walking back to the room. "Anna, there you are. You've got to tell me. How did you do that?"

"Do what? Look, I'm really, really sorry about being late. I lost track of time. I didn't even get to tell the story."

"But you had to have..."

"Had to have what?"

"You don't know?"

"Know what? Are you feeling alright? You're looking a little pale?"

Actually, he was looking very pale. "I think I need to go lie down for a bit."

"You do that." She looked at him in concern.

'Anna' continued to walk to 'her' room and unlocked it. Once inside, she removed the wig, made from Liska's hair. Speaking of Liska, she was lounging on the bed, still with furry ears and tail.

"How'd it go?"

"You made quite the impression," Kira admitted to her cousin. "Your friend Todd stopped me and tried to find out what was going on. I played dumb."

"Good. I just wish I could have seen the looks on their faces.

"It was something. In the third group, someone nearly passed out."

Liska's smile was predatory. "Shall we try it again next year?"

"You're incorrigible."

"You say that like it's a bad thing. Besides, so are you."

"We'll see. I don't know that we could pull it off twice. How are you going to explain this to anyone who asks?"

"Play dumb. If that doesn't work, I'll claim Halloween magic and leave it alone."

"Halloween isn't until next week."

"So?"

"Never mind." A quick glance at the clock showed it was now after midnight. "Happy birthday."

"It's not..." Liska stopped, blinked, and continued. "It is, isn't it? October 24?"

"Honestly, how do you always end up forgetting your own birthday?"

"I don't always!"

"This is the third time. Second year in a row, even."

"I was a little preoccupied last year."

Kira snorted. It was laugh or cry. "I'll say. I still don't know how you do this. You never forget mine but never seem to remember that yours is just a month later. How?"

"Practice?"

Chapter Twelve

The opposite of paranoia is stupidity. – The Kikitsutai Book of Wisdom

Kira's diversion seemed to have worked perfectly. Todd no longer appeared to think she was Cats-eye. Which was good, because she could have totally ruined everything with the Halloween prank. It was a stupid trick to pull, but just too tempting to resist. So far no one had caught on, so it should be fine. She hoped. Todd had tried to question her one more time, but when she again pled ignorance, he evidently decided he didn't want to know. Fine with her. Liska had bigger things to worry about. Lately she couldn't shake this nagging feeling that something was wrong. Nothing stood out, there was nothing to act on, just an edgy feeling.

Even right now, sparing with Todd, knowing they were the only two in the room, she felt paranoid. A threat was nearby. Not Todd, but something else. Speaking of Todd, he was getting better. She still won consistently, but his movements were getting faster, and he wasn't as predictable as he was in the beginning. He had also gotten better at reading her. Potentially dangerous, but thus far that ability only seemed to extend as far as her fighting style. Besides, while most people played to their strengths, Liska was taught a more flexible style, based around exploiting her opponent's weaknesses. So every time Todd adapted his style to match hers, she changed hers to challenge him. Something he found more than a little frustrating.

"You should be thanking me. I'm helping you improve your skills. Speed, reflexes, and mental flexibility."

Todd nodded, conceding her point. "Yeah. I met with my mentor last week. He's impressed. Says that my main problem was that I had a very static style. Seems that trying to beat you caused me to learn how to change my style enough to be less predictable." She could have told him that.

"Was your mentor the person you primarily sparred with?"

"Yes, why?"

"Then you developed your style as a way of countering his. I use a different style so you have to adapt."

"Probably."

"Your mentor went primarily for shots at the chest and head, didn't he? Not usually the neck, and rarely feinted."

Todd stepped back to avoid her swing. "Exactly. How did you know?"

"Because that's what you are best at countering. You developed a style based around that, which I took and flipped like a mirror. That shows me what you were taught."

"Wow. I never thought about doing that. Are you sure you're not the psych major here?"

"The world is full of amateur psychiatrists. Have you ever met a martial arts practitioner who wasn't one?"

Todd snickered, dropping his guard enough for her to score her second point. "Ow! Okay, you win."

"Another round?"

"Nah, you've beaten me enough for today. Besides, I wanted to show you something." Todd took off his armor and started to put it away. She did the same, putting away the *shinai* last. When she turned away to face him again, he was pulling something out of the storage closet. It couldn't be what she thought it was. It couldn't be!

"Is that..."

"A genuine Japanese Edo era katana."

For a moment she couldn't speak. "Where... How... Where did you get that?! Most of those were destroyed during the Meiji era." Todd shouldn't have been able to afford something like that. A rare artifact, where most specimens were in museums or in the hands of wealthy collectors? Liska had done some background research into Todd after finding out about Cats-eye. Neither he nor his family had the type of income to buy an Edo era katana. There were only so many ways he could have gotten that, and few seemed good. "There's no way you could afford that!"

"You're right. It's not mine. It's my uncle's. I'm just holding on to it for a couple days while he gets his security system upgraded. He said it would be safer with someone that no one suspected."

Security through obscurity. Not her favorite method, as it had a surprisingly high failure rate. In addition, judging from her research, Todd only had one uncle in the vicinity, and he wasn't rich either. He was, however, police. Perhaps the sword had been impounded? Had Todd told her about his uncle? "How did your uncle get it? Is he a millionaire or something?"

Todd laughed. "Would you believe he won it in a poker game?"

"Must have been a high stakes poker game."

"Not as high as you'd think. Apparently, the guy wagering it didn't realize what it was worth."

Well, that was safer than most of her thoughts. "You can't let anyone know you have this here. You shouldn't have even shown me."

Todd looked almost hurt. "I trust you." He did? Why?

"I'm honored, but you really haven't known me for long. You don't know how trustworthy I am." Wasn't that the truth? "I'm worried for you. That sword is extremely valuable. People have been killed for less. Who else knows you have it?"

"Jamal does, maybe Shahara."

"I *strongly* suggest that you don't tell anyone else and ask them to do the same."

Todd smiled. "I'll be careful. You want to hold it?"

Liska had to hold back a gasp at just how trusting he was. "Are you sure that's wise?"

"It's a sword. They aren't known for being delicate. The edge might be a little brittle, but I know you'll be careful."

She took it hesitantly, as if it would break if she dared breathe on it. Stepping away from Todd, she gave it a gentle swing, and then a better one when it didn't disintegrate in her hands.

Liska closed her eyes. She was almost there. Edo era Japan. She could all but see the battle. The chaos, confusion, shouts of men, sounds of horses. Blood, fear, pain, and death permeated the air. She was a soldier fighting for his country, unsure exactly what he was fighting for, but fighting with everything, nonetheless. With a deep breath she suddenly pulled back and was again in the gym. What was that?

Todd was looking at her strangely. She had to deal with that first. "Thank you. It was more of a gift than I can put into words. But please, please be careful. Tell no one else you have it."

"Wasn't planning on it." Todd took the offered sword and started to put it in the supply closet.

"You're trusting a school lock? Those things can be picked with a safety pin!" She knew, she had done it.

Todd smiled. "I don't know that they're that bad. Besides, no one knows I have it, right?"

"How many other people can get in that closet?"

He turned away to think about her question. "Well, technically, five people have keys to supply closets in the gym, and they all use the same lock, but that closet's mine. No one else has any reason to be in there."

She wanted to wince at the poor security, but that would be out of character. "I still think it would probably be best somewhere else, but for a couple days, it should be fine. I hope."

"It'll be fine. *You* won't tell anyone, right?"

"Of course not." Liska watched him lock it up. This did not seem like a good idea. But if she was looking for a valuable katana, the supply locker in the gym would certainly not be on her top list of places to check. "Anyway, if I'm going to get any breakfast before math class, I have to run." Just as she got to the door, she stopped and sniffed at the air. How odd. She turned to Todd. "Did you have chocolate before you came in?" Doubtful, she ought to have smelled it.

"No, why?" He approached while answering, before getting to the door. Judging from his wrinkled nose, he noticed what she had, even if he didn't smell as well as she did. The hallway smelled like chocolate. "How weird. Who eats chocolate in a gym?"

"A bulimic dieter?"

Todd shrugged. "Now I want chocolate. How about you?"

"Me? No, I'm violently allergic."

"That stinks. What happens, if I may ask? Hives? Swollenness? Nausea?"

"Convulsions. I can have a little chocolate without too much trouble, but I'm not entirely sure how much is too much, and am not interested in experimentation." She still remembered last time she guessed wrong.

He swallowed hard. "Ick. Yeah, I can imagine. I'll remember not to offer you chocolate then."

"You don't think anyone was listening, do you?"

"I doubt it. You're too paranoid."

True, but sometimes it was necessary. "You're probably right. Bye."

**

Ryoko, Ryoko-*Sensei* to most of his younger family members, considered himself a patient man. It came with long practice and was especially useful when dealing with children, a designation he now gave to most people under the age of forty. Though even he had to admit that his grandniece, under any of her personas, could be extremely challenging.

It wasn't that Liska tried to be difficult, for him at least. Indeed, she was highly respectful and obedient, as she had been raised to be. What she wasn't, was open and honest about what was going on. It had been obvious since she arrived in Florida, taking the persona Anna Andrews, that she wasn't telling him everything. Part of it was that she was undoubtedly aware that he was informing her father about the important things. Another part was her determination to prove herself. He could understand why perfectly. She had been backed into a corner by circumstances out of her control and retaliated by throwing herself into any challenge that came at her and one way or another working a way through or around it. Unfortunately, she had gotten badly hurt that way before and it was likely to happen again. All to prove herself to people, many of whom would never accept her, no matter what she did.

Ryoko strived to avoid favoritism. He had taught most of the members of the clan under the age of fifty and simply couldn't afford to pick favorites. But in many ways, Liska was a favorite. No, that wasn't quite accurate. It was more complicated than that. Yes, she was special to him, and he was more protective of her, but most of his feelings for her were tainted by his guilt.

Ryoko had never approved of his very promising nephew, the soon to be head of the family, marrying an outsider. To make matters worse, Liska was born so quickly afterwards that many speculated that she was the reason for the marriage in the first place. It didn't help that the outsider, Ann, still had trouble adapting to life in the clan. It was much worse back then. His nephew, Sejou, was almost unable to take his rightful place because of the marriage, and the transition was much more difficult than it should have been. It was hard not to see the child as a personification of the unrest of those early years.

That was the one thing Ryoko and his wife argued about. Yumi thought it was unfair to assume the marriage was one of necessity, and even more unfair to blame the child if that was the case. Slowly, he started to open up to the girl. Then Yumi died, and while the child wasn't responsible, she was a factor. Grief blinded him for years, as he blamed the girl. Only time allowed him to heal enough to realize how unreasonable it was to blame her for something that wasn't her fault. Something she likely didn't remember. In fact, considering the circumstances, Ryoko hoped she didn't.

He could almost see a bit of Yumi in her sometimes. Her determination and willingness to fight a losing battle, because it had to be fought, turning each loss into a determination to be strong enough and clever enough to win the next battle. All those factors together, it was impossible to treat the girl the same way as the others.

Liska knelt at his table, calmly sipping tea. There were a few things he wanted explained. Favorite or not, Ryoko intended to find out what she was doing. "It was nice having Kira here, wasn't it? Shame she had to leave so quickly."

"Hmm." Liska's face didn't change but her pulse increased momentarily before going back to normal. If he hadn't been listening for it, he probably would have missed it. So, Kira's visit wasn't a coincidence. He had suspected as much.

"You must miss her. I know you're closer to her than any of your other cousins."

"I do miss her. It was good seeing her again." That was probably completely truthful.

"She must miss you too. Taking the chance to show up so close, so quickly after you left. It's unusual for her to take... active work, isn't it?" Kira was more on the support staff side. Besides, Ryoko knew for a fact that whatever brought Kira stateside wasn't official orders. While side work was a possibility, usually approval was necessary first.

Liska shrugged as if unconcerned. "Doesn't mean she can't do it."

"True. I was never quite clear on why she was here or what she was doing in Miami. Did she tell you?"

"Not all the details. I believe there was a confidentiality contract."

"Since when has that stopped you two?"

A smile flashed before being hidden by her teacup. "We only break those when it's important. And only to those who need to know."

"I know." After all, there were degrees of confidentiality. Family came before any job. Still, this wasn't getting him the information he needed. Perhaps another approach. "Are you still practicing with that Kendo boy?"

He hadn't forgotten the boy's name; in fact, after his research he might know more about him than his parents did. Liska should know more though. If she had any sense she would have done at least as much research as he had, and she interacted with the boy on a regular basis. No, this was his way of making sure his grandniece remembered the difference between them.

Another spike of pulse, and a brief flash of emotion on her face, gone before he could analyze it. Oh dear. "Yes, he's getting better.

"Is he suspicious?"

"No." That wasn't the whole truth. It might fool a polygraph, but not him.

"Not at all?"

"I answered everything to his satisfaction." Still not the complete truth, but he wouldn't get anything else out of her right now. Liska was simply too good at lying. Even when caught in a lie, she seldom became flustered and usually managed to redirect in such a way that the person trying to trick her felt abashed at doubting her. He had taught her that, and she had surpassed him. It served her well, even if it made things fiendishly difficult for him sometimes. Time to let things go for now.

Perhaps it was just as well. If something serious had occurred, he would be duty-bound to tell her father. Sejou had made no secret of the fact that he wasn't happy with his daughter's plan to study abroad, leaving the work for an education she didn't truly need. Ryoko still didn't know how he had been persuaded to go along with it. If something went wrong, he might use that to order her back to Japan. Liska never went against her father's orders.

"We better finish up. I'm not at my best tonight."

"Yes, I remember."

"Good. Now, what card am I about to turn over?"

***

Todd looked around the room for the third time in the past ten minutes. He drummed his fingers incessantly trying to figure out what had him on edge. It was just a strange feeling, like something was going to happen. He didn't get those often, but when he did, he was usually right.

He abandoned the chair to pace carefully in the cluttered room. What was he uneasy about? Had anything new happened? Anna wasn't Cats-eye, but that was a long shot anyway, and a couple days ago. There was the tour he tried not to think about. The sword... That was it. The sword was making him uneasy. Why?

He was getting infected with Anna's paranoia. Everything was fine. But there had been the smell of chocolate in the hall. It must have been recent. He had laughed it off when Anna suggested someone might have been listening, but what if she was right? Maybe it would be a good idea to keep the sword here, in his room. Jamal wasn't in at the moment, so if he hurried, he could go get the sword, bring it back, and hide it before Jamal returned. It wasn't that he didn't trust his roommate, but... *Hurry. Get this done quickly. It was important.*

Todd shook his head to clear his thoughts. It was a good idea, and a light jog should help his restlessness. He only took the time to slip on his shoes and grab his gym bag before practically running for the gym. He couldn't explain the urgency he felt, so he just went with it.

The room used for Kendo was also used for aerobics later in the day, but that was over now. The room was deserted and the lights were out.

Stepping into the room, Todd fumbled for the light switch when a flicker of movement in his peripheral vision stopped him. Instinctively, he moved to the side, away from the lighted door, and tried to get his eyes to adjust as quickly as possible. Yes, he might be in a dark room with someone, but at least he wasn't a visible target anymore.

Seconds passed. Nothing happened. It must have been his imagination. Todd started to reach for the switch again when he did see something. No, someone. There was someone in the room!

Before he could react to that, he doubled over, a sharp pain in his chest. Air. He couldn't breathe. His legs gave out under him as he slid slowly down the wall. A little light from the door allowed his eyes to confirm what his mind had pierced together. It was the sword. Black encroached on his vision until he couldn't even see that anymore.

Chapter Thirteen

A wild spirit cannot be safely caged. – The Kikitsutai Book of Wisdom

In Liska's experience, coming home to find policemen at your door was rarely a good sign. While she couldn't be entirely sure they were looking for her, they were stopped outside her door and arguing with her RA. Besides, when in doubt, Liska preferred to operate on the assumption that 'they' were looking for her.

She quickly reviewed her options. No one had seen her yet, so she could walk away. Liska ruled that out quickly. If they saw her leave, she'd be in more trouble, her room was certainly not police safe, and they shouldn't have anything serious on her.

On the other hand, walking in there when she wasn't sure what they might believe wasn't the best option either. It's easier to claim innocence when you know what you're claiming to be innocent of. Then again, if she went in acting confused and nervous, maybe she could convince them they got the wrong person.

Simply standing there wasn't getting her anywhere, time to go forward. A quick check in a nearby side mirror allowed her to make sure Anna was firmly in place, looking confused and a bit intimidated. Taking a deep breath and walked up the stairs. Hearing her name mentioned, she almost changed her mind but kept walking. Second-guessing one's self was not a good idea.

They were blocking her door. "Pardon, is there a problem?"

The two police officers and the RA all turned to look at her. One of the officers, a man, probably six inches taller than her, Hispanic, looked like he was former military, spoke up. "Are you Ms. Andrews?" He might be shorter than his partner, but he was definitely the bigger threat. His name tag said 'Velazquez'. More worryingly, he was angry. Whatever had occurred, he was taking it personally, and she might well make an excellent scapegoat.

"Yes. Anna Andrews. That's me." College students questioned by the police should be nervous and unsure. Not calm and collected.

"Could you come with us, please?"

Not good at all. "Is something wrong?"

"We need to ask you a few questions down at the station."

So they believed her a reasonable suspect for a crime. Probably a serious one. "Of course I want to co-operate fully with the law." She bit her lip and moved in to speak quietly, trying to emphasize her height or lack thereof in a 'See, I'm harmless' manner. "Um, this is bit embarrassing, but I *really* need the WC. Could I just have a couple minutes? You could wait here."

The police gave her a look that clearly said, 'What do you take us for?'

"The RA has a key."

"She's right, and there's no other entrance or exit. Even the windows don't open." Karen folded her arms.

"You could have a gun in there," The other officer said. Also male, probably Eastern European background, though no accent. Taller than his partner, but probably newer to being an officer. His patch said Crane. He wasn't happy either.

"No, sir. Guns and other weapons are not allowed on campus." Both statements were true. She had no guns in her room. She did however have other weapons that were against school rules.

"You don't even have proof she's done anything yet!" Karen sounded exasperated. Anna fidgeted a little.

The police exchanged a look. "Two minutes."

"Thank you!" She let herself in quickly, slamming the door behind her. Grabbing her identity card, she rushed to the bathroom, conveniently the room furthest from the door, and pulled out her cell phone. This was so not a good night for this, but Ryoko-*Sensei* was the only one close enough to help her. Hopefully he hadn't changed yet.

"Hello?"

"*Sensei*, it's Liska. I have a major problem. There are two policemen outside and they want to question me about something. I don't know what. If they find 'proof' of whatever they are looking for, they'll check here. Can you make sure it's clean?"

"It's almost ten-thirty! This isn't going to be easy."

"I know, but it's an emergency. You remember where I live, right?"

"Of course. Good thing your dorm is so accessible. I'll do my best. You be careful."

"I will." They were wasting time. Liska hung up and popped a piece of gum in her mouth, chewing quickly. As she did, she took a plastic sealable bag out of her pocket and dumped her clothing card, her mobile and anything else she didn't want to be found if or when they searched her. Gum pliable now, she spat it out and used it to stick the bag to the inside of the water tank of the toilet. Ryoko-*Sensei* would know to look there. Her time was almost up, so she washed her hands, careful not to dry them completely. Of such small details an impression is made. Then she went back out to brave the inquisition.

Unsurprisingly, they were out there, looking as humorless as ever. Karen looked very worried. In addition, they were attracting a small crowd. At least she wasn't in handcuffs. Then again, she wasn't being arrested. Yet.

***

For being taken in for questioning, they hadn't asked her a lot of questions yet. They had taken her fingerprints though. Liska made a mental note to deal with that later. For now, she was trying to be low-key, confused, and innocent. The confusion part was easy. Not showing her impatience was harder. She needed to know what was going on. Ryoko-

Sensei would resist changing until he got her phone call, but he had to change by midnight. Then she wouldn't be able to talk to him until morning.

Finally, another police officer showed up. A woman this time, tall, curly hair, name of O'Malley. Hopefully she didn't have the stereotypical Irish hatred of the English. "Anna Andrews?"

"Yes, what's going on?"

"Do you have a lawyer?"

"No, I've never needed one."

"I'm going to read you your rights. You are under arrest."

"For what?!"

Her question was ignored until the woman finished reading the rights. "Do you understand those rights?"

"I understand what you read, but I don't understand what I did. Why have you arrested me?"

"Do you know Todd Kensworth?"

Todd? What about Todd? "Yes, he's a friend from school. Did something happen to him?"

"The school Kendo instructor?"

"Yes, yes. I know."

"You know he keeps real swords?"

"Well, yes. I presumed he had permission from the school to keep those." Perhaps someone stole the sword. She would be on the short list of suspects for that, but why take her fingerprints?

"Where were you tonight between nine and ten-fifteen?"

"Um, let's see. I was studying in my room until about nine-thirty or so before I took a walk around campus."

"Can anyone provide an alibi for this?"

Wouldn't these be the questions asked before they arrested her? That and she could demand a barrister. But she wanted to know exactly what she was accused of before she called Ryoko-*Sensei*. "No. I don't have a roommate, and I didn't stop to talk to anyone on my walk."

"So there's no proof you weren't the one who stabbed Todd Kensworth?"

"What!? Oh, how awful! Is he alright?" No wonder everyone was mad. They probably knew Todd. Surprise was easy. Concern was easy. The hard part was keeping the calculations off her face.

O'Malley moved in. "Suppose you tell me?"

"I think... I think I need to call my uncle. He can arrange a barrister." The officer eyed her a bit before nodding to the phone.

"You aren't calling England, are you?"

Anna gave a small upturn of her lips. "No, it's a local call." It was almost eleven forty-five. Talk about cutting it close. The phone would be monitored, so she dialed her own cell number.

It was answered half-way through the first ring. " 'Allo?"

"Uncle Ray? It's Anna. I'm sorry to call so late, but there's been the biggest mistake! My friend, Todd, you remember, I told you about him, he was attacked and the police think I did it, and no one will tell me anything, and I'm scared, and I don't know what to do..." She broke down in tears. Ryoko-*Sensei* would ignore it, but the police would hopefully be swayed. At least a little.

"Anna, Anna, take a deep breath. Just stay calm. Co-operate with the police but don't answer any questions without a barrister, I'll arrange one.

I'll take care of everything. Calling a barrister, watering your plants, contacting your parents, etc." So he had found everything. That's what the plants line was about.

"Okay, but I didn't do it!"

"Don't worry. Everything will get straightened out."

"Okay. I love you."

"Love you too, Anna."

They hung up at eleven-fifty-three. That was cutting it much closer than she ever wanted to again.

After making her phone call, they tried to ask her more questions, but she refused to answer anything without a barrister present. So she was led to a small holding cell for the night. She had no cell mate which was the only blessing. The hallway contained other cells that were not empty, and not all the inhabitants were quiet. The room was small but too open. It reeked of previous inhabitants, strong cleaners, and odors that even those cleaners couldn't remove. Every single possible bodily fluid had spilled in this room at one point or another. Then there was the fear, despair, and anger that permeated the air. She was fighting a headache trying not to imagine possible previous inhabitants. At least the sheets had been freshly washed, though she would rather not speculate over some of those stains.

Breathing through her mouth so she didn't gag, Liska feigned sleep trying to figure out who had attacked Todd and why.

Todd wasn't the type to make enemies. To get a little too curious, perhaps, but even then, she seemed to be the only one he was nosing about. She hadn't stabbed him, had she?

It wouldn't be the first time she had done something and not remembered it later. When that happened, it was usually over something very bad. But she wasn't missing time, she thought.

Rolling over, she brought her hand to her nose, still pretending to sleep, or at least try to. Inhaling deeply as she dared, she had to separate the room smells from the smells on her. There was no smell of fresh blood. That was something.

Second possibility, he had been stabbed because of her. While she didn't think anyone she knew would stab him because he was investigating her, it was a possibility. Also, someone might have stabbed him to frame her. Her prints were evidently there, and it was hard to do damage with a *shinai*. So it was probably the sword he had shown her that morning, well, yesterday morning now. Someone *had* been listening in! Not to mention, the police had picked up on her awfully fast. That suggested that they had been told to look for her. Framing seemed the most likely possibility.

Now, how could she prove she wasn't guilty? Or at least that there was an innocent explanation for her prints being on the sword? Jamal and Shahara could, if they believed her, testify that she and Todd were on friendly terms and he might have shown her the sword. If she could convince the judge, jury, whatever, of that, they shouldn't have enough evidence to convict her of anything. Unless, of course, whoever framed her had manufactured more evidence.

Still, it was at least the basics of a plan. How was Todd anyway? They said he was stabbed, not that he was dead. Was he dead? If not, might he die? If he didn't die, could he identify his attacker? So many questions, so few answers. She'd get nowhere if she didn't try to rest.

***

Her barrister arrived shortly before seven. Liska wasn't a morning person by any stretch of the imagination, but that was when she actually slept. The few snatches of rest barely counted. Besides, she was out of the smelly holding cell, to a slightly less smelly room. Still, it was a little surprising he had gotten there so quickly. Ryoko-*Sensei* wouldn't have been able to call anyone until after six.

First impression of her barrister included relief that he was obviously one of them. Not that she expected anything else. Being one of them, he was probably related to her. She hadn't met him before, but that didn't mean anything. True introductions could wait.

"I am Mr. Sakamoto. Your uncle hired me to represent you." He then turned to the guards. "May I have a few minutes to converse with my client?"

The request was granted and they were soon alone in the room. Further proof that he was one of them was that they shared the same paranoia. As soon as the police left and the door was closed, they quickly searched the room, looking for cameras, recording devices, or anything else. There shouldn't be any, since this was a room for suspects to meet with lawyers, but they wanted to be sure. Mr. Sakamoto even had an electronic hand-held device solely to stymie listening devices. Liska hadn't tried to bring hers.

"We're clean. Sit rep?"

"Unsure. I'm being accused of stabbing a friend from school."

"Did you?"

"If I wanted to kill a classmate, he'd be dead; and I wouldn't even be on the suspect list."

Mr. Sakamoto nodded. "Evidence against?"

"My fingerprints, apparently. And there's no reason for them to be present. In fact, there's no reason for me to be in the room that I suspect the weapon was in." She gave a quick summary of the Kendo sparring and the katana.

"Is your paperwork in order?" Did 'Anna' have a complete record, including birth certificate, passport, medical history, transcripts, financials, the things police would look through.

"Yes, and it's clean."

"Can you pass a polygraph?"

"Yes." She could pass a polygraph claiming to be Queen Nefertiti.

"Do you have an alibi?"

"Not really."

"Character witnesses?"

"Maybe. But they're Todd's friends, not mine. If they actually think I did it..."

"How long do we have?"

"Nine days."

Mr. Sakamoto grimaced. "Not a lot of time."

"I didn't decide to get arrested because I wanted to tour a jail cell."

"Do you know the layout of the prison?"

"No."

"Careless."

"I wasn't working. I didn't expect to be arrested. No, I don't have a plan yet."

"Start making one. This isn't going to be easy."

"You aren't hired for easy."

"Point taken. Okay, we'll bring them in. Let me do the talking when possible. You are in shock, confused, and upset. Understand?"

What did he think she was, some kind of rookie? "Of course."

Chapter Fourteen

The mind is a stronger cage than any steel. – The Kikitsutai
Book of Wisdom

"Jamal! You get back here this instant." Jamal winced at his sister's shrill tone but dutifully waited until she caught up to him.

"What is it, Shahara?"

"I know the police talked to you and you told them that you thought Anna might have attacked Todd and I want to know why."

"They asked. They said she had been arrested on suspicion and asked me a few questions about her. C'mon, girl, they found her prints on the weapon!"

Shahara's eyes widened slightly as her brother's accent came through on the last sentence. They had taken opposite attitudes to their accent after moving from Jamaica. She had cultivated hers, but he deliberately tried to get rid of it, believing it difficult for non-Jamaicans to understand. If he was slipping, then he had to be very upset. Not that it was a surprise, Todd was his best friend, had been for years. "The sword he told you about?"

"Yes."

"Maybe he showed her the sword."

"Perhaps."

"Did you mention *that* to the police?" Shahara tapped her foot.

"Sure."

"So why do you think she did it?"

"I said it was possible. I didn't say she did it. Look, Todd's in the hospital, still in critical condition. I want to know who put him there!" He tried to keep back the tears that threatened to escape, but it wasn't working well.

"So do I. But I don't think it was Anna." At least she was much calmer now.

"Ignoring her looks, her age, and her nationality, can you tell me three facts about her that you are completely sure are true?"

"What?"

"Does she have siblings? What are her hobbies? What's her major? What does she want to do when she gets out of college? Favorite animal? Food? Color? Movie? Do you know any of those?"

Shahara opened and closed her mouth a few times. "Um, I don't think she has any siblings..."

"But you don't know. Neither do I. We know *nothing* about her. And despite what Todd thinks, I don't think he knows much more than we do. Honestly? I can see her planning something like that. I have no idea why, but I can see her doing it."

"But what if she didn't? It's been two days already. Two days that she's been in jail. What if she gets charged and sentenced and she's innocent?"

"Then they'll find out and let her go."

"Oh, and they always catch the right person?"

"They will this time. All we need is for Todd to wake up and say who attacked him."

"*If* he saw."

Jamal nodded, before accepting the hug Shahara obviously wanted to give him. "I hope he wakes up soon," she said into his shoulder.

"So do I. Believe me, so do I."

***

Liska sat on her bunk, the top one, legs folded, eyes closed, trying to pretend she was somewhere else. *Anywhere* else. Well, almost anywhere. Other than being grounded by her parents, this was the longest she had been confined against her will. Being caged played havoc on her nerves. To add to the fun, the jail was over-crowded. There were currently one hundred seventy-five inmates in a space meant to house between ninety and one hundred. She had been 'lucky' in grabbing a bunk, since there was one more prisoner than bunk in her 'room'. Liska would have considered herself more fortunate for the bunk if it wasn't obvious that the woman who gave up her bunk for her was clearly expecting something from her later. 'Anna' was too naïve to catch on so far. She wasn't sure how long she could hold on to that though.

Then there was the sensory overload. Too many people meant far too many sounds and smells, mostly unpleasant ones. There was no escape from them. Well, there was one, maybe two, but she wasn't that desperate yet.

Then there was the delicate balance between Anna and Liska to maintain. She had to persuade the guards and the police that she was harmless, innocent Anna. But in order to avoid trouble from the other inmates, she needed to not be seen as an easy mark, and that meant letting Liska shine through. At the moment she was trying to avoid the situations as much as possible, and letting others take advantage of her in little ways, like cutting in line, giving up more desired places, ignoring it when someone took her food, etc. Ignoring the stolen food was actually the hardest.

There had been a preliminary trial, or whatever they called it. To see if there was enough evidence for a trial and set bail. That had been a disaster. Apparently, the reason the police went after her so quickly was there had been an anonymous tip saying she was responsible. When her fingertips matched those on the weapon, and she apparently matched the extremely vague description someone gave of a person wearing the scene (wearing black), well, the police decided they had their man. Figuratively speaking, of course. Even worse, due to the severity of the crime and the fact that she was an international, she was deemed a high flight risk and denied bail.

There had been two good points. One, Todd wasn't dead and might recover. He was still listed as critical, but the doctors were becoming 'guardedly optimistic'. Two, whoever tried to kill Todd had left a candy bar wrapper at the scene. The prosecutor was, with some success, trying to use that to portray her as completely heartless, eating a chocolate bar while killing a classmate, but Liska was slightly relieved to have conclusive proof that she couldn't have done it. Of course, she would have to find a way to prove that she was allergic to chocolate without giving the rest away. It wasn't like she could go to a normal doctor. Perhaps records from a family doctor. Still, proving the candy bar wasn't hers was hardly the same as proving she wasn't the attacker.

The most frustrating part, currently at least, was that she didn't have a clue who had done this or why and couldn't investigate while in jail. If she had been released on bail, then she would have had a chance. It could take months or years for something to go to trial; plenty of time to find, or if necessary, manufacture evidence to clear herself. Now, however, she had to hope for a trial quickly. She couldn't afford to be here long. Even if she wasn't changing in less than a week, her sanity would go if she had to stay.

One way she had taken to trying to keep sane was to make mental escape plans. She wouldn't use any of them unless she had to, but she had a few dozen by now, ranging from the sensible and plausible to the utterly absurd. Her personal favorite was one of the latter; there was no possible way to get that much Jell-O period, let alone in the water supply. Truthfully though, Liska didn't think this particular jail was too secure. In fact, she could have escaped at least twice already. But if she escaped the jail, she would also be leaving behind 'Anna Andrews' and possibly the whole idea of outside schooling. Not until she was desperate. But oh, she needed out!

***

After four and a half days in jail, Liska wondered if she had reached the point of desperation. It was all she could do to keep from starting to change from stress. The noise, the smells, the knowledge that threats were everywhere, all of it was keeping her from sleeping, from ever relaxing her guard. She was going to go insane if she didn't do something.

Part of meditation training was learning to retreat mentally to the extent of being partially removed from external stimuli. Liska could do this, and while it would be a temporary relief from over stimulation, it also meant being vulnerable to any threats that came along. Finally, she decided it was worth the risk.

She could set a time limit or a stimulus, such as a code word, to bring her out. Since no one was there to bring her out, she set a limit of an hour, to come out immediately if she sensed danger of any kind. One hour should be enough to keep her sanity in check. With a deep breath and a hope she wasn't being foolish, Liska mentally retreated.

An hour later, Liska woke feeling a lot more refreshed. She also woke up in the infirmary. That hadn't gone quite according to plan. She couldn't blame them though; to all appearances, she had gone into a coma. Luckily, they had just gotten her there and hadn't run any tests yet. That would have been a disaster. This way she just had to persuade them not to run any.

Fortunately, for her, if not for the jail in general, the infirmary was one of the places budget cuts were made. When she said it was just low blood sugar and she'd be fine if she ate something, they were willing to take her at her word. It got her out of there quickly, and supposedly 'fixed'. So they gave her a couple energy bars, had her stay there for an hour or two to make sure she didn't pass out again, then had her taken back to her cell. The guard was warned to keep a closer eye on her, just in case. Liska estimated that would last a day, two at most. Best case scenario, no one would steal her food during that time.

Ryoko-*Sensei* would be furious though.

***

Mr. Sakamoto wasn't thrilled either. "What were you *thinking?*"

"I was thinking that if I didn't get away somehow I was going to snap. Violently."

He stifled a sigh, conceding the point. "Are you alright now?"

"For now. You can't possibly get me out soon enough." She flashed four fingers at him. Four days until she changed.

"Give me a little time." He returned two. Wait two days. That meant she needed a serious plausible plan to not just escape but leave the area by tomorrow.

"Any progress?"

"We're checking the video cameras in the gym, trying to prove you weren't there."

"You aren't telling me something."

Mr. Sakamoto didn't look at her, instead folding the corners of some papers in front of him. Must be camouflage. That was the only reason Liska could think of for him needing a list of textile factories in Spain, written in French. "We did check, but the cameras in the gym had unexplained malfunctions for the time we need."

"Uh-huh."

"I know, I know, bad 'luck'. I don't suppose you were near any video cameras that can prove you were away from the gym?"

Liska thought it over. "I don't think so. I was outside the whole time, and I usually tend to avoid cameras when possible." Unless she wanted to establish her presence somewhere. "So, they're tech savvy, or walking techbanes."

Mr. Sakamoto shrugged. "Not enough to narrow down the list much."

Liska nodded. "Heard anything about Todd?"

"The doctors are now confident that he'll recover barring unexpected setbacks. They've reduced his medication and he should wake up soon. He may be your best chance. Even if he doesn't know who attacked him, he can at least testify that he showed you the sword. Without that, there is no real case."

Liska nodded, then scowled at the clock. This visit wouldn't last much longer.

"How are you doing? Really?"

"When I get out of here, I'm going to take a long, hot shower, then another, and keep taking showers until I *feel* clean again. Then I'm going to sleep until I'm not tired anymore. Then I'll deal with everything else."

"A wise plan." The guards were starting to come back. "Your uncle says not to worry, he's handling everything. Taking care of your plants, contacting your parents, etc."

"Good. I'm glad."

The door opened. "Your parents wanted to come but they can't make it."

"I understand." They couldn't come because Anna's parents weren't Liska's.

"I brought a package from your uncle, they've probably finished checking it over by now. Let me know if there is anything else you need." Tools, weapons, bribes, etc.

"That was very nice of him. Pass along my thanks."

"I will. Now, I better leave before the guards kick me out."

The two said their farewells, and she was given an obviously opened and searched package as she was led back to her cell. The package contained two books and a small tin of tea biscuits. Liska wasn't sure which she was more grateful for.

Almost as soon as the guard was down the hallway, one of her cell mates, the one who kept muttering about blood in her sleep turned on her. "You're one of them, aren't you?"

Liska put the package on her bunk so she'd have her hands free and faced the clearly unstable woman. Keeping her hands in plain view, slouching a little to look shorter, feet parted for free movement, Liska tried to seem non-threatening. "What do you mean?"

"You can't fool me! You're one of them! Trying to take over the world. Well, you ain't getting me." The woman leapt at her, a straightened wire hanger in hand.

Poor weapon choice. Should have been filed. Doubt she's currently open to criticism.

Chapter Fifteen

Healing comes in many forms of equal importance. –The
Kikitsutai Book of Wisdom

Consciousness came slowly, gradually, and not
without pain. The closer to consciousness, the more
pain. Somehow though, the pain wasn't as sharp as
it seemed like it ought to be. Judging from the
amount of fogginess, that was probably because of
medication.

When Todd regained consciousness, he
wasn't sure he was conscious. Putting thoughts
together was too much effort, even without the
bright lights drilling through him. Where was he?
Hmm, bright lights, blinky machines, medicine-y
smells, he must be in the hospital. That was good.

He wasn't sure why he was in the hospital yet,
but figured it was probably better than the
alternative. He could figure it out later, when the
place wasn't spinning so much.

Movement made him focus on the dark
shadow of a person in the corner. Todd squinted
trying to make it out. "J'mal?" Okay, voice wasn't
working yet.

The shape jumped. "T-man? You awake?"

"Wha' happen?"

"What do you remember?"

What did he remember? It was hard to think.

"Dun' know. Head all swirly."

"It's the morphine."

"Oh. Feels funny."

"Yeah, I believe it. They got you on the strong stuff. Do you remember anything?"

It was vague, but he was starting to. "Sword. Someone had. Stabbed me."

"That's right. Nearly killed you. Do you know who?"

"Barely saw."

"Police arrested Anna."

"Anna? Why? Not her sword." He closed his eyes briefly.

When he opened them again, Jamal was gone, and he could think much more clearly. They must have changed medication or something. Pressing the 'Please Help' button got a nurse who gave him a lot of technical terms over what happened to him. Todd barely understood two words in five, but figured Jamal could explain it later. What he did get was frightening. Punctured lung, infection, broken rib. It was sad when a broken rib was the least of your problems. Since he didn't pass out in that time, and remained mostly coherent, she allowed two police officers to come in and ask him questions. Todd was surprised that he didn't recognize them.

"Mr. Kensworth, can you please tell us what happened, to the best of your ability?"

Todd filled them in on the details of holding the sword for his uncle, and how Anna had been so

insistent that keeping it in the gym was a bad idea.
"I thought she was paranoid at first, but the more I
thought about it the more I decided she might have
a point. So I went to get it. She was right, it was a
bad idea. Someone was already there."

"Did Miss Andrews handle the sword at all
when you told her about it?"

"Yeah, for a little while." He was still too out
of it to try to interpret the look they shared then.

"Did you get a look at your attacker?"

"Not a good one. Just vague impressions and
an outline."

"What can you tell us about those
impressions and outline?"

"A little shorter than I am, probably about
five-eight or so. Definitely male. Um, medium build,
I think. That's really all I got."

"I see. Any questions?"

"Did they take the sword?"

"No, the sword was still on the scene. It's
been collected for evidence."

"Oh, wonder why they didn't take it." He was
starting to get foggy again, and the nurse chased the
police away. Todd started to tell her it was okay, but
it was just too much effort. He'd just rest his eyes a
bit. Not like he would fall asleep aga...

***

"You are positively certain she's alright?" Ryoko
asked for what was at least the tenth time.

"She's fine. Knocked the wire out of the woman's hands, then jumped onto her bed and out of reach until the guards came to settle things. She's perfectly unharmed and hopefully convincing the guards that she's non-violent."

Ryoko rubbed at his face. "What about the near coma?"

"Damage control is done, and I doubt she'll feel it necessary to do it again in the next few days."

"Speaking of, do we have a plan?"

"If she has one, she hasn't shared it yet."

"Then we better hope it doesn't come to that."

"Perhaps, though I don't see her going back to Japan to be a disaster."

"Not a disaster perhaps, but she would be disappointed."

"She can live with it." The words were dry and without sympathy. Obviously Liska's barrister didn't understand why she wanted to do this.

As he didn't completely understand her motivations himself, Ryoko decided to leave it alone and change the subject. "Any chance of a trial in the next couple days?"

"Not really. These things take time. Anything I could do to ensure a faster trial would have the adverse effect of getting declared a mistrial if anyone found out about them. I'm good, but..."

"But there's no guarantee that no one would ever find out. There's someone at the door. I'll call you back." Ryoko hung up the phone without waiting for whatever the answer would be. He would understand, just as Ryoko would if the places were reversed.

Ryoko wasn't expecting anyone. That, in and of itself, did not mean that there wasn't a perfectly ordinary and innocent explanation for the sudden knocking at his door. It could be a neighbor, someone who had gotten the wrong address, a package to be signed for, a salesman, etc. Plenty of options.

That said, he intended to be very cautious. He turned off the light in the living room, so that whoever was looking in had to look through the dark to see him. Knife in hand, he opened the door slightly and crouched behind it so he couldn't actually be seen. "Who's there?"

At the same time, he took a whiff of the air blown in by the slight breeze. Lots of people smells, industrial strength disinfectants, all the various and sundry and mostly unpleasant odors that flourished wherever large numbers of people were, but underneath all that...

He flung the door open in a heartbeat. "Liska?"

She stood there, looking distinctly rumpled, but with a slight smirk on her face. "Hello, *Sensei*. Are you going to let me in, or am I *persona non grata*?"

He didn't so much let her in as drag her across the threshold, slamming and locking the door with almost one movement. "What are you doing here? You were supposed to wait another two days. Were you followed? Seen? Do you need to run? Do you need supplies? Money?"

She held up both hands to stop the torrent of words. "*Sensei*, please. I wouldn't show up on your doorstep like that. I'd have gone to the back door.

No, I was released, more or less. Todd woke up and not only backed up my story but gave a brief description of his attacker. Nothing that the police can match, but enough to exonerate me. They gave a grudging almost-apology, and all but threw me out. They didn't even give me enough money for bus fare. It's over." She stepped back and leaned on the doorway as she finished.

Ryoko eyed her expertly, realizing she was almost in shock. Even her grasp of Liska was slipping. "You should have called, even collect. I would have come to get you."

"I spent almost a week primarily in a barred cage smaller than your living room with four other people. I needed the walk. It helped tremendously."

"I imagine it did. Now, why don't you make some tea while I call back your barrister? We will drink the tea, and you can rant and rave until you feel better. Then you are going to get some real sleep!" Normally he wouldn't try to command her like this. She may obey his orders, but she was too independent to be happy about it. At the moment, however, she obviously needed time to collect herself.

"Thank you, *Sensei*, I was hoping I could just hide here for a bit. Slight amendment to the plan, can I fit in a shower somewhere along the line?"

Considering their sense of smell, the shower was probably as much a physical necessity as a psychological one. "Right, shower first, then tea. Are you hungry?" It was too late for lunch, and too early for dinner, but he didn't care and doubted she did.

"I am. Prison fare is not overly satisfying." Nor did they take into consideration that she needed several smaller meals instead of a few larger ones. She simply couldn't eat too much at a time.

"I'll make something when I'm off the phone then." His call should take less time than her shower. "You know where everything is."

Liska didn't spend the night often, but there was a room she could use when she did. In that room was a set of toiletries for her, towels, and a few spare changes of clothes.

As Liska headed upstairs, Ryoko turned to the phone. Instead of a typical greeting, he got, "Is everything alright?"

"Better than alright. Liska's here. She's been cleared."

"What?"

"The victim woke up. His testimony cleared her."

He could hear the sigh of relief over the phone. "That is probably the absolute best solution we could have hoped for. How is she?"

"A bit shocky, I think. But she'll be fine. Just needs a little time."

"I understand. Prison is never a pleasant thing. So, you no longer have need of my services?"

"Indeed. How much do I owe you?"

"Nothing."

"But-"

"You're family. Besides, you would help me if I needed it."

"Of course."

"Exactly. Give her my regards and my business card."

"I will." They hung up soon after, and Ryoko went to make tea and something decent to eat.

Liska came down about half an hour later, drying her hair, and showing signs of using water that was too hot and/or scrubbing too hard. Ryoko debated and then decided against saying anything about it this time. If this wasn't extenuating circumstances, what was?

He also decided that one way or another Liska was spending the night here. She needed that retreat from the world. He could give her that, if only for one night.

Chapter Sixteen

The most dangerous enemy is he with a grudge. – The
Kikitsutai Book of Wisdom

Far from West Palm Beach, there was another who
had been following Liska's recent prison time. Why
shouldn't he? After all, he had arranged the whole
thing. It had taken a long time to get to this point,
but he was close to his goal. But to reach his plan,
the girl had to be eliminated as a threat.

It had taken a long time to find her again.
Interesting that it was a website that led him to her
current location. He had to risk coming in person to
verify it was indeed her, but even there fortune had
blessed him. He was certain she hadn't seen him
and it put him close enough to indirectly control the
human, sending him to fetch the sword, when his
servant had been waiting. The human hadn't been
killed, but he didn't matter either.

No, it was the girl who had to be destroyed,
one way or another. Revenge would make it sweet,
but her death, or at least diversion was vital. She
was no longer imprisoned. He'd make her wish she'd
stayed in jail. There were many who wished her kind
or her specifically dead. And there was at least one
easily manipulated right in the area. He doubted the
human would actually succeed, but maybe he would

get lucky. If nothing else, the girl would be distracted.

The times were changing and the fates help anyone who stood in his way.

***

It took a few days, but Todd was finally up and about, well, to a limited extent. He may be back in school, but he still wasn't supposed to push himself. Jamal and Shahara had visited him frequently, as had Uncle John and a few of the police officers. Even his dad had flown in for a day or two. Mom had temporarily moved down to West Palm, not wanting to be even an hour away. Anna had sent flowers but hadn't actually visited. When Jamal informed Todd, for the second time, since he didn't remember the first, that Anna had actually been arrested and spent almost a week in jail, he was surprised she even sent flowers.

Todd didn't blame her for not wanting to visit. In fact, he was trying to figure out whether or not he owed her an apology. True, he hadn't tried to be attacked, but if he had followed her advice, it might not have happened. Or if he had told Jamal he showed her the sword, she might not have been a suspect. Well, she might have, but they wouldn't have had reason to hold her.

It would probably be best to clear the air with her as soon as possible. Unfortunately, he didn't have any contact information for Anna, didn't share any classes, and due to his injuries, he wouldn't be running the Kendo club until next semester at the earliest. So how was he supposed to find her? According to Shahara, Anna was even more withdrawn now than she had been before.

Groaning in frustration, Todd decided to take a walk. Anna seemed to like the waterway, walking, running, or skating alongside it. There was a small chance he might find her that way. The intracoastal was directly across the street from the campus, so he was there soon. So, turn left or right? He was about to turn left, when he got a sudden hunch to turn right. Todd had gotten weird hunches from time to time as long as he could remember, but it had been coming more frequently since the attack. Still, he made it a point to pay attention to those hunches.

After about ten minutes of walking, Todd caught a flash of Anna's unique red-orange hair. Sure enough, she was nearly two blocks ahead of him. He tried jogging, but it only took a few steps to realize that wouldn't work. She couldn't possibly hear him from this distance, so he'd have to follow her. Hopefully she wasn't going too far.

It felt like hours but was probably only about fifteen minutes later that she spotted Todd. She had gotten to a street crossing and looked all around, clearly seeing him. Thanks to traffic, he had managed to catch up so he was on the same block with her, close enough to see her frown when she noticed him and start walking to him. Good thing too, considering he really shouldn't be walking that much yet. In fact, he was so grateful that he didn't even pause to wonder why Anna had looked all around before crossing that particular street instead of just looking at traffic.

"Todd? What are you doing out here?"

"Following you."

"You succeeded. Gold star for you. Why?"

Slightly winded by pain and loss of stamina, his speech was in economy mode. "Need to talk."

Anna frowned again. "Now really isn't the best time. Can we talk later? At school?"

One advantage to being injured was the ability to guilt most people into co-operating. Heck, he had gotten Jamal to carry his books to classes that Jamal wasn't even in. "Can't walk back yet." Todd tried to restore his normal breathing patterns. "I wanted to apologize."

"There's nothing to apologize for."

"But there is! You were arrested and spent a week in jail. It might never have happened if I had listened to you in..." Todd trailed off suddenly as the little voice in his head started screaming at him to MOVE NOW!

Either Anna heard his voice or she had one of her own, because she plowed into him, knocking them both to the ground behind a parked car. The pavement next to them splintered into little fragments. Having been fortunate enough to have never been shot at before and being in severe pain from the less than gentle landing, Todd went into shock.

Part of his mind started narrating as if explaining things in a movie. The sidewalk splintered because of a bullet. Judging from the impact point, the bullet probably would have hit one or both of them, if Anna hadn't just demonstrated that she could probably play pro football. The bullet had to have come from somewhere behind Anna, so she had responded without actually seeing the threat. The noise he heard wasn't what he would recognize as a gunshot, so the gun was probably silenced.

As she was hitting the ground, Anna reached into her jacket and withdrew a medium-sized throwing knife, which she threw more or less blindly in the direction the shot probably came from. The narrative part of his mind calmly critiqued her form and found it very good. Another part of his mind wondered which he should be more surprised at; that she was armed, or that she showed such proficiency.

As unexpected as these things were, they paled in consideration to what she did next. Anna was five-two in shoes, and thanks to trying to fit a costume for her, Todd knew she weighed approximately one hundred pounds, give or take. Todd was five-ten, and weighed about one sixty, though it was probably closer to one fifty at the moment. Anna suddenly scooped him up and started to run, while carrying him.

Their mysterious attacker tried to take another shot at them. Anna dodged. While not an expert at physics, the observant little voice in Todd's head was still trying to calculate the energy needed to dodge a bullet, or even to run while carrying someone one and a half times your weight. His mind kept coming up with an *Error: does not compute* message.

While Todd certainly agreed with the running part, he couldn't figure out why she was running closer to the sniper. She seemed to be headed towards a specific house. This suspicion was backed up when she shouted, "*Sensei!* The door!"

A door was opening. As they got close to the house, there was a rain of grayish dust. Anna swerved to avoid it, but some landed on them anyway. Most of it landed on him, but she had some on her arms. It didn't hurt at all, but that didn't necessarily mean anything.

The door slammed behind them as they dashed into the house. Anna basically dropped him on a nearby couch but didn't stop moving as she headed into the kitchen. Todd could hear water running. An older looking Asian man stood by the door, looking worried.

"Silver dust?"

"*Itai!* Yes. Don't worry, I didn't breathe in any of it," Anna answered from the kitchen.

That was Japanese for 'ouch'. Weird. "Do you know who that was?" The man asked.

"Not yet." Anna came back into the living room. Her arms looked like they had been splashed with acid. Her accent was missing, had been since she shouted.

"That's from the silver? Man, I didn't think that could happen. Not unless you're a Werewolf or something." Todd heard the words but it wasn't until the other two people were staring at him that he realized he was the one to say them.

Anna just looked at him a minute. Then she smiled the strangest smile and something changed in her eyes. They were glowing. Like a cat's eyes. "Werefox, actually."

"Oh." And with that, Todd very calmly fainted.

Chapter Seventeen

In the dance of death, take care not to misstep. –The
Kikitsutai Book of Wisdom

With Todd unconscious, Liska turned to her great-uncle. He was livid, even if he was giving her a pleasant smile.

"You told him?" The voice was mild, as if discussing the weather. Liska knew better. If she didn't spend several hours explaining *everything* that happened over the past few months, she'd be amazed. But that would have to wait.

"*Sensei*, I love and highly respect you, but isn't there a sniper on a nearby roof?"

"Well said. I'm a little old for a roof top chase. Do you want this dance?"

"Thank you, *Sensei*, I believe I will."

Liska closed her eyes and tried to mentally rewind to the initial shot. Once she had it, she tried to find the angle of the bullet. Where had it come from? Not this house, maybe two or three houses to the right? So it should be possible to climb to the roof of the house without being noticed if she was careful and had a bit of luck.

On the second floor there was a good-sized window on the left side of the house. Earlier experimentation had shown her that it was possible, just, to reach out and grab the roof if she climbed partially out the window. Liska had fallen the first three times and another two times since, but she could do it successfully. She wouldn't fall this time. She couldn't afford to fall.

It was a vulnerable position. One foot on the side of the frame inside, and one leg pushing up for height, before she could grab the roof with both hands. If spotted by someone with a gun... Tune it out. *Sensei* was behind her, so he could try to catch her if she fell. Tune it out. She was high enough up that a fall would *hurt*. Tune it out. Worry later. The only thing that mattered was her grip on the roof, and how to get up there.

Her grip hurt. Shingles sides are sharp, and not meant for grabbing like this. It didn't matter. She had as secure a hand-hold as she was going to get. That was what mattered. Move into a modified hopping position, deep breath, and PUSH. Experience was her friend; she landed on the roof on her feet. Good. Much better than the alternatives.

There he was. Two roofs over and to the front. He hadn't heard her. She was downwind, letting her catch a slight smell of blood. So she had hit him. He was focusing on that, not his surroundings. Liska smirked. Amateurs. Not that she was complaining.

If she could see him, then he could see her. IF he turned. He was at the front, and she was close to the back, and moving more to the back, low to the roof. She didn't want to be seen. Not by him, or anyone else.

They hadn't attracted any attention yet. Maybe it was just too hot for people to be out. She had been thinking that for ages. The house he was on seemed temporarily un-lived-in. Maybe they were on vacation. Didn't matter right now.

Slowly, carefully, Liska glided to the edge of the roof. There was about ten feet between this roof and the next, with the next being slightly lower. Not a problem. Focus on the landing, make it quiet.

The landing made her wince. Not the jarring, but the volume. Her hearing was better than a human's at any time. Adrenaline made her hyper-sensitive. To her, it was unforgivably loud. But the noise didn't seem to penetrate the fog of fury that the shooter was building up. She could hear him running through every curse word she had ever heard in the English language, and then a few.

The distance between this roof and the next, her target, was slightly less than before. Unfortunately, the roof vibrated under her landing, and one of the tiles fell off. Liska froze, teeth clenched, muscles taut, as the tile landed with a dull *plop* in the grass. Nothing happened. He didn't turn. No, he was muttering about demons in human form and why couldn't they all go back to hell where they belonged. Liska rolled her eyes. Had to be a Purifier. One of the pseudo-religious types too. She tried to respect people with all religious beliefs, but it was a little harder when their religion told them to kill her.

He was bleeding. She could smell it. Ah, there was her knife. Good. She wanted it back. For one thing, she hadn't been wearing gloves. Second, they were good knives.

He still didn't know she was there, and she planned on keeping it that way as long as possible. Playing dodge-the-bullets wasn't her idea of fun, even if she had been pretty lucky so far. Luck smiles most on those who depend on it least.

She was good at stealth, even on a tiled roof that needed repair. It did help that the target was preoccupied. He seemed to be trying to decide if he should leave, try to get in the house, or wait for them to leave.

Liska approached slowly, keeping her eyes above his head. It truly was possible to feel someone watching, and she didn't want him warned. This way she could still see him out of here peripheral vision. Her two dominant senses, hearing and smell, were closely focused on him.

Now would be a good time for a plan. Kill? It was safer. But she hated killing. Luna Liska was no assassin. Besides, she needed information. Capture it was then. Unless he spotted her and started shooting. Then she would do whatever she had to do.

Coming up behind him, she tapped him on the shoulder. He whirled around and instantly met her fist just under his chin. She grabbed his collar, and punched him again in the solar plexus. *Voila*, one unconscious shooter.

Of course, this left her with a very heavy unconscious man that she had to get off the roof somehow. Who was this guy anyway? She searched him. More proof that he was a total amateur. He actually had his driver's license on him. Only one, and anyone who was good enough to have multiple IDs, and smart enough to have a fake on him, would have been a better shot. Or at least vanished before she got there. So, hello, Richard Calloway. Liska memorized the information and continued looking. With the credit cards and his social security card in his wallet, she now had enough information to completely steal his identity. That might be useful later. What she didn't find was a permit to carry a gun. There was even the Purifier's membership pin inside his coat. Utter foolishness, on the both of them. Hate groups really shouldn't give out ways to identify their members, and those members really, *really* shouldn't carry them around to perform illegal acts. Well, she had his identification number now.

Perhaps the most troubling, to her at least, was the shoebox of silver coated bullets and enough silver dust to kill half a dozen Weres. She suppressed a shudder, as she shut the box with her shoe. Not touching that, thank you. They could stay here for now. Maybe later they could send someone up to retrieve it. Or she could, with the right precautions. That much silver should be at least semi valuable. Priorities. First, she had to get Mr. Sniper-wannabe down.

The house really did look like the owners were away for a few days. It was subtle, but she had been trained to accurately tell the difference between an occupied location and an unoccupied one at a glance. Besides, even with an ear to the roof and listening carefully, she could hear absolutely no people sounds. The house next door did seem occupied, but no one was outside. That meant she'd have to be quiet.

Calloway wouldn't stay unconscious forever, so Liska retrieved her knife and started scouting for the best way down. There was a ladder in the back, obviously how he got up, but there was no way to safely get him down the ladder. Chlorine tickled her nose, but a lot of houses in the area had pools. Now, if this was one of them... Ah-ha! Perfect. There was a swimming pool in the back yard. Thanks to a downpour of rain over the weekend, it was a trifle over full. The deep end said it was twelve feet, two story roof, and the guy was unconscious. It was risky, but her best option. For herself, she'd prefer to take the ladder, but that wouldn't work. If he woke up, she'd have to knock him out again. If he didn't, she'd have to get him out before he drowned.

Fortunately, it appeared the owners liked privacy. There were nice large shrubs on one side of the yard, and the house between this one and Ryoko-*Sensei*'s had a nice high fence. She'd have to drag the guy around it, but she'd manage. It wouldn't be easy, she was out of adrenaline. Worry about sore muscles later. There was work to do.

Liska rolled the man to the back of the roof, relieved he wasn't stirring yet. Once there, she had to actually toss him off the roof. The pool wasn't straight down. Don't miss! Good, perfect shot. And he was waking up. Liska jumped. In seconds she was behind him. A quick jab to a pressure point in his neck, and he was unconscious again. He hadn't cried out, but Liska still tread water quietly for thirty seconds to see if anyone reacted. Nothing happened.

So, she had been shot at, had silver burns on her arms, probably some bruising on her hand, was now sopping wet and she still had to haul someone twice her size around back to Ryoko-*Sensei*'s house. Oh, and explain things to Todd. Did this count as a bad day yet?

It took several minutes to get him there and help *Sensei* get the man into his car. The look she got from her mentor left her in no doubt that she had a lot of explaining to do. Then he drove off, leaving her temporarily alone with Todd. Just ducky.

Chapter Eighteen

Instincts are natural gifts that should be heeded, but not always trusted. – The Kikitsutai Book of Wisdom

Todd woke up slowly, groggily, and in pain. More importantly, something in his head was screaming, 'WRONG! WRONG! WRONG!' at him. Something had happened. Something important, but what? As he opened his eyes, the first thing he noticed was that Anna was there and her hair was wet. The second thing he noticed was that he didn't have a clue where he was. "Anna? What happ... ow!" Okay, sitting up was out for now.

"Easy, don't try to move yet." There was something wrong with her voice. If he could think clearly through the ache in his head, the fire in his chest, and the shortness in his lung, maybe he could figure out what.

Another movement made him decide that figuring things out could wait long enough for him to take a pain killer. "Do you have a glass of water? I really need to take this." He fished the plastic medicine bottle out of his pocket despite stabbing pain.

"I'll be right back." And she was. That glass of cold tap water was one of the best things Todd had seen in days.

Once he took the pills, Todd leaned back into the couch once he found a position that didn't send spots into his eyes. Now he just had to wait for the medicine to kick in. In the meantime, "What happened? Why are you all wet? Are you wearing different clothes?" She was wearing a red tee-shirt now, and he could swear she had been wearing green before.

"What do you remember?"

Todd stifled a groan. "Anna, I'm in pain. My ribs hurt, my lungs hurt, my head hurts and I'm seeing stars. I really don't want to play twenty questions."

"I can't tell you what happened until I know what you know."

"That means having to think. Thinking hurts right now."

"It's good to stretch your mind."

What did he remember anyway? It was so fuzzy. He had been looking for Anna. That's right, to apologize to her. Obviously he had found her. Yes, and she had tried to get rid of him. Saying it was a bad time, then what... "Someone tried to shoot us! We need to call the police. OW!"

"Stop moving! It's fine. We're safe now. You've been out awhile. He's gone."

"Gone? Gone as in left? Gone as in arrested?"

"Gone like arrested. Do you remember anything else?"

"Arrested already? How long was I unconscious?"

"About twenty minutes. People try to work fast when crazy gunmen are involved."

"I believe it." He was still forgetting something. What was it? "Why did he try shooting us anyway? Was it just some crazy guy shooting at random?" Was someone actually trying to kill him? He had assumed that the stabbing was because he surprised a thief in the act. But a second attempt? That was taking coincidence a bit far. But no one wanted him dead. He didn't think so anyway. Anna was talking again. Pay attention.

"I don't really know all the details. Just that he was taken away, and that no one was killed."

"Well, that's good. Anyone else hurt?"

"We seem to have been the only ones on the street."

"Oh, okay." But it wasn't okay. Things didn't mesh right. Some crazy sniper would have chosen a crowded place, somewhere in public. Besides, could the police have gotten there, taken out a sniper and left in twenty minutes? Even if they had, why wasn't anyone taking their statements? "Do I have to give a statement?"

"No, it's fine."

No possible way. That simply wasn't the way the police worked. He should be in an ambulance right now, with some officer waiting to take his statement as soon as he could string together half-way coherent sentences. Considering that he knew half the department, his uncle would probably be waiting at the hospital.

Anna was lying about something. But what and why? If she was telling the truth about the police coming, then even if she hadn't told them he was there, she should still be answering questions. She could be lying about how long he was unconscious. A clock was in his view. He didn't know exactly what time he met up with Anna, but the time seemed right. So what was she lying about and why?

What did he know? He was in a house, so not on campus. Anna seemed comfortable, not like it was a stranger's house. But her family lived in England. A family friend, maybe? Or maybe she had more poise than he thought. Not likely the case. She was wearing different clothes, and she hadn't been carrying anything that clothes would fit in. So she had spare clothes here, or someone here was her size and wore her clothing style. Her hair was wet. If she had taken a shower or gotten wet somehow, that might explain why she changed, but why take a shower now?

He remembered being shot at. There was more though. Well, chances were that it paled compared to being shot at. Next fact, Anna was calm, so there was probably no immediate danger. The house they were in was probably the one she had been running to. How had she managed to carry him anyway? Had to be adrenaline. She had remained in control. Hadn't panicked or lost her head. Did it mean something, or was she just one of those lucky people who kept their heads in a crisis? Not enough information yet.

She said the shooter had been arrested. She also said that they had been the only ones on the street. The gunshot hadn't sounded like one to him. If no one inside realized that a gun had been fired, then no one would call the police. That left Anna, and the person who owned the house to call. Anna was extremely secretive, at least somewhat paranoid, and had just recently been released from prison. If Anna had called the police, then he was Sigmund Freud.

Todd knew nothing about the house owner. However, if Anna trusted him, then it was more than likely he wouldn't call the police either. It fit. That's why he didn't have to give a statement. The police simply didn't know. If they had known, even if Anna hadn't said she had been a witness, they'd be knocking on doors, asking around.

So, Anna was probably lying about the shooter being arrested. Why? What happened to the shooter? What was going to happen to him? Think, Kensworth, think! There was no way that any rational person was going to leave someone shooting at them like that. Of course, the rational solution is to call the professionals. Anna hadn't, he was certain of it. Why would she lie about that?

One of the first steps to dealing with a character flaw was realizing it. One of Todd's flaws was being too trusting. He had been told that by multiple people, including Anna. Usually he didn't think it was too much of a problem. Right now, he was wondering if it would get him killed.

This was Anna, his friend! But she was also lying to him, had been arrested on suspicion of attempted murder, was extremely secretive, and that hypnosis theory was looking more plausible by the second. His mind, still sluggish, replayed the attack. Oh yes, not only had Anna picked him up and carried him, she had reacted before the bullet was fired. From a shooter who was behind her. How had she known? And she had thrown a knife. Armed and experienced with weapons. He never would have guessed that she carried a knife. Did she always have one, or had she been expecting trouble of some sort? Dare he ask her?

He didn't dare ask her why she was lying. Not yet. Not while she controlled the territory. Had he been kidnapped? It was a strange, sudden thought that popped up out of nowhere and seemed ridiculous even to him, but he couldn't completely disregard it. Not while he couldn't get up off the couch.

Todd might be in the living room, in full view of the door, but that didn't mean he could leave. Yes, his painkillers had kicked in enough that he could get up and walk. Maybe. With great difficulty. He would probably need Anna's help to even get off the couch. If she decided not to let him leave, he couldn't do anything about it right now. One sharp poke at his sutures would be enough to make moving the last thing on his mind.

"Todd, are you alright? You don't look well." Anna's voice not only brought him out of his thoughts, it also made him jump, pulling his stitches *again*. A strangled cry escaped him despite his best efforts. "Easy, don't move. Sorry, I didn't mean to startle you."

Her arms came up to steady him. Her arms that had little red irritations on them. Where the dust had hit her. The dust that she said was silver dust. His thoughts snapped together so hard he was privately amazed she didn't hear it. "You said you were a Werefox."

Someone was coming in. Anna moved between him and the door before seeing who it was, relaxing and backing down. But Todd was too focused to notice. "Your eyes glowed golden. You *are* Cats-eye!"

He did manage to notice that the man who came in, the same one who let them in, turn an intense look at Anna, who actually winced, and she wasn't even looking at him.

"Pray tell, who or what might 'Cats-eye' be?"

"I'll explain later, *Sensei*." Anna turned to him. "Better make yourself comfortable. This is going to be a long talk."

Chapter Nineteen

The truth is a rare and valuable commodity, to be treated with care. – The Kikitsutai Book of Wisdom

It wasn't until after he blurted out that she was Cats-eye that Todd realized that might be a mistake. Anna had clearly spent some time trying to conceal that fact and probably wasn't happy with him knowing. She might not have wanted the other person in the room to know either. However, it was too late now. At least she didn't seem angry. "Are you Cats-eye?"

"I never called myself that, but yes, most of the incidents that you credit to 'Cats-eye' are mine."

"How did your eyes glow like that? Why did you say you were a Werefox?" He had a million questions, but if he kept asking than she would never have a chance to answer them.

"Oh good, the easy ones first." She didn't sound like she thought them easy. "In reverse order, I said I was a Werefox because I *am* a Werefox, which is why my eyes can glow. Under the right circumstances."

What circumstances? "Werefoxes aren't real."

She smiled. "Are you sure?"

Todd would have answered her, but he had forgotten how to speak. As she spoke, she started to change. Her hands were held up as fingernails lengthened and sharpened to claws. She opened her mouth to reveal teeth changing into fangs. A wave indicated her eyes, pupils rounding and becoming slitted. Her ears didn't need any indication as they lengthened and came to a point, covered with red and black fur. He was not going to stare; he was not going to stare! Oh, yes, he was. That was a tail! "Dzyackger," was all that emerged from his throat, a strangled sound.

"I see you believe me now. Good. I must ask that you try not to pass out again, as this will be difficult enough to explain." She paused, perhaps trying to figure out where to begin. "I'll be blunt. Most of what you believe about reality is wrong."

Todd blinked at her. He had to be looking stupid, and he knew it, but he couldn't figure out how to stop. "Um, like what?" Okay, eloquent it wasn't, but it didn't make him look like a total idiot.

"Name something that doesn't exist."

Something that *doesn't* exist? That was different. "Um, zombies?" There, that seemed to fit with the whole Werefox theme. Jamal had been watching a zombie movie last night, and Todd ended up seeing more than he planned.

"Good. I don't believe zombies are truly real, but there are shades. They are a bit similar. Actually, they're probably closer to ghosts. Well, a mix between the two."

He was back to surprised blinking.

"Liska, you aren't doing it right. If you insist on telling him, at least do it properly."

Liska? Who was Liska? It didn't slip Todd's notice that the older man, whoever he was, did not seem surprised by this. Anna nodded. "You're right, *Sensei*. Let me try this again."

"Why did he call you Liska?"

"We'll get there. Okay, I need you to picture something for me. You're the artist, it should be easy. To begin with we have humans. They are very much in the majority, outnumbering the rest put together by three or four to one. They are or at least consider themselves the standard of normality. Because they are the majority, they don't have to hide and can walk freely in the metaphorical Day. So, we call them Days."

Todd nodded. He was still confused, but hopefully if he kept his mouth shut, she'd explain more. At very least he understood humans.

"Then there is what we call Night. Those who can't hide what they are, can't pass as human or 'normal'. They are not necessarily nocturnal, though some are. Nor are they necessarily monsters, though some do become that. Driven by fear, hatred, and jealousy, hating that they have to hide, they become twisted and desperate. Fortunately, only a very small percentage acts like that. Do you understand? Not, do you believe me yet, just understand."

"I think so."

"Good. Now, just as we have Days and Nights, we have those in between. The Twilights."

"Anything to do with—"

"No," Anna, or maybe Liska said firmly. "The name is a coincidence. The boundary between Day and Night. Twilights are humans with non-human abilities, mostly Espers, or people with ESP; or non-humans that can pass, such as Weres and vampires. No, I don't consider myself human."

"Vampires are real too?" Todd interrupted. She gave him a look. "Sorry."

"Yes, vampires are real too. Now, the thing about Twilights is that they never quite fit with Days or Nights. Nights are jealous that they can walk with Days or don't consider them 'other' enough. Days, especially the more perceptive ones, realize that there is something subtly 'wrong' about them. It isn't always a conscious reaction, but it is there. Espers don't seem to provoke as strong a reaction as non-human Twilights. You have remarked on my anti-social status enough times. It isn't that I don't like people, well, sometimes I don't. A large part of it is that people don't wish to associate with me."

"Man, that's too bad. Why do people do that?"

"As I said, it isn't always, or even usually, conscious on their part. Nor do most go out of their way to avoid me or be mean. Most just don't wish to be friendly. If I make an effort to be friendly, most are friendly enough back. But as you can imagine, in an effort to keep people from finding out my secret, I tend to be less social than average."

"Is that why you're okay with Jamal, Shahara, and me? Because we're friendly?"

"Mostly. I'm friends with them primarily through you. I'm friends with you through Kendo." Anna hesitated.

"What's wrong?"

"Are you feeling alright? Really?"

"Yeah, I think so. The painkillers kicked in a while ago. I'm still alert enough, right?"

"Yes, you're fine. How's your head?"

Back to the confused blinking. "Okay, I guess. Why?"

"There's something else you need to know."

"What's that?"

"Perhaps because it is difficult, though not impossible, for Twilights to manage friendships with Nights and Days, a Twilight will always recognize another Twilight. It's a deep sense of knowing."

"O...kay?"

"Do you remember the first time you met me?"

Todd rolled his eyes. "Not forgetting that any time soon."

"Did you get a weird feeling the first time you saw me?"

"Yeah! I did, actually. I thought, 'she's like me', but I don't know what that... means," The last word left his mouth slowly, a letter at a time. "No. Not possible. I can't be..."

"A Twilight? You are. An Esper, I imagine. Anything else, and you would probably be aware of your status. It's also why you were able to integrate so well with the Days."

It was at least a couple minutes before Todd said anything. She was right, this was a reality shift. "Let me see if I understand. You aren't human."

"Correct."

He looked over at the Asian man who had been watching silently. "Most perceptive. No, I am not human either."

Todd looked back to Anna. "You are a Werefox." She nodded. Then he turned to the Asian man she called *Sensei*, who nodded as well.

"You are also Cats-eye."

"More or less."

"There are things out there that I have never heard of and more that I thought were just stories that are real."

"That's right."

"ESP is real."

"Yes."

"Jamal always said it was. Guess he was right," Todd muttered.

"Apparently."

"And just to make things more interesting, I have ESP. Am I getting it so far?"

"Essentially." Anna nodded.

"I think I liked it better when I just thought you were trying to kidnap me."

For the first time, Todd saw Anna truly laugh.

Chapter Twenty

What is known cannot then be unknown. – The Kikitsutai
Book of Wisdom

"When did you think that?" Anna asked after a moment.

"When I woke up and realized you were lying about the shooter being arrested. Speaking of, what really happened to him and do you know why he tried to kill us?"

"He has been dealt with. It's someone else's problem now."

"But—"

"It isn't our concern." Anna's voice was quiet but made it very clear the issue was *closed*. Todd decided to drop it for now. "As to the why, I do have an idea."

"Oh, it wasn't random?"

"No, it wasn't random. It wasn't random at all." She closed her eyes briefly, as if to gather her thoughts. "Tell me something, why do you think this whole... matter," she waved her hands in emphasis, "is a secret?"

"Um, I hadn't actually thought about it. So you're left alone?"

"That is part of it. How long have you been friends with Jamal?"

Todd blinked at the random question. "Since the beginning of high school. About seven years. Why?"

"Yet he is black and you are white."

"So? You never seemed to care."

"I don't. It makes no difference to me, or to you, or possibly to him. Yet to some people, that is a big deal. Perhaps you should ask him sometime, if he could hide the fact that he was different, would he? I'm guessing that at least at times, the answer is yes."

"Maybe. But what does that have to do with anything?"

"Even as recently as the 1960s, segregation was legal and common place in *this* country. There are places where it lasted much longer or still exists. Even today, there are people who don't like people like him, possibly even hate him, for nothing more than the color of his skin, or the fact that he was born in a different country. Jamal and Shahara are human, completely. Imagine how complicated things become when you add non-humans to the mix."

"I think I begin to see."

"Exactly. As a famous sage once said, 'Three can keep a secret if two of them are dead'. Our secret is large and getting larger every day. While we have been having this conversation, there have probably been at least three to five births of Twilights and Nights, and two other conversations similar to this one. Someone who didn't know, is finding out. Some of those conversations will end well. Some will not. Some really will not."

"What do you mean?"

"You're a psych major. What is the most common reaction to the unknown?"

Todd winced. "Fear."

She nodded gravely. "Fear. Hence the secret. Despite that, there are many who know or suspect that not all the people they meet are as normal as they appear. This encompasses a wide range of people. Some are paranoid or mentally disturbed. Some are conspiracy theorists, some have no life and will believe anything, some have personal experience of at least part of the truth. Reactions vary widely too. Fear is a strong emotion, but so is curiosity. Some think the whole thing is 'cool', others stay quiet to protect themselves or others. Many who find some small scrap of truth brush it off thinking they must be wrong or keep quiet so they aren't thought crazy. Then there are those who consider our very existence a threat."

"Like the guy on the roof?"

"Precisely. He belongs to an organization called Purifiers. They desire to 'purify' the world from what they perceive to be a dangerous, possibly even 'demonic' threat. In other words, us. Yes, 'us'. If they found about you, they'd lump you in with the rest of us."

"So they tried to kill you because you aren't human, and me because of an ability I didn't even know about? I still don't know what it is." The whole idea seemed bizarre.

"That is pretty much the size of it."

"How would he even know?"

Anna frowned. "I'm not certain. Even the most perceptive Days generally cannot look at a Twilight, and realize they are a Twilight. It is far more subtle than that. I'll check the Purifiers' watch list to see if I'm on it. They probably weren't actually looking for you, you just happened to be in the area."

"That's twice in under a month," Todd muttered.

"Pardon?"

"Nothing, just thinking. That's twice in under a month I nearly got killed by being in the wrong place at the wrong time."

"I am sorry."

Todd waved it off. "Not your fault."

"Actually, it may be. Partially, at least." Anna looked a little guilty.

"Huh?" Wow, that was eloquent. But really, what was he supposed to say?

"I've made some enemies. The sword you were stabbed with was one I handled earlier in the day. It wasn't stolen, and I was picked up less than half an hour after you were found, because of an anonymous tip. You might have been attacked in an attempt to frame me."

Todd could feel his eyes bugging out. "What kinds of enemies do you have that would do something like that?"

"Ones you do not want to be involved with." For a moment, she just looked tired. Before he could say anything, she changed the subject. "Purifiers and others of their ilk are far from the only reason to keep this quiet. There have been a few attempts to weaponize Espers, possibly augment their abilities through experimentation, etc. This usually doesn't go well. For anyone. Ironically enough, this is one of the reasons everyone is so afraid of us." She smiled without humor.

"Are we dangerous?"

"Are humans dangerous? Are dogs dangerous? Birds? We have the potential to be, I don't deny it. But we also have the responsibility to use our abilities wisely. Don't get me wrong, evil exists. It exists in Days, Nights, and Twilights. But so does good."

"Then the fear..."

"Let me put it this way. Are you afraid of vampires?"

"I didn't believe in vampires twenty minutes ago," Todd pointed out.

"And I told you they exist. If I introduced you to a vampire, right now, would you be afraid?"

Pride wanted to say no, but Honesty demanded the quiet, "Yes."

"Why?"

"They're dangerous. They suck blood. They kill people!"

"Do they?"

"Um, I think so. Don't they?" It occurred to him suddenly that he really had no idea. All he had were stories and myths, but they probably weren't all that accurate.

"Yes and no. Yes, vampires do drink blood, but seldom human blood. They have their own little council/police force to prevent rogue vampires from going out and killing people. Though in all honesty, they are probably motivated more by a desire for secrecy than out of moral obligation."

"So they don't think it's morally wrong to kill people?" Todd tried to ignore the fact that the last statement came out a lot more like a squeak than he wanted it to.

She shrugged. "Some do. Most do, even. But just like humans, vampires like to believe themselves superior. And if they are superior to humans, why should they be bound by their ethics? Fortunately, those that feel that way are an unpopular minority. Before you get on your moral high horse, I would like to point out that human kill a lot more humans, *and* kill more vampires than vampires kill humans."

He tried to digest this. "So the secrecy is to keep yourselves safe?"

"It is for safety on both sides. There are just too many, on all sides, who aren't ready to deal with integration yet."

"Well, what if you cut the legs out from under them? Announce the whole secret? Then you could go through legal channels for any problems."

"No! No, that would almost certainly be a total disaster. Humans can't accept their fellow humans, and the Twilights and Nights aren't always much better. We can't make peace with each other if we can't even make peace with our own kind. There would probably be 'witch hunts' for those who don't fit. Blame for incidents would definitely not be fairly proportioned. And what of the Twilights and Nights who believe themselves superior and have no qualms about violent action? Right now, they are kept in check, either because they fear what might happen if the veil of secrecy was removed, or by others who fear the end of the secret."

"Are you sure it would lead to violence?"

"The path to change is always through violence to some extent or other. Most of the time, the path to change is washed with blood. A sad but proven truth."

"You can't hide forever," Todd spoke softly.

"No, we can't. But at this point in time, I believe that the end of secrecy would lead to war. A war that no one can win. The true war to end all wars. So I am dedicated to making sure the veil isn't torn asunder in my lifetime." The 'even if it takes my life' wasn't spoken, but Todd heard it anyway.

***

Liska was privately pleased that Todd was taking this so much better than she had feared. Even Ryoko-*Sensei* seemed pleased, which meant he might not tear quite so many strips from her hide over this debacle. Still, Todd seemed to be reaching his limit on how much he could take. "It's getting late. Maybe we should save the rest of the questions for another time. I'm sure Ryoko-*Sensei* would be willing to drive us back to school. Oh, I apologize; I forgot to introduce you. This is my mentor and great-uncle, Ryoko-*Sensei*."

"Uh, pleased to meet you, sir." Todd stumbled to a stand and tried to bow, even though it obviously hurt.

"Likewise." The older Werefox gave a small bow back. "Hopefully next time will be under less... intense circumstances."

Liska stifled a snort at her great-uncle's understatement. "So, are you willing to put off the rest for later?"

Todd nodded reluctantly. "I have so many questions."

"I'm sure you do. I'm equally sure that if we keep talking, you will start forgetting things. If there is anything extremely important, ask it now. Let the rest wait."

"I can't tell anyone about this, can I? Not Jamal, or Shahara, not even my mom?"

"It would probably be best if you didn't, at least for now."

"Am I a target?"

"I don't know. I do not believe so, and I intend to find out, but at this point, I simply don't know."

"You'll let me know what you find out?"

"Of course."

"So, where do we go from here?" Todd asked.

Liska bit back a smile. "Right now, the car. From there, the school?"

"And at school?"

"You go to your dorm and rest, while I do some investigating."

Todd gave a huff. "That's not what I meant."

"I think to the best of your abilities, you should try to pretend this afternoon never happened." He wouldn't be able to, but it would be for the best if he could. She threw a glance at Ryoko-Sensei, who nodded. If necessary, Todd would 'forget' everything. But they'd give him a chance first.

"So in one afternoon, I get shot at, find out one of my friends isn't human, find out I have ESP, something I didn't even believe in, basically discover that reality isn't anywhere close to what it was, and I'm supposed to pretend it never happened?"

"Exactly." Liska smiled, before opening the rear car door and climbing in.

"Oh, good. I was afraid you were going to ask me to do something hard," Todd muttered under his breath. He tried to offer her the front seat, but Liska was buckled in by then and waved him off.

Eventually he climbed in. "So, how much do I really have to keep secret? I mean, obviously I can't tell anyone about you..."

"Keeping in mind that I am completely paranoid and that my reaction should be taken with about a tablespoon of salt, I'd say don't tell anyone anything. If you want to tell someone you absolutely trust about being an Esper, that's one thing, and even then, you may want to wait until you can say what you can do. Everything else, I'd keep quiet about. You can always tell someone something later. Un-telling them is a lot harder."

He tried to turn to look at her. "Can you un-tell someone something?"

"*You* can't, I imagine. There are those who can do the next best thing. Don't go depending on it though."

"What about getting shot at?"

"Definitely keep that a secret. You have police connections. It wouldn't take long for them to realize there was never a call about this. That would probably be almost as awkward to explain as the rest."

Todd had realized he couldn't turn to look at her, so he pulled down the sunshade so he could see her in the mirror. Liska made a point of meeting his eyes in the mirror. "Can you handle keeping this a secret?"

"It won't be easy."

"No one said it would be. If it helps, anytime you need to talk, you can track me down."

"Or me." Liska's eyes widened slightly at her mentor's offer. "You know where to find me?"

"Um, sort of. It was a little hectic."

"I'm sure. Have 'Anna' give you one of my cards. It has my address on it."

Todd didn't seem to notice the subtle dig there. Then again, he didn't know *Sensei* like she did. He might even still think Anna was her real name.

"Okay, thanks. So what did happen today? Officially?"

"You were looking for me, right? Well, you found me. We talked. You bought me ice cream or something and now are quite sure I'm not upset at you about being arrested, and you are convinced I had nothing to do with your attack. I had, oh, strawberry, if anyone asks. Make up any other details you like. How's that sound?"

"Do I owe you ice cream?"

"No, it's just a little detail to make the story more convincing."

Todd grimaced. "I'm a lousy liar."

"I noticed," Liska drawled. Then she got serious. "Putting in little details helps. Like deciding what flavors we supposedly bought. So does actually believing it for the few minutes it takes to tell it. That's how the best do it."

"We're here. Todd, if you'll help me find your dorm, I'll drop you off first. I want to talk to Anna for a while."

Ah, yes. Interrogation time. She knew she wouldn't be able to avoid it, but that didn't mean she was looking forward to it.

It was rather like she expected. He gave her a massage while gently asking pointed questions. Who was Cats-eye? How did Todd know about her? What had she done to prevent this, and why had he not been informed? And why had she decided to tell Todd what she did?

Liska avoided the main points to the best of her ability, but it was obvious that her 'I had it under control,' wasn't going over well. She didn't tell him that Todd had suspected she was Cats-eye, that she had made a semi-botched hypnosis attempt on him, and finally had to call Kira in to help. Oh, Ryoko-*Sensei* probably suspected some or all of the truth; but what he didn't know, he didn't have to report. There was absolutely no way she was going to mention Korvou or anything he had said.

She wasn't sure how to answer why she had told him so much today. She didn't know. Maybe what Korvou told her was a factor, maybe she didn't think a second hypnosis attempt, even by an expert, would go over better than the first. Officially, she used the justification that Todd was an Esper, therefore had a right to know. She doubted *Sensei* bought it, but he was polite enough not to call her a liar to her face.

Liska had never tried interrogating someone while giving them a massage. It might be worth trying sometime. Tensing up was an unmistakable non-verbal cue. Liska had to work very hard on not tensing and therefore giving herself away, and wasn't sure how well she succeeded.

It didn't help that Ryoko-*Sensei* was as paranoid as she was. He followed the same rules. Everyone was lying until proven otherwise. The person you trust most says you have four eggs, you double check anyway. Assume that people you don't even know want you dead. It's probably true. Of course he doubted her. After the massage, he left and she could start investigating.

Chapter Twenty-One

Knowing your opponent is the first step to defeating them. –
The Kikitsutai Book of Wisdom

There were two ways to get information from the Purifiers. One way was to go to their local headquarters. Liska specialized in physical infiltration, but even she wouldn't hesitate to admit that Purifiers' HQ was more of a hassle than she was willing to take on if she didn't have to. They had dogs, guards who knew what they were doing, everything was color-coded, and there was silver dust, purified salt, garlic, and crosses in the air vents. Only the first would really affect her, and even the garlic and crosses were more annoying than damaging to vampires. The UV lights, on the other hand, would be an issue for them. Purified salt would probably only affect shades and some types of Fae. It was possible, but it would definitely be a difficult task.

Fortunately, the second way was much easier. Pulling a small metal object from her pocket, Liska sat at her computer, and typed in the web address of a junk website. It appeared to be the type the showed up when no website had been built. Clicking a hidden link led to another junk website, that led to another which said no such website existed. Finding the hidden link there, she was presented with ten squares. She had fifteen seconds to identify the red one, and they were arranged randomly.

Hovering her color sensor over the screen, already set to red, it beeped at the third square from the end. Liska clicked the square just barely within the time limit, then closed her eyes, turning away as the screen flashed very bright light for a few seconds. Then, and only then could she log in to the Purifiers' website. Membership was by referral only. She had been referred by one of her skulk. She wasn't sure exactly how he got a membership, but privately Liska suspected a good portion of the Purifier's membership was built up of Twilights and Nights trying to find out what they were up to.

The website had changed from her last visit. She'd have to check that out. First things first. The important thing was to see if they had been tagged. Fortunately, they had a 'Find known or suspected demon influence in your area' section. She typed in the zip code. That was odd; none of them were on it. In fact, at least a quarter of the list were straight Days. Checking another area, she looked up members to find Richard Calloway. Even more interesting. He wasn't high enough up to be given missions like that, and it was recommended against giving him that kind of clearance. There were a few reports about him being a loose cannon. Liska drummed her fingers against the keyboard, thinking. So what had brought Calloway out there today?

Staring at the computer screen wouldn't answer her question, so she turned to other parts of the site. What did they have on her anyway?

The answer turned out to be reassuringly little. They were pretty sure Liska was a Were of some sort, but prevailing opinion was that she was a Werewolf. Obviously they didn't have any linguists on their team. Why did everyone assume Werewolves were the only Weres anyway? They believed her to be European, which wasn't too surprising considering that the majority of her work had been there. They thought she was currently in Russia or that her home base was there. From the looks of it they had caught on to her Inge Tarna persona. Oh well, she hadn't used that often, it wasn't a big loss. It might, however, cause problems for the real Inge whose name she had partially borrowed. Maybe not, the last name wasn't exactly the same. Still, she should drop her a line and warn her.

What else did they have? This was new. There was a notice of a reward for any demon brought in dead or alive. They were especially interested in Vampires and Weres. Didn't they know that vampires didn't leave a body? Still, she didn't like it. Sounded like someone was interested in experimentation.

Interesting, they had a bounty set up for the most wanted demons. Knew him. Knew her. Tisiphone? She was dead going on three years now. She would have thought they would notice something like an absence of missions. Ah, well, Liska never credited them with being the best informed organization.

Liska wasn't surprised she was on the list, but was a little surprised she was number two on the list. She wouldn't have thought she was that well known. Though she had been given some high profile jobs. More disturbing was that she had never heard of Atolatar, the number one on the list. If they wanted him so badly, even with very little information on him, why hadn't she heard of him? Definitely something to look into.

***

"Atolatar? Doesn't sound familiar. How do you spell that?" Ryoko-*Sensei*'s voice echoed over the phone lines. Liska spelled it for him and waited. "No, nothing. Anyone else interesting on the list?"

"Sending you a copy now. Tisiphone is on there. Number seven. Not bad for a dead assassin, huh?"

There was a deep silence on the other end. Something was wrong. "*Sensei*? Are you still there?"

"I'm still here. You said Tisiphone? The assassin from a few years back?"

"That's right. I guess they don't know she's dead."

"It would appear."

"What's wrong?" He sounded so odd.

"Nothing. I'm just a bit distracted. Anything else?"

He should have a copy by now, but it wasn't worth bringing up. His eyes were probably bothering him again. Not something he would willingly admit to her. "Let's see, Ryo's on the list. So is Shinji. I already told you I was there. A few other people. You aren't. Sorry."

"It's fine." She could hear the smile there. "No doubt they think me dead or retired. Anything else on the site?"

"None of us were tagged. They don't know we're here. They probably don't know about Todd at all. You dealt with Calloway. What brought him out?"

"An anonymous tip."

"Another one? I'm beginning to seriously dislike these anonymous tips. What did I do to Anonymous anyway?"

"I don't know, but I suggest you stop. Could it be your picture?"

Liska snickered at that, thinking of the picture she had had taken of her standing next to the statue of Anonymous in Budapest, Hungary. "That must be it. I'll apologize next time I'm in the area. Does Calloway remember anything?"

"No."

"So making large purchases with his credit cards..."

"No, Liska."

"How about small ones?"

"Liska." He sounded tired.

"Alright, *Sensei*." Technically, that wasn't a 'no'.

"How much more do you plan to tell the boy?"

"As little as I can get away with. We'll have to test him to find out his ability. He should know the genetics of being an Esper, and maybe just enough about being a Were that he won't get wrong ideas about me."

"Will you tell him about your job?"

Would she tell him she was a ninja? "Not unless I have to." *If Korvou is right, I just may have to.* A new thought popped into her brain, driving the rest away. Korvou had said that Todd would play a major role, but he never said how or whose side he would be on. What if Todd was where the secret fell apart completely? Had she doomed the world? How much trouble had she caused anyway?

"Liska? You are still there?" Apparently it had been her turn to lapse into deep dark silences.

"Yes, I'm just thinking." She was being silly. If Todd didn't handle his new reality well, then steps could be taken. Many possible solutions, ranging from temporary to permanent. Some were quite unpleasant, but if Liska had to pick between the safety of her family, possibly even the world itself, or the safety of one person she had met a couple months ago, well, it was no contest. She would just have to try to keep it from coming to that point.

"Very well. I think it would be best if you have the boy here when you explain as often as possible. I need to know what you are telling him. Besides, having a second person to help explain can only help."

Plus, he'd be able to rein her in if she started to say too much. Or at least chastise her for it. "Of course, *Sensei.*"

"If he is available, bring him down tomorrow when you come."

"I shall try."

"Good. Oh, I heard from Yoshiro yesterday."

Liska fought back a wince and forced herself to relax even though she couldn't be seen. "Yes?"

"He's going to be working with a blood of vampires."

"That's nice. Where?" *Not here, please, not near here.*

"I'm not certain."

"Hmm." Operational security. They didn't need to know, so they didn't. "Speaking of Yoshiro, does he know where I am?" Most of the skulk believed her to be in England or close to it. More operational security.

"I do not believe so. You were the one to decide on the list."

"I didn't put him on, but Father might have."

"Probably not without telling you."

Father would do what he pleased whether she liked it or not and they both knew it. But it wasn't worth arguing over. "Perhaps not."

"Vampires can be tricky."

"Not if you know what you're doing. Yoshiro is many things, but not an idiot." Arrogant, cruel, and self-centered, but not an idiot, usually. After all, he was being groomed to take over head of the clan.

"Quite true. Very well, bring the boy down tomorrow, and we can explain some more."

Liska hung up, musing over her mentor's hidden message. He had definitely done it on purpose. Todd was temporary. Yoshiro was her future. Whether she liked it or not.

Chapter Twenty-Two

Discretion may be mistaken as cowardice by the rash. – The Kikitsutai Book of Wisdom

Todd was only able to carve out half an hour to be at Ryoko-*Sensei*'s, so they had to prioritize. Explaining would take a long time, so *Sensei* decided to go over the ESP tests. She was tested first, supposedly to show how the tests worked. Once again, she flunked with flying colors.

Todd didn't do much better. Until they got to the card test. When predicting what card would be turned over next, the average was about twenty-four percent correct. Her average was closer to twenty-two percent. Todd's first run was forty percent correct. With each correct call, Ryoko-*Sensei* became more and more excited. Even Liska was interested when the percentage was calculated.

Todd was less enthusiastic. "Only forty percent?"

"That's nearly twice average. Raw, untrained talent. Now that you know your talent, you can work on honing it." Liska shuffled the cards and put them away.

"Pay attention to your feelings and dreams. They may be trying to tell you something," Ryoko-

Sensei instructed. Even if he didn't have ESP, he was enthusiastic about studying it.

"Where does ESP come from?" Todd asked.

"Good question. No one truly knows. It seems to have a basis in genetics. If one parent is an Esper, there is a high chance the children will be as well. There is a possibility of an Esper being born to Day parents, and an even rarer possibility of a Day child being born to two Esper parents. But usually it's hereditary. Then there's the theory that everyone had some amount of ESP in various amounts but most never realize it or develop it." Ryoko-*Sensei* warmed quickly to one of his favorite topics.

"So my children..."

"Will probably be Espers," Liska confirmed.

"So, why did he test you? You're a Were, not an Esper, right?"

"Father is a Were, so I am a Were. My children will be Weres, regardless of who I marry. But Mother is an Esper. There is a possibility that I have some ESP capabilities because of that."

"So, being a Were is genetic too? What about spread by bite?"

Liska shook her head. That was always a sticking point. "Long story. The short version, being a Were is genetic and cannot be transmitted. It is a dominant trait, but that doesn't matter much. Marriages are nearly always within the Were community."

"But they can inter-marry with humans?"

"Certainly. My mother is a human Esper, as I said. Don't you have to get to class?"

"Sheesh, is it that late already? Yeah, I have to go. Need a ride back, Anna?"

"No, I'm staying for a bit, but thank you."
After the past couple weeks, she needed some time
to relax, let down her guard. She couldn't do that on
campus. Of course, she couldn't completely do that
here either. Not with Ryoko-*Sensei* trying to figure
out what else she might be hiding.

Sparring was a big help. She always felt more
alive when sparring. Some psychologists, possibly
even Todd, could probably get a lot of mileage out of
that, but it wasn't like she didn't know she needed
years of therapy anyway.

***

Liska was about halfway back to campus when she
felt the eyes. Someone was watching her. They were
good. She could tell that even before she started
looking for them. One side-step later, she had
bumped into a man carrying a huge stack of papers.
Predictably, they scattered. Apologizing profusely,
Liska was immediately down on the ground helping
him gather his papers before they flew away. While
picking them up, she discreetly looked around for
her new shadow.

Except, she couldn't find anyone. They *were*
good. On the off chance they hadn't connected Liska
leaving 12 Magnolia Drive with Anna Andrews on
campus, Liska went a few blocks out of her way to go
to the large bookstore near the campus.

Once inside, it only took her a few minutes to
buy a Chai, find the book she had been reading last
time, and find a comfortable place to sit on a

windowsill. The sitting by the window was weird. She usually preferred an out-of-the-way nook where she was unlikely to be noticed. But if she wasn't by the window, how would she know when her shadow left?

It took nearly two hours before she felt the sensation of eyes leave her. She stood up, threw away her trash, put her book away and left. Still no eyes. The feeling of being watched didn't return until she was almost on campus boundaries. So, they did know. Well, in that case, the best thing she could do was pretend not to notice.

It was hard to ignore something like that. It demanded so much focus that she walked past Todd, barely noticing him. At least, she barely noticed until he grabbed her wrist.

Wrist grabs were one of the first things Liska had learned to defend against. Both her instinct and her training said to make him stop NOW. She forced them down as much as possible. Rather than jerking her wrist away and following through with an elbow jab, she just turned to him. "Let go. Now."

He dropped her hand at a speed that may well have rivaled light. Backing up a few steps for good measure, Todd managed out a tentative, "Anna?"

Liska took a deep breath. Snarling at Todd wouldn't accomplish anything. "It would be best if you don't try to grab my wrist like that. I have too much training that considers that an attack," She muttered in a low voice.

"Oh, sorry."

Liska nodded. Then in a more normal 'Anna' voice, "Yes, Todd? Did you want something?"

"Uh, I have some more questions."

Of course he did. It was only natural. But where would be a good place to talk? He wasn't allowed in her dorm room or vice versa. Where did one find a private place on campus? Somewhere they wouldn't be overheard. "I'm being followed," she whispered. In a normal voice, she continued. "Sure, I'll go on a drive with you."

Todd stared at her for a moment. "Should I be worried?"

"I doubt it. Traffic isn't that bad."

He still wasn't getting it. "Um, okay?"

"Stop being obvious," She hissed in a low voice. "You have any other guarantees of privacy?"

Todd shrugged. "Sure. A drive. Anywhere in particular?"

"Doesn't matter. As long as it isn't suspicious. So, don't just drive around the block." Even just sitting in his car would get them some privacy but it would also look suspicious. Unfortunately, since Liska didn't have a car here, she didn't know too much of the area more than a couple miles from campus. "Along the water will do."

"Sure, I think I know just the place."

Liska followed him to his car, giving it a brief, careful look. It seemed safe enough, no sign of tampering. Out of courtesy and lack of experience with how much he would need to pay attention while driving, she stayed quiet until he spoke.

"Can I ask you questions now?"

"Does your radio work?"

"Um, yeah, did you want to listen to something?"

Liska turned it on; it was set on a Country Western station. She wouldn't have thought Todd the type. Not her preferred music, but it would do. She turned up the volume. "That will cover our voices if anyone is using a directional mic."

Todd blinked at her. "Is that really necessary?"

"Probably not. But better safe than sorry, right?"

"I guess."

"Your questions?"

"Oh, right. Well, to begin with, why did that guy, your great-uncle? Yeah, why did he call you Liska? Isn't your name Anna?"

Of course he would ask that. "Great, again with the easy ones. Very well, no, my name is not Anna, never has been. Though I do have some very official looking documents claiming it is. 'Anna Andrews' as you knew her, never existed. The background information I gave? Most of that is part of the cover."

"Like what?"

"Well, I told Shahara I was part Vietnamese on my mother's side? That was a lie. My father is Japanese, while my mother is British. Neither of them are college professors either."

"So, is Liska your real name?"

Sensei was going to love this. Then again, if he hadn't called her Liska in front of him, then she probably could have left him believing she was just Anna Andrews with a few extra secrets. On the other hand, if she really wanted to do that, she would have just told him that Liska was a nickname. "No, it's a working name. Actually, it's Luna Liska, or Moon Fox, frequently shortened to Liska."

"You make it sound like you're a spy or something."

She smiled because that was the only way she could avoid flinching.

Todd swallowed hard. "Are you a spy?"

"If I was, could I tell you?"

"Um..."

"I'm just here for school. Nothing else. So what I might have done before or what I might do after has no bearing on the situation."

"Right, okay. So, what's your real name?"

"You don't need to know that." He looked about to argue. "I don't mind answering questions about the world at large or Werefoxes in particular, but my personal life is... not always for public consumption."

"Okay, okay." He was quiet for a minute. "So, what else is real? I mean, I always thought Werewolves were a myth."

"How many different cultures ended up independently coming up with stories of humans changing into animals or vice versa?"

"Most, maybe all."

"And you thought this a coincidence?"

"Well, it seems unlikely, but it wouldn't be the only time. I mean, most cultures have dragons too, but-"

"They're Night."

"Dragons are real too?" He squeaked.

"Yes. But they're both rare and isolationist. I've never met one. Father has. He gave me a dragon scale from a dragon he helped once. It's supposed to be good luck. I sometimes wear it as a necklace."

"How about aliens? Are they real?"

"Haven't the foggiest. I've not met any, but I'm not ruling out the possibility."

Todd shook his head, before pulling to a scenic overlook. "Is this good?"

It was a place for people to stop and look at the scenery, so no one would be bothering them for a while. "This should be fine. What other questions do you have?"

He took a deep breath. "I don't want to offend you, but I'm not sure how to word this. How different is it being a Werefox?"

Liska was silent for long enough for him to get nervous. "I really don't mean to offend you..."

"I'm not offended, but I'm not certain how to answer. After all, I have nothing to truly compare it too. I've never *not* been a Werefox.

"Good point. But do you have some idea?"

"Some, but finding a common frame of reference is difficult. For example, I'm sure you know that a dog has a much stronger sense of smell than you do, but do you truly understand what it is like to have a dog's nose?"

"No, I guess not. Do you have...?"

"Right now, in this form, my sense of smell is much better than yours, but not as good as your average dog. In fox form, my sense of smell is the same as a fox, or an average dog. Not as good as a hound, but still quite good. Same with hearing. Before you start getting too jealous, my sense of taste is about a third to half of yours. My eyesight is a little more variable. I am nearsighted, and totally and completely color-blind. My night vision is excellent, so I consider it a fair trade."

"Wow, so you literally see the world differently than I do?"

She nodded.

Todd frowned. "Aren't some of those a bit of a drawback? Like too strong a sense of smell? Or no sense of taste? Or color? I can't imagine not being able to see color."

"No, I imagine an artist like you couldn't. I won't say that there aren't drawbacks. My food is usually pretty bland, unless I go for strong flavors. I cannot be an artist or an electrician. Strong smells are an annoyance or worse. Lack of color seems to be the biggest problem. Humans are very visually based, and many things are color orientated or coded. That doesn't help me much. I don't know if my clothes match. Clearly, judging from your snicker they often don't. However, there are ways around those, and there are advantages too."

"Like?"

"Even in this form, I can track a person by scent. I can hear your heartbeat, and smell if someone is lying. I can get an impression of what a person is feeling, even if they have the best 'poker face' in the world." That would do for now. He didn't need to know everything. Maybe later she'd tell him other things. Like how she could always instinctively find magnetic North. Or that she could jump at least twice, maybe three times as far as he could from a standing start. They weren't major secrets, but there was no point in showing all her cards just yet.

"So, you don't care about the disadvantages?"

Liska shrugged. "Some I don't care about, some I'm just used to. It's more of a problem here than at home. Here, in human society, things are geared to human senses. I have to pass inspection visually, which is difficult for me. And what is a comfortable volume for you may be painfully loud to me. Yes, like the radio. I'll cope. One the other hand, I can keep more secrets here. No one realizes when I'm eavesdropping on someone across the room, nor can they smell my emotions, or tell by smell whose company I've been in." He wasn't comfortable with this part. Maybe she was being too open.

"So, you know what I'm feeling right now?"

She looked at him, and he met her eyes, but it seemed to be reluctant. "Your heart rate is elevated; you may be looking at me, but your eyes keep flicking away. Your fingers are twitching on the steering wheel. You don't smell of fear, but you are clearly uneasy. So you must be nervous. Of course, a human trained in body language would come to the same conclusion."

He laughed at that, though it was a little shaky. "Good point. So when I said I saw you going to Food Mart...?"

"I knew you were lying and were suspicious. I wasn't sure why, though. My attempt at covering my tracks must not have been sufficient."

"The police got called in, and I saw the video footage of the front door."

Liska nodded. Made sense.

"So, how did you pull off a job in Miami, and be in West Palm within half an hour? You can't teleport, can you?"

She laughed, more to stall him than anything. She'd rather not tell him about Kira's involvement, but if she blew him off now, he might ask again in front of Ryoko-*Sensei*. That would just get her in more trouble. "No, there are a rare few individuals who can. Not Weres. I had help. Short version, there is a member of my family who looks a lot like me, especially when you can't see us both to compare. She was in Miami, wearing a wig made from my hair."

"That's how you did it! The Halloween trick. Which were you?"

"I told the story. If Kira had been the one quarter formed, her tail would be much darker than mine." Todd looked confused. Liska stifled a sigh. "Okay, this part will probably mean more to you than me. How much do you know about foxes?"

He shrugged. "About average, I'd say."

Probably very little then. "Okay, for whatever reason, and I don't know why, so don't bother asking; every Werefox, no matter where in the world they are, transforms into a *vulpes vulpes*, also known as the red fox. The kind you are most familiar with, I imagine. Okay, despite being called 'red' there are numerous color phases."

"I knew that."

"Good. Now, any color phase that a wild red fox can have, we can have. I change into a standard red fox, with fur the color you have already seen."

"Like your hair."

"According to Mother, yes. Now, not all match their looks in human form, though many do. Kira is what's known as a cross fox, a red fox with a black stripe down the back, and one across the shoulders. We have deep red foxes, light red foxes, cross foxes, silver foxes, even the occasional black fox. At least, that's what those who see in color tell us."

Todd nodded. "That's interesting. But what exactly is quarter formed?"

Liska snickered. "Remember what I said about sensing emotions? Proof I'm not perfect. I could tell you were confused and explained the wrong thing. Okay, the state I'm in right now, is called human state. I'm not human, not even right now, but I'm closer than any other stage. I can also change into a full fox, creatively enough called 'fox state'. Now, with very, very few exceptions, I can do that at any time. Now, think of the way most werewolf movies picture a transformed werewolf. Man-sized, vicious, bi-pedal, dangerous to everyone around him. Okay, I can do that too, but that is extremely dangerous, especially for me because I'm not a full Were. That's called half state or half formed. Now, the transition from human to fox, or fox to human, or human to half form, always goes in the same order. I can do it much, much faster than I showed you, but I was trying to prove a point. When you reach the point of having a tail and the furry ears, but you haven't yet changed the mental processes, it's called quarter state, or quarter formed. All Weres are born that way."

"Can I see pictures?"

"No, I didn't bring any."

"No, I guess you wouldn't. So how many of you are there?"

"Me? Just the one. Thankfully." The last thing the world needed was more of her. When he tried to argue, she cut him off. "I know what you meant. But it's need to know. And you don't."

"I'm going to hate that phrase, aren't I?" Todd sounded resigned.

"Quite possibly."

"So how does it work? You said you could be a fox at any time, but the half state was very dangerous. Is that what you do on full moons?"

"No, it's actually a lot more complicated than that. A *lot* more complicated. First of all, the moon actually has nothing to do with it, even though we only discovered that in the past hundred years or so. Okay, forget about the classic Werewolf, spread through bite. If they ever existed, and we believe they did, they're gone now. Being a Were is purely genetic. Now, every Were is born with two chemicals in them that have not been found naturally anywhere else. They both have long scientific names, but we refer to them as Lunerium and Solium."

"Lunerium helps you change? And Solium does... something?"

Liska bit back a smile. "We think Solium is what gives us stability, preventing us from uncontrolled transformations all the time. Lunerium builds up in the system of a Were, in an approximately twenty-eight, twenty-nine day cycle, coming to a climax on the last day, which because of timing, always falls on the same lunar phase. Hence the association with the moon. No, it's not the same lunar phase for everyone. When it comes to a climax, first quarter moon for me, between the hours of midnight and six in the time zone the Were is currently accustomed too, the Were cannot be in human form. They simply can't. They have two choices. They can be in the form of their animal, where they keep their human memories, filtered through the mindset of the animal. Or if they are not in animal form, they are forcibly shifted into a half state, where they do not have a rational mind or their human memories. The stereotypical dangerous Werewolf. Being in that state for too long, even without outside dangers, can lead to insanity, especially to anyone who isn't a full Were. That isn't the only way to end up in half state, but as you can imagine, most try to avoid it."

"Yeah, I'll bet."

"Now, like I said before, Solium prevents the change. It's most abundant in Weres in the late stages of pregnancy, when shifting can cause a miscarriage. It may also occur, naturally or induced, in a Were who is badly injured and at risk of dying during a change, or a Were in a coma."

"If it can be induced, and I'm guessing synthesized, why doesn't anyone try taking it all the time to avoid changing at all?"

"Well, first off, we were all born Weres, and most of us are raised in all Were communities. Very few would even want to do that. It has been experimented with though, enough to prove that while we might all have small amounts of Solium in us, large amounts become toxic eventually. *Maybe* one could get away with it for a year. Probably not longer. Besides, not being able to change seems to impact negatively on a Were's mind after a while."

"Ah. Do you change often?"

"Into a fox? It depends. Sometimes I use it a lot, other times I go a long time between non-essential changes. It can be very... freeing." There really weren't words for the joy of the hunt, the freedom of running under the moon, the security of the skulk around you. Non Weres simply didn't have a frame of reference for it.

"Does it hurt? Changing?"

"Not anymore. We have our first change about five. Then we change involuntarily at random times as we slowly gain control. Most reach 'full' control at about eight to ten. In the beginning, it hurts. But there are special pain medicines just for that."

'Hurts' was an understatement. Most Weres were of the impression that the reason the initial changes were involuntary was because no one would go through it twice if they had the choice. It was like every bone and muscle in the body tore itself apart and repaired itself simultaneously, forced into a body of a much different size than accustomed to. It took at least two or three changes before the average Were could even try more than twitching in their new body. Liska had been tortured and could honestly say nothing done to her so far had hurt more than her first change. Nor was her experience uncommon in the Were community.

"Fortunately, the more the Were changes, the less it hurts. I'm not sure if it's because our bodies become trained to handle it, or our pain tolerance goes up. Within the first month, there is only some discomfort from changing, at most. Unless I'm injured, the worst I face is a bit of stiffness if I change too many times in a short period. Otherwise, it's like stretching."

"Okay, what about silver? It obviously bothers you, but why? I'm guessing it isn't magical. Is it?"

She would not laugh. It was a fair question considering his whole view of life was changing. "No. Silver, and all other metals, are just that. Metal. Honestly, no one knows why Weres are so sensitive to silver, so we chalk it up to our unique bio-chemistry, which is pretty weird. That's why I can't go to a normal hospital. The minute they start doing tests, it's obvious I'm different. That and I have weird reactions to many normal medications. Silver is acidic to us." She showed off the spots on her arms where the silver dust touched them. "These itch and they hurt when it happened. But I have a lotion to help, and they are so small, they probably won't scar. I rarely scar, part of constantly transforming. Silver wounds are more likely to scar, but it's not true that I will only die from an injury from a silver knife or bullet. It would hurt more and heal slower than a regular knife or bullet, and scar worse. But the chances of it being fatal are only slightly better than the chances of the same injury from a regular bullet or knife."

"If you can't go to a regular hospital..."

"We have our own. Twilight and Night clinics. My home has doctors that, of course, specialize in healing Weres. That kind of thing. Weres don't need it as often. I don't get sick often, but when I do get sick, it hits hard. Though I do get a rabies vaccine at least once a year. I do heal faster than a human, though not so quickly it's likely to get noticed. Except nerve damage. That can take ages for a human to heal, and I'd heal in a couple weeks max.

No Were has ever ended up permanently paralyzed, and the odds of permanent brain damage is very much reduced as well. Most other injuries are much closer rates."

"So what kinds of physical differences are there? Are you stronger, faster?"

"Well, my bones are lighter, and more compact than a human's are. Yes, slightly more fragile as well, but barely noticeable. That lets me move faster, react quicker, and jump further and higher. Strength-wise, I'm stronger than one would expect of a human female my size and fitness level. About equal to a human female body builder my size."

"You carried me. While running!"

"Mostly adrenalin. I could pick you up, carry you a little, under normal circumstances, but it would hurt."

"What else is out there?"

Liska laughed. "More than you can possibly imagine. It's getting late. We should probably get back to the school." No matter what he asked, she didn't give another answer.

***

There was really no reason not to join him for dinner, since the cafeteria wouldn't be open much longer. Jamal and Shahara were already there. It was the first time she had seen them since being released.

"You're back! I knew it! I knew you were innocent!"

Liska stiffened instinctively, then forced herself to relax. This was a hug, not a tackle. By definition anyway. "Um, Shahara? Great to see you, too. Air would be nice though."

Jamal was quieter and a little sheepish in greeting her. So, he had suspected her. Not surprising. "Good to see you back."

"It's good to be back."

He rubbed at the back of his neck. "Look, I'm sorry..."

"Don't be. I know it looked pretty bad for a while. Even the police thought I'd done it, right?"

"Well, yeah, but..."

"You don't still think I'm guilty, correct?"

"No, of course not."

"Then we're fine." Liska busied herself with her napkin, deliberately not looking at anyone. When she was done, Jamal had composed himself. "So, how are midterms coming?"

That got the conversation away from her and onto school, a natural topic for a table of students. It was also a very safe topic, which was why she chose it. She congratulated Shahara on getting an A on her English mid-term, listened patiently while Jamal ranted about the Anatomy exam that pulled in all kinds of information that hadn't been mentioned in class, agreed to pose for Todd again in the near future, and thanked the others for their congratulations on nearly getting caught up with school work. Being in jail for a week really threw off one's schedule. Todd was having an even harder time.

Jamal was the one to almost ruin it, though in his defense, he couldn't have known. "So, any more work on Cats-eye?"

Todd choked on his drink and wouldn't look up from the table. "No, nothing yet." His voice was scratchy and a little too high.

Mentally Liška shook her head and promised to give him a few acting lessons. Besides, they needed to talk about Cats-eye at some point. "Oh, are you coming down with the cold that's going around?" She hadn't heard anything about a cold going around, but in a school this big, there was always something. "You really must be careful. Especially since..." She trailed off not mentioning his injured lung. He would still be very susceptible to infection.

Shahara jumped in. "Yeah, be careful. There were three people missing in my Math class this morning. And two more were coughing."

Jamal nodded. "If you're sick, I could get some soup from my mom."

Todd held up his hands. "I'm not sick. They made me get a flu shot before I left the hospital, just to be on the safe side. And I'm on antibiotics."

"That you're taking properly?" Jamal stared at him intently.

"Once in the morning, once at night. I remember your lectures."

Liska hid her smile. That was one conversation successfully avoided. "Anyway, it was a pleasure to see you all again, but I have to go. My history paper will not write itself, and I want to refresh my memory on some math formulas before tomorrow."

"Good point. I have some work to catch up on too." Todd grasped the offered lifeline with both hands.

Jamal and Shahara agreed, and they separated there. Todd did take a minute to whisper to her, "You did that on purpose, didn't you? You just threw me to the wolves?"

"Absolutely. You really do need to be careful though. We'll talk later." She slipped away before he could question her anymore. There was a small smile on her face as she walked to her room.

Liska debated on hiding the smile but decided against it. There was nothing suspicious about smiling. She had had dinner with 'friends', she wasn't being followed, and she was in a good mood. Why shouldn't she smile?

As she opened her room door, she spotted a note on the floor, face down. Probably from the RA. Liska ignored it for a few minutes, putting some more lotion on her silver burns. They were starting to irritate her a bit. A human would probably say that the lotion had no smell. Liska's twitching nose would argue with them. The scent might not be strong, but it was an unpleasant smell, that tingled in the nose. She washed the last remnants of lotion off her hands, then tried washing her face to stop her nose from feeling numb. Mostly she succeeded in getting water in her nose and eyelashes. Not the best of improvements. Still, when she dried her face, she was reasonably confident that her nose would mostly work.

Then she went back to the note. Despite being ninety percent confident that it was a note from the RA, probably about maintenance, or a floor meeting, maybe about the winter break, Liska would take every precaution. Kneeling on the floor, Liska sniffed carefully. Nothing out of the ordinary. She got closer. Still nothing. Paper didn't hold a scent well. Her head was a foot away. Liska could smell ink, normal computer ink. No paper. Nothing else.

Taking a pencil off her desk, she slipped it under the note then flipped the note so she could read it. Her breath caught in a gasp. It was not from the RA.

Sakaki,

Spending your whole day with humans? What would your betrothed think? You would be wise to separate yourself from the situation. Humans aren't worth it anyway.

A well-meaning friend.

Chapter Twenty-Three

A life based on secrets is always perilous. – The Kikitsutai
Book of Wisdom

Someone knew her name. Her real name! How? No one outside her skulk should know that. Well, Korvou might, she wasn't sure. Focus, calm. Who knew she was here, might know her name, and looked down on humans?

Korvou was out. This wasn't his style at all. He might enjoy annoying her, but he wasn't the type to try messing with her mind. Nor was he overly anti-human. He probably didn't know her name anyway. She had never told him, and he didn't seem to have much contact with others in her skulk.

Kira knew her name and where she was but wasn't anti-human. Besides, if she was in the area, she'd visit. If it wasn't safe to do that, she might leave a note but it would be a useful one with information, not specious threats.

Mother *was* human, and certainly not one to go through subterfuge like this. While Father was subtle, he didn't always bother with being subtle with her. Besides, having married a human, he couldn't be overly against humans. Ryoko-*Sensei*? Hmm. He wasn't truly anti-human, but he wasn't as welcoming as some she could name, nor would it be out of character for him to test her like this. But it didn't feel right. Her barrister, Mr. Sakamoto? She didn't know him well. Would he have her address? She'd have to ask Ryoko-*Sensei*, he'd get answers she wouldn't. Liska had some contact with the local blood of vampires, but only one of them knew her address, and none of them should know her name.

This was wrong. Totally and completely wrong. Part of her wanted to be in her fox form so she could raise her hackles and growl at the paper. Oh, she was growling, quietly. Liska briefly wondered how long she had been doing that, tried to stop, realized it wasn't working, then ignored it in favor of scowling at the deceivingly innocent-looking slip of paper.

It was typed, not handwritten. She wasn't tech-y enough to identify the type of machine just by appearance of type. There weren't any handy identifying marks either. For all she knew, it had been typed up in the school computer lab.

He called himself a friend. Liska didn't think this felt very friendly. No, it felt very much like a threat right now. It wasn't like she had any shortage of people wanting to threaten her.

Those who looked down on humans generally hated half-humans, like her. Even those who claimed not to mind humans often looked down on 'half-breeds'. While most in her skulk would say they weren't *against* humans, they generally considered themselves superior. Which meant that growing up a half-human in that community could be as awkward as being a cat in a dog show. She hadn't been lying when she told Shahara about it.

It didn't matter now. Her past was just that, past. The now always trumped the past. Putting on gloves, she checked the note for any unusual residues, powders, etc. Nothing. Waving the paper under her nose, she sniffed again. Still nothing but paper and ink. No sign of the deliverer. Perhaps whoever sent her the note was wearing scent concealer. Weres had come up with that ages ago. Still, it should mean there was nothing nasty on the paper for her to discover later. A brief dusting for fingerprints revealed nothing.

Biting back a frustrated sigh, Liska dropped the note on her dresser to show Ryoko-*Sensei* tomorrow. There was no way she was going to try to deal with this one on her own. Even she wasn't that foolhardy.

Throwing away the gloves, she tried to focus on her homework instead. The heavens knew she was still behind. Some of her teachers were nice about it, but some still looked at her strangely, and didn't seem to want to give her time to catch up. Math, she almost had to appeal to the Dean to get the classes she missed in jail to be counted as excused absences. Without that, she might have failed the class due to the attendance policy.

But despite the necessity, despite trying to focus on the influence of the French in the American Revolution, her mind kept going back to the note. After the third time she typed the word 'note' when she meant 'not', and one time when she meant 'Lafayette', she gave up to glare at/study the note some more. As her fingers made contact with the paper, the world changed.

She was picking up the note, freshly printed, staring at it in her hands. Except they weren't her hands. They were larger and differently shaped. And in color! It had to be color, but what color was it? Male hands. And strange feelings. These weren't her feelings. Resentment mixed with a touch of respect. Utter hatred. Then the note was passed to someone she couldn't quite see, and...

And it was over. What was THAT? What just happened? Nothing like that had ever... yes, yes, it had. When she handled the blasted sword Todd had shown her, she had vaguely seen a battle. Had there been color there? She couldn't tell. At the time, she had assumed the whole thing was just her imagination. But this certainly hadn't been her imagination. Maybe she truly had seen something. Unfortunately, she hadn't seen enough to identify anyone, or even a location.

Liska put down the note, then picked it up again. Whatever had happened before, didn't happen again. Not truly. She could still feel a little bit of the emotions, but she wasn't literally in someone's head again. No colors this time. Unable or unwilling to determine if she should be relieved or disappointed by that, Liska focused mainly on the fact that she'd have a lot to tell Ryoko-*Sensei* tomorrow.

***

Paranoia was as natural to Liska as breathing. Even Ryoko-*Sensei* didn't know all her 'bolt holes'. These ranged from a hollow tree stump that was just big enough for her backpack and herself in fox form, to a never used basement of some corporate building, to a legally owned apartment that she hadn't quite mentioned to anyone that she had. He might know of that one, but she doubted it. The Kikitsutai had two official 'safe houses' that she was free to use, though she hadn't yet. But she refused to be completely dependent on them.

Liska made sure there were at least four ways to get to any of those places. Four ways that were so memorized that she could find her way blind, injured and out of her right mind. She had six paths to get to Ryoko-*Sensei*'s though two of them she didn't use very often. Of the four she did use more frequently, she varied, trying not to use the same one more than twice in a row. The less frequent routes were harder, both to use and to explain if she was caught using. But knowing she had them made her feel safer.

This time she took path five. Over two walls, through a hole in a fence, up a fire escape, across four rooftops, climbing in a window of a quiet office building to go down the elevator, out the front door, cutting through the park, through the dry rain tunnel, up a ladder, down two alleyways, before ending up at his back door.

Ryoko-*Sensei*, knowing full well the type of path, if not the exact path she took, simply raised an eyebrow and awaited an explanation. She had called him that morning saying she had big news. He still seemed unsettled by the extent of her paranoia as she spent several minutes checking for bugs and finally turned on his radio, to a volume just slightly painful to the both of them. "That big?"

She just handed him the note. If it hadn't been so important, it would probably be rather funny watching his face go through some interesting contortions, while changing to what had to be unusual colors. Odd, she probably wouldn't have thought about the colors yesterday.

He put the note down. "Any ideas?"

She shrugged. "Theories only. Does Mr. Sakamoto have my address?"

The older Werefox frowned. "He may. Do you suspect him?"

"Not really. I simply am trying to figure out who might be a possible suspect."

Ryoko-*Sensei* shook his head. "I think not, but I will talk to him. He will answer me."

Liska nodded. "Thank you. Do you have any ideas?"

"No. Not yet. Were you aware you were being watched?"

"I realized it on my way back from here yesterday. They were good. I couldn't find him. There's more."

"This isn't enough?" He reached for his tea, looking drained.

"Apparently not. Something happened when I touched the note."

His eyebrows knit together. "You checked for residue first?" He probably didn't mean for it to sound that condescending but Liska had to force back a scowl anyway.

"Of course. Residue, smells, fingerprints, everything."

He nodded, an implicit almost apology. "Then, what happened?"

"I found myself seeing through another's eyes. The note writer. Then he passed it on to someone I couldn't see to deliver it."

She could smell his excitement as he realized the implications of that. "Retro-cognitive? Why didn't it show up in our testing?"

Liska had spent the better part of an hour wondering the same thing and had a possible answer. "You usually handed me an article of clothing. Had anything important happened while you were wearing that particular piece? I think that it may be something about emotional intensity that I'm," she paused, "drawn to?"

Ryoko-*Sensei* had abandoned his tea to dig out a notebook and was writing everything down, even while he argued with her. "One time isn't enough to suggest that. Has it happened more than once?" As he spoke he gave her a look that suggested that she had better have a very good explanation for keeping information back.

"I think it may have. I didn't put the pieces together until last night, but the sword, the one that Todd let me handle? The first time I held it, I felt like I was part of a battle. It was faint, and I thought I was imagining it, so I didn't say anything."

"But you weren't?"

Liska shrugged. "I may never know for sure, but I now believe I wasn't."

"In the future, you will tell me of these occurrences?"

"In the future, I will know I am not imagining things, and to take them seriously." It wasn't a promise. What she told him would depend on the circumstances. His disappointed look proved that he caught her evasion, as she knew he would, but he didn't press the point.

"What did you see? Location? Identity?"

"Definitely male, the hands told me that. He hates me, I can feel that. But he also slightly admires me or at least respects me. As for location, he didn't look around much. My senses are different. I couldn't hear or smell any better than," what should she call it, "my host could. Nor could I see in color, though I'm pretty sure he could. I guess my brain simply can't interpret color." She lied without a shred of guilt, even if she was a little unsure why.

"Makes sense." Liska could just see him trying to plot out more tests to determine her limits. "Did you have this experience every time you picked up the note?"

"No, only the first time I touched it without gloves on. The second time there was a faint emotional residue but nothing new. After that, nothing. Time may have been a factor, and I think I ended up touching it close to or in the same place or places he did. Another possible factor."

"Which might explain why you've not discovered this before." Notebook abandoned, Ryoko-*Sensei* was pacing. As excited as he was, one would think he was the one with the newly discovered talent. "We'll have to find a way to practice, hone this ability—"

"The sword." Liska winced as she realized she had accidentally interrupted, but her mentor looked more curious than upset. "The sword was probably my first experience, even if I didn't realize it at the time. I saw part of a battle from hundreds of years ago. If I could see something from that long ago, maybe I could see his attack, get a clue about his attacker.

"Yes," He drew the word out slowly. "Yes, I like it. Two birds, one stone. Can you get at the sword?"

"I don't know. I'll have to ask Todd. He should be able to at least find out where it is now."

"Do that." The older Were sat slowly before continuing. "He may know a little more, but he isn't one of us. He doesn't belong to our world. The gap is just too large. Don't forget that."

"I know, *Sensei*. I know."

"He can be your friend while you are here, but no more than that."

"Of course."

Weres mate for life. They both knew that.

Chapter Twenty-Four

Kindness may include calculated cruelty. – The Kikitsutai
Book of Wisdom

"What? That's it, this means war!"

Ryoko paused at hearing *that* in his niece's room. She had wanted to check the Purifier's website again, and possibly a few other places she didn't want showing up on her school computer's browser history. While neither of them *liked* the Purifiers, generally they were more of an irritant than an actual threat worth getting angry at. "Problem?" He asked, walking into the room.

Liska didn't look away from the computer. "Do you remember when I sent you a list of the Purifiers' top ten most wanted?" She was fiddling with a pencil in one hand, making it walk across her fingers. A nervous habit that she only had when very tense or thinking of a plan. At least it was a pencil instead of a knife this time.

"Of course, I printed a copy." He didn't say anything about her rudeness in not looking at him. If she was this upset something far more important than a little impoliteness was at stake.

"May I see it?" The voice was level enough, but she was clearly ready to strike.

He handed her the paper without a word.

She scanned it briefly. "Ah-ha! What number is Tisiphone on this list?"

"Number seven." He had known that without looking.

"What number is she on this website?"

He had to squint to see the screen. "Number six? Why move up a dead assassin? Did they get rid of the previous number six?"

"No, he's number seven."

Ryoko squinted harder trying to make sense of this. "I repeat, why move up a dead assassin?"

"Because they don't know she's dead. Look at this." She clicked through a few links too fast for him to follow. When she stopped, even he had to restrain his reaction.

"What happened?" The scene in front of him was a total massacre.

"They are crediting that to Tisiphone."

Utterly impossible. "When was this?"

"Recently. They aren't sure of the date, but it was within the last week or two."

"How many are dead?"

"I can't tell. At least four. I think more."

That matched his guess. "Tisiphone may have had a reputation for being macabre but she was never that brutal. Nor did she kill indiscriminately." He watched Liska carefully. It was definitely Liska. Sakaki wouldn't be able to take those pictures without flinching.

"I know. But someone calling themselves Tisiphone is taking credit for the kill."

He didn't want to ask. He truly, truly did not. "Are you positively sure she's dead?"

"Absolutely. I killed her myself. They are not bringing her back. Not like this." It wasn't a shout. It was a whisper. That made it worse.

Ryoko closed his eyes and silently asked for a forgiveness he knew would never come.

***

Liska made it back to the school without the feeling of eyes on her. When she was almost to her room, she spotted Todd. More importantly, he spotted her.

"Hey, Anna. Can I *talk* to you for a few minutes?"

Inwardly she shook her head. That boy simply had to learn some subtlety. Hmm, they couldn't go off driving all the time, it would spark questions. Besides, he had been low on gas yesterday. Private talks did not belong in public areas. She was almost to her room and no one was paying attention to them. Guys were not allowed in girls' rooms, but she'd probably only get a verbal warning, especially if it was obvious they were only talking. Besides, where else could she ensure privacy?

"Follow me." Surprise wafted off him as she let him in her room, but he wisely didn't say anything. Once in, she waved for him to be silent while she quickly checked to make sure her room was untampered with. Just to be on the safe side, she turned on her scrambler. Todd probably couldn't hear anything, but to her it was an annoying squeal. Still, it would disrupt listening devices pointed in their direction. "Room's clean. What is it?"

"Does the name 'Tisiphone' mean anything to you?"

Liska stilled. "Where did you hear that name?"

Todd looked at her startled. "Well, I'm pretty sure that's a mythological reference, but I can't remember off the top of my head."

"One of the Furies. Name means 'avenging murder'."

"Thanks. But I also got this weird note under my door that suggested Tisiphone was involved in my attack. I wondered if you might know anything."

"Do you have the note?"

"Yeah, here." He fumbled in his pockets for a minute before bringing out a crumpled piece of paper. Liska gave it a discrete sniff before taking it.

Once again, she was in someone's head. Not as strong, not as deep. Maybe time was a factor, or maybe the emotions didn't run as deep. Either way, all she got was a few emotional impressions. It was definitely the same person, but he didn't have respect for Todd, but not as much hatred either. Nothing visual this time, to her acute disappointment. Only so she could try to find the location, of course. Todd was looking at her strangely when she came out. She ignored him and read the note. Nothing he hadn't told her.

"Same person who sent mine."

"Yours?"

Seeing no reason to hide it, she showed him the note she found yesterday.

"You're engaged?" He practically squeaked.

"Betrothed. He still has to propose." Liska waved it off.

"Congratulations?"

She rolled her eyes.

"Should I ask?" Apparently, he had realized there was something odd there.

"No, most definitely not."

"Okay. Um, your name's Sakaki?"

"Is this relevant?"

"Just curious. Isn't Sakaki usually a last name? I think I remember reading that."

"Often, yes. It can also be a girl's name. We don't have last names in our skulk, we just combine our parents' names." Why were they still discussing it? It didn't matter.

"So, Sakaki is your first name?"

She just looked at him. "Do you know anything else?"

"What, oh. Not really. Do you know who Tisiphone is?"

"No. I knew who she was, but not who she is."

"Huh?"

Okay, in his defense, that had come out pretty cryptic. "Tisiphone was an assassin. She was killed two, three years ago. Someone brought back the name."

"Are you sure she was really dead?"

"I killed her myself. She's dead." Blasted bandersnatch! She hadn't meant to tell him that.

"*You* did?" That was definitely a squeak.

Might as well tell him. Then maybe he'd stop staring at her like she was a serial killer. "I'm a ninja. My entire skulk continues to train in the ninja tradition. We call ourselves the Kikitsutai. I think it means, roughly, the way of the fox spirit. Like I said, rough translation. We have our own form of martial arts, based off ninjitsu, passed down for a few hundred years. We... handle difficulties that come up between Days, Twilights, and Nights. Oh, and we usually call ourselves a skulk, from the term for a group of foxes, though we do use 'clan' occasionally."

"But... You *killed* her?"

"It was necessary. She was an assassin who went too far." Yup, definitely disturbed. Change the subject. "Do you know where the sword you were attacked with is now?"

He blinked, and she could almost see his brain rebooting. "Pretty sure it's in the police evidence room. Why?"

That would make things difficult. "Do you remember being tested for ESP?"

"Not going to forget that anytime soon."

"We've found my gift. I'm a retro-cog."

"What's a retro-cog?" Fair enough, the term wasn't used nearly as often as pre-cog.

"Basically the opposite of the pre-cog. You see things before they happen, I see them after. I saw through the eyes of the note writer when I handled my note the first time. I think I may be able to find out something about your attacker if I can handle the sword again."

"Oh. Well, congrats on the retro-cog thing. I don't know about getting the sword. I mean, I could ask my uncle, but I don't know that he'd go for the idea." He had an idea. He had an idea but was nervous to tell her.

"You have an idea. What is it?"

"I don't know that it would work."

"That's why you tell me, and we polish your idea."

His shoe scuffed at her rug. "There is a policemen's dinner and dance at the station. I have a ticket plus guest. If you came as my da... *guest*, it would get you in the station. The evidence room would still be off limits, though."

Liska nodded slowly. "That could work. Do you know the safeguards used? The layout?"

"A little bit. I can get the layout of the station easy, but there are cameras, locks, all kinds of things."

"Closed circuit cameras?"

"I think so."

"Okay, I need all the information you can give me." He was still nervous. "If I think there is the slightest chance I'll get caught, then I won't attempt it that night. I will not get you wrapped up in this."

"Um, no one will be in danger, right? I mean, I know a lot of the police—"

"I won't hurt anyone. That would go against my purposes. If I do my job right, no one will ever know I was there."

That helped him, but there was still a slight shadow of doubt and apprehension. "Will your *betrothed* mind?" Knowledge struck Liska like a snowball to the face. He had been planning to ask her. He had wanted to ask her out and the presence of someone in the wings was throwing him off. That and the knowledge she had killed. Perhaps it was best he knew now.

"It's for a mission."

"So he won't mind? Is hanging around with me, with us, going to cause problems?"

"He won't be happy, but I've done nothing wrong and if he's going to be upset, he's a hypocrite."

"What?"

"Nothing. Moving on." Yoshiro wasn't a topic she liked discussing at the best of times. This was nowhere near the best of times.

"But—"

"Moving on. Now."

"Okay, okay. It isn't any of my business."

"No. It isn't."

"You know, other than that time with the dog, I've never seen you this emotional." Liska knew he didn't mean it as an insult and tried not to take it personally.

"Training. Lots of training, and practice. I'm actually very emotional by nature. I've had to learn to control it so I don't end up in trouble. Emotions can be quite dangerous, especially to someone in my line of work. Unfortunately, several large things are happening at once, and I'm on edge."

"Everyone has their breaking point. Thanks for telling me. I know it wasn't easy." As if to prove that he did have some tact, he changed the subject. "So you *are* going with me to the Police dance?"

"When is it?"

"Two weeks from Friday. I meant to ask you before, but..."

"Things kept happening." Her change would be the Wednesday before. While she would be tired and a little sore on Thursday, she should be fine by Friday. "Yes. What's the dress code?"

"Fancy. I'm renting a tux."

Liska frowned. "I don't think I have anything that fancy."

"Well..." He paused, biting a lip.

"Spit it out, Kensworth." She wasn't in the mood for verbal sparring today.

He laughed. "Remember how Shahara is an image consultant in training?"

"I know she keeps looking at me like you look at a canvas when you have an idea."

"She needs some before and after stories. She's asked Jamal to ask me to talk to you about if she could give you a make-over. Tell her you need to do this and she'd drag you out shopping in no time."

She hated shopping but it might be necessary. "Fine. Could you maybe drop the hint to her that you found out I'm color blind. Tell her I'm a little sensitive about it, so don't mention it to anyone else. That should explain enough, don't you think?"

"Sure. I can do that. Are you sensitive about it?"

"Not in the slightest. But color blindness is a sex-linked recessive trait. It's rare for a woman to have it."

"Ah. I should probably go." Todd stepped toward the door before looking back at her. "You never told me. Who was Tisiphone?"

"Tisiphone was an assassin. That's all you need to know."

"But—"

"That's all you need to know."

Chapter Twenty-Five

Do not choose between honor and your life. Honor is your life.
– The Kikitsutai Book of Wisdom

The next day, Liska was about to head out to breakfast when her phone rang. She frowned at the caller ID. Ryoko-*Sensei*. How odd. Ryoko-*Sensei* seldom called her, especially on her room phone, and never this early. But it wasn't her mobile, so he wasn't worried about the line being tapped. Or he knew he was. Not knowing exactly what she was getting into, she settled for a neutral, "'Allo?"

"Are you alone?"

"Yes. Are you?"

"Yes. How soon can you get here?"

"That depends. Do you need me to skip class?"

There was a pause before answering. That pause worried her. If it was urgent, he would have answered yes immediately. But normally, he wouldn't advocate skipping class at all. "Are you doing anything important in class?"

"I have a test in History, ten o'clock. Nothing else after that until one, and I can skip that if necessary." Not completely true. She could skip, in that she knew enough to miss the class. But absences were a problem. It might be necessary to retake some classes.

"We should be done by then. Come by after your test. Just don't answer your phone or check your email until after we've talked."

Well, that didn't sound ominous at all. "Maybe I should come by now."

"No, no. Take your test. Focus. Concentrate."

"I know."

"You have been slipping lately." The reprimand was gentle, but it still stung.

"Thank you."

"It's true. I'm worried about you."

That made it a little hard to be mad. "I'm fine, *Sensei*. Are you going to give me a hint on what this is about?"

"No, I think not. Just come as soon as you can, safely."

In other words, take normal precautions. Slow and safe was better than fast and dead. "Very well, I should be there by eleven-twenty."

"I will see you then."

***

Anna was completely focused on her test and probably did quite well. Liska, on the other hand, felt about two hairs shy of a nervous wreck. A fact that was driven home every time she had to stop herself from chewing on her pen. Chewing on things was a carryover from the vulpine instincts. Most

Werefoxes would admit to a little chewing when nervous. However, while she might be able to get away with chewing on a pencil, chewing on a pen was more of a risk. She didn't need a mouthful of ink, or to leave behind her dental marks. Sometimes she could use gum as a substitute, but this professor was strict about not chewing gum in class. Besides, she didn't think it would work well this time.

Why was she so nervous anyway? It wasn't unusual to wait for information. She could usually handle the wait without becoming a nervous wreck about it. Was it Tisiphone being resurrected? The notes? Being followed? Being thrown in jail? All of the above? The lack of control? That was probably it. She had no control over any of this, and she hated that feeling.

Fortunately, the professor said they could leave after they finished their tests. Even after double checking all her answers, no one else had turned in their tests. The ability to tap into one's subconscious memory could be very advantageous. She could quote the professor's lectures back to him, word for word. Still, she didn't want to stand out, so she didn't. Liska pretended to work on her test until at least two other people had handed their tests in and was still out of the room by ten-forty.

In a compromise between speed and safety, Liska chose Route #2. It wasn't as clear-cut as Route #1, which was reserved for emergencies, but it was less convoluted than the others. Then she forced herself not to run, most of the way. She was still there by eleven.

"You're early. Did your test go well?"

"It was fine. We were allowed to leave when we finished."

"Did you check your work?"

"Of course."

"Would you like some tea?"

No, she'd like some answers. "Yes, *Sensei*, that would be lovely. Shall I make some?" It usually was her job.

"No, no. I'll make it." He still hadn't looked her in the eye.

This was bad. It was worse than just stall techniques. He was uneasy about her reaction. What could be this bad?

She drank her tea without comment and waited until he finished his. "You wanted to tell me something?"

"Yes, Sakaki. Would you like more tea?"

Sakaki? This *was* big. "No, thank you." He didn't say anything. "Are we at threat for war?"

"No." He looked up at her, startled.

"Is there a plan to release silver dust over Japan?"

"No."

"Is Bigfoot coming to call?"

"No. Wrong area of the country." He was smiling now.

"I do believe you're right. Well, I've had my three guesses. Are you going to tell me? Or at least give me a hint?"

"It's about Yoshiro."

"Ah. Him. Okay. Yoshiro... has decided to take up ballet?"

"No." He chuckled slightly.

Liska snapped once in mock disappointment. "Yoshiro... has decided to become a pacifist?"

"No."

"Oh, I know! Yoshiro wants to become the first Were on the moon."

"No. He... He ran away with another girl."

"Oh." She put down her cup, staring into the dregs. "Who?" Her voice sounded emotionless even to her.

"Chiro." There were three 'Chiro's in the skulk. But Liska still knew which one he meant immediately, and not just because one of the other two was in her fifties while the other was six.

"Poor girl." She thought of the young, shy girl who had followed Yoshiro around like a duckling. Chiro had specialized in medical training, she thought. Yes, that was one of the only ways the two actually spoke to each other.

"What?"

"This dishonors his family, her family, both of them, and to a lesser extent, my family, correct?"

"Correct."

"What is the proper etiquette for this situation? Do I send them a wedding card? Condolences to his family, her family, my family?"

"Never mind the etiquette for a moment. How do you feel about this?"

"I hardly imagine my initial reaction is appropriate for the situation."

"What is your initial reaction?" He asked nervously, as if it would be to hunt down the two of them. Actually, considering the rules and traditions of the skulk, she could probably get away with that.

"I want to do cartwheels up and down the hallway. That isn't exactly appropriate, is it now?"

He smiled. "Not exactly, but I won't tell. I promise."

A few minutes later she had sat back down and was straightening her hair. "So, now what?"

"Good question. Your father is wondering what to do."

"What to do, as in...?"

"Yoshiro and Chiro have left the skulk. Unless you choose to pursue things, likely nothing will be done." Liska shook her head. Leaving the community was punishment enough. "There is also who to arrange your marriage to now." A matter that would be more complicated since most of the eligible parties her age were betrothed to another. Chiro's betrothed, Shinji, was her father's sister's son, so they couldn't even be matched together.

"Do you think you could get him to wait? Until I finish college at least?"

"I'm not sure he'll want to wait that long. Why?"

"If we wait until I'm back, there's a higher chance of being able to marry someone I could get along with rather than just someone who can strengthen my standings within the skulk. Besides, my new betrothed may have a few issues about my finishing my schooling." Yoshiro hadn't cared because he didn't want to marry her any more than she wished to marry and they both knew it. Her being halfway across the world was a good reason to postpone the marriage.

"We could try. You do realize why he's so concerned."

"Yes." Father was head of the skulk. As a mostly genetic office, the role ought to fall to her, her parent's only child. Unfortunately, as a half-blood, she didn't have the political clout necessary to lead. The reason she was supposed to marry Yoshiro was that he was the oldest son of the second most influential family. Father thought it was quite fortunate they were born within five years of each other. The hope was that those who were reluctant to follow her would follow him. He was certainly charismatic enough... when he wanted to be. He had never bothered with her.

Of course, no one had ever bothered to ask her if she wanted to marry Yoshiro, or to lead the skulk, or even if she wanted to be one of the front-line fighters. Well, she enjoyed being a front-line ninja, most of the time; maybe after a while she would have learned to enjoy being married to Yoshiro, though she doubted it, or leading the skulk.

"Sakaki?"

"Sorry, just thinking." No point getting upset over things she couldn't change.

Chapter Twenty-Six

Trust is a valuable gift, made more precious by its scarcity. –
The Kikitsutai Book of Wisdom

The next time Liska went to pose for Todd's painting, it was obvious that he had a chance to talk to Shahara about a shopping trip. The Jamaican girl was composed enough to keep from bouncing but only barely.

"Okay, this may be a little rude, and I'm sorry, but I need to know so I don't put my foot in it. What colors can you see?"

Liska winced. She really hadn't wanted to go into that. But it was a reasonable question. "Okay, but you can't tell anyone."

Shahara nodded, a little confused.

"I can't see in color. At all. Cone monochromacy. It's really, *really* rare."

"I'll say." Jamal had apparently heard of it before. "How did you get it?"

"Same way anyone else does. Genetics. Shouldn't have. It's something that runs on my father's side of the family, but not my mother's. But apparently it was there, deeply hidden." Neither Todd nor Shahara seemed to recognize the term. "The inside of my eyes have a different proportion of cones to rods than you do. I can't see any colors, just black, white, and about twenty shades of gray. I also can't see in as much detail as you can. However, I can see a little better in low light, distinguish movement and differentiate between two similar shades better than someone with normal vision. I will admit to being more sensitive to brighter lights." While she didn't actually have cone monochromacy, it was close enough to work. Most of what she said was true for both, though her low light vision was a lot better than she said. Liska did not mention that she was also a little nearsighted. It wasn't a big deal.

"That's awful," Shahara barely breathed.

Liska shrugged. "It could have been a lot worse. It could have been rod monochromacy. Then I'd have terrible vision in addition to being color blind. As it is, I'm pretty sure my sight isn't much worse than the way you watch a black and white TV." Nor was there any reason to mention that degenerative vision disorders were prevalent in the skulk. She tried not to think about that. "Anyway, I try not to talk about it too much. Most people don't react well."

Shahara swallowed the rest of her questions. "Okay. Thank you for telling us. We won't tell anyone, right?" Jamal and Todd nodded a quick agreement. "Though, it does explain a couple things." She gave quick look at Liska's outfit.

"Everyone says that. Is my dress sense that bad?"

Shahara literally bit her lip, probably to keep herself from blurting out her first answer. "Well, perhaps while shopping for your dress, we can work on... updating your wardrobe a little. It's just, well, you don't always go for the most flattering choice. Um, is budget an issue?"

"Not too bad. My parents are Uni professors, so I find out about all kinds of obscure scholarships. Then there's my savings."

"Perfect. Saturday good?"

"Well, yes. But let's not go overboard."

"Todd, didn't you say you were going to rent a Tux then? You can come too."

Todd tried to get out of it, before Liska speared him with her eyes. If she was trapped, then he was coming too.

"This will be perfect." Shahara clapped.

"Do you think we have time to run?" Liska asked him.

"I think she'd hunt us down and drag us back."

"Ducky. Just ducky. Okay, why don't you distract her while I make a run for it?"

"How come I have to be sacrificed to the shopping demons?"

"It was your idea. Besides, you're the gentleman."

"I am not that bad!" Shahara protested, laughing.

Liska and Todd exchanged a look.

"Anna, would you like me to do your hair and make-up for the dance?" Shahara offered.

No, she wouldn't. But it was a generous offer, and it wasn't something she could do well. "Yes, I think I would. How much for the make over?"

Shahara seemed almost hurt. "I'm not going to charge you. Just let me take a couple before and after pictures and give me the gossip."

More pictures. Lovely. Then again, it was unlikely anyone who truly knew her would see them. "For your class, or personal use?" "Class, maybe personal, why?" "Nothing posted online, okay? It's a really long story." Shahara didn't get it. What could she tell her? "I had a cyber stalker once. I think I got rid of him, but..." "Nothing online. I promise. Wow, that must have been scary." Liska shrugged. Maybe if it had actually happened. Then again, there were more than a few people she didn't want knowing where she was. "It wasn't fun. Anyway, are you sure I can't pay you something? I know it can be a lot of work." As she hoped, the change in subject changed the mood, even if Todd was still watching her. "Don't worry, it'll be a blast!" "Famous last words," Liska muttered.

***

Shahara continued planning the shopping expedition and muttering things about make-up that Liska didn't even try to understand, but she had escaped the scary shopping lady's clutches and gone back to her room. Even though she had been there for over two months already, there were a couple boxes she hadn't unpacked. Odd, considering she really hadn't taken much with her in the first place. She couldn't take anything that would link back to Liska, or anything that she couldn't bear to have lost, damaged, or left behind.

Today, she was looking for something she hadn't needed as Anna Andrews, a catalog of spy equipment. Since she hadn't pulled a job here, nor had she intended to, she had brought only the basics. Breaking into a police evidence vault, on the other hand, would probably involve a little more than she had brought with her. Not that she had a plan, or the information to make a plan yet, but a little forethought and planning could only help.

The catalog was near the bottom of the box, so it wasn't likely to be found. Liska started to pull it out, only to pause when her fingers touched something wooden. There shouldn't be anything wooden in here. Taking a peek in the box, Liska was shocked to see a carved wooden box she didn't recognize. She had packed this box herself; there should not be anything in here that she didn't put there.

Pulling the box out, Liska looked it over. It was a simple box, with no elaborate decorations. About the size of a cigar box, with a small latch to hold it closed. Liska suppressed a shiver and swallowed bile. There was no reason to be afraid. She would just open the box, find out what it was, and everything would be fine. Her fingers brushed the latch...

Pain exploded in her head, so fierce she was literally blinded by it. Dropping the box, she dashed for the kitchen and started rooting around for the bottle of Were-safe painkiller she kept in the drawer. Thankfully, she had been smart enough to keep it in a place where there was nothing else that could be mistaken for it. Once she had the pill in hand, she grabbed a glass, not even caring about the sounds of cups falling in her blind haste.

Sink, where was, there. She turned on the water and soaked half her arm in an attempt to get enough water to swallow the pill. Once she had taken the pill, she stayed hunched over the sink, waiting desperately for the stabbing, throbbing pain to go away.

It felt like hours but was probably less than ten minutes as it started to ease. She could see again. More importantly, she could think clearly again, even if she didn't have her bearings quite back yet. She was back enough to realize she had left the sink running, and apparently she had turned it on hot instead of cold. Liska turned off the water and rubbed at her eyes and forehead. Cups, pick up the cups. She got three of them, leaving the one on the floor, because she was pretty sure if she bent over, then she wouldn't be able to get up.

She took a few minutes to just focus on her breathing. With every exhale, some pain receded. With every inhale, she gained some clarity, some focus. Just then, her cell phone rang. Liska checked her caller ID. Ooh, it was Kira. Good, she hadn't talked to Kira in over a week.

"Hello, Liska's House of Mayhem and Madness. This is Mayhem speaking."

"How come you get to be Mayhem and I'm stuck with Madness?"

"We flipped for it, remember?"

"You cheated."

"Did you catch me cheating?"

"No."

"Then I didn't cheat. It's only cheating if you get caught." Liska was smiling on her end, certain Kira's smile matched hers. In addition to being an inside joke, it functioned as an almost code letting each know the other was free to talk.

"Just to be sure, Ryoko-*Sensei* has already talked to you, right?"

"About what?"

The line was silent for a moment. "You are kidding, right?"

Liska decided to have pity on her closest cousin and best friend. "Yes, he told me about Yoshiro."

"Whew. Good, I was worried for a moment. Shouldn't have been. I know you."

"My condolences." Liska scooped up the last cup and put it away.

"I know. It's such a trial."

"What doesn't kill you..."

"Makes you stronger, I know. The trick is making sure it doesn't kill me first." There was a small silence, and even thousands of miles away, Liska could feel the mood change. "About Yoshiro. I'd say I'm sorry, but I'm not. The guy was a complete creep, and you deserve a lot better."

"Thanks."

"I mean it."

"I know you do. So, what's the talk back home like?"

"Well..."

"Come on, Kira, you're my inside source. No keeping quiet to spare my feelings."

"Your mother is firmly on your side. She never liked Yoshiro since the time he tried to hurt you when you were kids. Your father is taking it personally. Like it was a personal insult."

"Not truly surprising, either of them. How about the skulk at large?"

"Mixed. You are clearly the injured party, so most are at least sympathetic to you. There are some who are saying that it wouldn't have happened if you weren't halfway around the world for no good reason." Liska rolled her eyes to that. Kira was probably doing the same. "Or, if you weren't a half-Were." Kira never used 'half-breed', no matter how many times Liska told her it didn't bother her. Because Kira knew her better than anyone else, and knew she was lying through her teeth.

"Why am I not surprised?"

"Because you're smart enough to know which way the wind is blowing without anyone telling you?"

"There could be that, yes. Anything else?"

"Well, I didn't really want to tell you this, but your father's been acting... a bit strange lately."

"Strange? In what way?" Her eyebrows furrowed as she studied the ceiling. She didn't think Father seemed any different in their recent IM conversations, but it was easy to fake something over the phone, and even easier through type.

"He keeps going off and talking to people in secrecy, acting like he's making some sort of big plans."

"But you don't know what it's about?"

"Not yet. I'll keep you posted. So, how are you doing? Not upset about Yoshiro, right?"

"I have a date next Friday."

Kira laughed. "Are you kidding or is this a mission, or something?"

"Mission."

"Okay, tell me all about it."

Liska smiled, and sat down on the bed, relaxing. She barely noticed when she kicked something hard under the bed. Stretching out on the bed, she filled Kira in on the requested details.

"You have to tell me everything when you get back."

"Fine, fine. Anything else?"

"I... well, I heard about Tisiphone. Are you... okay?"

"It's a threat, and I'll deal with it. The fact that they're using the name of someone I've eliminated already just emphasizes that." Her voice was cold, harsh. It wasn't fair to Kira, even though she knew her cousin wouldn't take it personally.

"Fine, but how do you feel about that?"

"A bit stressed, worse than I should be. But I'll be fine. I don't have enough information to deal with it yet, so it will have to wait."

"Okay, let's talk about something else." Kira seemed almost as eager to change the subject as Liska was.

"Good idea." But to what? A thought popped in her head. No, not that. No reason to mention that. Except, she was. "It's probably nothing, but there is something weird."

"Oh?"

"I've had this recurring dream for a while. Past three or so years. In the beginning I had it a lot, then it faded to maybe once a month, twice. Now I'm having it once or more a week."

"Tell me about it."

"It's probably nothing." They both knew she didn't believe that.

"Then there's no harm in telling me about it."

Sakaki smiled. Sometimes she thought Kira was the only one she could be Sakaki with. Everyone else, she had to wear a mask. "I'm fighting someone, sword fighting. The whole area is full of a really dense fog so I can't see my opponent. I can't really hear or smell them either, so I don't know who I'm fighting. The fight is intense, clearly to the death. My opponent is good, and I'm struggling a bit. Well, maybe more than a bit. I'm slowly losing, until I manage a direct thrust to the heart. Then suddenly the fog's gone, the sword is in my chest, and holding the other end, I see myself, looking cold, emotionless... Then I wake up. So, do you think I'm trying to tell myself something?"

"Other than you being your own worst enemy?"

"I *knew* that."

"It's your dream. I dare say you know the answers better than I. Any other recurring dreams?"

Well, there was the one where she was standing in front of a mirror as Anna, or whatever current harmless persona she was using, only it was an actual mask. She'd take it off and find another persona underneath. After taking off several masks, she'd come to Liska, also a physical mask. Sometimes she'd try to take that one off and couldn't and the dream ended there. Other times, she'd take that off, see Sakaki and realize that was a mask too. She'd take that one off, even though she was trying not to, and underneath would be a monster.

Sometimes the dream ended there. Then sometimes, that would be a mask too, and underneath that was absolutely nothing. A void, a black hole...

Liska forced back a shiver and decided not to mention her mask dream. It wasn't like she needed help interpreting that one. "Not really." It was so much easier to lie over the phone.

"Look, you know you can talk to me about anything, right?"

"Of course. And vice versa."

"Good. Have you mentioned this dream to anyone else?"

"No, just you."

"I'm honored. But maybe you should tell Ryoko-*Sensei.*"

"I'll think about it." And she did. For approximately five seconds before rejecting the idea.

"Okay, this phone call is going to cost a fortune if I don't get off. Remember to call me anytime you need to."

"I will if you do the same."

"Absolutely. Let me know if you figure out your dreams."

"I will." Liska hung up the phone and tried to remember what she had been doing when Kira called. She was sure she was doing something. Oh yes, catalog. Time to look through that.

Chapter Twenty-Seven

Crowds bring safety and danger simultaneously. – The
Kikitsutai Book of Wisdom

Shopping Saturday, as Liska thought of it, dawned
bright and early. Far too early. Shahara's
enthusiasm led to her knocking on Anna's door at
seven-thirty in the morning. Any attempts to explain
that this early was a bad time fell through. Despite
Liska's protests, Shahara insisted on coming in and
seeing her wardrobe first, so 'we'll know what you
need'. Liska knew what she needed. A dress. She was
getting by just fine with the rest of her clothes.

While she didn't mind (much) letting
Shahara in, she had a feeling that letting the other
girl pick through her clothes would be a less than
uplifting experience. She was right.

"This won't work. This won't work. This looks
awful on anyone. This is just wrong for you. Yuck.
This won't work. Definitely not. This isn't bad.
This... nah. No way. Yuck. Nice style, wrong color.
Bad idea. Ick. Nah Uh. This one's fine. Blah. No. Not
worth it. I like this one. Nope. Nope, nada. Not bad.
Maybe. This will work with the right top. Perhaps.
Okay. Nope. Any more clothes?" It was like watching
a tornado. A highly critical one.

"You discarded almost everything."

Shahara shrugged. "You have unusual coloring. And apparently a habit of picking clothes that fit rather than clothes that made you shine. Ready for a shopping expedition?"

"I like having clothes that fit. It's much more comfortable than the alternative." Her usual shopping trips were something like picking out a few tops, and pants when she could find the right size, at a thrift store or other discount store. She did have some dressier things, but for the most part she didn't care. It wasn't a matter of cost, she simply didn't want to be bothered being very concerned about clothes. "This is going to take longer than I thought, isn't it?"

"We'll find you clothes that fit! And it shouldn't be more than a few hours or so."

"Oh, goody."

Her lack of enthusiasm did not deter Shahara in the slightest. Liska found herself practically dragged from her room and to Walters, one of the guys' dorms on campus. Todd's dorm. "Um, we're not supposed to be in here," Liska pointed out, following in Shahara's wake.

Shahara completely ignored her. "Three eleven, three eleven. Here it is!" She started knocking on the door.

A half-awake Jamal stumbled to the door and blinked at them for a moment. When his still asleep brain registered no immediate cause for alarm, he slammed the door in their faces.

Liska snickered slightly, while his sister scowled indignantly and pounded on the door some more.

"If there isn't an emergency, go away!"

"No way! We have a shopping trip to do, and Todd's coming."

Sounds of a struggle could be heard on the other side of the door. After about a minute, a very sleepy looking Todd was pushed out the door with a shirt partially over his head. "What time izzit?"

"Almost eight. Get a move on!"

"Eight? I'm going back to sleep." Todd fumbled with the doorknob, only to discover it was locked. Before he could pull out a key, Shahara dragged him away.

"We are going shopping. Now!"

Liska, who had been quietly chuckling the whole time, started to slide down the wall. Normally she wouldn't let out her emotions so much, but Shahara wouldn't think twice about her laughing like this.

"You're coming too." Liska was told as she was hauled unceremoniously off the floor.

"This is your fault," Todd grumbled at her.

"My fault? It was your idea."

"But did she have to start this early?"

"I assure you, I am as thrilled as you are."

"Why do I have to come anyway?"

"Considering how much of my wardrobe was judged lacking, you'll probably be playing packhorse."

"Yay, my favorite pastime."

"You don't do sarcasm well when you're half asleep."

"And you do?"

"Enough chatter, you two. Get a move on!" Shahara called back.

"Yes, Sir, General Shahara, Sir!" Liska snapped off a perfect salute that was partially wasted due to the fact that Shahara had her back to her.

Despite the time she had spent in major cities, Liska realized that she had never been in an American mall. In fact, she could only remember three previous mall trips period. Perhaps not too surprising. After all, she disliked crowds with an intensity bordering on phobia, even if she appreciated the anonymity a crowd could give her. Lots of people meant lots of sounds, lots of smells, and lots of chances of running into a threat. Yet another reason she had a reputation for being a loner in all her incarnations.

Malls didn't carry much that she couldn't get other places, often much cheaper. Books, maybe. Toys? Not really. Electronics? Her sources were better. Toiletries and 'scent'-y stuff? She was too sensitive to constantly be around something with a scent. Clothes?

Work clothes were important. She was willing to spend a lot of money to get quality clothes that suited her purpose. She even had a few pairs of pants that were actually designed to have a flap of cloth that hid a blade along the length of each leg between ankle and knee. Liska loved those pants even if they were unfashionable and perhaps ugly, judging from Shahara's reaction. Other than that, she really did just grab whatever fit, even if it was some t-shirt advertising some business she had never heard of. So what, wasn't that 'college chic'?

"Whose car are we taking?" Todd asked, once they were outside.

"Mine's a bit small for three people, especially if we're buying a bunch of stuff. Anna, do you even have a car?"

"No. I don't have an American driver's license either." She had a motorbike stashed at Ryoko-Sensei's, but no car. In truth, she did have a license or two, but none in Anna's name. Including her motorcycle license. Besides, she'd rather not explain some of the bike's special features. Like the rotating license plate and the button that made her invisible to radar. The fact that it was very quiet for a motorcycle might require some explanation as well.

"Then I guess it's mine. Nice to have a little bit of warning," Todd muttered, though he didn't sound too put out.

"Todd, we're going to use your car," Liska deadpanned.

"Thank you, L-Anna."

Shahara didn't seem to notice the slip, but Liska gave him a look that could have sliced diamonds. Todd flinched under her glare and hurried to unlock the car.

It would be too conspicuous to give the car a thorough search, checking for explosives or other traps. The slight smell of oil in the air didn't help her nerves any. However, a quick look under the car showed a small puddle that would explain the scent. Nothing else seemed amiss.

To be on the safe side, she touched the car, trying to make herself receptive to what it was that gave her those flashes of the past. Nothing happened, which could have meant just about anything. Everything was probably fine.

The next sign that this wouldn't be her day, was that, despite not being open an hour yet, the mall parking lot was already at least half-full. Goody, goody gumdrops.

Even before they got to the door, certain scents reached out to invite them in. Probably even Todd and Shahara could smell some of them, like coffee, cinnamon, and other scents from the food court. Liska could smell all those, and more. Ink from the books, industrial strength cleaning products, perfumes, soaps, candles, plastics, fabrics, and lots and lots of people scents. A few animal scents from the pet store became noticeable when they finally entered. Liska trailed behind, pausing briefly on the threshold, before smiling a small wry smile.

She wasn't the only Were here. There was a Werelynx around somewhere. Male, probably forties or fifties. She wondered briefly if he had as much trouble adapting as she sometimes did. Bit south for a Lynx. Oh well, she probably wouldn't even run into him.

They entered the mall through a large bookstore. Liska neither noticed nor particularly cared which chain it was. They tended to be more alike than different in her opinion. If she was alone, she probably wouldn't have left the bookstore, but that wasn't the intent of this expedition, so they didn't even stop to browse.

It quickly became apparent that Shahara was, to put it mildly, a bit compulsive at shopping. Liska started to blank out when surrounded by clothes for sale, so it was easier to let hurricane Shahara take charge. After they established a few ground rules.

Rule one, no overly revealing clothes. Weres aren't body shy, and Liska was no exception, but she didn't like the way people looked at her when she wore revealing clothes. Rule two, nothing too conspicuous. Rule three, machine washable, unless it's absolutely worth the extra care. Other than that, they made things up as they went along.

"No, Shahara, I am not wearing that many sequins." "No, I don't think a halter top is my style." "I'd really rather not wear something with little sheep and hearts on it." Fortunately, Shahara caught on pretty quickly to Liska's 'style' though she did despair at her preference for darker colors.

"It's too hot down here, you want lighter colors. Besides, you walk at night, I've seen you, and you don't want to be hit by a car or something. At least you wear reflective gear if you run or skate."

Liska covered by telling her that she belonged to a group that played games like capture the flag in the dark, and she needed to blend in. It certainly wasn't Shahara's style, so she didn't need to worry about the girl asking more information.

"Maybe, but do all your clothes need to be dark?"

"Some of the games are spur of the moment. I like to be prepared."

"Fine, most dark, but a few lighter, okay?"

"Fine. But no neon, okay?"

"Deal."

The second problem was that for some reason, the clothing industry seemed to have an inflated sense of how tall the average woman was. Liska knew she was petite, barely making five-two in shoes, and she was fine with that. But it was irritating that even most of the clothes marked 'petite' were too big for her. Shopping in the Juniors section got annoying, especially because most of those clothes were designed to stand out.

"Okay, so we need clothes that fit, you don't want anything too memorable or noticeable, clothes that let you participate in active games at a moment's notice, but don't make you look like a little girl. Fine, but we need at least some fancier things, okay? Maybe some dressier tops. And your gown, of course. How often do you wear dresses?"

Liska shrugged. "It's been a while. I do have one, though."

"I saw it. You should never, ever wear pink. Okay? We'll find you one. Never know when you might need one. What do you have in way of jewelry?"

"Does my hair ornament count?" She had never really cared about jewelry. She couldn't wear silver, gold was too memorable, and there was little point in forming an attachment to items that could easily get lost or left behind in one of her escapades. "I have this bracelet." She waved the wide plastic band on her wrist. Come to think of it, she couldn't remember the last time she took it off.

Shahara looked at her skeptically. "Is that it?"

"I have a necklace or two. You know, kid stuff. It's just not a major deal."

"You're hopeless." Shahara sighed. "Let me see the bracelet." Liska held up her wrist. "I don't kn..." The word cut off suddenly, as she examined the bracelet. "On second thought, why don't we just we just leave it well enough alone?" There was something very odd and slightly strained in

Shahara's voice. What could have caused... Ow! Sudden, sharp pain invaded her head.

Liska rubbed at her temple and had to ask Shahara to repeat herself. "I'm sorry? Yes, I'll be fine. Why don't we just get started?"

It took less than thirty minutes for Liska to lose any interest she might have had, and she had to force herself to pay attention. It was important because Shahara was sensing her lack of interest and tried suggesting a few items that were very much not her taste.

"I look enough like a little kid already; I am not wearing things with little bunnies on them."

"Even if the bunny insults people?"

"Especially if the bunny insults people."

After another hour of this, and an interminable time of trying on everything Shahara and occasionally Todd picked out, Liska finally had enough.

"Are we done yet?"

"Not even close."

"Can we at least take a break for lunch? I haven't eaten yet today, and it's almost twelve."

Todd, carrying enough clothes to have trouble seeing his feet, quickly backed her up.

"Alright, alright, we'll take those clothes out to the car; then break for lunch."

Chapter Twenty-Eight

Truth remains truth regardless of perception. – The Kikitsutai
Book of Wisdom

Todd had noticed Liska's strange reactions to
shopping, but he didn't have a chance to ask her.
Shahara was too close, she'd hear them. Besides, he
doubted she'd answer in public.

They were coming back from the car when
they were stopped by a man with a clipboard.
"Excuse me please, would you mind answering a few
questions for a survey?"

Todd and Shahara looked at each other while
Anna, have to remember to call her Anna, narrowed
her eyes slightly. "What kind of survey?"

"We are taking a survey of how people in the
age range of eighteen to twenty-five view religion.
Are you all in that category?"

All three nodded. The man asked them some
questions about how they felt about religion in
general, certain religions in particular, and religious
faith. Finally, he asked how they qualified
themselves religiously.

"Christian, Baptist," Shahara responded
immediately.

"Christian, I usually go to a Presbyterian church at home," Todd answered.

Anna just smiled. "Jedi. May the Force be with you." Then she walked away, leaving a rather flabbergasted survey taker.

"Um, I think she's kidding. You may want to leave her out of your survey," Todd said before hurrying after her. He could hear Shahara apologizing for them before she caught up too.

"That was rude. You're going to skew his results," Shahara scolded.

"How do you know I'm not part of the Jedi church?"

"There's no such thing."

"Uh, I think there is," Todd said.

"There is. Though, I admit, I am not actually a member." They split up briefly for food before meeting up again in the food court.

"There's really a Jedi church? Does anyone truly believe that?" Shahara seemed to still be in shock.

"Not being able to speak for them, my guess is not really. Most probably join it for fun."

"That's a silly reason to join a church." Shahara frowned at her cup.

"Hey, it's silly, but they have fun, right? I'm sure none of them truly believe it." Todd took a sip. "And even if they do, so what? Shouldn't we respect their beliefs?"

"Not this again. Not the 'as long as you're sincere' argument." Shahara shook her head.

"Not quite, but that's a good point." It was something he had debated with Shahara and Jamal more than a few times. Mostly Shahara.

"Let me see if I understand you. You are saying it doesn't matter what someone believes as long as they are sincere in that belief?" Liska asked. Or maybe Anna. Or maybe it would be easier to think of her as Sakaki. After all, whether she was Anna or Liska, she was still Sakaki.

"Well, that's my view. Shahara disagrees with me."

The red head smiled. "What is this?"

"A spork," Todd answered.

At the same time, Shahara spoke up, "A perversion of a serving tool."

"No, I think it's an elephant."

The two looked at her.

"It's a spork," Todd said quietly.

"No, it's an elephant. See, here are the tusks, here's the tail, and it's gray. Therefore, it must be an elephant."

"Actually, it's blue; those are tines and a handle." He tried to ignore Shahara giggling at them.

"But to me, it's gray and has tusks and a tail. Therefore, to me, it's an elephant."

"But... But you're wrong!" Todd couldn't help blurting out.

"But I sincerely believe it's an elephant. So, shouldn't it be an elephant?"

"As I think Anna is pointing out, sometimes believing something doesn't make it so." Shahara finally stopped laughing.

"If it did, exams would be a lot easier. After all, as long as we believed something, there would be no wrong answers." She looked at Todd still shaking his head. "If you like, I can go to the second floor and claim to believe I can fly. Would you be 'respecting my beliefs' or trying to get me to get down?"

"But that's dangerous," Todd pointed out.

"Yes, it is. And from my standpoint, so is not being a Christian," Shahara answered.

"I can see that. If I understand correctly, your religion claims to be the only way to heaven. If you truly believe that, then surely any decent Christian would wish everyone to convert, am I right?" Anna asked.

"Exactly! So, what do you believe?"

Todd listened closely himself. Would she answer truthfully?

"I'm not sure." She frowned. "I can't believe everything happened by random chance any more than I believe this spork-elephant was formed by an explosion at a silverware factory. So, somehow, somewhere, what we know was created. Some credit it to aliens, but that just moves the problem back a few steps. Where would the aliens come from? Anyway, there's a creator, but as to what kind or the nature of the creator, I'm not sure. Other than that He, She, It, or They have a sense of humor. Nor am I sure if they are still involved in their creation, though my hunch is 'yes'. The problem is, if I go much further into this, I reach the issue of a creator that I probably have some obligation to, and I'm not sure I'm ready to handle that."

"At least you're honest about it." Shahara smiled. "If I gave you a Bible, would you read it?"

She was quiet for a moment. "I'll try, but no promises, okay?"

"Great. Now, if I can only get Todd to listen."

"Hey, I go to church, remember?" Todd protested.

"You go when you're at home or when my brother guilts you into coming with us. Do you actually listen, pay attention, or think about any of it? Have you put as much thought into what you believe as Anna has?"

"Well..." How much had Sakaki actually thought about it? Was what she said even the truth?

"Alright, I don't know about you two, but I think now might be a good time to change the subject. Besides, we're all finished, right?"

Saved by the red head. "Sounds like a plan." Todd got to his feet and started gathering his trash.

Shahara reluctantly dropped the subject and they left the food court, Shahara quickly seeking out one of the mall directories. Behind her back, Todd noticed Sakaki make eye contact with an older man. When he scowled at her, she raised an eyebrow, smirked slightly, and gave an abbreviated nod. He seemed to deflate slightly and nodded back. Then he continued walking. By now Sakaki had noticed Todd watching and mouthed, 'Later'. He shrugged and they both followed Shahara into a store.

The conversation topic might have changed, but Todd was still thinking about it. How honest had Sakaki been? She must have lied to them about a lot of things in the time she knew them. True, most of that was probably necessary, but the problem with liars was that even when they told the truth, people didn't know if they could believe them.

"What do you think of this dress?" Shahara asked, pulling Todd from his musings. How deep had he been thinking if he had missed Sakaki changing? Why did Sakaki feel like a better name for her than Anna or Liska? Maybe he should ask her what she preferred to be called. As Shahara got his attention again, he turned to look at Sakaki. Then promptly felt his jaw try to drop.

The dress was a deep blue, bordering on black, embedded with rhinestones like stars in the night sky. The skirt was straight, reaching practically to her ankles, with a slit to just past her knees. The top came all the way up, ending in a high collar, also slit. There were no sleeves, and the whole dress had a bit of an oriental flavor to it. Appropriate.

"Oh my. It's, uh... really nice." His fingers itched for his sketch pad.

"You think so?" Sakaki looked a little doubtful.

"I think it's lovely." Shahara sounded satisfied.

"It's a little hard to move in this."

"Can you dance in that?" Shahara asked.

"I think so. As long as I don't have to use too long a stride."

"You'll be fine. How about the collar? Is it too much?"

"No, the slit keeps it from triggering my phobia."

"Excellent! Now all we need is shoes and accessories."

Shoes were a bit of a problem. One, Sakaki had small feet, even for her size, so they had to make do with what they could find in her size. Two, Sakaki didn't want any heels on the shoes at all, and Shahara didn't believe shoes were dressy unless they had really high heels. Preferably stilettos. Besides, a little heel to the shoe would make her look taller.

Todd tried to stay out of the argument, though privately he was on Sakaki's side. After all, she was the one who had to wear them. Besides, it wouldn't be fun at the dance unless she was comfortable.

Of course, he couldn't forget that she was going to the dance for information, not a date. She was spoken for. Off limits. And don't you forget that, Kensworth. At least she didn't know how much he was attracted to her. He would have to be very careful to keep that a secret. Even if she wasn't engaged, it would never work. Would it?

Somehow shoes were decided and agreed upon without causing distress and great bloodshed, with compromises on both parties. The heels were higher than Sakaki claimed to be comfortable with, but still shorter than Shahara liked. More importantly, they were wide enough that Sakaki could actually walk in them without holding out her arms like she was on a high wire.

"By the way, do you know how to dance?" Todd asked, suddenly realizing he didn't know.

"Of course. Mother approved of dancing as a way to make me more graceful, and Father thought it good exercise and that it would make me better at reading people." Todd and Shahara blinked at that. Sakaki quickly changed the subject. "Are we done now?"

"Not yet. We still need accessories and jewelry."

"Do I need accessories and jewelry?"

"Yes!" And hurricane Shahara struck again.

***

Finally, finally, all the shopping was done. Sakaki seemed to be falling asleep in the car, but Todd doubted she would actually let herself sleep with them around. He couldn't blame her for being tired though, he wouldn't mind a nap himself.

At least they got all their shopping done. Sakaki had a wardrobe that she could wear without hurting other people's eyes, she had a dress to the ball, and he had a tux.

When they got back to the school, Shahara volunteered Todd to help Anna sort through her new clothes and ducked off somewhere. If Sakaki realized Shahara's less than subtle attempt at matchmaking, she didn't say anything.

Well, he could at least help her carry everything up to her room. Shahara had gone just a little overboard.

"I do appreciate the help." Sakaki paused to sniff at the door before unlocking it. Maybe he could ask her about that later. Or not.

"It's no...Ooof!" Todd walked into Sakaki's back as she stopped suddenly. She seemed to be looking at something. Something on the floor. He looked over her shoulder to see what had made her stop. There was another note on the floor.

Chapter Twenty-Nine

Those who play with fire should stock up on burn cream. –
The Kikitsutai Book of Wisdom

"Another note?"

"Yes." Liska tried to keep back the growl, but doubted she was very successful. Then she moved out of the way so Todd could pass her and get in the room. Once he was past, she investigated the note. No unusual smells, didn't appear to have any residue. She put on gloves and tried a few other tests, before taking them off and seeing if her new trick bore any fruit.

It wasn't as strong as the first time, but it was clearly the same person. Again, no clues on where he was. It was dark, and his night vision wasn't as good as hers. Was that a clue? There was a bit of color though. Very interesting. The deliverer was not the person she was picking up on, though she thought she could get just a slight feel from him too. Why was that? Perhaps the deliverer simply wasn't as emotionally involved. Maybe even unaware of what he was carrying. Unlikely though. It was an open sheet of paper, not even in an envelope.

Todd was shifting about nervously and had already asked her what it said at least twice. She read it out loud.

Sakaki,
The ink on your formerly betrothed's wedding certificate is hardly dry. Making your move on another man already? Are you hoping to force Daddy into letting you marry a human as well?
Your well-meaning friend
"It's the same person."
"What does he mean 'formerly betrothed'? What wedding certificate?" Oh, right, she hadn't told him yet.
"Yoshiro ran off with another girl."
"Oh. Um, I'm sorry?"
"For what?" She asked absently, still looking at the note.
"Any hurt he may have caused you."
Liska shrugged. "I attempted to restrain myself from doing cartwheels only because it disgraced several good families."
"So, you aren't upset by this."
"Yoshiro and I never got along. I doubt marriage would have changed that."
"Do you have a new betrothed now?"
"Not yet. I'm asking my father to wait until I finish school. We'll see what happens."
"Right. When did this happen?"
"I found out about it within the last few days. Ryoko-*Sensei* told me. Speaking of *Sensei*, I need to inform him of this latest round. Excuse me."
He didn't pick up the phone, leaving it to go to the answering machine. "I got a new note from my secret admirer. He keeps mentioning our mutual acquaintance and knows about the change in status. I'll show you when I come over for dinner." There,

that should tell him what he needed to know but not give away too much in case anyone else heard the message.

Todd was waiting, still seeming uneasy. "Do you have to leave?"

"He wasn't home. I'll go by later. You were going to help with the clothes?"

"Yeah." He helped her sort through the clothes. "Quick question. That man at the mall, what was that?"

Liska smiled. "He was a Werelynx. He challenged my right to be there, I challenged his right to challenge me. Because it was neutral territory, we were able to both leave without getting into a dispute."

"All without a word?"

"Who needs words?"

"Personally, I find them very useful. Okay, let's start here."

They went through the clothes, with Todd telling her every color, even if the name meant nothing to her; what it would go best with, and her marking them, making a list of what was marked how. Shahara would be disappointed, but Liska still insisted on salvaging some of the clothes that Shahara had discarded. Mostly clothes she could work in.

Speaking of work. "Did you get the layout of the police station yet?" She opened the bottom drawer of her dresser and pulled out a key that she kept taped to the bottom of the drawer above it. The key went to the padlock of the suitcase in her closet. In the suitcase was her work laptop, which was linked to her biometrics.

"Yes, but it wasn't easy." He pulled out a flash drive. "I had to look six different places to get all the info."

Liska pulled up the info on her work laptop. Saving the files to her computer, she opened them and looked at the layout, embryonic plans forming and being discarded as she pondered her options.

"You've been in the station, multiple times, right?" She asked Todd.

"Yeah, but not all. Never the evidence room."

"Can you?"

"Get in the evidence room? I doubt it."

An idea sparked. "You get along well with your uncle, right? And he is a high-ranking police officer."

"That doesn't mean he'll let me in the evidence room."

Liska just smiled.

***

"So, this is Anna? We never really got a chance to meet before." The meeting was about as awkward as any she'd had where no one wanted to kill anyone else. Nor was she the only one to feel that way, from the looks of it. Todd kept shifting from foot to foot. His uncle, John Kensworth, was smiling at her, but it was the smile of someone wishing he was far away, doing anything else.

Liska shook the offered hand politely, smiling her best smile. "Perhaps for the best." She didn't know exactly why she hadn't met the man during the investigation in Todd's attack but suspected that it was very deliberate. Perhaps he had stayed away, afraid his presence could be called interference during the trial, or perhaps he didn't trust himself to be around the person he thought had tried to kill his nephew. Equally as likely, protocol had kept him away, forbidding him entrance. Still, it did mean that their meeting, awkward as it was, was perhaps not as bad as it could have been if they met first in an interrogation room. "Still, I am pleased to meet you now. I've heard a lot about you."

John gave a look to Todd. "I've heard of you, too. But," he folded his hands, "I'm a little confused by your... *request.*"

Todd opened his mouth, but Liska spoke first. "Well, it is a little hard to explain. I know that the case is still open," she ignored to hardening of the older man's brow. The case was officially cold. "And I have a lot of faith in the police to ferret out the truth eventually. But I'm sure you'll agree, 'eventually' can take a long time in coming sometimes. Todd and I, well, we're looking for a bit of closure. A bit of... I'm not sure, just something concrete."

John was silent for a little while. "We will find the man who did this. And I can't have anyone tampering with the evidence in the meantime." Again, Todd looked ready to speak but cut off at Liska's look. "However, I suppose it wouldn't hurt to show you the box in the evidence room."

"Thanks, Uncle John. We really appreciate it." Todd beamed in relief.

"C'mon, kids. This way." Liska allowed the men to walk ahead of her, trailing slightly behind so she could look around subtly. This could work out better than she hoped.

Her trailing behind had another advantage. It gave John Kensworth enough confidence to whisper to Todd, "Are you sure you trust her? I mean, we don't have proof she was involved in your attack, but..."

"I'm certain. Very, very certain."

Liska ignored the slight tickle in her chest at that. Todd probably knew she could hear them. Before she could think about it anymore, they were led to a large metal door. There were at least two cameras pointing in that direction. John swiped a key card before tapping 29096010 into the keypad. Liska memorized the number.

The evidence room was like a vault. Steel all the way around, even Korvou couldn't walk through that. Not that she planned to ask him. There was another camera focused on the door, and one to the room at large. The camera for the room at large had blind spots though. They trusted the cameras at the door to get all the information needed. The room was cool and dark. Then brightened as they walked in. Lights on motion sensor? That wasn't so good. "Where are the motion sensors?" Liska looked about, trying to seem confused. Innocent.

John smiled. "We've got to keep some secrets." He wasn't good at it. She noticed his eyes flicked low to the side. She spotted them then. On the ground. Hmm. Possible complication, possibly not. She gave him an appreciative smile, like a young child seeing a magic trick.

Whatever organization there was in the Evidence room, it was a confusing one. Even John

Kensworth seemed to have trouble figuring out where to look. The evidence box for Todd's case turned out to be about three quarters into the room, two shelves down from the top.

The camera was a problem, as she didn't think this was one of its' blind spots. She'd have to check. Still, there were ways around that too. Yes, her plan was solidifying quickly.

"So, does this help? Seeing the box?" John asked, after giving them a few minutes.

"You know, I think it does." Todd looked at her. "What do you think?"

"Yes, I'd have to agree," Liska said.

***

It was five-thirty on Friday when Todd went to pick up Sakaki. He smoothed back his hair, trying not to be nervous. He really hadn't seen her since Tuesday. She had said that she needed time to plan, plus she changed on Wednesday, and would be tired and out of it on Thursday. Not seeing her had only increased his nervousness. Well, he now knew he was really not cut out to be a spy. Sakaki had promised him three times that she'd keep him out of it, as much as possible, and he was still a nervous wreck. Or was that because it was a 'date'? Don't think about that.

He had never worn a tuxedo before, and he couldn't help feeling ridiculous. He tried to pretend he was an ultra-cool, suave spy, but honestly, he felt more like a penguin. Was everything ready?

He had his corsage, a creamy white rose, pink-tipped, and a spray of baby's breath; the car was ready, he had taken in through a car wash and filled the tank. He had put on the complete suit, he'd checked twice. Had keys to the car, had his tickets, knew where the place was, he should be set. Taking a deep breath, he knocked on her door. Camera! He forgot a camera!

Todd didn't have time to think about that, because just then the door opened and out stepped a vision. He'd seen the dress before, but not like this. He'd seen her with her hair tied up, but not like this. He'd even seen her in painting sessions wearing make-up, but never like this. It took a few minutes before even the word, "Wow," could escape his mouth.

"You like?" Sakaki asked, sounding at the same time demure and sultry.

She was wearing the blue dress, and a necklace that looked like braided gold. Her earrings looked like diamonds, though he knew they weren't. Her hair was in an upswept chignon. Her make-up was subtle, but knowing what she normally looked like, he could see it was there. Shahara had even slipped a gold bracelet over Sakaki's usual green plastic one. Why she had done that, he didn't know, but he didn't ask.

"You look gorgeous," Todd said sincerely.

She actually blushed. Todd didn't think he'd seen that before. "Oh, here. This is for you." He handed her the corsage.

"Thank you. It's beautiful. And it smells lovely." Sakaki smiled and tried to put it on. Evidently she didn't have a whole lot of experience, because after a moment of fumbling with it, Shahara sighed impatiently and put it on for her. Todd hadn't even realized she was still there. Before disappearing back into the room, the Jamaican girl handed Sakaki a red carnation. "Oh, right. This one is yours." Sakaki held it out.

"Psst! You're supposed to put it on him," The shadows whispered loudly.

"Oops, sorry." Sakaki put it in his buttonhole.

"Say, Shahara, did you bring a camera? I forgot mine," Todd asked the room at large.

"Of course I brought my camera. Now get in here, you two."

After that, there were a lot of pictures. Pictures together. Pictures separately. Pictures Shahara had them pose for. Pictures Todd had them pose for. Pictures that had to be retaken because one or another blinked. Pictures in case other pictures didn't work out. Finally, Todd called an end to it. "We're going to be late if we don't leave soon."

"Alright, have fun you two. Don't do anything I wouldn't do!"

"Does that include drag racing in police cars?" Sakaki asked, as Todd offered his arm for her to lean on. It wasn't that she couldn't walk in her shoes; it just wasn't always easy.

"Yes!"

"Well, there went my plans for the evening." Todd sighed.

"Bye, kids!"

"She does know you're older than her, right?" Sakaki asked Todd.

"She ought to. She's been to several of my birthday parties. Heck, I'm a little older than her older brother." By then they were at the car. Todd knew that some people who were going to the party were renting limos and had considered doing the same. But it was expensive, he was a student, and several other things had cropped up. Part of him knew, though, if she had agreed to go with him, just as a date, not to gain information, he would have found a way to get one and not thought twice about it. Still, he didn't say anything about it, and neither did she.

He did remember to open the door for her, and to walk slowly. "How do you want to play this?"

"Do you know the schedule?"

He smiled at her pronunciation of 'schedule'. "We should get there around six-thirty. Dinner is at seven, and there is dancing until ten."

"I see. We'll have to play this by ear, but probably closer to the end, when people are tired and not paying as much attention. Will alcohol be served?"

"I think so, but aren't we both underage?"

"I'm not suggesting we drink. But if those around us are, they will be less watchful."

"Right. Good idea." Would they dance? Probably. It would look out of place if they didn't. Surely Sakaki didn't want that. The sad thing was, even knowing it was just an act, he would take it. Just for one night.

"Remember, I am Anna Andrews there."

"I remember." Maybe, just maybe, he should take the risk and tell her how he felt. There was no betrothed in the works now. Maybe...

"You are certain you can do your part?" Her voice jarred him from his thoughts.

"Sure. I'm just the distraction." He still didn't know quite what she planned. She refused to tell him beforehand, saying *maybe* afterwards. He still wasn't sure if he wanted to know. "Hey, question for you. You seemed to sniff around the car before getting in. Why?"

"Because I'm paranoid. Given my druthers, I would search the car before getting in. Doesn't work in this dress."

"Do you drive?"

"I can, but I do not own a car at present. I do have a motorcycle though. It's at Ryoko-*Sensei*'s house."

"I wouldn't have pictured you for the biker type. What kind?"

"It's custom built, made of lightweight materials. It has to be for me to steer it well. I'm stronger than I look, but not superhuman. It's also really fast, maneuverable, and efficient for long distances. It also has a few other fun features. On the downside, if I hit something solid, it could cause a lot of damage."

"I'd be more worried about you than the bike."

Sakaki shrugged. "I'm a Were. We generally heal well and completely. *Che*, I once took a really bad fall and broke about two-thirds of the bones in my spine. I was up and about again in six weeks, trying to build up the stamina to go back to my normal routine."

Todd tried to force his fingers to relax on the steering wheel. Or at least stop clenching so hard it hurt. "How far did you fall?"

"Oh, about forty feet."

"You're lucky you weren't killed!"

"I do know what I'm doing." He could just see a small smile.

"Right, just... be careful."

Sakaki, or was she Liska right now, froze. "I don't tell you how to paint; you don't tell me how to do my job." Her voice was ice slivers.

"Sorry, sorry! I just— You're my friend. I don't want you to get hurt."

"Don't get too close. Neither of us can afford it."

At that moment, they pulled into the station parking lot.

Chapter Thirty

In dancing and in sparring, choose your partner carefully. –
The Kikitsutai Book of Wisdom

Liska took a moment to center herself before exiting the car. She really shouldn't have gotten into a fight with him, not just before the dance, or before an op. While she was confident in her skills to carry on as if nothing was wrong, Todd was a lot more open about his feelings. More than he realized. Besides, he was simply concerned. Unfortunately, few things raised her hackles faster than someone implying that she couldn't handle herself as a ninja. She had worked so hard to prove herself to a doubting skulk. Sometimes it felt like she could never please them. Or Father.

But that wasn't Todd's fault. He just had a gift for pushing some of her more sensitive buttons. When Todd came around to open her door, she forced herself to apologize and mean it. "I'm sorry. I shouldn't have snapped at you. You were only showing concern and I bit your head off. It just, well, you hit some issues I have."

"It's okay. I probably should have left well enough alone." He smelled surprised though. The reaction to the apology seemed to be automatic. He helped her out, and she got a good whiff of his smell. Paint, some ink, various toiletries, the same smells he usually had, but underneath it was his unique scent; warm and welcoming, rich and deep in a way the average human would never know. Never in a million years would she admit to liking that scent. He had skipped cologne. Had he guessed that being around strong scents like that irritated her nose?

He was clearly in a better mood. That should make the dance less awkward. Well, except for the fact that he kept growing more and more attracted to her. Even finding out she wasn't human hadn't stopped that. It made her feel awful about using their 'date' to get information, but she had been completely honest with him. Which was more than could be said for some other times she had used someone's attraction to her advantage. Maybe she should buy him a ticket for a singles cruise or something. Muse later, work now.

Then they were inside. It was obviously a gym, but it certainly didn't look like one now. There were balloon sculptures, ribbons galore, fountains of punch, and a live string quartet, plus piano. There were also a lot of people. A whole lot. Many of whom were in law enforcement and probably almost as paranoid as she was. She could handle this.

Todd was popular here, and seemed to be constantly introducing her to people. If she hadn't trained herself to bring up subconscious knowledge on demand, she probably wouldn't have remembered any of them. A few were giving her strange looks, undoubtedly remembering how she had been the initial suspect for her current date's attempted murder. She couldn't blame them. There were stranger ways to start a relationship, but she couldn't think of many off the top of her head.

"Toddy! How are you, my boy?" John Kensworth appeared, booming voice heralding his presence. Both Liska and Todd winced. Liska at the sound, Todd at the welcoming slap on the back.

"Hi, Uncle John. You remember Anna. Anna, you remember my uncle."

John's brows furrowed. "I do remember. I hadn't realized that she would be your date, though."

He didn't trust her. Not that she was surprised or bothered by that. Still, it would make things much easier on Todd if his uncle wasn't suspicious of her. "Yes, I must say it's nice to see the precinct under a happier time. This room looks amazing." Todd had mentioned that John Kensworth was on the committee for planning this event.

John relaxed slightly, a proud smile curving slightly at his lips. "It does, doesn't it? Well, why don't you two hit the dance floor for a while?" He clapped Todd on the shoulder, mouthing something about a talk later, then left.

"So," Todd began, "What do we do now?"

"Now we dance." He smelled a bit surprised. "It makes sense considering the surroundings, and by looking over each other's shoulders while moving about the room, we can scan the whole place and watch each other's back."

"Oh, right." She could smell his disappointment. It made her feel like she had been kicking kittens.

"And because I want to." She took his hand and led him onto the dance floor, secretly savoring his surprised pleasure with just a bit of hope. One night. They could both pretend, if only for one night.

***

Whatever Sakaki was thinking, Todd knew better than to ask her. She turned out to be a superb dancer. Not to mention surprisingly good at small talk. When seated at dinner with his uncle and his date and another officer and her date, Sakaki had been very good at keeping the conversation light and moving without answering any personal questions or seeming to manipulate it at all. After eating, they danced some more. It was then he realized that whatever it was that made her come alive when sparring was present to a lesser degree when she danced. It was a relief to see that. He had missed that spark of life, of spirit; being unable to practice Kendo until he was completely and fully healed. Another month or two to go.

While he wasn't sure of it, he thought his pre-cog abilities might be helping him dance. He had been trying to hone them, and they seemed to give him little clues on how to move, how she would move, and how not to bump into people. It was working well enough that after the second dance, she relaxed and let him lead. They had done a bit better when she led, but no disasters occurred.

"Someday, can I paint you dancing?" Todd asked while giving her a spin.

"I don't know. Can you paint motion?"

"Well, not quite. But I want to watch you dance and try to paint my impression of it."

"We'll see. I have to be careful who would see a picture of me."

"Why are you so paranoid?"

"You would be too if as many people wanted you dead."

Now wasn't that a mood killer. "I suppose you're right. You often are."

"We'll see. If it's just for private use, or one of your classes, I might agree."

Todd just smiled. "I appreciate it." He truly did. The more he learned about her and how secretive she was, the more he appreciated that she opened up to him at all. He knew he was quickly becoming more open to her than anyone else.

It probably had to do with having to hide. Sakaki had always had to hide who she was around most people, so she was secretive. On the other hand, Todd had always been pretty open. But when Sakaki opened his eyes to another world, he had to keep it a secret. It was just so much easier to stay with someone he didn't have to pretend around. Besides, the more he learned, the more curious he got. And sometimes, she would tell him things that he never would have noticed or imagined.

"Say, didn't you... um, you know, the other day?"

"Change? Yes. Why?"

"Would it be safe... could I see you sometime?"

Sakaki raised an eyebrow millimeter by millimeter. Todd was ready to take it back, apologize for breaching some unknown rule of etiquette, but she spoke first, "Perhaps." Before he could say anything, she continued. "What time is it?"

"Almost nine. Why?"

Sakaki looked around slowly. "Why don't you show me where the WC is?"

It took him a half second to recognize the planned signal. "Right. This way."

The rest of the police precinct was manned by a skeleton crew. There were a few people in fancy dress, obviously come from the dance, but for the most part, it was empty.

Todd led Sakaki to the ladies' room she had specifically mentioned earlier. She had a plan. Sure, she hadn't told him the whole plan, but he knew she had one.

Sakaki disappeared into the restroom, only to come out a moment later with an 'Out of Order' sign that she taped to the door. "Okay, you know what to do. If I'm not back in twenty minutes, something went wrong. Leave without me."

"But..."

"I have ways to get out that will suffice for me, but not for another."

Todd nodded. Besides, he had promised to do exactly what she said. "Okay. Be... I mean, good luck."

She gave him a chilly smile and ducked inside. Todd went a little ways off and tried to look like he wasn't waiting for anyone. He would have to get the story from her later.

***

Liska wished she could lock the door behind her, but like most public multi-stall restrooms, it didn't have a lock. Since the door opened inward, she settled for dragging the large trashcan in front of the door. Her little sign wouldn't work as a diversion for long. Time to get moving.

Heading to the stall in the middle, she took the lid off the water tank and was relieved to see that the waterproof bag she had planted during her earlier tour was still there. There wasn't much time.

Liska had researched everything she could possibly think about and discovered some interesting facts about the security of the building. For being police, they didn't have the best security. Probably didn't think they would need it, since anyone who wanted to break in would have to go past literally dozens of police officers before getting anywhere important. Budget was also a factor, she was sure.

But the thing about infiltration was it didn't matter how many ways you *couldn't* break in, as long as there was at least one way you could. Liska had devised three plans that had an eighty percent chance or more of success. After some consideration, she decided to go with the way that was least likely to link back to Todd.

She stripped off her dress, and quickly slipped on the uniform she had hidden in advance. It hadn't been hard to figure out where the police ordered their uniforms from, and even easier to get a uniform in her size. A brass name badge was the next step. As a private joke, the name said 'A. Moon'.

The wig was a little harder, but she had practice, and was soon satisfied that her own hair wasn't visible under the black wig. Liska wished she could trade out the shoes, but there simply wasn't a way to stash sneakers somewhere where they wouldn't be discovered for a few days. Still, there were no regulations that said women couldn't wear heals.

Liska stashed her dress and the waterproof pouch in the trash can under the bag, then slipped on the latex gloves. The last prop was a mobile phone in an evidence bag. Then she moved the trash can out of the way and strode purposely toward the evidence vault.

Someone had tried very hard to secure the room; cameras, motion sensors, key cards and codes. But they didn't think of the budget. The cameras were stationary, and everyone used the same key card and code. If Liska had another week, she probably could have gotten her own key card. But she didn't have a week, so she had to make do.

No one looked twice at yet another uniform walking briskly. People in a uniform were invisible, and people in a moderate hurry clearly knew where they were going and what they were doing. When she cut across a bullpen, a few people glanced up as she passed their desk, but most didn't give her a second thought.

It only took one person to be a security risk. One person who left their key card unattended, and someone always did. It was on a desk, about halfway through the bull pen, near the edge of the desk. She would have preferred it if the desk was unoccupied, but one couldn't have everything.

As Liska swept past the desk, the displaced air stirred a precariously stacked tower of papers. Both Liska and the desk's owner moved to steady the papers. When they were certain the papers wouldn't move, she met the officer's eyes, gave him a brief nod and kept walking. He never noticed that his key card left with her.

Leaving the bullpens, Liska got to the hallway the evidence vault was off of. Someone else was heading towards her, and the evidence vault. Oh, she hoped he wasn't going in. No, he walked past, but he was eyeing her. Liska didn't say a word, maintaining the air of one too busy to notice other people around them.

"Are you new?"

She allowed herself a small start, as if drawn from her preoccupied thoughts. "Yes. It's a temporary assignment." Liska used an accent she had picked up from a family of Chinese immigrants who had lived in New York City for several years.

"Oh, do you need a tour?"

Ah. She should have guessed. "No, I've picked it up by now. Thank you, though."

He frowned a little but persisted. "Well, can I interest you in some coffee?"

"Thank you, but I'm engaged."

Eyes flashed to her hands, and he raised an eyebrow. "No ring."

"Oh, I don't wear it at work. I'm afraid of it getting lost or damaged. But it's beautiful." She smiled wide, trying to be 'bubbly'. "He was so romantic. Ron took me to my favorite restaurant, and he got the musicians to play my favorite song, and there was candlelight—"

The police officer's eyes were already glazing over. "Well, glad to hear it. Congratulations. I... You.... Don't you need to get that to the evidence vault?"

"Oh, yes! Thank you." She ignored his semi-dignified retreat and let herself into the evidence vault.

Once inside, she went straight to the box of evidence from Todd's case. Liska ignored the cameras. *Don't look at them, don't look like you're avoiding them.* She blocked the camera's view of the box, then carefully slit the evidence tape.

***

Todd was trying very, very hard not to act like he was up to something. He was not good at it, at all. His job was two-fold. He was the distraction, and the lookout. Make sure no one went in the bathroom she had put the sign on while she was gone and try to distract the officer watching the surveillance tapes. He had only caught a glimpse of her in costume, and he hadn't recognized her at first. Hopefully that would be enough to fool someone who didn't know her.

Fortunately, he knew Officer Velazquez and knew that while he was a very good officer; he hated watching the security tapes. Too boring. Not that Todd blamed him.

"Hey, Officer Velazquez. How'd you get stuck watching the tapes tonight?"

The Hispanic man smiled at Todd. "Hey, Todd. It was this or go to the party. Sad when boredom is the better option, huh? What are you doing here? Party's in the gym."

"Yeah, I know. My date wanted to, er... freshen up, a bit." That was a decent excuse, right? Todd tried to eye the screen showing the cameras without being obvious. He saw her get stopped in the hallway, but she managed to get past that quickly. She was in the evidence room now. At least, he thought it was her. The camera quality wasn't great. Which was probably something she was counting on.

A laugh distracted him. "Yeah, that's chicks for you. So, you really asked that redhead?" The voice was light but there was something in those eyes.

"Well, yeah. Anna's my friend."

Velazquez eyed the screens. He didn't seem to think her being in the vault was anything out of the ordinary. Even Todd couldn't see what she was doing, and he knew roughly. "I saw her a couple times, when she was here. Was one of the arresting officers, actually. There's something... chilly about her. You be careful, Todd. Last person I got that feeling about... well, that case gave me nightmares for weeks. And I don't get nightmares very often."

Todd nodded slowly. It made sense that some people would read the predator in her. "I know she has her..." darker side, "rough spots; but she is a good person. Truly."

"Sometimes they're the most dangerous."

***

Inside the box, on the very top, was the inventory list, saying what was supposed to be in the box. Since she wasn't taking anything for keeps, it wouldn't matter. Moving that aside, there were papers and photos. It wasn't until she had dug through those that she found the sword.

Liska pulled it out. Nothing happened. Then again, she had never gotten a response through gloves before. She didn't have time to go through all of these papers to find out if they had recorded where fingerprints were.

Forcing back a growl, she stripped off one glove and took hold of the sword at the tip of the hilt where she knew she hadn't touched it. Where it was unlikely anyone had touched it. Before she could worry if it would work, she was thrown headlong into another mind.

Dark. Waiting. Chocolate is good. Not as good as blood. He'll come. Just wait until he comes, then blood. Bloodbloodblood! If I do well, I'll be rewarded. Blood! Sweeter than chocolate. Hurry, hurry, come so I can kill. Killkillbloodkill. Get rid of the fox. Danger. Hiss. Don't like fox. Spy. Watch. Make sure fox is blamed for death. Then she cannot interfere. Don't want her. Here he comes. Wait. Not yet. There! Atolatar will be happy now. ATOLATAR!

Liska pulled back with a strangled gasp. That was the strongest she had felt yet. Nothing to see, but that was okay. She had everything she needed. Liska put her glove back on, wiped the box and the tip of the sword hilt, and concentrated on putting everything back the way it was. She didn't have time for this.

***

Sakaki, no, definitely Liska at the moment, had been gone for fifteen minutes. Todd knew because he couldn't stop counting them. She had said twenty minutes, but maybe he should give her a grace period. Or not. If something did go wrong, then things could get worse quickly. He really hoped she'd hurry. Fortunately, she seemed to be almost done.

He was still chatting with Officer Velazquez, but it was obvious that the Hispanic cop knew something was off. Hopefully he just thought Todd was nervous about his date. Oh, he hoped Liska didn't get caught. She had made him promise that if something did go wrong and she got caught, he was to deny any knowledge of what she was up to. He didn't want to break a promise, but he wasn't sure he could do that.

It was almost too late that he noticed someone else heading to room. A cop he didn't recognize, holding an evidence bag. No points for guessing where she was going. Liska hadn't left yet.

Todd swallowed hard. Should he do something? Could he do something? Before the officer entered her code, she stopped and turned. Oh, she was talking to someone. Good. Keep talking.

"Todd?"

He managed to keep back the jump, barely. "Yeah?"

"You okay?"

"Yeah, fine." The other cop was leaving and the first one was entering her code.

Out of the corner of his eye, Todd could see Officer Velazquez trying to figure out what he was looking at. "The monitors aren't that interesting."

Todd forced a smile. "No. They aren't."

Liska walked out as the other cop opened the door.

Chapter Thirty-One

Do not start a fight where there are no exits. – The Kikitsutai
Book of Wisdom

Liska was mentally muttering every swear word she was willing to use. It wasn't many. Mother had pressed on her a dislike for profanity. She had taken too long to get out of there.

Werefox ears were sharp enough that she could pick up the conversation on the other side of the steel door. She had taped the box back and stuffed the phone in an evidence bag into her pocket. There was some evidence that this wasn't the original tape, but one would have to look for it to notice. Besides, there were a lot of people who had access to and reason to look through the box. No one would catch on.

Still, she managed to leave as the other officer came in. That was a little risky simply because it was more memorable. But it shouldn't matter now. As long as she was able to get changed before anyone realized anything was off. Then, even if someone did notice something was off, *and* figured out it was related to the new police officer, they'd be looking for the wrong person. She just had to get back to that bathroom.

The woman who was entering the vault as Liska was leaving seemed mildly surprised someone was in there but not astounded. They shared a quick, professional nod, and both continued on their way.

She 'dropped' the keycard in an unwatched corner and took a different route back to the bathroom. It didn't stop her from overhearing someone complaining about losing *another* keycard, and how they would probably get chewed out for it. She had thought he seemed the careless type. Good to see she was right. Maybe he'd find it later. Liska would have dropped it back off, but she couldn't come up with a good reason for taking the same exact path, stopping by the same desk.

Liska was three minutes late getting back to the bathroom. Had Todd left, or had he waited? She had told him to go, but she had a feeling he was going to be, as Father put it, 'stupidly loyal'.

He was there and mouthed the word 'Clear'. "You were supposed to leave." She didn't give him a chance to respond. "Give me five minutes." She could hear him say something, but she ignored it to focus on changing back. Switching out her uniform for her dress was quick enough, but removing the wig and fixing her hair into something that resembled a deliberate hairstyle instead of a rat's nest took longer. Compressing the uniform into something that would fit back into her pouch took even longer.

Hiding it back here wouldn't work; how would she get it back? It was all things she could replace easily, but it had her fingerprints, her hair, her DNA all over it. So she couldn't leave it here. Hmm.

Liska walked out the door, tearing down the sign as she did so. The sign could be thrown away. "Do you have any interior pockets in that suit jacket?"

Todd blinked at her in confusion. "No?"

She looked between the packet and Todd again. It wasn't a form fitting jacket. "Can you tuck this under your shirt in the back? Just until we get out of here."

Todd took it with a frown. "Why is it wet?"

Liska rolled her eyes, and ducked back in the restroom for some paper towels. Good thing there were no cameras by the restrooms. She had checked that too.

Todd took the package back after it was dry and tucked it down his shirt like she had asked. "What is this, anyway? It's definitely not just clothes."

"Tell you later. Do we need to stick around, or can we go now?"

"We can leave."

"Good. I'll explain everything when we get to Ryoko-*Sensei's*."

***

Todd managed to hold his curiosity until they were in the car and moving. "Did you find out who attacked me?"

"No."

"So, it didn't work?" All this effort for nothing?

"Did I say that?"

"Well, no."

"Then don't assume." She continued looking straight ahead, no sign of anything. Her fingers were tracing the sides of the pouch he had given back to her when they got to the car.

"So it did work?"

"Did I say *that*?"

"Not really."

"Then don't assume. I don't know who attacked you, but I know what and who they're working for."

Well, that was something. "So I was attacked by a non-human?"

"Yes."

"Anything I would know about?"

"I said I would explain at Ryoko-*Sensei's* house."

"Right, sorry."

"I've figured out what I'm doing wrong." Sakaki seemed to be reading the street signs.

"What?"

"You have lots of questions and I keep answering most of them. That gives you the impression I will keep doing so."

Todd laughed. "Is it getting annoying?"

"There's another one."

"Sorry."

"It's not too bad, but some of them are personal."

"Okay, I'll try to stop making you uncomfortable. Just keep in mind, unless I really have to know, no one is forcing you to answer."

Sakaki's answer was a half shrug.

This wasn't a good time to ask, but he had to know. "Can I try sticking my hand in the hornet's nest again?"

"Can you?"

"Do I have your permission?'

"You may try, though I don't know why you'd want to."

"Who was Tisiphone?" He couldn't explain why he wanted to know, but he couldn't shake the idea that it was important. That if he knew the answer, other things would make sense. It was probably stupid. After all, it wasn't like he knew any assassins. He hoped.

Sakaki leaned back suddenly as if she had been stung herself. Before he could ask if she was alright, she spoke in a mechanical, emotionless voice. "Ask me no questions and I'll tell you know lies. Where ignorance is bliss, 'tis folly to be wise."

"Does that mean you won't tell me?" Todd asked, hoping she'd stop looking so much like she had been chiseled from ice. Even fury would be better than this. Maybe.

"It certainly does. You do not need that information at this moment. If it becomes necessary you know, I'll tell you. Not before then."

"Not even a hint?"

"You are dangerously close to getting stung."

"Fine, fine. I've got to stop talking to you in the car. It leads to difficult conversations."

"No, the conversations are more or less like the others we have had since you found out about the whole Twilight thing. The difference is that there is no distance. Neither can leave to calm down. Besides, I think you subconsciously consider this your territory, so you don't back down as quickly and press your points farther."

"Maybe. Which way do I turn to get to your Uncle's?"

"Right on Hydrangea."

***

The rest of the ride was silent except for directions. Liska was able to concentrate on forcing her claws back into fingernails and toenails. She just barely managed it before they arrived.

Ryoko-*Sensei* greeted them quietly, not saying a word until both were inside, and was immediately in business mode. While Todd's uncle had watched them, he tried to be subtle about it. *Sensei* didn't bother with subtle, knowing Liska would know anyway. As for Todd, Liska thought he was trying to intimidate Todd slightly. From the smell of things, it was working. Or he was just nervous about what she may have seen.

"What did you see?"

"Tea first?" Liska asked, partially because she wanted some, and partially to get back for all the times he insisted that she have tea before he told her what she wanted to know. *Sensei* shook his head, sighed to let the world know how put upon he was, and went to make some tea.

As she took her third tea cake, Todd spoke up. "You just ate; how can you be hungry already?"

Liska swallowed her cake. "In the wild, wolves have large stomachs. When they can find it, they eat enough to make up for times when they can't. Foxes, on the other hand, have small stomachs. About big enough for a small rodent. It means that they eat small meals frequently. Now, our stomachs aren't the size of a fox's, but they are smaller than yours. So, I don't eat a lot at a time, but I will be hungry two hours later." Another reason for her habit of caching food for later.

"Ah, sorry."

"You apologize too much."

"Sor..."

She couldn't help it, she giggled slightly. Ryoko-*Sensei* gave her a look. She covered her giggle by finishing her tea. This, however, left her with no more room to stall. "Everyone done? Good. I need to explain what happened. I did see through another's eyes, but there wasn't much to see. I also picked up thoughts as well. I have a theory as to why, but we'll go into that later. As I suspected, this was an attempt to frame me. Your attacker, he?" She shrugged. No way to tell, nor did it matter. "He had been waiting for you to come in. Eating chocolate while he waited. He was very eager for this, anticipating the blood especially, but also killing you. He's not working alone, because he kept thinking of his master, Atolatar. I'm ninety-five to ninety-eight percent sure it was a shade, so Atolatar is probably a vampire. Any questions?"

"Okay, I'm going to go out on a limb here and assume that since this guy tried to kill me, I'm actually entitled to some information. What are shades? How do you know this is a shade? Who is Atolatar and how do you know he's a vampire? Will that do for a start?"

Liska ignored the sarcasm. "Let's start with shades. Shades are... well, it's difficult to define. No one is quite sure what they are. They aren't quite alive, not like we are at least. Their whole existence is entwined with death. In fact, some say they come from death. As far as we can tell, they don't actually reproduce on their own. They just appear, usually in an area where there were violent deaths, or at least one violent death. Some think they are the spirits of those who died, but there's nothing to prove that, and a few things to suggest otherwise. On their own, they do very little and do not go far from the place they originated from. About seven hundred years ago or so, vampires learned that they could get shades to act as servants. A shade on its own may have no ambition, but when promised blood and an opportunity to commit violence, that shade will usually follow that person to the ends of the earth. No one knows why they are so obsessed with blood and death, but it seems to be an inherent trait in shades."

Todd shivered and hunched forward slightly. Not that she could blame him, but he didn't even know the worst of it yet. "What do the vampires get out of it?"

"Servants with undying loyalty. Spies. A shade can become invisible, preventing most people from ever realizing that there is a shade around.

Shades can go out in daylight, something vampires really do have trouble with. Though it seems to have more to do with UV radiation than direct sunlight. I digress. A shade is a perfect scapegoat. Order the shade to do something and then deny any connection to it. If ordered to keep secrecy, a shade will never talk. They also don't have fingerprints, so it's hard to tell when a shade has done something."

Yes, he was definitely more frightened now. "Can shades be killed?"

Liska waved her hand in a 'so-so' gesture. "In a way. As I said, they seem to be the result of violent death. If you can figure out the particulars of which death, you may be able to put things to rest. Burying a body, consecrating a field, etc. Purified salt works pretty well too. Also, killing the one who gives the shade orders neutralizes the shade."

"I thought you said, you didn't believe them to be spirits of the dead. So why would that work?"

Liska shrugged. "They have absolutely no connection with the life of those who died. No interest in the survivors or family, or even revenge for the death. One prominent theory is that it leaves a residue or a stain that some weak spirit entity harnesses, maybe channels. Perhaps that's why it works. It's really hard to study shades."

"Okay, how did you know it's a shade?"

"The thought processes. If you ever find yourself unfortunate enough to hear a shade speak, you'll notice they seem to have the capacity of a mentally deficient three-year-old. They have obsessions, mostly with blood, death, violence, and their master. I tried getting some information from a shade once, and in the twenty minutes I talked to it, I don't think its vocabulary exceeded thirty-five words. Mostly it kept saying the same thing in various ways. This one did mention making Atolatar happy. I'm not sure who he is, except that he's number one on the Purifier's hit list."

Todd frowned at the mention of the Purifiers. "They don't know what he is either?"

"They aren't the most accurate sources. They think I'm a Werewolf."

"Wait, they know about you?"

"Not nearly as much as they think they know." Liska waved it off. "Anyway, if he's using a shade, odds are good that Atolatar is a vampire. Especially if you consider the chocolate."

Ryoko-*Sensei* nodded while Todd looked at her confused. "Chocolate?"

"Okay, for some reason, or perhaps various reasons, most Twilights, not including Espers, do not like chocolate. Many can't eat it at all, like most Weres. One notable exception is a particular blood of vampires that very much enjoys chocolate."

"Blood?"

"That's what we call a group of vampires. Well, my skulk calls them that. They may well call themselves something different. If so, they haven't shared and don't seem to mind being called a blood."

"So, you know what blood Atolatar is in?" Todd leaned forward, excited.

"Maybe." Liska held up a hand to calm him. "There was a split in the blood a few years back, so he might be in the main blood or the offshoot. Also, it is not impossible that someone trained a shade, including getting them to like chocolate to cast suspicion on them."

"Is that likely?"

"Likely? No, not really. But it is possible. Either way, we have a place to start. Actually, I'm going to look up some things while I'm here." She started to stand before looking at Todd. "You can go home if you like. I may be awhile."

"How would you get home?"

"I can walk. Or Ryoko-*Sensei* can drive me." Liska didn't look away from the computer.

To her surprise, the older Werefox disagreed. "Actually, it might be wise to stay together, especially at night."

Todd swallowed hard and nodded. "Yeah, vampires and invisible assassins. I think I'll stay here."

Liska bit her lip to keep from laughing. He had a legitimate concern. "I don't think you are actually much at risk. I don't believe Atolatar truly..." She stopped typing and stared at the screen.

"Liska? What is it?" *Sensei* asked, concerned.

"The top three on the Purifier's hit list are, in order, Atolatar, Luna Liska, and Tisiphone.

Chapter Thirty-Two

Choose your friends with caution and your allies with care. –
The Kikitsutai Book of Wisdom

"Um, what exactly does this mean?" Todd asked.
"I truly couldn't say. Nothing good, I'm sure."
Liska glared at the screen.
"What do they know of Atolatar?" *Sensei*
asked.
"Not much. He's keeping a low profile, but
actions suggest he's leading up to something. He
also seems to have a ruthless disdain of humans. But
they can't even pinpoint a location, just whispers of
rumors and rumors of whispers." Liska huffed then
started another search.
"What are you doing now?" Todd asked.
"A general search on 'Atolatar'. What have
other people heard? What does the name mean?
What language is it? Where are his rumors most
prominent? Things like that."
"The name?"
"Sure. I doubt his parents named him that.
He probably chose it, which means it has meaning
for him. The name you choose for yourself means
more than the one you were born with. Take 'Luna

Liska' for example. That means Moon Fox. Liska is Czech for 'fox'."

"Why did you choose that?" Even *Sensei* looked interested in her answer.

"Honestly, I liked the name."

"Doesn't it give too much away?" Todd asked.

"Not really. I mean, 'fox' is a common code name. Unlike say 'Atolatar' which apparently means 'Hateful Venom' in Anglo-Saxon. Hmm."

"Maybe he, or she, took the name when they became a vampire?"

Point. Other than the Purifier's website, they didn't have proof about Atolatar being male. "Good point about the gender. The name part is possible but unlikely. Eighty-five percent of all current vampires were born vampires. If they weren't effectively immortal, the percentage would be higher. But vampires live a long time and they only cracked down on regulations a few centuries ago."

"Immortal?" She could feel Todd shiver.

"Unless the heart is destroyed. Then they turn to ash. Anything else they can survive and heal from. It is possible for a human to kill a vampire and you don't need a wooden stake to do it, but I wouldn't recommend it." She gave Todd a look. "I think you may want a UV flashlight. Just in case."

"That helps?"

"Won't kill them, but it will weaken them. And shows them you aren't easy prey. Might be enough to change their minds."

"Right, changing the subject before I become a gibbering wreck. Vampires reproduce? Like have baby vampires?"

"Not quite, but close. Why is this a surprise?"

"I thought they just turned people into vampires."

Liska went back to her search. "Too much paperwork involved."

"Paperwork?"

"Yes. In order to get permission to turn a human into a vampire, you have to fill out a ton of forms, in triplicate. That's their way of trying to keep down requests. You don't even want to know the penalty for turning someone without the proper paperwork done first."

"Paperwork. I must admit, I hoped there were better safeguards than that."

"I've seen their paperwork. It's enough to stop all but the most dedicated. Believe me, the most complicated lawyer-speak in the world is simpler and clearer than a vampire contract. They also reserve the right to turn down requests without specifying why."

"But, seriously, paperwork?"

"Vampires have a depth of loyalty that most humans don't truly understand. Particularly since that loyalty is not always willing. A turned vampire's deepest, first loyalty will always be to the one who turned him. The young are wraiths who must drink the blood of a vampire to become full vampires. Their loyalty will be to that vampire. They may not like that person. They may be unwilling. But their loyalty will lie there until one of their deaths. An unauthorized turning is a serious offence and often ends in the death of both." Liska looked at Todd, allowing herself to think briefly of the Blood Hunts, the arena fights, and some of the other ways vampires had been known to deal with the rare traitor.

Todd shivered and changed the subject quickly. "So how was there a split in that one blood?"

Liska turned back to the computer. "The leader died. That changes a lot of loyalties. Leaves a vacuum."

"Why is Liska number two on this list if one and three are so dangerous?"

"Because Liska is more mainstream, even hired by the Days sometimes. The demon who seems to be on your side can be more dangerous than the one clearly against you. And no one knows anything about Atolatar!"

"No one who is posting anything, anyway," *Sensei* pointed out.

"Yes, we'll have to ask around now. At least we have a starting point." The Werefoxes exchanged a look. They knew this step and knew it well.

"Ask who?"

"I thought I'd try calling information." Todd stared at her. "I have some contacts with the local blood. They may or may not tell me anything, but I can certainly ask."

"I thought Weres and vampires didn't get along?"

"Forget the movies. It isn't that simple. We actually have sort of an uneasy truce. We are in similar situations, and can and do work together, but there is little in the way of trust. Our mindsets are different and our blood fights each other. Both vampires and Weres can inter-mate with humans but not with each other. The offspring doesn't survive more than a couple months in utero. A Were cannot be turned into a vampire. They would die in agony as the Were blood and vampire blood intermingles. The vampire might not survive either, drinking too much Were blood."

Todd clearly had loads more questions, but as Ryoko-*Sensei* pointed out, it was getting late. Time for sleep.

***

Todd tried to escort Liska back to her room, but she insisted on walking him back to his. She would actually know if shades were around, something he couldn't know. Come morning, she would have to see what could be done about that. Once that was done, Liska went to her room.

Yes, it had been heavily implied that she should sleep, but this was more important. Liska dialed a number that she hadn't even told Ryoko-*Sensei*, the number she had hacked into the local telephone company to make sure it didn't get cut off. It was hard for vampires to hold a day job. Anyway, she preferred being able to call than to visit whenever she wanted information.

"Hello, Van?"

"Who is this?"

How many other people used this number? "Liska."

"What's wrong now?"

Liska smiled at the slight irritation in Van's voice. "What makes you think something's wrong?"

"We don't exactly get together for social interaction. We only contact each other when something's wrong. Or when you need information?"

"I need information."

"The usual?"

"This may be bigger. I may need permission from your chief."

"He doesn't like you."

He didn't either. Liska wasn't sure why, but it went deeper than the usual Were/vampire tension. "Does he like the fact that I keep him and his blood from being exposed to Days?"

"What is this about?"

"Atolatar." Silence. "Van? You there?"

"Come by tonight, around one. You know where, right?" Liska took a quick look at the clock. Thirty minutes. She'd be cutting it close. That was probably deliberate.

"Of course." It was hard to hide a vampire den, especially from a Were.

Van took this as confirmation and hung up. So she did know something. Something that had her very on edge. If Liska was to go to the den, then Van must plan for her to see the chief. Who honestly did not like her. What fun.

***

Liska arrived about five minutes early, but Van was waiting anyway. The pale, slight vampire was uncharacteristically silent, and twitchy. This might be bigger than Liska had initially suspected.

Van was a turned vampire, one of the few Liska knew of. Born Vanessa, last name unknown, sometime in the eighteen hundreds, she had taken to being a vampire well. Apparently the first thing she did was decide to go by Van. Names were important, so Liska made sure to call her that.

The fact that she had been human meant she often had a different perspective on things, including not having an innate distrust of Weres, or the prejudice that vampires were superior to humans. That made her an ideal contact for Liska.

"Follow me."

Liska gave her a slight nod and followed into the building. From the outside, it was a dilapidated, unmarked building, presumably for offices. There was a reception area, manned by the wraiths who could take sunlight and radiation better than full vampires. They were the ones to turn away the curious, the lost, and the salespeople.

Two wraiths manned the desk. The lobby was dingy, poorly lit, and certainly not meant to be welcoming. Both wraiths eyed them carefully but said nothing as Van led Liska down a corridor, then inside the Heart of the Blood.

Stepping through that door was like stepping into a different world. It was dark here, lit only by scattered candles. Tapestries hung on the walls, rich and vivid. Liska doubted the vampires could smell the mold. Could they hear the skittering of spiders and other insects, that even she couldn't see in the darkness?

Music was playing, somewhere. A harp? The scent of blood permeated the air, many different kinds. Including a little human.

Liska straightened and kept her face emotionless. This was a danger zone. Do not forget that. She had been invited, that included safe passage out. Provided she followed their rules. The rules that were a tangled mess of tradition and custom that would make the Gordian knot seem like a simple slip knot.

Van's route was not clear-cut and was designed to confuse. She had probably been ordered to do that. Of course, being sensitive to the magnetic pole, Liska had a rough compass in her head at all times. No need to mention that.

Finally, she was led to the inner chamber. Seated on an ornate chair, that was undoubtedly as black as they could make it, was the Chief. A tall man, wearing silk and velvet, plus at least five rings. A vain man, and proud. Liska had never learned his name, but he tended to call himself *Rex Magnus*. Great King.

There was a goblet in his hand, the scent of blood unmistakable. Human blood, at least some of it. If Liska criticized, then she was in violation of the rules of guests. Her protection would be stripped away, or she would be allowed to leave only by the 'great mercy' of the chief. He was goading her. Or at least testing her.

She bowed as she approached. "Great Chief, may the nights be long and prosperous."

"And may the moon ever be generous to you." A little different from the traditional greeting, but more fitting because she was a Were. Rex stood, looking down in a regal pose. "You seek information on Atolatar?"

"Yes."

"Why? What reason have you to get involved? To interfere?"

"I have been drawn in. Atolatar attempted to kill a friend of mine, to frame me. Perhaps even more. Besides, it is my job." The Kikitsutai had worked for centuries to keep balance between Days, Twilights, and Nights. Not everyone liked that, but it was generally considered better than the alternative.

She kept deliberately silent on Atolatar's gender. If Atolatar was female and Rex knew that, then if she said male, he'd know she didn't know anything. Never let on how much or how little you know.

"Perhaps. Or perhaps it is meddling. If it wasn't for one of your kind, Atolatar might not be out there now."

That was news. "May I ask why you say that, Great Chief?"

With a snort, Rex moved closer, pacing. The royal pose was gone. "He was a member of the Lyonoko blood." Liska nodded, having figured that out. "The Lyonoko blood followed the controversial teachings of Ryasmus."

"Peaceful integration of Days, Nights, and Twilights," Liska confirmed.

"You disagree?"

He wanted a particular answer, but she wasn't sure what answer that was. "A lovely dream. I fear, though, it is not easy to accomplish."

"No doubt." His lip curled, fangs peeking out. "Tisiphone considered the dream too dangerous and killed him. A leaderless blood is a dangerous thing. Some looked on Ryasmus as a martyr, trying to follow his path. Others believe that his mistake had been pacifism and they must take recognition by force. In the past year, Atolatar has taken head of this group."

Right, this was bad. Unless she was misreading him, even Rex was worried about this. "Where?"

He waved a hand, rings glinting in the candlelight. "I know not. Nor do I know why I should tell you if I did."

"If, as you say, it was the meddling of one my kind that started this, then is it not merely right that another one fixes it?"

There was no immediate answer. The vampire chief stared into the candle light as if transfixed. "They say you are the one to have killed Tisiphone."

"Do they?"

Rex gave a toss of his head. "Why would you do such a thing?"

"All I can say on the matter is that I would not do such a thing unless I felt it truly necessary."

Rex gave no answer to this.

"Do you know why Tisiphone killed Ryasmus?"

"If you do not, how could we hope to? I imagine she was paid to do so. Was she not a common assassin?"

Liska bit her tongue, literally. She wanted to argue with him that Tisiphone was not just some common assassin. But why did she object so strongly? Besides, arguing with the chief was not a good idea. She was still a guest. Being rude to the host might be enough to forfeit her protection. "Do you know who Atolatar was before this?"

"No. He, his past and weaknesses, are now known only to him. Ryasmus or Tisiphone might have known, but I doubt either could give you an answer now."

"You," *fear*, "distrust Atolatar, nearly as much as I do. I have told you my reasons, what of yours?" That was borderline impertinence. Careful. It wouldn't take much to be declared in violation of the rules of being a guest.

Rex stalked over to her with a swish of his cape. "You even ask? He is mad! He makes mockery of our way of life and endangers us all. He would strip us of our traditions, our protections, everything!"

In the candlelight, she could see that the cape was moth-eaten. The rings were costume jewelry. The silk was stained and the velvet was velour. Even the chair was painted, not black wood. This was the 'wealth' of the vampires.

"Yes, you are right. I must take my leave. May your hunting always be plentiful." She bowed.

"To you as well."

Liska let Van lead her out, wondering how much more damage and disrepair was hiding in the dark. "He means the best, for all of us," Van surprised her by saying as she left.

"I know." But that way was dying. It couldn't be sustained forever. Neither could the Kikitsutai. Yet the way forward... it couldn't be done. The alternative was even worse. Wasn't it?

She spent the ride to Ryoko-*Sensei*'s house to drop off the motorcycle and the remainder of the walk home, Liska pondered the questions in her head. It wasn't the first time she had such thoughts, and it wouldn't be the last. But she had no answers. Never did.

She didn't tonight either, as she got back to her room and realized someone was already there.

Chapter Thirty-Three

Matters of the heart must be given careful thought as well. –
The Kikitsutai Book of Wisdom

"You know, it's generally considered rude to enter a person's living quarters without their permission. Especially if they aren't there." Liska glared at the intruder.

Korvou shrugged back, looking unconcerned. "You weren't here."

"Yes, I do believe that was my point."

Korvou didn't answer her.

"It's late. I've had a busy day and am not interested in sparring with you. If you aren't here to try to kill me, then say your piece and get out."

"And you said I was rude."

"You are rude, and this is my room." Her territory that he had no right to without her permission. Unfortunately, a borrowed college dorm room that she had lived in less than three months and had no attachment to wasn't 'home' enough to keep him out. No real 'threshold'. Not unless she lined the door and walls with iron or steel and there was no way to do that and keep her security deposit.

"I heard about Yoshiro."

Wow, she had been so busy, she had almost forgotten about him. "Of course you heard about Yoshiro. Everyone's heard about Yoshiro. I've received condolence notes from Peru to Mongolia." Well actually, it was emails. There were two, one from Peru, and one from Mongolia.

"I think he might still have a place in this."

Great. Yoshiro was one of the last people she wanted contact with. "Or maybe his leaving was his place."

"The possibility exists." Korvou nodded to concede the point.

"Tell me, have you ever heard of someone who calls himself Atolatar?" Liska asked on a hunch.

Korvou paused and looked down absently, trying to think. "Not that I can recall. More information?"

"Vampire, formerly of the Lyonoko blood. Left when they split, seems to be a leader of the offshoot."

Korvou closed his eyes suddenly, as if in pain. Liska waited. This was how he usually reacted when certain pieces came into place.

"I think—" He cut off suddenly.

KNOCK! KNOCK! KNOCK!

"I think you'd better answer your door."

***

Todd sighed, hoping he wasn't making a nuisance of himself. He knew it was late, but her light was on.

Hopefully she was still awake. He tried knocking quietly but wasn't sure if he succeeded.

Sakaki opened the door quickly, and she was still dressed though she had changed into jeans and a t-shirt. "Todd? What on earth are you doing here? You're supposed to stay inside after dark, not go wandering about at two, sorry, three in the morning."

He winced. "Sorry, I didn't realize it was that late. But you're still awake, right?"

Sakaki sighed. "No, Todd. I'm asleep. I always walk and talk in my sleep. I even answer the door in my sleep. Don't you?"

She seemed stressed. "Is this a bad time?"

"Yes. Come on in."

Todd entered the room and froze when he spotted the other male in the room, lounging on the bed. "Um, hi?" What had he interrupted?

"Right. Todd, Korvou. Korvou, Todd. You're both Twilights."

Korvou stood up, and up, he was at least six-foot-four. His hair was as black as any crow, his skin pale, and his features angular. He moved like a predator, eying potential prey. After a moment, he let out a, 'hmm', leaving Todd to feel he had been sized up and found wanting.

Perhaps that wasn't surprising. Todd was only about five-eleven, and while he could generally take care of himself, he certainly didn't exude an aura of danger like this guy did. While not stocky or heavy, Todd knew he had gotten a bit out of shape since his injury. Sandy brown hair and a typical tan finished this picture. If this Korvou was Sakaki's type, then he didn't stand a chance. Who was this guy, and what was he doing here?

Sakaki said she wasn't involved with anyone right now, but she might not tell him if that changed. Or if she was seeing someone she wasn't supposed to be with. He was sitting on her bed. But there was only one chair in the place. Both Korvou and Sakaki were fully dressed and neither looked like they had thrown clothes on in a hurry. But why come here at three in the morning? On the other hand, he had a perfectly legitimate reason to be here at three in the morning. Well, semi-legitimate.

"So, who are you exactly?" Todd asked, only slightly surprised that this Korvou guy started to say the same thing at the same time.

"An annoying thorn in my side," Answered Sakaki from the kitchenette. She must have gone in while the two men were staring at each other. In fact, now that he thought about it, he seemed to recall hearing her muttering something about needing tea.

Korvou smirked. "If that's what he is, then what am I?"

A wet tea bag hit him in the side of the neck. "Target practice."

"You know, attacking when I'm not looking isn't very honorable." Korvou rubbed at his neck.

"Neither is going in a lady's room in her absence."

"What are you doing here?" Todd asked.

"I could ask you the same."

"At least I waited to be invited in," Todd retorted, eyes narrowed.

"Yes, at three in the morning. How did you know she would be awake?" Korvou's eyes were pinpricks through furrowed brows.

"Her light was on."

"How often do you come by for a midnight tryst?"

"That's none of your business," Sakaki said, coming in with a tray holding three mugs of tea.

"How often do *you* come by in the night?" Todd asked, ignoring the Werefox offering him a cup of tea.

"That's none of *your* business." Sakaki continued, glaring at him.

"You do realize that your being here could be considered impinging on her honor, don't you?" Korvou asked.

"And what about your visits?"

"Boys..." Sakaki started, sounding weary and annoyed.

"I have done nothing I would be ashamed to have known," Korvou answered.

"Neither have I."

"I won't be ashamed of what I do to the two of you if you don't knock it off, either."

"So why are you here?" Todd repeated.

"Why don't you tell me first?"

"Why don't you both leave?" She was ignored. Again.

"I believe I asked before you did."

"Perhaps, perhaps not." Korvou didn't back down and looked like he was enjoying himself.

It was then that Todd got the sudden urge to duck. Doing so, he saw Korvou hit in the head with a pillow that Sakaki was wielding. It would have hit him in the face if he hadn't moved. Sakaki whacked him with it anyway. "Okay, you two, listen up! Neither of you are in a relationship with me or have any dishonorable purpose in being here. You both came to talk, right? Fine, talk or leave, I don't care. But I refuse to be part of a territorial dispute! Besides, it may be just a college dorm room, but for now, this is my home, and you are my guests. Sort of. I have even offered refreshment. Could you please respect me and my home?"

Todd was pretty sure he was blushing, but this Korvou actually winced. "Sorry."

Korvou gave a slight bow. "You are right. I apologize. It will not happen again. As for tonight..." Korvou looked at Todd again, as if trying to read something in him. His eyes unfocussed slightly. Then they focused again and he smirked. "Who am I to stand in the way of destiny? I bid you both good night." With that he walked past Todd and through the door. The closed door.

Todd blinked at the door a few times. "Did he just..."

"Yes."

"What is he?"

"An annoyance."

"Not what I meant."

"Fae. And all that goes with it. He'll never lie but never trust anything he says at plain reading. Also, word to the wise; never, ever, utter the words 'I wish' in front of a fae. Any fae. Even if they like you, and want to help you, they cannot resist messing around a little."

"Um, okay. So, what exactly is he to you?"

Liska drained her tea, looked at the spare mug for a moment, then decided to drink that one too. "Complicated. We're sworn to kill each other, but we've worked together far more times. I'd regret it if he died, and I think he might feel the same towards me. I'm pretty sure that at this point, neither of us would seriously try to kill the other unless ordered to. There are times, though."

"But you two aren't..."

"No. There has never been and never will be anything between us. In fact, for a fae, Korvou is still very young. It will probably be another couple centuries before he's even interested in anyone in that way."

"Okay, good."

Sakaki raised an eyebrow at that. "I fail to see how either my or Korvou's potential relationships is any of your concern."

"Well, I... I guess it isn't." Come on, tell her. There might never be another chance. She didn't look welcoming though. If he didn't tell her now, who knew when he'd get the courage to try again? "It may not be my business. But I'd like it to be."

Her face became stone. "What do you mean?"

"I," *think I love you*, "am extremely attracted to you. I care about you a lot. I like you a lot. More than a friend. I was wondering," *if you could love me too*, "if there was any chance you could eventually feel the same way?"

Sakaki sighed bitterly and turned away from him. "No."

"Why not?" Todd tried to keep his despair out of his voice. He didn't think he was very successful.

"Werefoxes mate for life. We only fall in love once in our lifetimes. We are only *capable* of falling in love once. And when we do, it is forever. No matter what happens to that other person. Should that person die, or leave, or betray me, I will still love them; never able to give that love to someone else."

Had she fallen in love with someone else? "You haven't..."

"Never. I've never dared. Honestly, I'm not sure I ever will. Love is frightening, painful, and dangerous. Love is beyond me. I can like you as a friend, but I cannot fall in love."

"After all you've done, all you continue to do, how can you be afraid of love? You aren't afraid of pain or danger."

"You're right, I'm not. But they can only hurt my body. That's as much as anyone can do without my permission. I grant no one the power to hurt my soul."

"Is that so? What about Kira, and your parents, and your other relatives? Can't they hurt you inside?"

"I can't choose my family. I was never given that option."

"You love them, right?"

"Of course. But that's different."

"How so?"

"They are my family. I have to love them. I can choose not to be that vulnerable to someone else."

"Someday you are going to realize that love isn't a weakness."

"Someday you are going to realize that I'm not worth it! I'm cold, hard, bitter, ruthless and inhuman. The impossible love story may work in books, but in real life it only leads to heartache. You'll change your mind, and you can walk away. You'll never forget me, but you can fall in love again. If I fall in love, that's it for me. I'll never be the same again."

"No one is ever the same after love. I won't change my mind and I'm willing to take the chance."

"You will, and I'm not."

There was silence for a while at that. He couldn't do much except respect her choice. The risks were greater for her than for him.

"Why did you come here tonight, Todd? Please don't tell me it was to confess your undying devotion," She asked in a tired voice.

"No, um, I just wanted to know what to do about vampires or shades. Since I can't see the shades, and I imagine I can't fight off a vampire."

"You might be able to, but I wouldn't recommend it." Sakaki went to her closest and started to pull some things out. "Here, UV flashlight, carry it around whenever you go out. This is blessed salt. Put some on your thresholds, it will keep out shades and might give vampires pause. You can try a little garlic, but it actually isn't that useful. Don't invite strangers into your room. Oh, and wear this. I can't promise it will help, but it's supposed to be a protection charm." She handed him the items without looking at him.

"Thanks. You really think this will help?"

"You've been left alone this long, I doubt he'll go after you again. He probably doesn't believe you to be worth the effort. But if he does, this should help. Especially if you don't do stupid things like wandering around by yourself at night. Get security to escort you back. You aren't far from their office."

"Right. Thanks again." She still wasn't looking at him. "Goodnight?"

"Goodnight, Todd."

He left then. As he left, he saw her through the window, staring sadly into a mirror.

Chapter Thirty-Four

Those who know you, know your sorrow. – The Kikitsutai
Book of Wisdom

Ryoko was slightly surprised that Liska called him instead of coming over, as she usually did. Perhaps she was simply tired. Or perhaps she was hiding something.

"You talked to the local blood last night." It wasn't a question and he didn't bother giving his grandniece the time to answer or lie. "I was trying to give you a chance to rest."

"You know me, *Sensei.* Once I have an answer to a problem; I have to follow as long as I can. You knew I would."

He huffed softly. "Yes, I did. Can't blame me for hoping though."

"You sent us home early so I'd have time to contact them."

"Am I that transparent?"

"Am I?"

"Sakaki, child, I know you better than you know yourself." There was a bit too much truth there.

"Oh, really?" There was an edge of challenge there, but only an edge. He was her respected elder, after all.

"Well, in some ways. Other ways, you can be harder to understand than quantum mechanics. But enough of that. What did you learn?"

"Atolatar was indeed from the Lyonoko blood before the split. He is the current leader of the new group, the one that feels that Ryasmus's mistake was pacifism."

"I see. Do they have a location?"

"Not so as they told me. No location, no past. Nothing."

"Pity we can't ask Tisiphone," Ryoko said carefully.

"Yeah, well, unless you want to try a Ouija board, we're stuck without her."

"Quite." He pulled the phone away and covered it to let out a shaky breath.

"Say, you may have a point."

Ryoko froze. Now what?

"Tisiphone supposedly came back not long after Atolatar started making waves. Todd got a note saying that Tisiphone was involved in his attack, which we now know was done at Atolatar's orders. What if they're linked somehow?"

There was a thought. "The possibility exists, but right now we have no proof."

"Not yet." Ryoko could hear furious typing on the other end of the phone and remained quiet for whatever his grandniece was up to. "Ah-ha! According to the Purifier's website, at least three of the last five Tisiphone 'sightings' were within a fifty mile radius of Atolatar's suspected location. Then they lost sight of Atolatar."

"A little strong for coincidence, but it isn't proof yet. "Ryoko answered, opening his email inbox. Sure enough, there was an email from Liska in under a moment.

"A little out of my normal range. Do you have any contacts in any of those areas?"

Ryoko increased the magnification so he could read it. "Checking... yes. Romania. I have a contact in Romania who might be useful."

"Romania's as good a guess as any. Wasn't the original Lyonoko blood in Switzerland? If he couldn't stay too close, and didn't want to go too far, he would probably stay in Europe. But aren't there two other powerful bloods in Romania?"

"Yes. So he probably didn't set up there. But he may have some help there. Do you know the exact location of the original Lyonoko blood?"

"That information may have died with Tisiphone. Especially if they moved afterwards."

"Why would Atolatar resurrect Tisiphone?" Ryoko wondered aloud.

"Not sure. If she truly is responsible for the death of his mentor, than he probably has ample reason to hate her. Maybe to ruin her reputation? The new Tisiphone is ten times worse than the old one. Or maybe he's trying to intimidate others. If he claims to have her under his thumb, that increases his reputation."

"Perhaps. I've emailed my contact. The only thing we can do now is wait." Now came the true test. "Did anything else happen last night?"

"Like what?" Something did happen.

"You aren't sounding like yourself." *And you're hiding something.* She wouldn't tell him. He was sure of it. Anything she did tell him, he would be honor-bound to inform her father.

"I'm tired. I didn't sleep well. Perhaps that's it."

"Perhaps." Time to do a little digging. "Did you have fun at the dance?"

Brief silence. "It had its moments. We were successful in our objective. That's what matters." Her voice was as clinical as she could make it.

Oh dear. "And that Kendo boy?"

"His name is Todd. What about him?" She had never said anything about the boy's name before. This wasn't good.

"Did he understand your reasons?"

"Of course."

"And he knows that there is a very wide gap between you two?" From the first time he met the boy, he could tell the Esper was attracted to his grandniece. There was no way Liska didn't know. The sooner he understood the impossibility of anything happening, the better for everyone.

"He knows." There was absolutely nothing in her voice.

"Sakaki?"

"If it's quite alright, *Sensei*, I'm rather tired. Can we talk later?"

"Certainly. Take care of yourself."

"You as well."

The aging ninja shook his head sadly as he hung up the phone. Liska was on the edge of something possibly more dangerous than she had ever been in; and there was absolutely nothing he could do about it. Perhaps it was time to talk to Sejou.

***

She ought to be resting. It was the sensible thing to do. Resting or investigating, doing something productive. Maybe practicing her *katas* so she would be in good shape if trouble came. Or homework. School wasn't slacking off just because she was concerned about vampires and phantom notes.

Instead, Liska sat on the edge of a parking lot directly over water, staring into the intracoastal, hugging one leg while letting the other swing. Every once in a while, she'd scoop up a rock or several and throw them into the water.

Other than that, she just stared. There were fish swimming in the water, occasionally glinting in the sun. Little round jellyfish with no tentacles moved like partially inflated balloons. She could hear the wild parrots in the trees, but they blended too well to see them most of the time. She could smell them though.

A great blue heron waded nearby, walking like something prehistoric. Briefly, Liska wondered what blue looked like, then discarded the thought. While she had gotten a few glimpses of color in her retro-cog visions, she had no way of knowing what color was what and hadn't mentioned it to anyone.

Had she been over sand, she could have watched the fiddler crabs, scrambling in and around the shore. She liked watching the asymmetrical creatures sometimes. The smell of salt and water, permeated with plant and animal smells filled her nose, mostly blocking out the human and machine smells. The heat pushed down like heavy blankets, and despite a cool breeze from the water, she was starting to sweat. There were hints of rain in the air.

But none of that mattered right now. Liska tossed another stone. She had come out here to think. Or perhaps more accurately, not to think. Thinking had kept her up most of the night. That was not so bad in and of itself. If she had been thinking about Atolatar and Tisiphone, while it still would have been foolish, she wouldn't be kicking herself over it. But she hadn't been. Atolatar, Tisiphone, vampires and shades; all of it had barely crossed her mind.

No, her thoughts were on Todd. On how much it hurt to talk to him last night. How much it hurt to hurt him. How when he talked about love, she was almost willing to risk it. But she couldn't.

Liska sighed and looked up at the clouds. Part of her training had been in meteorology. It would rain soon. Perfect. Then she could sit there getting wet. A fool who didn't even know enough to get out of the rain. And she was a fool. Had she really believed that she could keep him from saying anything about his attraction? Did she really believe if they both ignored it, it would go away? Worst of all, did she really believe it was entirely one-sided?

Perhaps the whole confrontation was for the best. A small hurt now to stop agony later. He'd leave it alone now and find someone else. Someone better. Leaving her alone. Again. She threw another rock, even harder.

"So, what happened last night?" Asked an annoyingly familiar voice as someone sat down next to her.

"Hello, Korvou." Was it her imagination or did her voice just sound dead? Maybe he wouldn't notice. While she was dreaming, maybe she could re-do all of yesterday. Or maybe the whole school year.

"That good, huh?"

"Did you want something?"

"I told you what I wanted. To know what happened last night. It was something big, I could tell."

"Nothing happened." Liska didn't bother looking in his direction as she threw another rock.

"Right, and I'm a water nymph. He loves you, doesn't he?" Korvou, the showoff, tossed a stone that skipped four times before sinking. Liska had never managed skipping stones.

"Go away." There was more force in that throw, but the voice was still level.

"He told you he loved you last night, didn't he?"

"What makes you say that?"

"It fits certain patterns. So, what did you say?"

"Would you please leave?" That may be the first time she had ever said 'please' to him. He didn't seem to notice, but she was sure he had.

"Well, you don't seem to be rejoicing in the first blush of love. So you told him no, huh?"

"What do you think I told him? You know it's impossible!"

"Ah-ha! I was right! He does love you."

Maybe it was the sleep deprivation, or perhaps the stress she was under, but Liska snapped under her rotten mood. It was an impulse, but without thinking about it, she shoved him off the edge and into the water.

He stood up, sputtering water and glaring indignantly at her.

"You did say you were a water nymph, didn't you?" Liska shrugged, not feeling an erg of guilt. Weird that he couldn't lie, but he could use sarcasm. Not well, but he could.

"That wasn't nice."

Liska huffed a laugh. "How long have you known me?"

"About four years."

"And what, in that time period, has given you the impression that I'm a nice person?"

"Absolutely nothing."

"There you go." On instinct, Liska looked around. Then she sighed. She was not up to this. "Better get lost. Looks like I've got more company coming."

Korvou swam off somewhere, apparently to a dock. Five minutes later, Shahara sat down in his vacated spot without ceremony. "Alright, what on earth is going on here? What do you think you're doing?"

"Sitting, mostly. Throwing rocks in the water. Care to try?"

"No, I do not care to try! What happened last night?"

"You'll have to narrow that down a bit. Last night was fairly busy."

"All I know is that last night, two of my best friends went on a date with each other. They seemed happy. Today, they seem miserable. I want to know what happened."

"I'm one of your best friends?" Odd. Shahara had lots of friends, on campus and off. Who would have thought that quiet, almost aloof Anna would be on the best friend list? Sure, if Liska was counting friends, Shahara would be one of her best friends at school, but Liska didn't make nearly as many friends as the other girl did.

"Didn't you know that?"

"Can't say I did."

"Well, you are. A fact that won't get you out of answering the question."

"What did Todd say?"

"He won't talk about it."

"Well, if he won't, what makes you think I will?" She launched another rock in time with the 'will'.

"Jamal is working on Todd. I decided to try you." Liska remained quiet. Shahara sighed. "I'm going to have to play Sherlock Holmes, aren't I? Okay, did you have fun at the dance?"

"Yes." Liska was mildly surprised to realize that was completely true.

"Did something happen at the dance?"

Not like you mean. "Not really."

"After the dance then?"

"Shahara, please! I really don't want to talk about it."

"Too bad. You're hurting. Todd's hurting. I'm betting you're avoiding each other, so you won't work this out yourselves. As a best friend, it's my duty to help. You'd make this easier if you'd co-operate."

"It wouldn't make a lot of sense to you. There are too many things I can't talk about."

Shahara's face twisted, and when she spoke, it was softly and with concern. "You can tell me anything, you know? I want to help."

It was all Liska could do not to break out in hysterical laughter. She had no idea. "I appreciate that, I really do. But there are some things that I really, really can't talk about."

"Okay, what can you tell me?"

Liska sighed. Shahara wouldn't leave her alone until she had something believable. Maybe, just maybe, it would help to talk a little about it. Shahara was probably the closest she could find to a neutral party. Now, how could she frame a believable story? "He said he cared for me a great deal and wanted to know if I felt the same."

"Well, duh. I mean, he took you to the fancy ball. Didn't you know?"

"I suspected. I just kept hoping he'd find someone else."

Shahara was grinding her teeth. "If you *knew* he liked you, and you didn't like him, why did you go with him to the dance?"

"I had my own reasons and was entirely up front with those reasons even before I agreed to go."

Shahara lost a little of her fire but was still clearly upset. "What kind of reasons?"

"Way too complicated to go into."

The Jamaican girl bit her lip. She had a suspicion. A suspicion of what, Liska wasn't sure, but since the odds on her figuring out anything close to the truth were miniscule, Liska left it alone. "Okay, we'll drop that one for now. But, unless I'm mistaken, I think you like him too."

"I like him as a friend. That's all I can do."

"No chance of something later?"

"No." She threw another rock and watched it sink. Looked like she scared some fish this time.

"Why? Is there someone else?"

"No, not really."

"Are you into girls?"

Liska burrowed her head into her knee. "If I say yes, can we skip the rest of the lecture?"

"Um... well..." Oh, right. Homosexuality was outlawed in the Bible, and Shahara was a Christian, apparently of the fundamentalist type.

Liska took pity on her, interrupting Shahara's attempt to convince her that she was still her friend. "No. I'm not interested in girls."

"Okay, then what?"

How to explain this? "Do you remember my telling you about growing up in a very insular family, where my father broke tradition by marrying an outsider?"

"Yes."

"I managed, only by the narrowest of margins, to be semi-accepted by most of my family. My insistence on leaving the country to go to school certainly didn't help. If I got involved with an outsider too; well, that's it. I would never be welcome there."

"So what? If they can't take you as you are, who needs them?"

"Easy to say, hard to do. Tell me something, if Jamal disproved of your choice in suitor, seriously disapproved, would you really be able to ignore it so blithely? Or your parents?"

Shahara, to her credit, thought about it quietly for a minute or two. "Okay, it's an obstacle, I admit. But if that's the only reason—"

"It's not. Not even close. But it is the easiest to explain. I gave my reasons to Todd last night. He accepted them."

"He's upset."

"I'm not thrilled either. He was my first friend in this country. The first one I made who liked me for me, not for..." *my family*, "well, it's complicated. I don't like hurting him."

"Then why turn him down so firmly?"

Liska closed her eyes. This was *so* going to blow up in her face. "Promise to keep this a secret? No going back and telling your brother or Todd? Or anyone else, ever?"

Shahara sobered. "I promise."

"I have several reasons why starting a relationship with Todd would be a terrible idea. But I'm afraid, that if I'm not careful, if I let him try to win me over, that he'll succeed. That I'll fall in love."

Shahara smiled. "Would that be so wrong?"

"Yes. Yes, it would." The seriousness in her voice broke through to the other girl. Shahara sighed.

"Okay. I assume you know what you're doing. I won't tell anyone. But I still wish..."

"In a different world, maybe. As things stand now, I'd have a better chance creating a masterpiece. And for the record, I am hopelessly lousy at art. Can't draw to save my life."

Shahara smiled again. "Maybe with Todd's help."

***

A quarter of a mile upstream Korvou hid in the shadows; unseen, but able to hear every word perfectly. Silly Werefox, forgetting how sound travels over water. So that was what he was seeing. No wonder the paths weren't settled yet. For all Liska's protests, she hadn't made her final decision yet.

So much depended on which way Liska went. It was already obvious that the whole thing wasn't over yet. It could have ended last night, the bond the two were cautiously, unwittingly forming. But it hadn't. The human wouldn't let things rest. And Liska was more on the edge than she realized. A decision would have to be made soon. Now, what was he going to do about it?

He could leave it alone. Let them flounder around trying to work things out or not work things out on their own. Perhaps the fairest route, even if it was the least fun. Or he could take a more active part, one way or another. The human girl had promised to leave things alone. He had made no such vow and was free to act as he wished. Encourage or discourage this relationship. A pattern seer he might be, but he couldn't see the future. There were possibilities of good or harm, which ever happened. It was too early to tell which would be best. So very many options. But first, he had to figure out which side he was on.

Chapter Thirty-Five

Those who truly want, will always find a way. – The
Kikitsutai Book of Wisdom

Liska almost made it back to her room before the
expected downpour. Almost. Getting soaked did
nothing to improve her temper, even if she
acknowledged that she could have avoided it if she
tried. Perhaps especially if she acknowledged that.
To top off her cheerful mood, there was another
note under her door. Goody goody gumdrops. How
close was she to a nervous breakdown by now?

This one was face up, so she could read it
before doing her tests.

Sakaki,

*Have you figured out who I am yet? Are you
even trying? Did you really think you could escape
from your past? Perhaps you should ask Tisiphone.*

Your well-meaning 'Friend'

Liska had never trusted the notes, or the one
leaving them, but this was more hostile than before.
They weren't even trying to seem friendly. Tests
first, she could think about the contents later. Again,

no residues, fingerprints, nothing in the ink or typeface to give away the user. Taking off the gloves, she picked it up to see if she could 'see' anything. At some point, she'd have to come up with a name for trying to read something with retro-cognizance.

The trace was faint this time, nothing to see, just a vague feeling. Still the same person, with just a hint of the one who delivered it. That felt familiar. Liska closed her eyes and concentrated. Where had she felt that before? It was recent. Not just on the previous notes.

Which meant it had to be the sword. Yes, the one who delivered the message was the shade who attacked Todd! So, Atolatar was sending her notes, or ordering someone else to do it. Vampires didn't share shades, so he pretty much had to be involved. But why? What purpose did taunting her have?

That said, what did this stupid note mean? Escape the past? Liska was well aware that her past wasn't a pleasant one, but what did Atolatar know of it? How was she supposed to ask Tisiphone anything unless he planned on killing her to send her to talk to the dead assassin in person? That wasn't worrying or anything.

So, how did this mysterious vampire know her real name, her location, or anything about Yoshiro? This was the first note that didn't mention him. Did that mean something? There was something else, but she couldn't quite put her finger on it. She'd have to think about it. But she wasn't going to find answers by staring at a slip of paper.

It was far too early to expect Ryoko-*Sensei* to have any new information, but he should still know about this. She dialed the number with reluctance.

This whole mess was affecting him more than usual. On the other hand, it was affecting her more than it ought to also. Going it alone was not only ill-advised, it could well be suicidal. Liska frowned as she got a busy signal.

More waiting. Wonderful. Despite her sudden shower outside, she was still hot. How could it be this hot in December? Perhaps it was a mistake to choose a school in Florida. Ah, well. Done is done. Maybe a nice cool shower would help.

It was reaching for a shampoo bottle that Liska noticed she hadn't taken off her watch. Or her bracelet, the one she always wore. Come to think of it, Liska couldn't remember ever bothering to take them off for a shower. Well, if that was the case, then once more wasn't going to hurt. The watch was water resistant, and it wasn't like a plastic bracelet was going to be damaged by a little water.

Out of the shower, Liska changed into clean and dry clothes, and was trying to brush and dry out her hair when she saw her answering machine blinking. She must have missed a call. She pressed play then went back to drying her hair.

"Anna, this is Uncle Ray. I received the phone call a lot earlier than I expected. Could you come over please?"

Ugh, she hated putting her hair up when it was wet. It took forever to dry that way. But she didn't actually want most of the school knowing how long her hair really was, just in case.

Liska filled out a quick index card about her new outfit, grabbed her new note and left. Sometimes it felt like she spent all her time trying to go from one place to the other.

Before she could step foot off campus, she could feel eyes on her. So her watcher was back, was he? Probably the same shade who attacked Todd. Liska ignored it, ignoring the childish urge to wave. She couldn't figure out where it was coming from, and it would just make her look ridiculous.

This time, when she got to *Sensei*'s, he was the one checking for bugs. She wasn't the only one getting more paranoid.

"So, what did you find out?" Liska started.

"There is talk of Tisiphone working under Atolatar. He is also looking for more followers, not just vampires." Liska raised her eyebrow at that. That was unusual, vampires were generally isolationist, seldom even accepting vampires from other places, let alone non-vampires. "He claims he can change the world so that Twilights and Nights will no longer have to hide."

"A tempting thought for many. Does he say what he intends to do in order to make that change?"

"No."

"I'm not surprised." Liska closed her eyes, feeling physical pain at the thought of how much violence would probably have to happen in Atolatar's plan. "Any idea of where he is now?"

"Europe. He's still in Europe as far as anyone can tell. Probably Eastern Europe."

Liska nodded. "Then he must be using someone else to send the notes."

"What do you mean?"

She handed him the newest note.

"Ah, I see. This isn't good. More hostile, at the very least. But do we know there is a definite connection?"

"The same shade who attacked Todd delivered this. I felt it."

The older Werefox nodded slowly. "Interesting. Your skills as a retro-cog are improving. Keep working on it. So, what is the purpose of all this?"

It was all she could do to keep from snarling. "I don't know! This doesn't make any sense. What does he mean about escaping the past?" *Sensei* held up a hand as she stood up and started to pace. "Why bring Tisiphone back? How does he know my real name? Or about Yoshiro?"

"I do not know." The calm answer took the edge off her anger.

"No, of course not. You wouldn't know any better than I. Forgive me."

"There is nothing to forgive. But you must restrain your anger. An angry enemy..."

"Is easy to defeat. I know. But a furious one is hard."

"If you use your anger, then you become stronger. If your anger uses you, then even if you win against your enemy, you have lost to yourself. Do you remember what your father told you, long ago, when you attacked Yoshiro for insulting you?"

"That I carried the seeds to my own destruction and should be careful where I planted them. I remember." She didn't like thinking of that fight.

"Perhaps you should practice your calligraphy for a while."

"Yes, *Sensei.*"

Calligraphy had long been practiced as a way to relax and center oneself. In order to do the strokes properly, one must have an absolutely steady hand. So one learned to put away stress, frustration, anger, and fear in order to concentrate solely on the Kanji.

It took three tries to still her hands enough to work. Telling her to practice calligraphy had been one of Mother's favorite punishments for her. Sakaki had been too impatient to want to sit still that long, too emotional to keep a steady hand, and hated making mistakes. So it taught the lessons Mother wanted her daughter to learn, using a task Sakaki disliked, and wasn't potentially dangerous like some of the training regimens that Father would assign for punishment.

After half an hour of practice, Liska stopped, deciding it had helped as much as it would. Now she needed some tea. Another ritual that helped calm her. Even just making the tea was relaxing and reminded her of home.

Ryoko-*Sensei* was in the practice room, performing his *kata*. Another excellent way to get rid of stress, but it would make her more wound up. Counter-productive after all the effort she had put into calming down. So she stood on the side and waited for her great-uncle to finish and take notice of her.

It was another five minutes. "Feeling better?"

"Yes, *Sensei.*"

"You know I'm just trying to look out for you."

"Yes, *Sensei.*"

"I do understand, you know."

Saying 'yes, *Sensei*,' again felt too repetitive, so she just nodded.

He smiled softly at her. "You didn't get enough sleep last night. I know you never sleep properly when you are on your own, away from home. Why don't you get some sleep now? I'm on watch."

He was right. When she was on her own, she could never fully sleep, having to remain on guard. It was deep enough sleep to keep her going for the most part, but it had to be light enough that any disturbance woke her, at least woke her enough to figure out if she had to fully wake up and deal with it. The opportunity for real sleep was too good to pass up.

Liska woke up four hours later. It might have been longer if she hadn't had that dream again. Still, those four hours should last her awhile.

***

Todd frowned at his sketchbook. In front of him was a lovely bird-of-paradise flower. Somehow, in his attempt to copy it into his book, the flower had become hair. A very familiar shade of orange-red hair, flowing down the back of a very familiar person. Someone who probably wasn't talking to him right now. He sighed and slammed the book shut.

He couldn't stop thinking about her. Especially after talking to Shahara. Whatever Sakaki had said to Shahara had confused her into not knowing what to think. It made him wonder about a lot.

How did he truly feel about Sakaki? How did she truly feel about him? Was there anything that could be done, or should he just accept what she said last night and try to remain friends?

Todd's initial thought was that he should respect her wishes and leave the whole subject alone. To do otherwise would be being a jerk. But just as he decided that, he realized something. Sakaki hadn't made a decision based on her wishes. She hadn't said anything about what she wanted, only that he would eventually change his mind.

She hadn't even said that she felt nothing for him, only that she hadn't fallen in love. Which, based on this new information, only made sense. Nothing in the argument was about him personally, it was fear, and perhaps because of what was expected of her. It had nothing to do with him, and perhaps little to do with her.

So, if she had rejected him because of fear, if he could help her past that fear... then what? But he had to think this over carefully first. If Weres truly mate for life, if she really was only capable of falling in love once, then before he had any right to try to convince her that she could open up to him, to trust him; he had to be sure that she could.

Did he love her? Truly and forever? Was this just an infatuation, based partly on adrenaline? Would it fade with time and someone new? Forget what he wanted, would opening up to him really be better for her?

Yes, Todd had a lot of thinking to do.

***

Four hours of real sleep had been a huge help. Except for the fact that she couldn't fall asleep now. Chamomile tea hadn't helped. Counting rabbits hadn't helped. Mentally going through her genealogy, the periodic table of elements, and various other things she had memorized hadn't helped. Finally, after at least two hours, she drifted off to sleep.

When she was promptly disturbed by a knock on the door.

Eyes closed, the mostly asleep Werefox stumbled to the door. "Who's there?"

"Van."

A little more alert, she opened the door enough to see out of it. Didn't bother opening her eyes yet, though.

"Are you awake?" An amused voice asked. Sounded like Van.

"Do I need to be?"

"Yes."

Like a shot of adrenaline, Liska was suddenly the rest of the way awake. Van was alone; not injured, but upset about something. The campus was mostly still. No feeling of being watched. "What's up?"

"Is that even safe? Answering the door while asleep?"

"Didn't invite you in, did I? Trust me, slightest threat, and I'd be awake."

"You've got to show me how to do that sometime." Van shook her head.

"It's a gift. One I don't think you came here to discuss."

Van sobered instantly. "No. We intercepted part of a message from Atolatar to one of his followers. Unfortunately, it was just one word. Written, not spoken. Nobody knows what it means. I made you a copy, but I can't get you the original."

"Thank you. I take it the chief doesn't know about this?"

"He does not," Van said firmly. "I have to go before I'm missed."

"Thank you." It wasn't adequate for the risk that Van was taking, but the vampire wouldn't appreciate Liska going on about it.

"Just stop him, okay?" Van almost glared at her.

"What's wrong?" This wasn't normal behavior for her.

Van hesitated. "My sister's great, great, great granddaughter was killed by his followers. She was three." Liska hadn't known she kept track of her former family.

"I'm sorry," Liska said sincerely.

"Don't be sorry. Just stop him."

"Working on it."

Van looked like she was thinking about something. Liska could see the moment she made a decision. "You want to thank me? Swear, on your honor, that you will stop this... this leech."

Wow. Just wow. It was a well-known fact that for the Kikitsutai, swearing on one's honor was as serious as a vow as one can make. No one with even a shred of honor or decency would willingly break such a vow. Some said the only oath stronger was to swear on one's honor and life; others said it was the same thing. Van knew this. She knew what she was asking.

"You really want that? Someone will stop him, even if it isn't me. Do you really want *me* to swear this vow?"

"I do. But I will hold the vow void if, through no fault of your own, someone else finishes him off first."

"Very well. I swear, upon my honor, that I will do everything in my power to stop him from killing more or die trying. Will that meet your satisfaction?"

Van's lips tightened. "It does." Then she slumped. "Perhaps it isn't fair to ask this, but..."

"I understand."

The vampire nodded, then turned, jumping from the balcony to the ground before dashing off, slightly faster than a human could.

"Hope no one was watching," Liska muttered quietly. She threw on yesterday's clothes so she didn't have to fill out a new card. *Sensei* would want to know this immediately. There was no time to wait until morning.

Liska's dorm was on the edge of campus, meaning she could have left campus almost immediately. But *Sensei*'s house was the other direction. The campus might not be walled off or anything, but it was a little more secure than the city outside. Might as well walk on campus grounds as long as convenient. Which was how she ran into Todd and Shahara.

"What are you doing up this time of night?" Liska asked. Hadn't she told Todd, just yesterday, not to go walking about campus at night? It was nearly two. Besides, while not aggressive, there had already been one vampire on campus tonight.

"My fault. I had to go to Fort Lauderdale to visit a friend and had car trouble on the way back. When I called, Jamal couldn't come and get me, so Todd did. Then he insisted on walking me back to my dorm. I told him he didn't have to, but he insists." Shahara was smiling.

Todd had a slightly odd look on his face. "I had a feeling it might be a good idea."

Well, she wasn't going to argue with a pre-cog on hunches, not even a fledgling pre-cog. "I'll walk with you. Which dorm?"

"Oh, you don't have to. Shouldn't you be sleeping, too?" Shahara asked.

"Can't. It's no problem, really."

"Williams. We're almost there," Todd said.

"That's on my way." Then she could walk Todd to his dorm. That would only be a little out of her way.

"Where are you going?" Shahara asked, though they did continue toward the dorm.

"I..." What could she tell her? Oh, that would work! "Remember I said that I was part of a team that did spur of the moment 'capture the flag' games? I just got the call."

"At two in the morning?"

"It is Saturday, well, Sunday now. At least there are no classes tomorrow." Liska shrugged. Wouldn't have stopped her even if there were, but it would make her excuse a little more flimsy. Todd wasn't buying it, but she didn't expect him to.

If Shahara had any more questions about it, she didn't ask, possibly because they got to her dorm then. She wished them both goodnight, and Todd and Liska watched through the glass door until she got on the elevator.

"I'll walk you back to your dorm," Liska said as soon as Shahara was gone.

"I remember what you said about walking around at night, but I really thought I should go with Shahara."

"You thought you should go with Shahara, or you thought Shahara shouldn't go back to her dorm alone?"

Todd thought about it for a moment. "I'm not sure. I think it was I should go with her. But I could be wrong."

She could see the UV flashlight in his pocket, and he was wearing the protection charm. At least he wasn't being foolish about it. "I understand. Any idea about why you should escort her home?"

"No, nothing."

"You may never find out. But you should probably listen to those instincts anyway."

"So what are you really doing up, anyway?" Todd asked.

"New information. I have to get to *Sensei*. But first, let's make sure you get home."

"Wait, do you need a ride?"

It would be awkward. Especially after yesterday. But she was in a hurry. Besides, it would probably be best to act as close as possible to the way they did two days ago. "Yes, I would like that. Thank you."

On the way, she filled him in on most of the new information and reassured him that her mentor wouldn't be upset at them for waking him at this time of night. No, he'd be far more upset if they didn't.

True to Liska's prediction, while less than happy to be roused out of bed, as soon as she said there was new information, the older Werefox ushered them in quickly.

"What do you have?"

"Copy of part of an intercepted message. One of my contacts brought it over. They don't know what it means either."

She pulled out the note and looked at it for the first time. It simply said, '*HET*'.

Chapter Thirty-Six

Troubles never come alone. – The Kikitsutai Book of Wisdom

"What language is that?" Todd asked.

"Good question. Our sources say he's in Europe." Sakaki glared at the paper, as if willing it to be more helpful.

"So, it's Russian," The older man said.

"Could be Russian. It could also be Dutch." Sakaki rubbed at an eye.

"The two languages share a word?" Todd asked. Odd, he wouldn't have thought they had much in common.

"Not exactly. But in Russian, the 'N' looks like your 'H'. If it's Russian, that says '*nyeit*', or 'no'. But in Dutch, I believe 'het' means 'the'. I'm afraid Dutch isn't one of the languages I know," Sakaki said.

"How do we know which one this is?" Todd asked.

"From what we have here?" The teacher asked. "We don't. If we knew whether this was the full message or just a fragment, we might have a clue. After all, 'no' can be a complete message. 'The' isn't."

"True, and even if we knew which it was, it really only tells us that he is communicating to someone in a country that speaks the language, or a person that knows that language. Dutch would be easier to narrow things down. I'm not sure it's actively spoken in large numbers anywhere other than Holland. Russian, on the other hand, is among the top ten most commonly spoken languages."

"Do you know where it came from or was going?" The older man, whose name Todd could not remember for the life of him, asked.

"My contact didn't say."

"Your contact didn't give you a lot of information," The man grumbled.

"And yet, my contact took great risk to bring me what information we do have. Going back to ask for more may put my contact in danger. I can't do that."

The man nodded. "Well, it may not be much, but it is progress. You have better contacts in the Russia area, start sniffing around there. I'll see what I can do in former Soviet Union countries, and try to find someone in Holland. In the meantime, I think you two need to get some more sleep. Liska, you have enough belongings to spend the night if you wish. Todd, you may not have clothes here, but I do have a spare room if you wish to stay."

"Oh, um, thanks, but we didn't sign out at school. Well, I didn't. We could get in trouble if we stay out all night. Jamal would be frantic." Todd rubbed at his hair.

"He's right. Better go back to school." Liska sighed. "Goodnight, *Sensei*."

"Goodnight, sir."

"Goodnight, kits."

Briefly, Todd wondered how he was supposed to react to being called a kit, but he decided to ignore that. Next on his list to ignore, was Sakaki's reluctance to get in the car with him again. Still, when he opened the door, she did get in.

"I've been thinking." Todd pulled away from the curb, waiting for her reply.

"Should I be impressed?" Sarcasm as a defense mechanism. Not surprising.

He ignored it and continued, "I didn't realize I would be complicating things so much for you. You skipped the whole 'Weres mate for life' when you were giving me my lessons. So, I realized that it wasn't fair to ask you to take that kind of a risk until I knew my own feelings. Do I really love you, not just infatuated; and am I willing to stick around forever? That isn't something I can discover in a day. So, I'm going to spend a lot more time thinking about this. But to warn you now, if I realize I'm sure I do love you, forever, then I'm going to come back to try to convince you to give me a chance. Just a chance."

Sakaki sighed and buried her head in one hand. "Todd, you don't even know me that well."

"I know you well enough."

"Do you? If you truly knew me, you would be staying as far away from me as possible."

"Convince me."

"What?"

"You want me to drop this whole thing, right? And you say knowing more about you would do that. So tell me. Drive me away."

"Todd..."

They were at a red light, so he turned to her. "I'm not afraid of the truth. Are you?"

She stilled. A statue of a girl-woman. He could just barely see emotions trying to flicker across her face before being forced back. She opened her mouth to respond.

There was a harsh banging below his open window. Todd spun to see a punk with a knife. There was something familiar about him. Maybe he'd be able to figure it out if he could look away from the knife. "Both of you, outta the car. Now!"

Todd had started to associate his precognition as a trickle in the back of his mind. A whisper usually. Right now, it was a shout. On instinct, he flattened himself against the seat of the car. Then there was a sword under the attempted car-jacker's chin. White faced, he barely managed to gasp out, "You again?"

"Yes. Me. Again." The edge in Sakaki's voice was one Todd hadn't heard before and truly hoped never to have directed at him.

The kid backed up and started to run. Todd couldn't swear to it, but he thought he heard, "That's it. I'm going straight. This is just too dangerous."

"Was that the same person from the grocery store?" Todd asked, trying to be calm as he turned to Sakaki. She was tucking the short sword, a *wakizashi*, if he wasn't mistaken, into a velcroed compartment in her pant's leg, from knee to ankle. Stay calm, he could do this. She did it all the time.

"Light's changed. Yes, he was. This, this isn't the way back to campus."

Maybe this was a bad time. He certainly hadn't anticipated the guy with the knife. But when would they get another time? "No, it isn't. We need to talk, and if I take you back to campus, you'll avoid the whole issue. Come on, I can deal with the truth." Was this really helping her? Was this the right thing to do? He probably wasn't in the best shape for this either. But he had to, didn't he?

Something in her snapped. "Can you? You really want to know the truth? The truth is that I enjoyed that. I liked scaring him! The truth is that I'm not a nice person. You really want to hear? Then listen up, you'll learn a lot."

She took a deep breath. "You already know I saw death for the first time at age four. I was seven the second time. One of my uncles stepped in front of something meant for me. A handheld ball containing silver dust. Do you know what happens when silver dust gets into a Were's lungs? The lungs start to bleed. And bleed. And bleed! They eventually choke to death on their own blood. It can take about twenty to thirty minutes depending on how much they've inhaled. His blood is on my hands."

"That wasn't your fault! You were just a kid. He knew what he was doing and chose to save you."

"If I had been faster, more careful, he wouldn't have had to."

"You were seven! No one expects—"

"I was nine the first time I killed."

"Nine?" Todd squeaked.

"Nine. My father took me with him on a job. I was just supposed to observe what he was doing with some ghouls. But it was a trap. They knew he was coming and there were so many more than he thought. They were going to kill him. Until I killed the leader. I didn't even think. Just grabbed a knife and stabbed him."

"Did you mean to kill him?"

"I... I don't know. I truly don't know."

"It was self-defense. Well, I think so. Justifiable homicide at the worst." He'd have to look up the law in a case like that, but he was certain no jury would convict a nine-year-old for killing someone trying to kill her father.

"Do you really think he's the only one I've killed?"

"Have you ever set out to kill someone?"

"What do you think I am; an assassin?"

"Are you?" Why was he asking? Did he really want to know?

"Luna Liska is no assassin."

"I'm not asking about Luna Liska. Liska may be very interesting. But it's Sakaki I care about." It had taken a little time and a lot of observation, but he'd finally realized the reason he couldn't get a good reading off Anna or Liska was because they were only fragments. Sakaki contained both of them, and probably many more. That's what made her so fascinating.

"Sakaki couldn't handle it. Sakaki can't handle a lot of things. That's why she forms personas to handle things she can't."

Todd nodded. "I'm not driven away yet." Uneasy and trying to hold back shivers perhaps but not driven off.

"I've lied to every single person I've ever met."

"Now that's a challenge. Tell me something, since I've found out about the whole Were thing, have you lied to me?"

"Yes."

"When we aren't in public?"

There was a long pause. "I don't recall."

"Anything else?"

"Isn't that enough?"

"The truth shall set you free. I'm listening."

"I know I need years of therapy. I'm rather Machiavellian. There are few things I won't do if I feel it necessary."

"Like what?"

"We're talking about my flaws and dangerous traits, not whatever good points I may possess."

"I had figured most of this out already." It was only a slight exaggeration.

"Then why haven't you started running yet?"

"Do you want to know what I see?"

"Why not? After all, the truth shall set you free," Sakaki answered mockingly.

Todd pulled out a small mirror he kept in the glove compartment. "Take a look." Sakaki did so, reluctance obvious. "I see a woman who has seen more trouble and evil than many people twice her age. I see the little girl who remembers great pain, grown into a woman trying to prevent others from feeling that pain. I see someone who has torn herself apart trying to do what she believed was right. I see an angel of vengeance who hurts with every act but continues anyway. Do you wonder that I think I love you?"

While he talked, she stared into the mirror, as if searching for what he saw. Her hands, were they trembling? "Don't put me on a pedestal; you'll only be disappointed when I fall."

"I'm just saying what I see."

"Then get your eyes checked!" She dashed the mirror away as if unable to look anymore. It hit the floor and broke. Shards scattered over the carpet. There were ten, twenty Sakakis. Then there were none. "I'll walk from here. Get back to the school, and in your dorm."

"Sakaki, wait!"

"No! Leave me alone!" She hesitated before turning back. Sakaki put a hand in her pocket and pulled out something, looked like money. "For the mirror." She dropped the ten-dollar bill on the seat and walked away rapidly. "Get home, get inside."

Todd sighed and lifted his head, facing the ceiling of the car. He'd pushed too hard. He looked back at the broken mirror. Had he shattered their friendship like she shattered the mirror?

***

There had to be a limit on how long a person could mope on the same problem. After all, hadn't she spent all of yesterday moping over Todd and his declarations of almost-love? Shouldn't she be moped out? Then again, he had pushed the point. Why did he have to say those things? Why did he have to see her like that? Why did she have to—

RING RING! RING RING!

—answer the phone.

"Hello?"

"Anna, it's Uncle Ray. One of your cousins is over. I thought you might enjoy a visit."

"Okay, I'm on my way." What could that be about? Cousin, huh? That didn't narrow things down much. All Werefoxes were pretty much related to each other, so every adult who wasn't her parents or grandparents, she called Aunt or Uncle. Those who were her generation or younger were cousins. So this cousin could conceivably be anyone in the clan under the age of thirty. Who could it be?

More importantly, why was someone here? If there was a job to be pulled in the area, unless it was out of her range of abilities, she should have been offered it first. Even if it was, normally she would be informed that someone would be in her area. Perhaps they informed Ryoko-*Sensei*, and he decided to keep it a secret. That was more likely. He had to suspect she was hiding a lot, even if he hadn't called her on it. Perhaps he had decided to be more circumspect in what he told her.

She took route 4 this time. A little more out of the way than some, but it didn't involve anything harder than scaling a fence. About twenty-five minutes after leaving campus, she was there.

As soon as she got to his walkway, the tang of bleach was rife in the air. He really did want to surprise her. Wiping at her nose, she tried to remember his exact words on the phone. He hadn't said anything to indicate something was wrong, none of the codes to say he wasn't free to speak, except of course, that it wasn't a secure line. This should be completely safe.

All the same, she palmed her telescopic baton as she knocked on the door. The door opened a minute later; and Ryoko-*Sensei* wasn't the one to open it.

"Kira!"

The other girl laughed and hugged her. "It's good to see you again! Were you surprised?" Kira moved out of the way, letting Liska follow her into the house.

"I certainly was. I didn't think I'd see you again so soon. How are you?"

"I'm great. And you?"

"Fine." For that moment, she almost was. Kira was eyeing her, skeptically. Time to distract. "What are you doing here?"

The other girl sobered. "Uncle Sejou sent me. He said it's time for you to go home."

What? It was almost time for exams. "Home? For how long?"

"Permanently."

Chapter Thirty-Seven

When torn between loyalties, there is no victory. – The
Kikitsutai Book of Wisdom

"What?" This couldn't be happening. Not now.

Kira wouldn't meet her eyes. "I know you wanted to do this; get schooling and everything. But your father says, and I quote, 'She's had enough of this nonsense. It is time for her to start learning the important things.'" Normally, hearing Kira try to imitate her father would make Sakaki smile, maybe even laugh. Not this time. Kira sighed. "I am sorry."

"When does he expect me to leave?"

"He anticipated it would take some time to wrap up loose ends but was hoping that you could leave within the week. You might be able to talk him into letting you finish the semester, if you try."

Liska motioned with her head to the room where she could hear Ryoko-*Sensei* moving around quietly. Kira nodded. So, this had to do with something he had said to Father. Either she wasn't as discreet as she thought, or he had been more worried than she realized.

"What time is it?" Liska looked at the clock. Ten in the morning. Meaning it would be eleven at night in Japan. It wasn't too late to call yet. *"Sensei,* may I borrow your phone?" The older man hadn't come out to greet her yet, probably figuring it would be better to let Kira explain. Liska had to agree.

"Certainly."

She had an international calling card so she wouldn't be racking up his phone bill. Fortunately, she had it on her. Using the time between dialing and the phone being answered to calm herself, she was able to sound reasonable when Father picked up the phone.

"Moshi-moshi?"

"Father? It's Sakaki."

"Ah, I take it Kira has talked to you?"

"Yes, about that—"

"I've humored you long enough. It is time. You have responsibilities to the clan."

How were her responsibilities any different now than they were six months ago when she convinced him of her plan? "I also have responsibilities here."

"Your schooling is not a necessary responsibility. It is time to learn to lead the skulk." No, no, no. Not yet.

She had been hoping not to mention this part, to anyone. "I swore a vow, on my honor, to stop someone. I have to fulfill this before I can even hope to take up a mantle of leadership."

There was a pause. "This is about Atolatar?"

"It is."

"You swore on your honor? Why?"

"I was asked to."

Another pause. "I see. Very well. Finish your task. Kira can stay while you do that. Afterwards, you will return here."

"I understand, Father." Both hung up. Well, that bought her a little time. She had to use it wisely. Not waste it thinking about stupid things, like how her first thought when Kira said it was time to go, was to wonder if she would see Todd again.

"Sorry, Kira. I seem to have gotten you stuck here for a while."

"I don't mind. I like America. It's different." A pause. "Someone really asked you to swear on your honor? Did they know what they were asking?"

"Yes. We both knew."

Kira nodded. "And it keeps you from having to leave." Okay, there was just the slightest touch of jealousy.

Both girls ignored it.

***

Todd fumbled with the books in his arms, wondering if he was being beyond stupid. He had exams to study for, final projects and papers to work on, even his painting to finish up. But he had checked out two books on foxes, one on Japan, and one on the psychology of love. When was he going to find the time to read these? But he already knew he would do his best to make time. Better get back to his dorm before he ran into someone who questioned his reading choices. Especially Sakaki.

"There you are. Just the person I was looking for. It's Todd, right?"

Todd turned and looked at the intruder. The stranger from two nights back. "Yes, and you're Korvou, aren't you?"

The dark haired fae hopped off the low wall he had been perching on. Why was no one staring at him? He then took a look at the books in Todd's arms. "Interesting reading choices."

Todd tried to fight back embarrassment with irritation. "Did you want something?"

"I did. Walk with me, will you?" He started to walk away without a backwards glance to see if Todd would follow.

With a challenge like that, how could he not? "What do you want?" Todd asked as they got to a quieter area. A fountain with flowers around it. Wasn't this where he had tried to sketch the bird-of-paradise plant?

"I want to know what happened between you and Liska the other night. I want to know what got Liska emotional to the point where her steel grasp of control cracked and she pushed me in the water. I want to know," Korvou somehow managed to disappear only to reappear directly in front of him, "how you feel about her."

It wasn't easy, but Todd managed not to back down. "Why should I tell you?"

"Including or excluding the fact that I could kill you in a heartbeat and cover it up so that no one would ever find your body?" Korvou was smiling, but his eyes glittered dangerously. Todd didn't doubt he could do exactly that. He still didn't move. The fae nodded approvingly. "Good, you have spirit.

You'll need it. Now, consider me her honorary big brother. If I approve, I'll help you out. I've known her for years. That's a lot longer than you have."

"Why would you help me?"

"I'll tell you once I'm satisfied with your answers."

"I thought you were sworn to kill her. And she was sworn to kill you."

"We are. Doesn't mean I can't want her happy in the meantime."

Todd shook his head. "You two are weird. What did you want to know?"

"What do you feel for her?"

Good question. "I'm not completely sure."

"Fair enough. What do you know?"

"I've been fascinated with her since the moment I first saw her." Korvou nodded. "The more I found out, the more attracted I became. Some of that might be the adrenaline, I know. Emotions run deeper when in life threatening situations, but I know that's not all of it. As an artist, a psychologist-in-training, even as an Esper who is just realizing how wide this world is, she's... indescribable. I know she has problems, deep ones. I want to help her with them, but the fact that I know she has these problems and still want to be with her probably means I have problems of my own. But if it's best for her, I'll leave her alone. How's that?"

"Sounds like love to me. Mind you, I've never been in love. Are you sure, absolutely sure, that you'd leave her alone if it was for her own good?"

He hadn't been doing so well at that so far. "I'd certainly try."

"Are you sure this isn't some teenage crush?"

"I'm not a teenager anymore. I've been through crushes. This started with a crush, I know, but it's deeper than that now. It could be so much more if she'd be willing to give me a chance."

"How is she responding?"

"She keeps trying to drive me away. Last night she went into a whole laundry list of reasons why I shouldn't want anything to do with her."

Korvou smirked at that. "Oh, what did she say?"

Todd sat next to the fountain, putting his books out of range of the spraying water. "She listed a few traumatic childhood incidents, tried to pass herself off as an eviler female version of Lex Luther, then when I told her that despite everything I thought she was still on the side of the angels, she broke a mirror and left."

"Did she throw the mirror at you?"

Todd blinked. "No, just the floor of the car."

Korvou perched on the edge of the fountain, like a gargoyle. "Looks like she's half-way to love herself. She'd have thrown the mirror at me in a heartbeat. Then again, you've never tried to kill her." For some reason, he seemed to think that was funny. "Did she tell you about the first time she killed?"

"At age nine? Yeah." He really didn't like thinking about that. Didn't seem like she did either.

"I'm right. The main obstacles holding her back are fear and her skulk." Then Korvou got serious. "Did Liska tell you what I can do?"

"No, not really."

"I see patterns. As events transpire and people make decisions, certain things become more or less likely to happen. I can see, not what will happen, but often where and who will be most directly involved. You two have some sort of destiny. That's all I know. It could be good, bad, happy, or tragic. You two may get together, you may not. Even whether that would be good or bad, I don't know. This destiny could be life-long or resolved in a few months or even weeks. Think about that when you make your decision."

"I don't know how she feels about me!"

"She told some human girl that she was afraid of falling in love with you. Think about that, too. We'll talk later." Korvou smiled. Then he disappeared.

***

Liska was enjoying catching up with her favorite cousin and best friend. They talked about everything and nothing and everything in between. "Okay, now you have to tell me all about the dance," Kira insisted.

Liska sighed. She didn't really want to go into that. But it was Kira. "What do you want to know?"

Kira grabbed a sketchbook. "Everything. Start with your dress and his tux, then tell me what the ballroom looked like."

"Well, it was a dark dress, I think someone said it was blue, with rhinestones..." Getting caught up in memories, Liska was a bit surprised how much detail she went into. Finally, she finished.

"Like this?" Kira handed over her sketchbook, letting Liska look through the pictures. Anyone would swear that she had been there to see it.

Liska swallowed hard at the last picture, Todd and her dancing. "Yeah, that's it. Perfectly." She even had the hairstyle right. It was their gift. Kira could draw anything Liska told her about as if she had seen it herself, even when Liska was skimpy on the details. Neither could do that with anyone else.

Kira saw she had hit a nerve and took back her book. "So, are you involved in the upcoming political talk?"

"Political talk? Sorry, I'm a bit isolated here." Liska leapt at the new subject.

"Haven't you heard? It's Day business. All pretty hush-hush. Supposed to be leaders from over forty countries going to this peace summit. I wondered if they had asked you to help with security. You have a good reputation for it."

"I've been avoiding major jobs. I don't... didn't want anything traced back here. Besides college classes are hard enough when you have time to study and aren't worried about breaking into heavily fortified buildings. Or guarding them as the case may be."

Kira laughed. "I imagine you're right."

Something was niggling at the back of her mind. "Hey, do you know where the talks are supposed to be?"

"Well, it hasn't been officially announced..." Both vixens rolled their eyes. As if that stopped anyone who paid attention. "Saint Petersburg."

Liska froze. "Saint Petersburg, Russia?"

"Yeah. That's why I was surprised. You're one of the experts on Moscow- St. Petersburg."

"Would you excuse me for a minute?" Her voice sounded odd, even to her. Kira was looking almost alarmed. Liska ignored it and made her way to the computer. Time to write an email.

'Dear Fiona,

Hi, how are you? Is everything going alright? I hope your job is going well. I have a favour to ask. You may remember our friend, Jack Atolatar? I heard something about him being in your area right now. Could you look into it and let me know what he's up to? Thanks,

Selene.'

Fiona wasn't one of her normal contacts, so they didn't have a regular code. But she would be the best planted for this, if she'd agree to help. Unfortunately, the Russian government insisted on being able to access all communications in, to, or from the country. So anything that even looked like a code could put Fiona in danger. She was smart, she'd know enough to read between the lines. This would have to do. For now.

Chapter Thirty-Eight

There is no liar like one who lies to himself. – The Kikitsutai
Book of Wisdom

The political talks were set to begin Dec. 15th. Today was the 7th. That did not provide a lot of time. Preparing to travel to Russia was time consuming, but she couldn't start her preparations yet. She still wasn't sure she was right about this. Oh, it made sense, it fit, but there was no evidence. So Liska found herself checking her e-mail every ten minutes or so unless she forced herself to do something else. Making herself stop left her free to think about other things.

How was she supposed to explain dropping out after one semester? Would any explanation be made, or would she just disappear? No, that was rude. She couldn't care less what the school in general thought, but she owed her few friends more than that. Liska sighed. She was going to miss them more than she would have anticipated in the beginning of the year. Yes, she knew the tendency of Werefoxes to form a substitute skulk when away from family for long periods of time, but she hadn't thought they would become that substitute skulk. Jamal and his wry humor but sympathetic ear.

Shahara with her bubbly enthusiasm and her determination to help; whether you want it or not. And Todd. Todd and...

How long did it take to find out information? Even a hint that he might be there, and she'd find a way to get there. Fortunately, she had the connections to get a Russian visa in hours. Normally, that took weeks. Ryoko-*Sensei* had better contacts with airlines, letting her get last minute tickets. But first she needed confirmation that she wasn't sniffing around the wrong tree. Or maybe she should just start the process anyway.

She was second guessing herself. That was never a good sign. *Deep breaths, girl. Deep breaths.* Okay, if she hadn't heard from Fiona by this time tomorrow, she would go ahead and get everything started anyway.

Liska growled to herself. She was focusing on the wrong things. There was enough to do with getting ready to go back home. Packing was the biggest issue, but it was manageable. Liska had tried not to take much to college in the first place. In her line of work, one couldn't afford too much attachment to belongings. Some things she could get rid of, they were only here to help her fit in, or because she needed them here. A few things she had to have on her, most of those would go with her to Russia, or wherever. There wasn't much else.

She could put some things in her apartment, the one no one knew about. Maybe she'd tell Ryoko-*Sensei* about it. If he stayed in the area, then he could probably use an extra den. Then again, he was here because she was. Odds were he'd leave when she did. It was possible neither of them would ever be back here. And it was possible they would.

Liska huffed. She didn't want to pack, didn't want to think about the future, didn't want to think about leaving. A quick glance at the room told her that her packing was ahead of schedule. She could take a break.

Her skates called to her. Liska didn't have the willpower to resist. Soon she was skating the main campus walkways. Oh, there was Shahara. Liska stopped when it was obvious the other girl had seen her and was headed over.

"Hey, girl! What's up?"

"Hi, Shahara." She gave the girl a smile, but it didn't take a mirror to know it was hollow.

"What's the matter? You seem upset. Final-itis?"

Liska sighed. "I wish. I have something really major, not school-related, that I have to deal with. It's getting complicated. Then I found out yesterday that something happened and I may have to go back home after this semester."

"Go back home? As in quit or transfer schools?" Shahara stared at her in wide-eyed shock.

"Yeah, supposedly I'm needed back home."

"Why?'

"I don't know. Just that I have to go home."

"You... don't seem happy about this." Shahara was trying to be either subtle or tactful. Perhaps both. It was still mild prying.

"Let me put it this way, I chose to go to a school in another country, on another continent, for a reason. Many reasons, actually."

Shahara winced. "Does Todd know?"

"I haven't seen him since I heard. Could you tell him for me?"

"He's smitten with you, girl. Don't you think he should hear it from you?"

"I don't know that he wants to talk to me right now. We kind of got into a fight on Saturday. Well, I got mad and walked away."

Shahara shook her head. "What am I gonna do about you, Anna?"

"Talk to Todd for me?"

"Oh, I'll talk to him, all right. And tell him he needs to talk to you! And you, you will be polite and not run off. You can't leave for England with this mess between you."

"Shahara..."

"I mean it!"

"Fine. I'll try. He just..."

"Just what?"

"He brings out more emotion in me, all emotions, than most people can."

"And you still deny he's meant for you?" Shahara had a hopeful smile.

"I'm moving away. Remember?"

"Is this for certain, or just maybe?"

"As things currently stand, it's almost certain. How's that?"

"I wish you weren't going."

"So do I. Believe me, so do I."

***

Todd glared at his textbook. He was supposed to be studying it. However, he couldn't seem to make his eyes focus on the words for longer than a minute before he was back to thinking.

Korvou had come back and insisted on talking to him for a while, supposedly to 'give him a little balance'. According to the fae, one of Sakaki's strongest traits was her protectiveness and loyalty to those she cared about. He called it the flip side of her ruthlessness. Hurt someone she cared about or wanted to protect, and there was little that would stop her from turning you into hamburger.

She also tried to make herself sound worse than she really was. The more a person thought she'd be willing to do, the less she would actually have to do. The Kikitsutai had a policy of spreading misinformation to the point that ninety percent or more of what people knew about them was either exaggerated or understated. Liska was no exception.

Korvou's fae clan, or whatever they called themselves, had more contact with the skulk than most, so their information was (or ought to be) better. In fact, Korvou said he was impressed that Todd's view of the Werefox was more accurate than he had expected. He seemed to think it was a good sign.

But, encouraging as that was, it wasn't helping him study. Neither was the phone ringing. Huh, it was Shahara. "Hey, Shahara. Jamal's not here."

"I'm not looking for my brother. I want to talk to you."

"Okay, do you need a ride again?"

"No, that's covered. I need you to talk to Anna."

"Anna?" Who... Oh! Right. He was getting entirely too comfortable with her as Sakaki.

"I ran into her earlier. She told me about you two having a fight. Well, she described it as pretty one-sided on her part. Anyway, she's sorry now, and has something to tell you."

"What do you mean?"

"Talk to her, not me!"

"Yes, Ma'am. Oh, the fight wasn't completely her fault. I've been pushing her buttons all weekend."

"Glad you think so. Todd?" There was something hesitant about that last word.

"Yeah?"

"Do you think... I know she's hiding something. She has to be. But do you think she's in the Federal Witness Protection program or something?"

"What?" That was so not what he was expecting.

"It makes sense. You have to admit it. Maybe she told you something."

Todd took a deep breath. "Shahara, if Anna were in the Federal Witness Protection program, she wouldn't be able to say anything about it. I recommend not even asking."

"Right. Okay. We won't mention it again."

"Good plan."

"Good. Great. Now, call her! She should be back by now." Shahara hung up, not giving Todd enough time to say that he didn't have her number. Oh well. He'd try her room.

What could she want to tell him? How would she react to him now? How should he react to her? Maybe she needed a little space for a while. Maybe *he* needed a little space. He still wasn't one hundred percent sure he was ready to consider forever, with her or anyone. Did he truly love her? Sheesh, at twenty-one, did he even know what love was?

It was nine o'clock. He hoped she wouldn't mind him coming over so late. She hadn't been too upset when he went over at three in the morning. Well, she had minded, but that seemed to have less to do with the time than the reason.

Todd had just gotten to her door, hand raised to knock, when the door opened. Sakaki seemed almost as surprised as he was. "Oh, hi," She said in Anna's voice. Made sense since they could be overheard. He liked her real voice better.

"Hi. Um, sorry to bother you. Shahara said we needed to talk."

She sighed. "Shahara's right. Unfortunately, I'm leaving now."

"Do you need a ride?"

"On a night like this? It's beautiful. I plan on walking."

"Alright, do you mind if I walk with you for a while?" He fell into step with her, determined to walk with her unless she insisted he leave.

"No, I suppose not." She was quiet then.

It was a beautiful night. The moon almost full and there was just enough wind to rustle their hair. It was cool enough to be slightly brisk, but Todd was perfectly comfortable in his light jacket, and even if she was silent, the company was nice too.

Finally Todd broke the silence. "So, what does Shahara want us to talk about?"

Sakaki closed her eyes. In the harsh light of a streetlamp, her face looked drawn, tired. "I don't want to get into another fight. Not tonight. Can't we talk about it tomorrow?"

"I suppose. Provided we actually talk about it."

"We will. Say, you wanted to see me in fox form, right?"

"Yeah."

"Do you still?"

"Sure!"

"One of my cousins, Kira, you may remember my mentioning her?"

"The one who looks like you?"

"That's right. Anyway, she's over for a visit. Tonight is her night to change. I plan on being with her."

"As a fox?"

"Yes. If she's willing, you can watch."

"That would be great, thanks!" He paused. "Do you actually, hunt?"

Sakaki laughed. "Of course. That's most of the fun."

"What happens to the animals you hunt?"

"Don't ask questions you don't want an answer to."

"Right. Standard fox behavior. Got it."

"Oh, maybe you shouldn't mention in front of Ryoko-*Sensei* that you've seen Kira before. He doesn't know about our Halloween prank and might be upset."

"Oooh, blackmail," Todd kidded.

"Please, kitsune are experts at blackmail. And I know a lot more about you than you know about me." She was smiling, but Todd didn't doubt it was the truth.

"Oh, what do you know about me?"

"Let me put it this way. When I started to meet with you for Kendo, I did a lot of research on you. When I found out you were interested in my activities, as Cats-eye, I dug even deeper. Not to mention, I may have asked Shahara for embarrassing stories about you."

"I could ask Kira about you."

"She wouldn't tell you."

"Shahara would. Very well. I concede the point, gracious lady." Then they were there. 'There' being a park that was closed after dark. Todd didn't say anything as he followed her over the gate, then further in to the park, where two people were waiting.

Sakaki explained what he was doing there quickly. The other two didn't seem pleased, but they weren't rude either. Kira, who looked scarily like a black-haired Sakaki, agreed to let him watch. Well, he could watch them after they had changed.

The male Werefox explained while the girls disappeared. "As I'm sure you realize, foxes are a lot smaller than humans."

"Yes, I had noticed that."

"Clothes do not grow or shrink with you."

"Ah, right. Waiting right here then."

Two foxes came back a few minutes later. One was orange-red that exactly matched Sakaki's hair. The other was a cross-fox with black streaks in the fur, and a darker orange. "Let's see. You must be Sakaki, and you're Kira." Both foxes nodded at him.

"Okay, so you can understand me."

"Yes, in fox form we have all our human memories; we simply filter it through the focus of the fox," Ryoko explained.

"Got it."

The two vixens had evidently decided that he was less interesting than the surroundings and were sniffing around. Sakaki was sniffing by his feet, as if pondering his shoelace. Todd couldn't help it, he reached down to try and pet her. At the last moment, he remembered that she wasn't just a fox, and might not appreciate it. She looked up at him and tilted her head.

"May I?"

She nodded. Very slowly, very carefully, he lowered his hand. "Try to avoid her neck." Ryoko said.

"Right. I remember that. Anything else?"

"Be careful of the tail. She doesn't usually like anyone touching it. And she loves having her ears scratched."

She did seem to enjoy that, nudging into the hand. "She's so soft. You're lovely, did you know that?" He smiled at her. She tossed her head lightly as if to say, 'Well, naturally.' Todd laughed. "Thank you."

She made a foxy noise that was probably closest to a bark before running off to join her cousin. The foxes ran around, play wrestling, pouncing on each other, chasing each other and everything that moved. Ryoko even brought out a laser pointer for them to chase for a bit. Until the vixens worked together to steal the device.

Todd laughed. "Good thing cats don't figure out that part."

"They'll give it back. Eventually."

Suddenly Sakaki was at his side with something in her mouth. Something moving. "Um, what is... Is that a frog?" She dumped it in his hands. It was indeed a frog. "Uh, thanks. What am I supposed to do with this? I'm not supposed to eat it, am I?"

Okay, foxes could snicker. Good to know. Ryoko was smiling too. "But you'll hurt her feelings if you don't."

Todd eyed the struggling amphibian. "You're kidding, right?"

"Yes, I'm kidding. The frog isn't injured, so this is catch and release. Thank her for the frog, praise her hunting skills and let it go."

That he could do. "Great. Good job. Frogs are hard to catch." He put it down and rubbed some hand sanitizer on his hands. "Yay for the mighty huntress." More scratching behind the ears.

Sakaki ran after a noise he couldn't hear, so Todd turned back to Ryoko. "Why didn't she kill it?"

"She didn't want to. Maybe she wasn't hungry or just didn't want frog. We aren't complete animals. One of the rules of hunting is you don't kill what you don't plan to eat. Caching for later is allowed, but you have to plan to come back for it."

Todd nodded. "Makes sense."

They were playing in the leaves now. Todd sat back to watch, storing up the memories.

***

The voice of the fox was always in Liska's head. Sometimes quieter, sometimes louder. It predominated in fox form, but tonight it was even louder than usual.

Hunt good. Hunt with skulk better.
<u>*Yes.*</u>
Silly Human can't hunt.
<u>*No. No, he can't.*</u>
He's here, though. He wants to be mate.
<u>*Yes.*</u>
Mate must be equal and alpha. Can he be?
She glanced at him. <u>*I don't know. I truly don't know.*</u>
Do we want him?
<u>*Aren't we supposed to be hunting?*</u>

***

The night ended with them all going back to Ryoko-*Sensei*'s house. To Liska's surprise, Todd had stayed the whole night. Well, that meant she could tell him that she was leaving when they walked back to campus. Right now, she had other things on her mind. Like checking her email. And yes, Fiona had written back.

'Selene,

Sorry about the late reply. I was out of the country on visa renewal. You are correct, your good friend Jack is in town, though I haven't seen him. He seems to have gotten involved in politics and poetry. Look forward to hearing from you soon.

Fiona'

They may not have a firmly established code, but there were some things pre-set. 'Poetry' meant something that involved Days, Nights, and Twilights. Politics suggested he probably was interested in the political talks. 'Look forward to hearing from you soon', meant 'call me'.

It was eight in the morning eastern standard time. Add another eight hours, and it was four in the afternoon in Saint Petersburg. Hopefully she was home.

"*Allo?*" A nervous voice asked.

"Fiona? It's Selene."

"Oh, hi, Selene."

"So, you've heard about our mutual friend?"

"As I said."

"I was wondering if you could keep a bit of an eye on him. Maybe offer to help out." Can you do some infiltration? "I'm not asking you to do anything you don't want to. Feel free to stop if you want." I don't want to put you in danger. Get out if it turns dangerous.

"I think I could. Are you planning a visit soon?"

"Certainly looks that way. We can talk about politics and poetry."

"Okay, see you then."

"Keep in touch."

"You too." Both hung up.

"I'VE FOUND HIM!" came ringing through the house seconds later.

So, he was in Saint Petersburg, and probably had plans to wreck the peace talks. That gave a time and place to find him. Now she just had to get there. Unfortunately, with that problem, came other problems.

***

Todd knew he should have gone home hours ago. He hadn't even called Jamal to tell him he'd be out all night, so please sign him out. Mostly because he hadn't planned to be out all night. But he had been, and now needed some kind of explanation. Todd wasn't sorry though. This was worth it. Worth the lack of sleep, the awkwardness, the stiffness in his back from sitting so long, even worth lying to Jamal over where he had been.

Watching Sakaki in fox form had told him that he was absolutely correct. She was a vibrant, passionate, even playful woman. It was just that she spent so much time trying to hide it that she came off as cold and emotionless. But she wasn't, she was fiery and warm. Once again, he found himself wanting to work past her walls. Or at least put some doors in them.

Since no one had kicked him out, or even hinted that he should leave, Todd stayed, listening to their plans about Atolatar. Finding out that the current plan was for Sakaki to face him alone was worrying. But as had been made quite clear, this was her job, and she had a reputation for being very good at her job. That reassured him a little.

Less reassuring was his sudden pre-cognizant instance that he was to go as well. Todd tried to ignore it. No one expected him to go, they probably didn't want him to go. He didn't know what to do. Even if he wanted to go, it wasn't like he could help. However, the little voice didn't go away, it just got louder.

"I'm going too." Drat, he hadn't meant to say that out loud. The other three stared at him.

"No. No, you are not." Liska, it was definitely Liska now, stared him down.

"I have to."

"You most certainly do not. You have no training or skills in this, and you aren't involved."

Well, that wasn't true. "I am involved. Maybe not like you are, but I've helped you figure out the clue, been attacked twice, and even gotten one of those notes. And I'm going." Whether either of them liked it or not.

"You can't," Liska said firmly.

Todd closed his eyes for a moment, listening. The voice was insistent. "You'll need me."

"What was that?" Liska asked.

"You'll need me. I'm not sure why, how, or when, but you'll need me."

"Didn't you say he was a pre-cog?" Kira asked.

"Yes, he is." Liska stared at him, but he didn't look away. Then she shot a look at her uncle. He shrugged. "Alright. If, and I do mean, IF, you come, I'm in charge and you have to listen to what I say. Especially if I tell you to stay put. I'm not getting you killed if I can help it."

"Fine with me. I'm in no hurry to die."

"Might happen anyway. I can't promise anything."

Todd nodded slowly. Well, he had wanted her to be honest with him. He should have expected that some of that honesty would be painful.

"He's coming," Liska said, exchanging a nod with Ryoko.

"I'll start travel arrangements," The older man said. "Bring me your passport, today would be best, definitely no later than tomorrow night. I'll need to get you a Russian visa. You do have a passport, right?"

"Yes."

"Good. Liska, I'll be using your Selene Reynard passport."

"Fine."

Todd was ushered to the side and his picture taken for the visa. Liska said she would have to wait until she was in her Selene disguise.

"Tickets for the 11th, ten in the morning, from Miami to Moscow. That's the best I can do." Ryoko said, after a few minutes.

"It's fine," Liska said.

Kira agreed to take Liska's place in school; Liska joking that this was the best way to take exams. For Todd, they arranged it to look like he won an art contest and was invited to an international competition in, surprise, surprise, Saint Petersburg.

"That should be everything," Ryoko said.

"No, it isn't," Kira cut in.

"It isn't? What else?" Sakaki asked. She had finally released her grip on the Liska mask.

"Not now," Ryoko argued.

"We agreed. It has to be done. She'll need the time." Kira said.

Ryoko shot a glance in Todd's direction.

"What is going on?" Todd could catch only the barest bit of nervous tremors in Sakaki's voice. But the fact he could hear any at all said volumes.

"Now isn't a good time," Ryoko said.

"He may need to know too," Kira said.

"What's going on? Now isn't a good time for what?" Sakaki was getting more insistent and agitated.

"Look, if you need me to leave..." Todd tried to offer.

"No!" Both vixens snapped, still looking at Ryoko.

The older man sighed. "Very well. I could wish for a better time, but we won't get one. Before this begins, Sakaki, I would like to say that I am so terribly sorry."

"Sorry about what?"

"We need to bring Tisiphone back." He wouldn't look at her. Sakaki stared at the man, puzzled.

"She's dead."

"Sit down, please," He continued as if she hadn't spoken.

She didn't sit, so much as collapse on the chair. Ryoko stood, looking into her eyes. "Breathe deep, look at me, and do not fear. Who was Tisiphone?"

"Tisiphone was an assassin," She said emotionlessly. "You know that—"

He cut her off. "Who was Tisiphone?"

"Ask me no questions, I'll tell you no lies. Where ignorance is bliss, 'tis folly to be wise." Again, emotionless. Mechanical. The same answer she had given him. The life started to come back in her face as she started to ask again but was once again cut off.

"I must ask you these questions, so please tell me no lies. I realize ignorance is bliss, but now I must be wise. Who was Tisiphone?" A tear ran down his face.

That was nothing compared to Sakaki. The calm, cool mask she wore shattered to a thousand pieces right before Todd's eyes. Tears were streaming down her face, and she was barely able to answer. "Tisiphone... was me!"

That's when she started screaming.

Chapter Thirty-Nine

The scariest and truest monster is the one that wears our face.
     – The Kikitsutai Book of Wisdom

Todd was quickly and quietly ushered out of the room by Ryoko, while Kira stayed with Sakaki, who was still screaming, in between sobs.

"I don't understand. What happened? Is she okay? What did she mean she was Tisiphone?"

"Before Sakaki took the name 'Liska' she used the name 'Tisiphone'. As Tisiphone, she was an assassin. This was for about six to eight months. I'm sure there were signs beforehand; signs that she wasn't handling it well, but we missed them. It wasn't until she came home, shaking, claiming that Tisiphone had to die, that we knew anything. She... she cut her wrists at one point. Using a silver knife." Ryoko swallowed hard, then continued. "You do not know the agony that causes, but it says volumes about her state of mind. We found her in time, but she still has the scars. After surviving that, she spent two months as a fox, coming close to forgetting she wasn't just a fox. When we did get her to change back, she started talking about Tisiphone as if she were another person. A person she had killed. She was actively repressing the memories."

"So, you hypnotized her so she'd forget?"

"No, we hypnotized her so she would remember. If it ever became necessary, we could remind her. The problem is the hypnotism puts her back at the same emotional point where she was when she was originally hypnotized."

"Where she was almost suicidal?"

"Yes."

"Why did you make her remember? She's about to go confront Atolatar!"

"Exactly. Somehow this Atolatar knows about her being Tisiphone. We don't know how, but he knows. We couldn't send her into a fight not remembering. If he told her..." Todd winced. "We couldn't do that to her. We did it now, as opposed to later, in hopes that this will give her time to deal with it before fighting Atolatar." The man sighed. "Perhaps it is just as well you were there. Keep an eye on her? She'll need all the friends she can get."

"I will." He took one last look through the door before it closed. Kira was kneeling on the ground, holding Sakaki who was crying into her shoulder. The Werefox was definitely broken.

***

Sakaki, she didn't even want to think of herself as 'Liska' at the moment, had cried herself to sleep at some point, still leaning on Kira. When she woke up, in a bed in *Sensei*'s guest room, with Kira dozing

nearby, she was struck by the feeling of not wanting
to move. Her head hurt, her throat hurt, and her
heart and ribs ached. It only took a few seconds for
her to remember why. Then she had to stop from
crying again. Nineteen-year-old ninjas don't cry!
Neither do assassins. That was too much for her.
She dissolved into sobs, waking Kira in a heartbeat.

"Shh, it's alright. We know. We're here. It's
going to be okay."

"It's not. It can't be. It shouldn't be."

Kira just held her. Words wouldn't help.
Nothing was said for a long time.

"What time is it?" Sakaki asked, looking at
her watch. Her watch with the extra wide band to
hide the scars. Same with her bracelet. No wonder
she never took them off.

"About three in the afternoon. You're staying
here tonight. No way on earth I'm leaving you alone
tonight."

"Thanks." Okay, so it was part support, and
part a low-key suicide watch, but if they didn't
mention that part, she could pretend she didn't
know. So many things were falling slowly into place.
Why her wrists were always covered and she got a
headache whenever she wondered why. Her dreams,
why she couldn't remember what Tisiphone was
like. Her mind was conspiring against her to not let
her know the truth.

Shahara had seen her wrist. That's why she
went pale and insisted that Anna could tell her
anything. How ironic. She had been so concerned
and Sakaki hadn't known why. Because the
headaches came in when she tried to think about it,
just like when she touched that box... The box!

Sakaki stifled the emotions quickly, before Kira could get suspicious. After a few minutes, she spoke.

"Hey, Kira? I need to get some things from my room. My wig, so you can use it. Clothes, water the plants, and sign out for another night."

"You don't need that today. I've got extra clothes and so do you."

"I do need to sign out for another day. I could also get my notes for school." Kira was watching her. Kira always could read her. "I'll just be a few minutes. I'd say you can come, but you can't be seen on campus."

"What if I went as you?"

"The wig, oh, yeah. You have the wig. I forgot." Not a good sign, forgetting things like that. "Anyway, I'm fine. Well, not fine, but I promise not to do anything stupid." Kira was still giving her that look. "I need to do this."

"Then I'm going with you." Kira held up a hand before Sakaki could interrupt. "I'll stay off campus, but if you're gone longer than ten minutes, I'm coming after you."

"Deal."

***

Kira waited across the street from the campus, 'reading' a large newspaper and keeping an eye out. Sakaki had gotten her to promise not to come in as long as she was visible every few minutes. Hard to do that inconspicuously, but Sakaki suspected that wasn't her cousin's main concern.

She signed out for another night on the sign out sheet and even stopped by the RA's room. Karen, her RA, was very sympathetic about her sudden family emergency. Leaving the RA's room, Sakaki made eye contact with Kira, then went to her own room. She had her emergency travel bag packed, like always, and decided to grab the suitcase she had packed for Russia. It was possible she wouldn't come back to this room. There were only three days until she left country, and she couldn't see Kira letting her out of sight much during that time.

The wooden mystery box was under her bed. Sakaki tucked it in her emergency bag, under her clothes. This was neither the time nor place to go through it. She might need someone there. Last thing she grabbed was a notebook. Making notes to help Kira pass as her would at least keep her mind busy and fill the time.

She couldn't have been in her room for more than five or six minutes, but Kira was practically vibrating in impatience. More problematically, Kira was making her way to her before Sakaki even crossed the street. "I'm here, I'm fine. I have a mission, remember?"

Kira almost slumped at that. "And after the mission?"

"There's always another mission."

***

While she was actually in Ryoko-*Sensei*'s house, her watchers were more relaxed. They probably counted on their other senses to tell them if she was edging into dangerous waters again. So, it wasn't too hard, as in easier than quantum physics, to get a few minutes to herself.

Sakaki locked the door. It was futile gesture. The lock was flimsy, and either of them could and would break the door down in a heartbeat if they thought it necessary. But it would buy her a little time. Taking a deep breath, Sakaki slowly opened the box.

On the top were two long thin cords of metal, almost invisible when used right, with a wooden handle on one hand. They were razor sharp. Razor Thread, Tisiphone's signature weapon. Beneath it were papers. Tisiphone's notes and newspaper cuttings about some of her jobs.

Sakaki looked in the mirror. Tisiphone looked back at her. "I will defeat Atolatar, even if I have to use you to do it. Then you are gone for good," She whispered. Sakaki shuddered, then turned away.

***

Sakaki was able to hide the box and its' contents and pass as semi-normal under the circumstances before she unlocked the door. From appearances, no one had overheard her. Good, that wouldn't be easy to explain. Now, how did she deal with this?

If she seemed too fine, neither *Sensei* nor Kira would believe it, and they'd assume worse than if she couldn't stop crying and refuse to let her out of their sight. If she lost control too much, they would assume she couldn't handle it and refuse to let her out of their sight.

How did she really feel? Not counting whatever it was that was gnawing through her stomach from the inside, the severe headache from crying, the sore throat from the same, and the feeling the world was ending. Well, other than that, she probably felt fine. But she had to control herself. She had a job to do.

Ryoko-*Sensei* and Kira were in the living room. Both looked up when she walked in, obviously trying to analyze everything about her. She'd probably have to get used to this for a while.

"I remember Ryasmus. It was Tisiphone's last job. The whole thing felt wrong, but I did it anyway. It was only afterwards that I learned he wasn't really a threat. I had been used. I'm not sure which of his followers Atolatar was, or who followed him, but I can remember enough to handle it."

"Good. How are you feeling?" Ryoko-*Sensei* asked.

Awful, but that's okay. I'm a murderer, I deserve to feel awful. She couldn't say that to him. For one thing, saying that would get her classed as unable to work. She couldn't stop now, she had sworn a vow that she'd stop him. For another, *Sensei* had been an assassin many years ago. She didn't want to sound like she was judging him. "I'm... recovering. I won't go to the lengths I did last time. But I definitely feel worse than yesterday. Todd went home?"

"Yes, hours ago. He says he's still your friend," Ryoko-*Sensei* said.

Sakaki nodded. If she had known what was going to happen, she'd have insisted he leave first. So, would he avoid her or want her to talk about it? On the other hand, this would probably get rid of all his ideas about liking her. That could only be for the best, right? After all, who could care for a monster?

***

Before Todd even got back to campus, he knew classes were a wash today. Fortunately, one class was just a review, and another, the teacher didn't even take attendance. Jamal wasn't in, so he didn't have to explain anything yet. He had a headache from staying up too late, and possibly from this morning's news. Todd forced himself to push the whole issue aside for now and took a nighttime pain pill for his headache and to try to catch some sleep.

As a result, he got about four hours of disjointed sleep and some extremely odd dreams, the only part he could remember later was that they were weird, and he was pretty sure there was an emu involved. Feeling slightly more alert, Todd made himself a double strength coffee, and sat on the balcony of the lounge to think.

He knew it wasn't a good idea to try to make major life decisions while sleep-deprived and slightly drugged, nor did caffeine seem to aid rational thinking, but Todd had a lot to think about, and it couldn't wait much longer.

This Tisiphone revelation had completely floored him. He hadn't expected it and didn't have a clue how he was supposed to deal with it. Todd had always prided himself on picking the difficult truth over the easy lie, but this.... His first reaction was to wish he'd never found out.

Gradually, he changed his mind. Yes, it was a difficult concept to swallow, but it also slid a few things into place; and maybe, just maybe, he could help her somehow. He certainly wouldn't be able to help her very much if he didn't know.

Did this change what he felt about her? Did he still love her? It was love he felt, he was almost certain now. On the other hand, he wasn't so wrapped up in emotion that he was blind to her faults. He owed it, to both of them, to see if he could handle this new revelation before talking to her. What he needed was more information. Fortunately, he knew where to get it.

He went back to his room. Jamal was there now. "There you are! I was worried. Did you even come back last night?"

Todd rubbed at his hair. "No. Something came up unexpectedly. Sorry to worry you."

"Something came up?" Jamal arched his eyebrows, waiting for more information.

"I was helping a friend with something. Not my story to tell."

"This about Anna?"

He really was transparent, wasn't he? "Don't ask her. Seriously, this is... I don't even know."

"Shahara thinks she's in trouble."

Shahara was very perceptive. "I really can't say."

"But you do know." Jamal was just as perceptive.

"Jamal—"

His roommate threw up his hands. "Fine, fine. I'll leave it. But be careful, okay? Don't let whatever trouble she may be in put you in danger."

It already had. "I'll be careful." Todd found his folder of important papers and rummaged through it until he found his passport.

"Okay, what do you need that for? Exams aren't that terrible."

Todd managed a small chuckle as he tried to remember the cover story. "I found out yesterday, so I haven't had a chance to tell you yet, but one of my paintings won an art contest," that the Werefoxes made up on the spot, and declared him the winner of, "the next stage is that it gets entered into an international contest. I forget the name, but I have to be there. It's only a few days away. I'm talking to the professors today."

"Wow, that's awesome, Bro!" Jamal gave him a hearty smack on the back. "Why didn't you tell me you entered this contest? What painting?"

"It was last minute, and I kind of forgot about it. It was the painting of the Intracoastal on the eve of a hurricane. Remember that one?" It was one of his best, so they had decided that was the winner.

"Did you ever name it?"

"Yeah, it's *On Storm's Edge.*" Sakaki's idea. "Anyway, I really got to go."

"Right, good luck. Let me know how you do. Where is this anyway?"

"Saint Petersburg, Russia. I leave on the 11th."

Jamal clearly had a lot more questions, but Todd slipped out the door before he could ask any more.

His first stop was Ryoko. While the older man was pleased to have the passport, he was less pleased that he wanted to talk. "The girls are asleep. Let's not wake them. Come, we can talk in the park."

The park was the same one they were in all night, only about a block from the house. Todd wouldn't be surprised if that was a significant factor in buying or renting the house. It was also quiet for an early afternoon. Perhaps kids were still in school. Whatever the reason, they were able to find a quiet bench and privacy. "What is it you need to know?"

Todd wasn't fooled. Whatever Ryoko thought of him, good, bad, or indifferent, his first priority would be for Sakaki. So, this may not be the most accurate of information. But it was a start. "Everyone agrees Tisiphone was an assassin. How exactly are you defining assassin? Is it basically the same as a hit man?"

"No. Not in the least. A hit man or contract killer will kill almost anyone if they are paid enough for it. Tisiphone was an assassin and a highly selective one at that. She only went after those that the law couldn't or wouldn't deal with. This would include non-humans who endangered the innocent but couldn't be arrested, terrorists that conventional troops couldn't catch, and certain dictators or the powers behind a throne. She likened it to killing one to save many. You may disagree with her actions, but she wouldn't take a job unless she was convinced that removing a target would be necessary. We are all taught to respect life, and resist taking it unless it absolutely must be done."

Todd winced as he thought about the internal conflict she must have faced. "An assassin with a conscience. No wonder she fell apart."

"She was neither the first nor the last of us to be assassins, and most of us have a conscience." Ryoko looked at him as if he were a bug.

"How many started as a teenager?"

"That... is a much smaller number. She was one of the youngest. You may have a point."

"Who assigned these jobs?"

"Some, especially in the beginning were assigned by the skulk. Some she was hired by outsiders, such as various councils or governments. All contact was through intermediaries, so none of them knew how young she was or often even that she was female. It's safer that way."

First rule of assassination, kill the assassin. Todd nodded. "What happened to... well, everything?"

"We don't know. She won't talk about it."

"Right. Got it." He had a few other questions, but most of them were ones he'd prefer to talk to her about, not a third party. Plus, some simply weren't his business. After all, did he truly need, or even want, to know things like how many people she had killed?

Ryoko saw that he was done. "Sakaki will probably stay at my house until it's time to leave, but we'd like your help integrating Kira into the school."

"Sure."

"That will be tomorrow likely. It won't take much, Sakaki will inform her of the major things.

You'll be very busy as well. We've informed your school about your contest, so you need to talk to your professors about exams."

Todd nodded, glad for the first time that circumstances had prevented him from taking more than twelve credits this semester. He was pretty sure he'd have to retake Mental Development anyway, so it didn't matter if he missed the exam. Classical Painting Techniques had a final project instead of an exam, and he was nearly finished with his Greek gods' paintings. He had Dr. Keith for the last two classes, and she'd probably be willing to work with him. "I better do that now."

"Best of luck."

It was a relief to know that Sakaki had never been conscienceless, but they still needed to talk. That wouldn't be easy.

***

Ryoko turned out to be completely correct. As far as Todd could tell, Sakaki didn't leave the house until early Friday. She called him a few times but hung up whenever he tried to talk about anything other than plans for leaving. Kira had taken her place as school, with Todd briefly showing her around and trying to inconspicuously introduce her to people Anna should know. Fortunately, since it was the week before finals, most people were so busy with their own projects that a bit of memory loss was not remarkable, when some people seemed to have trouble remembering their own names.

Todd hoped Kira was managing well, but he was too busy to think much about it. Dr. Keith agreed to let him take his exams early. He couldn't do that in Mental Development, but on the professor's advice, he would retake the class next semester. Between the exams he could take and finishing his final project, he barely had time to think.

Being so busy was sometimes useful, as it kept him from answering too many of Jamal and Shahara's questions about his art project. Shahara wanted to do a party to celebrate, the three of them and Anna, but Todd convinced them he was so busy it wouldn't be possible. Maybe after Christmas Break. That made Shahara extremely unhappy, more than he thought it should, but he didn't have time to question it. She couldn't have been too mad. She bought him a Russian-English dictionary and made him promise to take lots of pictures. Jamal gave him a travel kit, with his usual toiletries in travel size. He had great friends. If only he could tell them the truth.

Busy as he was, Friday came before he realized.

***

Sakaki was already in her Selene Reynard disguise when she met Todd at the Tri-rail station. The train ran from a little north of West Palm Beach all the way down to Miami. It would take two hours, but it was cheaper, and sometimes faster than driving. From there, they could take a shuttle to the airport.

Todd hadn't seen her as Selene before, and it took her a moment to recognize her. Despite everything, that amused her a little. That and the look on his face when he did realize who she was. "You look really different," he greeted her.

"I'm supposed to."

"No offense? You don't look quite right as a blonde."

She shrugged. "It will do. Many go blonde who don't look right as blondes."

"True. Are your eyes blue?"

"They ought to be. Are they?"

"Yeah, it's... different. Not bad! Just, I like your normal look better."

"Thanks." Sakaki shrugged.

"Really." She could barely hear him over the sound of the train coming in. It was early morning and this was the second stop of the line so the train was nearly empty. They boarded. "How about we go to the top level?"

She agreed and led the way to the top of the three-level train car. It would be more private, and she liked the vantage point of being high up. Sometimes that was a tactical advantage.

The car was empty. They chose a seat with a small table, and Sakaki sat down. Todd sat down next to her instead of across from her. She opened her mouth to tell him they should sit across from each other, so they could watch each other's backs, when he spoke first.

"We need to talk." So that's what he was up to!

"Isn't that usually a girl line?"

"Who cares?"

"This isn't a good place."

"It's as good as we're going to get. You are avoiding the issue. You can't now. I figured this would be preferable to talking on the plane where we could be overheard." Or a hotel room in Russia where there might be listening devices. Captive audience. He was right about that. The only way out was past him and their luggage, and even if she managed that, there was no place to go. The train was in motion and even if she got off, she'd have to wait an hour for the next one. This was at least marginally better than anywhere else they could talk.

"That's not fair." Since when had she cared about fairness?

To his credit, he didn't call her on that. "And letting you hurt yourself is? Look, I'm worried about you, and I'm not the only one."

"You shouldn't worry about me."

"You're blocking it again, aren't you?"

"I have to. I have a job to take care of."

"You're on the verge of giving yourself Dissociative Identity Disorder."

"You don't know that."

"I'm a psych major. I may not know much, but I recognize a major problem in the making. Look, you don't want to talk to me? Fine. As long as you are talking to someone else. Are you talking to someone?"

"Yes." No.

"I don't believe you."

"Then how am I supposed to talk to you?"

"Maybe by telling the truth?" She glared at him. "Will you tell me what happened?"

"No."

"Please?"

It was a word. A simple word that she had heard and used thousands of times. So why did it suddenly have such power over her? Every wall, every defense she had shattered like glass. Sakaki didn't answer at first, she couldn't. Breathing was a lot harder than she remembered. Control, she needed control. "I was sixteen. I was too young. Far too young."

Inhale. Exhale. Inhale again. "I really couldn't take it. But I had to. I'm not like the rest of my family, being only a half Were. I've always felt so much pressure, trying to prove that I could be just as good. Maybe better. So, I always took the hardest paths. Not many of us choose that path, but those that do are respected... as long as they don't go too far."

Todd nodded, saying he understood. At least as much as he could.

"I was falling apart. Getting sloppy. I think... I think I wanted to get caught. I couldn't say, 'No, I won't do this'; but if I got caught, or badly hurt, or it became obvious that I couldn't do this anymore, then it would end. Of course, that just proved that I wasn't as good, but I wasn't thinking this through. My last job, Ryasmus..." Todd nodded again. He remembered. Good.

"I did the job, even though it felt wrong, and was leaving. This is the part I haven't told anyone. Ever. I was leaving, and I was spotted. By a child. No witnesses. There aren't supposed to be witnesses."

She heard his gasp of horror, could smell it on him. But it was too late to stop now. "I had two contradictory teachings. First rule of an assassin: never leave a witness. First rule of the Kikitsutai: never harm a child. So I did the one thing neither was supposed to do. I froze. It was a boy, maybe eight years old. We stared at each other for maybe twenty seconds. It felt like forever. Then he saw my sword. The blood on it. He started to scream. I panicked. I pushed him to the side and started to run past him. It was my fault. I knew there was a staircase there. I didn't even think about what I was doing.

She had to stop. *You can't cry here!* "I turned to look. He had fallen down the staircase and was on the ground. Not moving. I wanted to go down, see if he was okay, but we had caused a commotion, and I had to run before I was spotted again."

"Did he die?"

"I don't know. I don't know what happened to him at all." She stopped again. Another deep breath. "Am I a monster?"

Chapter Forty

A helpful word at the right place is better than a wise word at the wrong one. – The Kikitsutai Book of Wisdom

It wasn't long into her story that Todd found himself overwhelmed. He might be a psych major, but he didn't have his bachelors yet, and this wasn't something they taught in class. But someone had to talk to her, and he was the only one available. Then she asked him, "Am I a monster?"

He didn't answer immediately. An off-the-cuff answer could make things worse. Praying he was saying the right thing, he spoke, "Did you mean to do that? Push him down the staircase?"

"No!"

"Do you fear becoming a monster?"

"Yes."

"Then you aren't one. If you regret what happened, which was an accident, by the way, and fear becoming a monster, then you can't be a monster."

She didn't answer for a while. When she did, he had to strain to hear it. "Thank you."

"You're welcome."

They didn't talk again for the rest of the train ride.

***

By the time they got to the airport, Sakaki had herself under control. Now they were waiting to go through security. Fun. Sakaki hated commercial flying. So much could go wrong that she had no control over. Besides, she had to be careful about security, not having anything they could find.

Her swords and a few other weapons were in her check-in bag, along with a document stating she was carrying them for a museum. The razor thread was in the bottom of her carry-on, in a box labeled 'computer wires'. Even then, they wouldn't realize her stone hair ornament could double as a dagger. It wouldn't slice, but it could pierce. She still felt vulnerable.

To make sure she didn't get singled out for extra security measures, she made sure all her paperwork was in order, and that she had no metal at all on her. If necessary, she could try a little insta-hypnosis on the guard.

It wasn't necessary. The guards seemed bored, and tired. Her papers were in order, and her carry-on didn't look too suspicious. They didn't know what was in her check-in, so they didn't think to look for more weapons. She didn't set off the metal detector and was past the security checkpoint quickly. Todd had little less luck. Apparently, his belt and watch were enough metal to throw the detector off.

Selene waited for him on the other side, eyes closed. It was time to sink into Selene. Twenty years old, born in Bordeaux, France, living there most of her life, though she spoke more of the Paris pronunciation of French. Had dreams of being a poet (not very good, though), dreading being forced into the family business of owning a vineyard. Her family had been most displeased about her alcohol allergy and reluctance to join the family business but were currently being tolerant. (It probably said something that most of her personas had strained relationships with family.) Fluent in French, English, and Spanish. She had come to the United States to represent the family wine in a wine tasting contest, which had conveniently been close to a poetry convention she wanted to go to. Her trip to Moscow was a little harder to explain, but she had family in the area.

Most of this would never get said to anyone, but she had it to fall back on if anyone asked any questions. Other than what she was doing in various places, most of Selene Reynard had been settled over a year ago when she first used the identity. It wasn't a hard identity to maintain, even if it involved changing her looks. Her French was naturally the Paris pronunciation, though there were a few other dialects she could pull off if she tried. She had memorized a lot about vineyards and wine, knowing the terms, and could identify a lot about a wine from the smell without tasting it. She also learned about poetry and had some truly awful samples to regale anyone who asked. That kept most people from digging deeper.

"How did you get through security so easily?" Todd asked when he got close enough.

Selene answered, the French accent clear in her voice, which earned her a raised eyebrow. "By making sure to seem totally above board. Beware of the ones that look too clean."

"So you are... prepared?"

"A little." So little that she felt naked. Vulnerable. But he didn't need to know that.

***

While Sakaki was not fond of commercial flying, she did like the amenities that first class offered. So when she had to fly, she always splurged for an upgraded seat. It was one of the things that made flying bearable. Even discounting that it was more comfortable, it was more private, and she liked being able to pre-board. It was only a little bit of reconnaissance, but it made her feel a little more in control.

They had two seats that made up an aisle row, so they had some privacy. First class wasn't full. Evidently, that was a sign for Todd that it was safe to talk some.

"I have a question that's been bugging me since the train."

"Yes?"

He lowered his voice. "Ryasmus was a vampire, right?"

She nodded.

"So, wouldn't the little boy be a vampire too? You said vampires could only be killed when their heart was destroyed, then they turn to ash. Shouldn't you know, one way or another?"

"No, but I see your logic. The boy was too young to become a vampire. He'd be a wraith. Wraiths have a different physiology. They don't need to drink blood and have a higher resistance to sunlight, but they aren't as invulnerable as vampires. And if killed, they don't turn to ash. The coming of age ceremony generally doesn't happen until their fifties, which is like late teens to early thirties to humans." It was so much easier talking about it in abstract.

"What are you two talking about?" Asked a man sitting in front of them. Early fifties, dressed in expensive suit, probably traveling for business. Definitely a Day.

She could smell Todd's fear, and spoke up quickly, before he could blurt out something stupid. "It's a LARP." The man nodded.

"Sounds interesting. What's it about?"

"A power play in vampire aristocracy. Think Dracula meets Game of Thrones. Complicated to explain though."

"Ah. You enjoy it?" He seemed... envious? Must be a closet geek.

"I do. But my character got killed off."

That was enough of an explanation for the man, as he gave her a brief 'sorry' then turned back to his papers. Sakaki pulled out a note book, and wrote down a message where Todd could see it. *No more talking about this in public.*

Right. Sorry. A LARP?
Live Action Role Play
I know. I'm just a little surprised you knew.
Not the first time we've used that kind of excuse. Not by a long shot.

"So, changing the subject," Todd started, "About us-"

"Not now. Please, I can't..." She took breath. "I need to focus on this. We can talk afterwards." *If we're both still alive.* "Why don't you get some sleep? I intend to. It's a long flight, and we don't have much time to get used to the time zone difference."

"Fine, but we *are* going to talk later. What is the time difference anyway?"

"They are eight hours ahead of us."

"And we're flying into Moscow, I noticed. How are we getting to Saint Petersburg?"

"Overnight train ride. I've done it a lot. Easiest way to get from one to the other."

The rest of the plane ride was long, but uneventful. Sakaki had told as much as she was willing to, and more. They slept most of the rest of the way.

***

Todd's first impression of Sheremetyevo airport in Moscow was that it was a depressing welcome to the country. According to Sakaki, it was the most depressing airport she had seen as well. Airports tended to be painted white, with lots of light and windows to make it seem spacious. Sheremetyevo walls were rust brown, with a copper hive design on the ceiling, making the place seem smaller. There weren't many windows, and no one seemed to understand the concept of a line. Sakaki pulled him along as she weaved through the crowds or he might have been there for hours.

Passport control was especially aggravating, as he was certain that in thirty minutes, despite fifteen people going through the passport control booth, his line never got shorter. He was figuring out why Europeans didn't smile for passport photos. Certainly no one was smiling now.

Passport control took long enough that baggage claim was easy. Was it his imagination, or did Sakaki seem calmer when she got her suitcase? Customs was even easier. Sakaki noticed that no one was in the green channel, for nothing to declare, and led them straight through. Then they got outside.

Todd was shivering instantly. Not a surprise, it was December, and he was from West Palm Beach. Good thing Ryoko was able to hunt up a nice warm coat approximately his size.

Hunched over, he followed Sakaki through the cold and snow, hoping she had some idea of what to do. Apparently, she did. She eyed the line of taxis speculatively, until she started heading for one in the middle. The driver looked at them, first blankly, then with recognition. "Sasha!"

Sakaki gave a small smile. "Dmitri Ivanovitch. *Kak dela?*" If he remembered the guidebook correctly that was 'How are you?'

There was an indistinguishable flurry of what Todd presumed was Russian for a few minutes. He wasn't surprised that a few minutes later, the driver was helping them load their luggage into his truck. Todd made it a point not to talk until they got to the train station. Sakaki paid the man in American money, which he seemed pleased about. Then she handed her suitcases to Todd and told him to watch them for a few minutes.

He was just starting to get concerned when she came back. "Okay, we've got some Russian money, I bought our tickets, and we can store everything in the locker room. We've got over six hours before our train leaves, what would you like to do?"

"I don't know. I really don't know much about Moscow. Any suggestions?"

"Red Square and maybe the Kremlin." Sakaki didn't even hesitate.

"Sounds good. Do you know your way around the city?"

"Of course. I've spent a good bit of time in the Moscow-St. Pete region." She led them unerringly to a Metro stop.

"Why did the taxi driver call you 'Sasha'? And how did he recognize you as a blonde?"

"I told you I've spent a lot of time here. He's a contact, of sorts. Sasha is a very Russian name, so it can work for more than one look. No talking about it in the Metro." She opened the door to the station, and Todd felt heat hit him in the face.

Todd quickly discovered he loved the Metro system. It wasn't anything like he was used to a city subway system being like. It was clean, with a small army of people sweeping up trash. There was little to no graffiti. Sakaki told him it was fairly cheap, though, she was complaining that it used to be much cheaper, but as long as one didn't go above ground, they could ride all day. Best of all was the art! Some stations had statues, some had stained glass, or mosaics. They didn't see it, but Sakaki swore that one stop had a fountain. The trains were between three and five minutes apart, so they didn't even have to worry about missing one.

He might have been happy to spend the free time exploring the metro, but he was glad to see Red Square. Sakaki filled him in on various details. The church that everyone associated with Russia in general, and Moscow in particular was called St. Basil's cathedral, and it was built during the time of Ivan the Terrible in the 1500's. The little church in the corner, painted in a garish shade of yellow was actually torn down under Stalin because it was only two hundred years old, so it didn't qualify as historic. It was only rebuilt in the nineties.

The weird squat copper-bronze building was Lenin's mausoleum, where they could actually see Lenin's preserved body if they had any interest in doing so, which they didn't. A long white building was GUM (pronounced goom), and was a major mall in Moscow.

Best of all was that they were able to buy tickets to go in Saint Basil's. Todd never had a lot of interest in history, but knowing he was in a building built before Jamestown was settled was amazing. The art was even more so, as they covered every square inch, including ceilings, with paintings and icons. At least twice Sakaki had to remind him to watch the stairs before he tripped and fell. Since the stairs were stone steps, high, narrow, and uneven, she probably had a point.

"Red Square is actually a mis-translation. The Russian word for 'Red' is almost identical to the Russian word for 'Beautiful'. It was supposed to be Beautiful Square." Sakaki led him out of the building. "Come on, the Kremlin is right next door."

"Inside the wall?"

"Exactly. 'Kremlin' means 'fort'."

"These are not the most creative names." Todd tried to burrow further into his coat.

Sakaki shrugged. "I didn't name them."

There were different tickets that could be bought at the Kremlin. One let them walk the grounds and one let them walk the grounds and go in the churches. Much to Todd's disappointment, they didn't have time for that. "Maybe on the way back? There might be time then."

Sakaki was non-committal. He wondered about her sudden change of mood but got distracted when she again started playing tour guide. Even the outside grounds were beautiful, though he would have enjoyed it more if it hadn't been so cold, or snowy. Fortunately, before he was too frozen, they finished their tour and went to get dinner in the underground mall. "They built this to celebrate Moscow's eight hundred fiftieth anniversary," Sakaki informed him.

"Wow, Moscow is old. When was that?"

"1997. Pretty sure they built this to be the biggest underground mall in the world. They were going to build it eight stories down, but psychiatrists told them that people would get claustrophobic, so they decided to do five. I think they only had three done by the celebration." She stopped to have some of her drink. "There're still large empty parts. Came in handy once or twice." Sakaki's face was very like a cat that caught the canary. Or would that be a fox who caught a plump mouse? Maybe he could get her to tell that story later.

"Russians like to have the biggest. Remember the Tsar Bell and the Tsar Cannon that you saw in the Kremlin? Biggest in the world and neither of them have ever been used. The Tsar Cannon would probably break if you tried to use it. Besides, it was made for grapeshot, not cannon balls like the huge decorative ones next to it. And the Tsar Bell? They made that thing knowing that not only did they have nowhere to hang it, they couldn't even get it out of the mold! It took over a hundred years for some Italian genius to figure out how to get it out. In the meantime, Moscow had one of its' many fires..."

"I think I see where this is going."

"Oh yes. The mold caught fire. People were pouring water on it, and the bell was getting red hot. When they finally got the mold open... CRACK! Out came the chip you saw."

"The one as tall as you?"

"That's right. I can hide behind it too. It weighs fifteen tons. The bell altogether weighs about 220 tons."

"Wow, that's huge. Why'd they build it?"

"So they'd have the biggest."

***

Todd wasn't arguing when Sakaki said they should go back to the train station. He was wiped out. It was nearly eleven o'clock, and he fully intended on sleeping as soon as possible. "So what's the train like?"

"We're in first class, which isn't nearly as nice as first class on the plane. Basically it means we get a door on our cabin. The train is divided into cabins, each with four bunks. I purchased enough tickets for a full cabin, so we'd have privacy, and it would be safer." She shot him a careful look, as if daring him to say or do anything inappropriate.

"Even if I were not a gentleman, and exhausted, I know you can and would crush me like a soda can."

"You are quite correct."

The train came close to midnight. Their cabin wasn't bad, though it was hardly luxurious. Like Sakaki said, there were four bunks, two on each wall. Sakaki grabbed the top bed on the right side, while Todd took the bottom on the left. There was a thin mattress and some bedding. It was cold, apparently the heat only worked when the train was running; so they quickly made the beds. All bunks had a small wrapped Styrofoam tray with food. Breakfast. Great. They slept in their clothes, though Todd did notice Sakaki pulled a fifteen-inch sword from one suitcase and slipped it under her pillow. Definitely not a good person to wake up early in the morning. It was probably the same sword she usually kept in her pants leg. Sleep. In the morning they would be in Saint Petersburg.

Chapter Forty-One

Allies are to be treated with respect and caution. – The
Kikitsutai Book of Wisdom

Todd found the rhythm of the train hypnotic.
Coupled with his exhaustion, he fell asleep quickly.
All the same, he didn't feel well rested when he woke
up, jolted by a sharp lurch.

A quick peek told him Sakaki was awake,
sitting on her bunk.

"What time izit?" he mumbled.

"About five-thirty."

"I'm goin' back to sleep."

"We arrive in half an hour."

Todd moaned and pulled himself to a sitting
position, bumping his head lightly on the bunk
above him. "Does that mean I gotta wake up?"

"More or less. The train provides this as
breakfast. It's not spectacular, but it is food. We can
get something warm when we get to the city. After
all, we can't even check in until eight or so."

"Great. What is it?" Todd poked at the tray of
food.

"I believe that is what's known in some elite
circles as 'bread'. There's butter on the side. Some

yogurt, mine was strawberry, yours might be too. A bit of cheese, a bit of meat... *Preyatna appateetna.*"

"What kind of meat?"

"Don't know. Not asking."

"Wonderful. What's that mean, what you said?"

"Good appetite, basically."

"Is this edible?"

"I ate mine twenty minutes ago. I haven't dropped dead yet."

Well, that was semi-encouraging, and he was hungry. He decided to skip the meat though. "You promise we can get something else in St. Pete?"

"We'll certainly look. I want some tea. And we might as well find some place warm to wait for the hotel to open."

Sounded good to him. "What's on the agenda for today?"

"I figure we'll look for a café or something until we can check in. After check in, we can get some more sleep, and I'll contact Fiona. After that, we'll see."

Things went basically as she had planned. Todd practically fell asleep on her shoulder as they waited for the hotel to open. They didn't have reservations, but apparently Sakaki had 'arrangements' with a relatively nice hotel to stay there when she wanted. The hotel was called the *Moskva*, which Sakaki assured him was the Russian word for Moscow. Tired as he was, that seemed hysterically funny. Almost as funny as the 'Jewelery' kiosk in the lobby. Their rooms were next to each other. Before she let him in either of the rooms, Sakaki insisted on searching them. Finally deciding they were safe, she let him in. After warning him three times not to drink the water, or even brush his teeth with it, they separated, agreeing to meet up in the afternoon. Todd barely managed to pull off the covers and climb into bed before he was back to sleep.

***

About eleven a.m. local time, Liska decided to get to work. Fiona should be home. She dialed the number.

"*Allo? Kto tam?*" Hello, who's there?

"It's me." That should be enough for Fiona to recognize her voice. She wasn't that social.

"Oh, hi. What's up?"

"You up for company tonight?"

"You're here?"

"Tonight, the usual?"

"Sure, what time?"

"Eight?" Seven.

"Okay. See you then."

"See you."

So she had eight hours. There was a knock on her door. One hand grabbed at a throwing knife. "*Kto tam?*"

"Sakaki?"

Liska shook her head, as she put the knife away then unlocked the door. "It's Selene for now," She said after letting him in and shutting the door.

"Right, sorry." Todd rubbed at his face, sheepishly.

"It's fine. These rooms are clean. But be more careful. Have a nice sleep?"

"Yeah. Now what?"

"I called Fiona. We're meeting her for dinner at seven. Until then, we are on our own. Want to do a little sightseeing?" It gave her the excuse to do most of the reconnaissance she needed.

"Yeah, okay. But it'll be cold."

"It's winter, near the arctic circle. Get used to it. Actually, it's warmer here than in Moscow, because we're on the water."

"It's still cold."

Liska didn't roll her eyes, but she wanted to. "Next time, I'll tell the bad guy he should stick to warm climates."

"You do that."

***

Unlike Moscow, where the beautiful and historic parts of the city were all over, most of the tourist parts of Saint Petersburg were in the same general area. So it didn't take long to sight see in St. Petersburg, which was a blessing considering it was barely ten degrees Fahrenheit. Liska was most interested in Saint Isaac's cathedral. Not as beautiful as the Church of the Spilt Blood (a more elaborate and much newer version of Saint Basil's) nor as historic as the Hermitage, but it had something neither of them did. An indoor staircase leading to the roof, where you could get a panoramic view of the city.

Liska walked around the roof three times, taking pictures, mentally identifying points of interest, trying to map out possibilities and plans. Todd was next to her, shivering. To his credit, he hadn't complained. Yet. "You can wait inside. I want to see this."

"What are we seeing?"

"The city."

"So?"

"I need to know where everything is."

"I thought you knew this area."

"I haven't been here in two years. Things change." She took another picture. There actually wasn't much in the way of differences. But she'd rather double check than go on her memories and get caught off guard with a change.

"Can't you get a map?"

"I have maps. They won't tell me what my own eyes will. Besides, it's against Russian law to make or own a map that's too accurate." Not that she didn't have them, but no point mentioning that here and now.

"That's odd."

"No, that's Russia."

One more walk around and she allowed herself to be dragged inside. It was cold, but Liska had a higher than usual resistance to cold. Unfortunately, she wasn't nearly as good with heat. It made living in Florida an interesting experience.

Todd much preferred the inside of the cathedral. Since it was made in a very different era, it had a much different art style than the cathedrals in Moscow. This cathedral didn't have every square inch painted, though there were some paintings on the ceiling. Todd claimed the colors were much brighter here, too. She'd take his word for it. Art wasn't her thing. Eventually, it was time to meet Fiona.

***

"Here's what you need to know. Fiona is a Wererabbit. That means she's a vegetarian and really does not like the smell of meat. That's why we're going to the only vegetarian place I've ever seen in Russia. Being part rabbit, she's on the timid side. Gets very nervous, especially with people she doesn't know. Even though she knows me, she sometimes gets uneasy around me when I'm physically there. It's a Were thing. We deal with it by concealing our scents. I've asked her to find out what our good friend is up to around here. Okay?" Sakaki filled Todd in while leading him to the meeting place.

"Gotcha. There are Wererabbits?"

"Yes, Todd. There are Wererabbits," She answered, sounding slightly exasperated.

Fiona was already there. A small woman, just a little taller than Sakaki, with light brown hair. Todd could pick her out even before they got to her. She was the woman who kept looking around, wiping at her nose. Sakaki and Todd sat down in the booth opposite her, Sakaki on the outside.

"Hello, Fiona." She was speaking English, even if it was with that French accent.

"He...Hello. Who's this?"

"Todd. Friend of mine. He has great foresight." Fiona nodded, apparently getting what Sakaki had hinted at.

"Pleased to meet you." She turned back to Sakaki. "Hate to ask, but I'm out of perfume, could I..."

Sakaki handed her a small spray bottle. The same one she had sprayed herself with before coming in the restaurant. Fiona thanked her and excused herself.

Todd frowned. "I don't smell anything."

"Exactly." Sakaki smiled. Then filled him in by whispering, "More of an 'anti-perfume'. It hides scent."

Fiona came back, seeming a little more confident, though her hands still shook a little.

"So, what's our good friend up to now?" Liska asked. Todd had almost seen Sakaki transition to Liska.

"You were right, he's up to something. He's talking a shakeup of epic proportions. A world where those who hide can be in charge."

"But how's he going to get there?"

"I'm not sure, but he's talking about something being revealed with a bang in three days."

Liska and Todd shared a look. That was when the political talks started. "Okay, tell me about him personally."

"I've not seen him. He's paranoid, and almost no one knows anything concrete. There is a second he seems to trust. Haven't met him, but I'm told he's a moon lover." That must mean a Were. "Other than that, it's mostly shades of people." Or just shades. "I don't know that even they know what's going on."

"So, if someone stops him before then, nothing will happen?" Liska asked.

"I don't know."

"I see. Anything else?"

Fiona hesitated. "What he's saying? The things he's promising? It sounds good. Many are interested."

"Even after realizing what it will take to get there? How many will be hurt, even die, on all sides?" Liska's voice was so low, even Todd could barely hear her. Fiona must have heard though, because she was looking very pale.

"Would it really be like that?"

"Yes, I think it would."

Fiona put down the fork she had been fiddling with and deliberately folded her hands. "I was afraid of that."

"Look, I understand. I hate this too. We all get tired of having to live a lie. But it's not time yet. We aren't ready. Any of us."

"When will it be time?"

"When it won't result in death, destruction, and possibly the war to end all wars."

"Good point." Fiona shuddered.

Not surprising. Sakaki had mentioned that Fiona was a pacifist.

"So, where is he?"

"Took me three days, but I've got the address written down. Here."

Liska took it, then glared at the paper. "Why that cheating copy-cat." Her voice was a fraction too loud. But no one seemed to be looking.

"What is it?" Fiona asked.

"That's a school building. Well, used to be. It got closed a few years back because of budget constraints. I've used it a few times myself."

"Well, then you should know the layout pretty well?" Fiona asked hesitantly.

"Yes, I still have my notes. Ideas for best time?"

"I really don't know."

"Okay, that should be everything. Thanks, Fiona."

***

"So, what's your plan?" Todd asked as they headed back to the hotel.

"I'll have to go after him. Tomorrow night, I think. *You* will wait in the hotel."

"How will you stop him?"

Liska gave him a look. "Let's see, I can't talk him out of this, and prisons can't hold him. Whatever shall I do?"

"You'll kill him?" She could tell he was trying not to act horrified. He wasn't doing a good job, but she appreciated the effort.

"I'm open to suggestions."

"Is there like a prison for vampires?"

"Nope."

"Why not?"

"Vampires don't imprison one another. As for why there isn't a prison for Twilights or Nights, well, that would require everyone to agree on what should count as crimes and what justice should be for them."

"Well, how do they deal with issues like this?"

"You really don't want to know. Let's just say that we could make a solid argument for my way being more merciful."

Todd shivered but didn't back down. "Is it really necessary?"

"Would you prefer he do something to kill off all those world leaders?"

"Are you sure that's what he's going to do?"

"Absolutely positive? No. But that's the most logical explanation. 'Revealed with a bang', that's probably literal. Atolatar has shown a blatant disregard for human life, so I doubt he's going to go and politely ask that Twilights and Nights be recognized and have equal rights." Even if that was his plan, she might still have to kill him.

"So, a bomb, or multiple? Couldn't you just find and defuse them?"

Liska shook her head. "This isn't a movie. It's not that simple. One, I don't know what building the talks are going to be in. Two, I don't know he *is* planning a bomb. Even if I did, I'd have to find a way in, find a way to search the building, and find whatever traps he is planning. There could be one bomb, or fifty. He might have planned poisonous gas. He might send in his shades to kill everyone there. Too many possibilities. And even if I could defuse this plan, all of his possibilities, do you really think he'll just give up? Just say, 'Curses, foiled again,' fold his hands and disappear?"

Todd was staring at her, pale.

She deflated. "Look, believe it or not, I don't like this either. I don't want to kill him and wouldn't do this if I didn't believe it was one hundred percent necessary. I know my job. Leave me to it." What did he think ninjas did anyway? Teach origami?

Okay, so what if Todd was quietly re-evaluating their entire relationship? She had done everything short of spell it out for him that she wasn't normal and was certainly no angel. Besides, when this was finished, she had go back to Japan. Hmm, she still hadn't told him that. Well, if the job went well, there would be time afterwards. If it didn't, then it wouldn't matter. She wasn't going to tell him there was more than a sixty percent chance of both of them winding up dead. He didn't need to know that yet.

Chapter Forty-Two

Prepare for every battle as if it were your last. One of them will be. – The Kikitsutai Book of Wisdom

Todd left Liska alone, at her request, so she could work on her plans. The first thing she had done was dig out her old notes and memories of the building. On her first trip, Liska had mapped the place thoroughly. Studying the maps, she tried to bully her brain into remembering every detail. Where were the windows in this classroom? How far was the stairwell from that classroom? What rooms would he use the most?

The most obvious rooms to set up in would be those without windows. True, windows could be covered or even painted over, but someone might notice that and start wondering about the 'abandoned' school. Both the gym and the auditorium were large rooms without windows. The basement had few to none but was small and cramped. She wouldn't rule it out, but it was less likely to be his choice.

So, would he prefer the large emptiness of a gym, or the dramatics of a stage? The auditorium also had some small rooms or partitions without windows. Both had their advantages and disadvantages. Ideally, she'd prefer to find him before he knew she was there. She didn't even know how many followers he had on the premises. This was beginning to feel more and more like a suicide run.

Nothing she could do about it now. She had a job to do, even if the odds were against her. Liska half formed various plans and portions of plans, not committing herself to any, but having something to use if the opportunity presented itself. Plans had a way of changing in the heat of battle anyway.

She went through her supplies for the eighth time. Everything was in fine working order. The only thing she could do now was wait. Liska had spent half the night working on her plans, but she knew she wouldn't sleep again until this was over. Sleep was always hardest in the final stages of mission. Between worry, adrenaline, and her restless mind trying to figure out additional plans or cautions, rest was out of reach.

Okay, the chances of survival were low. Grudge matches were the hardest fights, and he was clearly holding a grudge against her. Plus, Atolatar knew more about her than she knew about him. A lot more. That was highly unusual for her, and she didn't like it at all. What else did he know about her? He was also a leader. Even if she got rid of him, what about his followers? Painful as it was to admit, she simply wasn't going into this at her best. True, she had faced worse odds, and made it out alright, she still wanted to make sure all contingencies were taken care of.

Despite her attempts to keep Todd out of it, if she died, he probably wouldn't make it out of the country. Sure, she told Fiona and Todd that if she didn't come back in the morning, they were to take her plane ticket and skip the country, but if she failed, even that wouldn't keep them safe for long. That was assuming they actually managed to leave. It should give them a little time before the attack, if they left immediately, because the country would probably lock down all travel afterwards.

So, ten hours to go. Liska closed her eyes and just took a few deep breaths. It was a habit of hers on the final day of the mission, if there was time, some weren't as considerate to give her prior warning, to contemplate worst possible scenarios. It helped her prepare for them, at least mentally. More importantly, it allowed her to figure out what to do so she could die without regrets. So, if this were the last day of her life, how should she spend it?

It took her less than a minute to decide. Todd immediately answered the door to her knock. "You should check before opening the door. After all, you didn't know it was me."

"Huh? Oh, yeah. I guess you're right."

"I usually am. Now, grab your coat. Let's go."

Todd picked up his coat while giving her a confused look. "Where are we going?"

"Out."

"Out where?"

"We are less than five miles away from the world's largest art museum. If we survive this, you are going to beat yourself up for the rest of your life if you miss this." Okay, she wasn't sure of the exact location, but he'd get the point.

"We're going to the Hermitage?" He asked excitedly. Apparently he missed or ignored the 'if we survive' part.

"Exactly. Let's go." Todd dragged her out the door. She was pretty sure her feet touched ground somewhere along the line but couldn't swear when and where.

***

Liska spent hours in the Hermitage, listening to Todd enthuse over various pieces. Quite frankly, she was bored most of the day, but that didn't matter. This wasn't for her. This was for him, and it definitely made his day. Hopefully it wouldn't be his last.

She had to shake that. Go into a fight thinking you'll lose and you probably will. Unfortunately, going into a fight thinking you'll win wasn't nearly as reliable. Would be nice, though.

The Hermitage used to be Catherine the Great's winter palace, and the museum started from her extensive art collection, but had become even bigger and grander over the years. It was the largest art museum in the world, and it was said that if you spent a few seconds on each piece, you would be there for seventy years. She didn't know if that was true, nor was she particularly interested in finding out. They might not have seen everything, but Todd seemed quite happy with the five or six hours they spent there.

In all fairness, there were some things she enjoyed. Some of the sculptures were positively fascinating, the armor was interesting to look at, and there was a Rembrandt painting that she swore made her heart stop for a moment. It was Abraham being stopped from sacrificing his son. She was familiar with the story, even before recently reading it in the Bible Shahara had given her. If she could actually tell the girl that she had been here, Shahara would probably appreciate hearing that.

All in all, she didn't have a terrible time, and some parts were enjoyable. Todd's reactions were often more interesting than the art itself. The look of awe on his face when he saw some of the Renaissance paintings, like Leonardo da Vinci or Michelangelo. Or the way his fingers twitched as if looking for a non-existent sketch pad. While she wouldn't admit it, even under torture, there was something... exhilarating in the way he'd look at a portrait of a beautiful lady, look back at her, and she just knew he was substituting her in that picture.

Sakaki stifled a sigh. Perhaps it was a good thing she had to go back home. She was just too close. Space was probably for the best. Before she truly did fall in love with him. She was closer than she'd ever anticipated. He'd given her one thing she'd never been able to get from anyone outside of a very select few of her close relatives. Acceptance.

Todd waxed lyrical about various exhibits as she dragged him out of the museum and to dinner. She had to keep him from walking into people and various objects, get him to sit down, order for him as he didn't seem to realize they were in a restaurant, and put the food in front of him. He did eat, though he didn't seem to pay any attention to what he was eating. Liska tested it by pouring sugar in his drink. Even though he was looking straight at her, he never noticed, not even when he was drinking it.

Finally, he pulled himself together. "But didn't you have to work? I was trying to leave you alone so you could."

"And I appreciate it. But I went over everything twenty times. I'll have to improvise when the time comes. First rule of combat; no plan survives contact with the enemy. Fortunately, I'm pretty good at improvising."

"I guess you're right."

"I know I'm right. I have done this before, you know."

He shivered slightly. Yup, he knew. To cover the shiver, he took a sip of his soda, then made a face. "Wow, this is really sweet. Do they use a different recipe up here?"

Liska shrugged, not mentioning the five sugar packets she had added. "No idea. Ready to go?"

She saw him to his door, while he tried to describe the golden carriage as if she hadn't seen it herself two hours ago. Once he was inside, she gave her final advice. "Stay here, lock the door. I'm not kidding, I will not bend on this. You stayed longer than you were supposed to at the police station, and I didn't say anything then, but you *must* listen to me this time. Do **_not_** leave this room."

She waited until he nodded. "Stay here, got it."

"Good. Do not let anyone you don't know in. If she doesn't hear from me by morning, Fiona will be here. The plane tickets, and some money is in my room, and I'm leaving you my room key. If I don't come back, take everything of use in my room and get out. She'll help you out of the city. My notebook goes to my family. Ryoko-*Sensei* or Kira, if you can manage it. If someone knocks on the door, the phrase is '*Kto tam?*' If you don't recognize them, don't open that door."

Todd nodded again. "Why are you telling me all this?"

"Because I have to realize there is a chance I won't succeed. I might die out there. Hopefully, I can make sure you don't. So, no opening the door?"

"No opening the door. But you will be alright, won't you?"

"I fully intend on it." Sakaki gave him one last look. "I..." *am so glad I met you. I wish things could be different. I wish I could give you what you want. Stay safe. Be careful.* "I have to go now. I'll let you know when I come back."

***

She didn't leave right away. Instead, she went to her room to take inventory. She had propped her door before seeing Todd safe in his. While it went against all her instincts to leave her door open especially while she wasn't in immediate view, she had to leave him her key, and it would be best that he didn't see her like this.

Did she have everything she needed? She had her sword, throwing knives, razor thread, shuriken, UV flashlights, purified salt, even a smidgen of silver dust. Some plastic ties and a little rope finished her check. It was always a balance between carrying what she might need, and what she could actually carry and still move freely. Still, hopefully she was ready for anything and everything that the night might throw at her.

She looked at the mirror, but was unable to tell who was looking back. Was it Liska? Was it Tisiphone? Both? Neither? Or was it Sakaki? Whoever it was had a job to do now. Stop Atolatar by any means necessary or die trying. She only hoped whoever was in the mirror was up to the task. She walked out the door and into the night, to face whatever was out there, waiting.

***

Todd paced the room, making his twelfth or thirteenth circuit. He had tried multiple times to stop pacing, but it wasn't working. Sakaki was out risking her life, and there was nothing he could do! To make things worse, if there was one thing this entire mess had shown him, it was that he truly did love her. Sure, he wished she didn't have to go out hunting crazy terrorist types, but he understood it. But she was going out and he had to stay here. If he did follow, he'd ruin her plans and put them both in more danger. What was the point of even coming?

There was a knock on the door.

Todd jumped a foot. What was the phrase Sakaki taught him? "*Kto tam?*" There that sounded right.

"Room service," came a voice with a thick accent.

"I didn't order anything."

"*Isvenitsye pazhalsta?*" What did that mean?

"I didn't order anything."

He just got the same phrase back again. And again. And again! Finally, he walked over and opened the door. "I didn't..." The words died as the sharp point of a sword rested on the hollow of his throat.

Looking beyond the sword, he saw a man about his age, probably Asian. "If you will please to come with me." It wasn't a question. The man smiled. It wasn't a nice smile. This was very, very bad.

***

There are two ways to get through a place without being noticed. One is to duck into every shadow, hiding whenever anyone came by, even traveling through ducts and pipes at times. The other is to walk through like you belong there and are doing exactly what you are supposed to be doing. Both have their advantages and disadvantages. She used both, depending on where she was.

She hadn't bothered to hide her approach until she got close to the school. Once on the grounds, she was more subtle, staying out of sight as she climbed a tree to get onto the roof. From there, she climbed into one of the heating vents. A quick glance and sniff convinced her that no one had disturbed the vent since her last visit. Good.

The heating vent let her into a storage closet, which was not booby-trapped, but did contain a more than comfortable hint of bleach. Someone had been in here, but she couldn't tell who, or when. Not great. Well, no one was here right now. Hopefully the bleach scent was only in a small area, because she was hoping to sniff out Atolatar.

Since her sense of smell was not at its best, she spent a little more time listening at the door than she would otherwise. Nothing.

Well, if she couldn't sniff him out, she'd simply work her way through the school top to bottom. That put the gym as one of the first on her list. Ideally, she would be able to get through the place, kill Atolatar, and get out without anyone being the wiser. That was Tisiphone's plan. Liska favored a modified version. Get in, confront Atolatar which would probably lead to a fight to the death, and then get out without anyone being the wiser. Liska didn't feel right killing the man, vampire, without him knowing she was there. Sakaki was struggling between those, and decided to put it aside until she actually found him. This would be a lot easier if she had met him before.

Werefoxes didn't rely much on appearances. Maybe it was because their sense of sight wasn't very good, or maybe it was because they were shapeshifters themselves. They remembered people best by scent. A picture wouldn't be a perfect help, though it might be some. Even if it would help, she didn't have one. She'd just have to deal with what she had.

Opening the closet door, she was struck in the face with the heavy odor of ammonia. It was everywhere! Either the place had just been massively cleaned, Atolatar was having a fight with his second, or they were expecting her or someone like her. She dropped her chance of survival to twenty percent.

A germ mask helped against the stench but between what was around and the bleach in her nose, she couldn't rely on her sense of smell at all. Not good, especially since smell was her dominant sense. Her eyes wouldn't stop watering. She found a pair of safety goggles in the closet, which helped, but cut down on her peripheral vision. Normally not a major problem, but without her sense of smell... Maybe fifteen percent.

It was dark. Her night vision should be better than a vampire's or even a shade's though it would be close. At the moment, it was her only advantage. Why was this place so empty? Atolatar had followers, where were they? She couldn't see or hear anyone at all. While some might say she shouldn't look a gift horse in the mouth, Sakaki was a firm believer in 'if it seems too good to be true, it is'. So, if she couldn't find anyone, that meant either they were really, really unprepared, she was better than she thought she was, or this was a trap. Her money was on 'trap'. She hated walking into traps, especially when she knew they were traps. Unfortunately, trap or not, she had no choice but to continue. This was worth so much more than her life. First things first. She had to find him.

So, how was she supposed to find him? She eased her way into the darkened gym. The lights shot on, blinding her. "Hello, Sakaki. How kind of you to join us." Oh, that's how.

Chapter Forty-Three

No battle is every truly fought alone. – The Kikitsutai Book of
Wisdom

Well, she had found him. Not the way she had hoped
to, but she still had found him. Or he found her.
How had he gotten the drop on her? Ah, video
screens. She hadn't realized the cameras were on. In
fact, she had disassembled them a couple years ago.
He must have fixed them and probably got quite a
show. It didn't matter now.

Sakaki took off the mask, though she left the
goggles. Protecting her eyes might come in useful.
The bleach wasn't in here, but it was still in her
nose. It would be a good twenty minutes or so for it
to settle and her sense of smell to be back to normal.
Most fights don't even last five minutes.

Face blank, Sakaki studied the vampire on
the second level running track. There was something
vaguely familiar about him, but she was pretty sure
she had never met him before. Perhaps a relative.
"So, you're Atolatar?" She asked casually, while
scouting out the room. It was mostly open and
empty, but there were stacks of crates in several
places, the video screens were against the wall
behind her, and there were cords on the floor as a
tripping hazard. She also had a strong feeling that
they weren't alone in the room. Important to know.

"I do answer to that name, yes." Why were they speaking in English? It wasn't her first language, or his. She spoke German, if not fluently, then close enough. Perhaps it was for someone else's benefit. More evidence that they probably weren't alone.

"It's a new name for you, isn't it?"

"Fairly new." He smiled a vicious smile at her. "Now tell me, what brings you here?"

"I hear things. I've heard that you're planning something. A new world. One where we don't have to hide. I want in."

"Do you? Do you indeed? Why? You seem to have dedicated your life to your clan's ideals. Secrecy and hiding."

"And where has it gotten me? The skulk looks down on me for being part human; the humans avoid me for being different. I'm an outcast wherever I go. Nothing I do can change that. You can. The old ways are dying, even if nothing is done. Might as well get in with the new while I can."

"How do I know I can trust you, and why should I risk it?"

Liska smirked. "You have no idea the connections I have. You want a world where you can roam free? You'll need enforcers to make sure of it. My skills are unparalleled, surely even you realize that or you wouldn't have targeted me. As for trust, well, what I want is something only you can offer." Not a single word was a lie.

"There would be a test first."

Of course. "Name it."

"Kill Tisiphone."

"Did that once. You resurrected her."

The vampire smirked, leaning slightly over the edge to pose. "Well, if you can't seem to kill Tisiphone, then maybe you can kill him."

Sakaki was already turning the minute she caught movement from the corner of her eye. She stiffened briefly but forced it back before it could be noticed. How had this happened? "Which? Todd or Yoshiro?"

"You say that so calmly, Tisiphone."

"No, I'm pretty sure neither of them is Tisiphone."

"Enough banter. If you really want in, then kill the human."

"He's an Esper. That makes him a Twilight too."

"He was given his chance and refuses. Therefore, he must be eliminated."

Sakaki gave an abbreviated shrug before drawing a knife and stalking slowly to the bound Esper held helplessly in her former betrothed's arms. Todd was struggling but it would do no good, Yoshiro was stronger. The closer she got, the more Todd struggled, his scent screamed of fear, shouted of disbelief, and whispered of trust. He was trying to say something but had been gagged.

He didn't seem to have been hurt, but he wasn't going to be getting out on his own unless someone untied him, even if Yoshiro did let go. Even if he was untied, he'd still have to get through who knew how many of Atolatar's followers.

If she killed him, it might allow her to take Atolatar off guard. If she didn't kill him, they would probably both be dead within ten minutes. She came to a stop a foot from him, her face expressionless.

He met her eyes, trying to send a message. Had she figured out what she had? It didn't matter. She knew what she had to do.

Todd's eyes squeezed shut as she swung the blade.

Yoshiro fell back a step, dazed from being hit with the butt of her knife. Sakaki ripped Todd from his loosened grasp and pushed/threw Todd to the stack of crates. She was trying to get him to land on top, which he did, briefly, but momentum and the jarring of the crates caused them to unbalance, dropping Todd on the floor. Sakaki hid a wince but didn't have time to check on him. Yoshiro had recovered.

She dodged his initial lunge, drawing her sword as he hit what was left of the stack of crates. This brought another one crashing down, wringing a pained, muffled cry from behind. Sakaki barely had time to register that, when Yoshiro turned back to her. That put Yoshiro between her and Todd, and she had her back to the vampire. Not good.

Speaking of the vampire, "I knew you were treacherous." He hadn't moved yet. Well, at least something was going right.

"No, you just have to know what side I'm truly on."

Yoshiro tried to take advantage of her divided attention to move towards her, but she hadn't let herself get distracted enough for that. It was a risk, but she jumped forward, enough distance from him and high enough that they effectively switched places. It was a quick move, but it left her vulnerable while she was in the air. That was why Yoshiro hadn't expected it. Now she had Todd behind her, and the angry Werefox and the vampire in front of her. Not a two-front fight, but she couldn't afford to move much either.

Sword met sword for the first time, the reverberations running down her arms as she tried to figure out a strategy. Yoshiro was taller, stronger, had better reach on her and truly was very good, even if he saw himself as better than he really was. But he was mostly blind in his left eye, thanks to a vicious fight with her some years ago. She was more agile, faster, better at reading people, slightly better stamina, and was just slightly better than him, as years of experience had proven. More importantly, neither of them could afford to lose.

The fight was fierce, dirty, and brutal. When he tried to stab her shoulder, she ducked under and kicked at his kneecap. He stepped back, tripping slightly on the wires, only to force her to dodge a sweep of the sword. She landed a kick to his stomach but didn't regain her balance in time to avoid the handful of broken glass thrown at her face. Good thing she still had the safety goggles on. He parried her thrust, leaving her open enough for him to grab her arm. She retaliated by stomping down on his foot, and hitting his left ear, hard.

Yoshiro drew away from her for a moment. They were both bleeding, but it was minor. She risked the quickest of glances up. Atolatar was still watching from the top, clearly enjoying the show. Todd was moving around behind the crates, probably trying to get loose. Good. In any case, he must be mostly okay.

Yoshiro jumped at her again, only to flinch back when she shined the UV flashlight in his eyes.

He might not be hurt by the radiation, but all Weres were photosensitive. Sakaki advanced, aiming the hilt of her sword at his skull. If she could just knock him out long enough...

He grabbed her hand with both hands, turning her wrist sharply. The sound of broken bones was almost drowned out by her yelp of pain, and the clatter of her sword against the floor. She was disarmed. In a sparring tournament, she would have lost. Were there rules, she probably would have been honor-bound to surrender. But here there was just one rule. Kill or be killed.

Yoshiro smirked at her and reached for her throat. A sign of dominance and power. Sakaki snarled and transformed. Not to a fox, small and not too strong, but still under her control. No, she turned to a half-state. The true Werefox. Bipedal, wild, fanged and clawed, running purely on instinct. Everything went white.

It was a voice that pulled her out. Todd's voice, calling her. He must have gotten the gag out somehow, Sakaki thought as the fog of instinct and rage receded and she changed back to human. What happened? What had she done? There was blood everywhere; she could smell it even through the bleach. There was blood on her hands, on her clothes, in her mouth. Where was Yoshiro? She looked down and nearly threw up.

It was the sound of clapping that forced her to pull herself together. With a growl, she turned her attention back to the vampire. Yoshiro was no longer a threat. "You find that amusing?" Sakaki scooped up her sword with her left hand. She wasn't truly ambidextrous, but sufficient training made it close. Would close be good enough?

"Immensely. As I predicted, you have once more become the cold, heartless assassin. You even killed your own betrothed, Tisiphone."

Yoshiro wasn't dead. In fact, he might be able to make it. Provided he could get medical attention in twenty minutes or less. Were-safe medical attention. The nearest Twilight/Night clinic was about forty minutes away. She didn't answer him.

How was she going to get to Atolatar? There was a ladder to the running track, but she really didn't trust him to leave her alone to climb it. Maybe she could get him down to her level. For now, though, he was still talking. "I've been planning my revenge against you for years, you know." She raised an eyebrow. "Oh, yes. Years. Even this whole 'reveal ourselves to the humans' was done at least partially in revenge."

"Why on earth do you hate me that much?"

His face went from an amused smile to a stony, hateful glare. "Don't you know? It meant so little to you, that it didn't even stick in your memories, what you did to my brother?"

"Your brother?" She studied him, then gasped, freezing in place. "The little boy."

"Oh, you do remember. Good. I would hate to kill you without you knowing why. Well, actually I'll be glad to kill you no matter what. But I want you to know why. Bad enough that you killed Ryasmus. An avowed pacifist who meant no harm to anyone; he could at least defend himself. But what happened to the legendary honor of the Kikitsutai? You attacked a child, and suffered no punishment for it."

He had no idea. "It was an accident! I never meant to hurt him." She closed her eyes briefly. Then she steeled herself to ask the question she was most afraid of. "What happened to him?"

"You didn't even stop to check!"

There was no defense. Not really. "What happened?"

"You don't know? Then you never will. I certainly won't tell you. I will tell you that you were the one who made me Atolatar. This, all this," he waved his hands at the room, "all I've killed, all I will kill, all the destruction that happens. This is your fault. After what you did, my anger, my rage nearly destroyed me. But I took that anger and became strong. I told Ryasmus that peace was for the weak and those that have no other recourse. I bet he wished he had listened to me. I won't make his mistakes again."

"That is such a cop out!" Todd's voice, still from behind the crates, startled them both. "You chose this path. You chose to become Atolatar, to target us, to target the talks. She didn't make you do anything. Millions of people lose a sibling, a teacher, or someone close to them, and don't go on a killing spree. Bad things happen to everyone, and only you can choose how to react to them."

Atolatar snarled. "You will not leave this room alive, human. Unless you are in a hurry to hasten your death, keep quiet."

"Leave him alone. He has nothing to do with this." It was a waste of her breath, but she had to try.

"He has to do with you. You deserve to pay for your crimes, and I intend to see that you do. Now, you are going to watch everything you care about, everything you've worked for, fall to pieces around you."

An idea came to her. It was stupid. It was suicidal. It was all she had. "You want vengeance? Fine! Take it! But take it against me. Not against Todd. Not against Yoshiro. And not against millions of innocents who know nothing about this!"

Atolatar tilted his head to the side. "What did you have in mind?"

"Let Todd go, find someone to help Yoshiro, swear you won't do anything to the political conference and I'll surrender. Completely and utterly. You can do anything you want to me."

The vampire stilled. "You would do that?"

"As you say, it is my fault." Todd was protesting, and she could feel Yoshiro's eyes on her. She ignored them both. If Atolatar agreed to this, her life was a small price to pay.

"You haven't shown yourself to be very trustworthy."

Sakaki took a deep breath. "I swear upon my honor, if you honor your part, I will honor mine." She took her sword and threw it to the side, fighting the urge to wince when it clattered to the floor six feet away. That was one vow she could never break.

***

Yoshiro knew he was dying. It left him surprisingly introspective. He had never liked Sakaki, feeling it beneath him to wed a half-breed, and insulting that she disliked him, the eldest son of the second most important family of the Kikitsutai. She wasn't truly one of them, an outsider, but she was known as a rising star, one of the most promising of their generation. It should be him!

For that matter, he had always chaffed at the restrictions that he was expected to follow. Never particularly fond of humans, he hated that they didn't have to hide, and he did. When he was approached by Atolatar and offered the chance to be his right-hand man in a world where humans were the ones hiding instead, it seemed perfect.

His new 'friend's' desire for revenge against his betrothed didn't sit easy with him. Sure, Yoshiro didn't like her and probably wouldn't mourn too much if she should happen to disappear off the face of the planet, but actively trying to kill her? Then Atolatar told him the tragic story of his brother. She hurt a child. The biggest taboo of the skulk and no one knew. She deserved this.

He had taken a little too much glee from kidnapping the human. Shades assured him they were close. That had been an insult too. She had not cared for his leaving at all, and even thought to replace him with a human? How could she? A crazy human at that?

"Who are you? Why are you doing this?" The *human was clearly frightened but trying not to show it as they drove to the school. He was bound, as a precaution, not because Yoshiro thought he could be a threat.*

"My name is Yoshiro."

"Sakaki's betrothed?"

He wasn't sure if he was more surprised that the human knew his name or that he knew hers. "How did you know that?"

"The notes you sent her. How did you know where she was?"

Yoshiro smirked. "Handy thing, the internet. Especially when someone tries to record sightings that match a red-haired Werefox. There aren't many of those, and Liska is distinctive." He suppressed the urge to laugh at the tidal wave of guilt and fear that suddenly welled up in the boy. "As for why? You have a choice, and that only because you are a Twilight. Join Atolatar. Or die."

The human's eyes flashed. "If Sakaki's right. Atolatar's plans will lead to death and destruction."

"Perhaps, but we'll win."

"No one wins a fight like that. Sakaki is willing to give her life to prevent such things. Weren't you taught the same?"

"Just because I was taught one thing, doesn't mean I can't find out the truth later. And Sakaki is a dishonorable coward."

The human shook his head. "Man, you don't understand her at all, do you?"

Yoshiro snarled. "I've known her a lot longer than you have, human."

"Doesn't mean you understand her."

Only the fact that Atolatar wanted the human alive stopped Yoshiro from killing him that instant. "You side with her."

"Yes." He seemed to be restraining himself from answering 'Always'.

"Then you will die with her." He gagged the human then, to prevent himself from killing him too

early. "We will see who truly understands the half-breed."

But if she was such a dishonorable coward, then why this? He could somewhat understand her concern for the humans, certainly for the human in the room, but why mention medical attention for him? They both knew that she had tried not to kill him during their fight. Why? Why surrender? Only one answer made sense. The human had been right. He didn't understand Sakaki at all. But that realization had come too late. There was nothing he could do now, was there?

***

Atolatar leapt from the track and approached her slowly. When she didn't move, he smiled, grabbing her neck and slamming her into the wall. The breath left her body, and she couldn't get enough new air in. Instinct and reflex said to fight him off. She dug her nails into her good hand. She had submitted to him, he had the right to touch her neck.

"Do you know what I'm going to do?"

She wordlessly shook her head; not sure she could speak.

"I'm going to break your neck, carefully. That should paralyze you for what, three weeks, four? Long enough. You can watch as I drain the human dry, watch your betrothed bleed out, watch as that veil of secrecy you've spent your whole life protecting is torn completely asunder. I'll make sure you get all the news while we wait for your nerves to heal. A week, two? Then, and only then, will I move on to killing you. Slowly."

***

Yoshiro made his decision.

***

Struggling against the hands slowly crushing her neck, Sakaki felt the movement before she saw it, and was reacting before she could analyze it. Yoshiro, lying on the ground, bleeding to death, had managed to get enough energy to leap at Atolatar. It took the vampire a mere three seconds to fling the badly injured Werefox away like a gnat and turn back to her. Those three seconds were enough that he met the light of her UV flashlight in the face.

He pulled back with a yelp, covering his face but recovered quickly, swiping the flashlight away. That was fine, it gave her all the cover she needed to get at a dagger and plunge it into his chest. "You said—"

"I said 'if you honor your part, I'll honor mine'. IF." She forced the dagger in and twisted it.

His body dissolved to ash, proving his death. She ignored it, running to Yoshiro.

Yoshiro might have been able to survive what she had done, with medical attention that he was unlikely to get. All the medical attention in the world wouldn't save him now and they both knew it. He had minutes at best.

"Why?"

"Ask the human. I have a few favors to ask." He was speaking Japanese. Remembering his dislike of English, and the mindset some of her countrymen had, that what was said in English 'didn't count', she replied in kind.

"Name them."

"Tell Chiro I loved her." They both knew he hadn't, but it was a small lie and would harm nothing.

"Why did you marry her?"

"She loved me, and it would make our parents unhappy. What will you tell them?"

"The truth. That you died honorably, facing a difficult foe, and without your aid, I would have lost." That was mostly true. She had planned on Atolatar betraying her, but Yoshiro's distraction may have been the deciding factor. It certainly made things easier.

"Thank you. I don't deserve it but thank you. Atolatar planned on using shades to set off explosives, but only he or I could give the order."

She nodded. Good. They would do nothing without that order. "Anything else?"

"He has at least one follower in Florida. I don't know who."

"It's fine." With her going back to Japan, they would probably leave.

"Will you mourn me?"

"Of course." It was no less than deserved that someone should howl for his death.

"The human, do you love him?"

"I'm afraid to."

"He's good for you. Don't tell him I said that."

She smiled sadly. He was fading, so fast now. There was no point in telling him it was impossible. "Anything else?"

"Be free. As free as you can. And tell Chiro something. You'll know what to say. She's carrying my kits."

That explained a great deal. Poor girl. "I'll tell her." He was almost gone.

"Please, I want to hear it."

She nodded, and took a deep breath. Then she forced out of her abused throat the loudest, most mournful howl she could manage. She didn't stop until she could no longer breathe. By then, Yoshiro, whose name meant 'free son', was finally free of life and all the troubles therein.

Chapter Forty-Four

Confronting family can be more difficult than confronting an enemy. – The Kikitsutai Book of Wisdom

Todd stretched out slightly in his seat, having trouble believing everything that had happened in the past ten or twelve hours. Despite being injured, Sakaki had tried to take care of everything herself. Todd finally got her to agree to being treated by pointing out that she was dripping blood everywhere. Besides, her wrist had to be hurting her.

After they were both patched up and her wrist was splinted, Sakaki insisted on getting rid of the evidence. Yoshiro's body they actually put in a freezer so it could be transported back to Japan for his family. Atolatar's ashes weren't a big concern, but Sakaki said they shouldn't just leave them there either. Todd didn't know if that was out of respect for the dead, or because bad things could happen if someone else found them. Most difficult was the blood. That had to be cleaned up or at least rendered unreadable.

Since neither of them had the time or energy to clean the whole place, Sakaki ruptured a few pipes to flood the place. That way, even if someone did find out there had been blood, between the water and the ammonia, they wouldn't be able to tell anything about it.

Then she made a few phone calls. One to Fiona, to tell her they had been successful. One as an anonymous tip to the security of the peace talks, mentioning the threat of a bombing. The last was to arrange transportation to Japan.

That's what they were on now. A weird-looking, little private plane, with a pilot who Sakaki greeted by name and with a quick hug. She said he was one of her more distant cousins, named Tora, and apparently he was betrothed to Kira.

Tora assured them that they could have some privacy while he was in the cockpit, but he also said that the plane could actually make it to Japan without refueling. Todd thought he was kidding, but Sakaki said he was serious. Apparently, the plane was a sub-orbital, capable of leaving most of earth's atmosphere, allowing them to get to Japan much faster than normal. Take-off was rough, but once they leveled off, it was extremely smooth.

Todd was a little surprised by the side trip to Japan but figured he shouldn't be. Sakaki would have to report in, and this would take a lot of explaining. She reassured him that he'd be back in Moscow by the time of his return flight. At least until he realized that the 'you' was singular.

"What happened last night?" He asked her. He'd work up to the trip back.

"At which point?"

"What did you and Yoshiro talk about before he died?"

Sakaki was leaning back, facing the ceiling. He was pretty sure she hadn't opened her eyes. "His last wishes. Mostly messages to be passed on. When I asked him why he got involved, he said to ask you."

"I just talked to him." What did he have to do with anything?

"Like you talked to me?"

"Sort of."

Sakaki nodded, then looked at him. "I didn't get a chance to tell you, but you talking to me helped. Tremendously."

"Really?" He would have expected 'a bit' or 'some'. 'Tremendously'?

"I was trying to ignore being Tisiphone, and would have been easy prey to his emotional manipulation if we hadn't talked on the plane." She sighed. "I did need you. Last night. Your words snapped me back to myself. Twice. And if you hadn't been there, I think I really would have reverted back to being Tisiphone. If that happened, I would never have been free."

"Then I'm glad I was there. Even if I am sore today. Hey, question."

"Yes?"

"You said I'll be back to catch my flight. Don't you mean, we'll be back?"

Sakaki glared at her wrapped wrist. "I meant to tell you. But things kept coming up. I'm sorry. I've been ordered back to Japan. For good. Father says it's time I learn to lead the skulk. I'm sorry."

Todd took a deep breath and tried to push away his emotions. This wasn't about him. This was about her. "Do you want that?"

"No, I do not have the organizational and leadership skills necessary to do so."

"There's a difference between wanting to do something and having or not having the skills to do it."

"Fine, I'm also happier where I am now. As a ninja, an active one."

"So tell him that."

"I couldn't possibly!" She sounded horrified.

"Why not?"

"He's my father. His word is law."

"He's your father. Chances are he wants you happy."

Neither of them spoke for some time after that. When she did break the silence, it was small talk. Todd let it go, for now. After all, it was her life, and he couldn't tell her what to do. He wanted to, but it simply wasn't his decision. He did make up his mind though. One way or another, before he left, he would make sure she knew how he felt.

***

Shortly before landing, Sakaki talked Todd into helping her put Yoshiro in the coffin Tora had supplied. "We can't bring him out in a freezer! Think of his family!"

Todd clearly had no love lost on the Werefox who had kidnapped him, but he was too much of a gentleman to leave her to struggle with the body, especially with a broken wrist. Perhaps the thought of Yoshiro's family helped too.

They were greeted by an unusually high number of the skulk. Foxes, partials, and human looking alike. But Sakaki ignored them all, looking for Chiro. It wasn't easy. She was hiding in the background. Disgraced.

The first thing Sakaki did was give her a hug. Chiro stiffened, before realizing that Sakaki wasn't going to attack her, physically or verbally. Then she melted into the embrace. Like Yoshiro said, she was pregnant, only a few weeks along. The girl had been so easily led.

"He asked me to tell you that he loved you. That you need to go on. As long as you remember him, he isn't truly gone. Carry his kits, let him live through them. Then he will be there, always."

"He... He said that?" Chiro looked at her through her tears.

"His last thoughts were on you." Sakaki lied, utterly without remorse.

She could hear the mumbling. Chiro and Yoshiro had disgraced themselves, her, and the entire skulk. What did she think she was doing?

"Yoshiro died a hero! Without him, we would have lost. By now, the world would know of us! He died to protect what we are! As for Chiro, she loved him, and must now carry his kits alone, is that not punishment enough?" Chiro, slightly younger than Sakaki herself, would never again be able to fall in love. As far as Sakaki was concerned, that was far more than enough.

"She's right." Kira? When had she gotten here? That was fast.

It was turning into an argument. "Silence!" Father. He turned to her, his 'I am the chief and you

WILL do as I say' persona in place. "Sakaki, you say that Yoshiro died a noble death?"

"I do."

"You say that Chiro should not be blamed for marrying the man who was promised to you?"

"I do."

"You renounce any rights or claims to vengeance?"

As if she had any plans for that in the first place. "I do."

"What do you recommend then?" As the one most affected by the whole mess, her suggestion would hold the most weight. It didn't mean the skulk would necessarily go with her suggestion, but there were good odds.

"I see no reason why she should not be treated like she is. The widow of a hero!" More murmurs surrounded them.

Father looked at her, as if daring her to back down. She didn't. "So be it! We have a funeral to prepare for. Chiro, you take the place of honor."

***

Father waited until the day after the funeral to talk to Sakaki. He probably felt it would be improper to do so beforehand.

Fortunately, Sakaki was able to talk to a few other people first. Kira and Ryoko-*Sensei* had come earlier the same day she had, after Kira finished the last exam. She and Kira had a very long talk that left Sakaki thinking about a number of issues. Todd also wanted to talk to her, but she was trying to politely avoid him, at least until she had some things straightened out.

Most important was the conversation with her mother.

"They told me you had to remember being Tisiphone." While she had never said it, Sakaki knew that Mother had been horrified by her becoming an assassin. Mother wasn't happy about her being a ninja either. She hadn't been brought up in the culture, and it had been hard for her to adapt.

"Yes." Sakaki braced herself for recriminations and 'I told you so's. They didn't come.

"I don't think I've told you often enough; but no matter what happens, no matter who you become, I love you. And I'm proud of you." Sakaki stared at her. "I mean it. I may not understand how or why you do these things, but I know it isn't easy for you. But you do it anyway, convinced it's the right thing to do. So, I'm proud of you. And I always will be."

The hugs after that were tearful and long. Yet over all too soon as Father walked in. It was time to take care of business.

"You are uninjured from your mission?"

"Mostly." It took deliberate effort not to twitch her now professionally-bandaged wrist.

"You kept your vow."

"Yes."

"Then you agree that it is time to put aside your foolishness and accept your rightful place here. Training to be the next head."

She took a deep breath. Todd had an even greater impact on her than she had thought. "Do you want what is best for me?"

Father blinked. "What?"

"Do you want what is best for me?"

"Yes, of course I do. You are my daughter and I love you. But there are other considerations..."

"Do you want what is best for the skulk?"

"Yes, of course. I'm the head. It is my responsibility."

"What if I told you that what is best for me and what is the best for the skulk was the same thing?"

"Wonderful. The best thing is for you to take your place."

This was either going to go really well or really badly. "I am in my place. My place is doing what I am doing. I cannot become the head."

Father clenched his jaw shut and stared at her. He was probably counting. Finally, he was able to speak, though anger still vibrated through his words. "What are you saying?"

"They won't accept me as the leader. They never have; they never will. Putting me as the head could cause a split that would destroy us."

"You are my daughter. Your role is as the chief." He wasn't growling, but that was only a step away.

"They won't accept a half-Were, and you know it." *And it is at least partly your fault. You married a human without doing any work to change their view of humans. How could you possibly expect me to succeed?* She didn't dare say it, she felt disloyal enough to even think it.

He knew anyway, and it hurt, to see the pain in his eyes. But what else could she do?

"Listen to her." Mother broke in, much to the Weres' surprise. "You have decided her path her entire life. Enough. Let her chose her own. She's right. We don't fit. Not quite."

Father sat down. "What would you have me do?" He asked the floor.

"Make Kira your apprentice." Dubious looks met Sakaki's suggestion. "It's perfect. She's your twin's child, almost the same as if she was yours. She's a little older. She's a full Were. She had the gift of leadership and is a born nurturer. The skulk would follow her to the ends of the earth without complaint. I'd be lucky if they would follow me to the meeting cavern. Then she can work on changing views."

"You would swear allegiance to her, giving up all rights of leadership?"

"I will revoke all rights of leadership now, before the skulk, and swear allegiance when the proper time comes. I will not cause trouble. You know that." Even ignoring the fact that she didn't want to do anything to cause trouble in the skulk, the last thing she would do want would be to hurt Kira.

"I've failed you."

"Father?" She had never expected to hear something like that from Father. Never.

"If I had worked on changing beliefs, then you wouldn't have this problem now."

Okay, that was partly true. "We don't know that. But the past is closed. And even if they didn't mind being led by a half-blood, there is still the fact that she has the gifts required, and I do not. We have to do what is best. For everyone."

Father stood and looked at her. He was still sad, but he would get past it. "If that would be best for all involved..."

"It will be. I have complete faith in that." For the first time in years, Sakaki and her father embraced.

***

Shock was the order of the day when Sakaki publicly gave up any rights she would have to lead the clan. When it was announced that Kira would be the next leader of the clan, most got past their shock quickly. Kira did not. Sakaki politely refrained from laughing in the vixen's face, but it was difficult.

"Me?! Me? I can't..."

"Of course you can. Much better than I could. Besides, you've always wanted it." It was the one thing that had marred their friendship. They both knew that Sakaki was destined to lead the group. And they both knew that Sakaki didn't want to, and Kira did.

"But I never dreamed... You will be my right hand, won't you?"

Sakaki had expected no less. "As long as you need me."

"I'll always need you." It was a choked laugh that was more amazement than humor.

"Then I'll always be there."

"What about him?" Kira gave a discrete nod to Todd in the distance. He was watching them, not wanting to intrude, but still wanting to be there.

"What about him?"

"You like him."

"We only fall in love once. I don't dare do so until I know it's forever." No point in mentioning she was half-way there already.

Kira nodded. "Are you going back to school?"

"Looks like it. I want to get my degree. It's important to me."

"He'll be there."

"For a while."

"He's good for you."

"You're the second person to tell me that in the past few days."

Kira's brows furrowed. "Who was the first?"

"Yoshiro."

"Yoshiro doesn't even like humans. Didn't. Sorry." Sakaki nodded. "If Yoshiro thought he was good for you, then he must be special."

"You know it's not possible."

"Oh?" Kira raised an eyebrow. Sakaki opened her mouth to argue, but she continued. "I know that Sakaki, next in command under Sejou the Dragonclaw, could not marry a human. Sakaki, right-hand of Kira the whatever, can. At least, as far as I'm concerned. If you truly want this, I'll find a way to make it acceptable to the skulk at large." Kira smiled. "You're on your own convincing your parents, though."

Sakaki laughed. "Convincing Father would be harder than convincing the skulk at large, and you know it."

"Are you going to give him a chance?"

Sakaki looked at him. "I might. I just might."

Kira smiled, then sobered. "What about Tisiphone?"

"It's time to take care of that. Permanently. Get Todd for me, will you?"

***

When Kira led Todd to Sakaki, she was making a small wooden boat. From the looks of it, she was almost done. She then took a piece of paper and drew what Todd assumed to be Japanese kanji.

After she was done, she set the boat and paper aside, looking up at them for the first time. "I am burying Tisiphone. I thought you might like to be here for that." Both nodded, Todd somewhat hesitant. From the looks of it, Kira might be as well.

Sakaki went to her bag and pulled out some papers. Some seemed to be newspaper clippings, some were clearly handwritten notes. Sakaki put them in a metal bowl and pulled out a box of matches. "These papers are clippings of her jobs, her notes, and the like. Kira, would you like to do the honors?"

Kira nodded solemnly, as she took the matches, then lit the pile on fire. The three stared silently as it was reduced to ash.

Once the bowl was cool enough to touch, Sakaki poured the ashes into a tiny paper box which she put into the boat. She tied the paper strip with the kanji to the mast and walked out the door, waving the other two to follow.

They followed until she got to the edge of the island, where she stopped. Then she started to sing. Todd didn't know the words, but he recognized a dirge when he heard one. Kira must have known the song too, because she joined in.

When she finished, she turned to Todd and handed him the boat. "Would you like to send Tisiphone on her final journey?"

With a half-smile, he took her hand and knelt in the sand. She knelt too. He gently pushed her hand, and thus the boat, into open water.

Silently, the three watched until it was out of sight. Only then did they start to head back.

"What did the paper say?" Todd asked.

Sakaki smiled. He liked that smile. It was a smile that bid goodbye to an old life, and hello to a new one. "*Tisiphone: Dead but not gone. Buried but not forgotten. Remain at Rest.*"

Bonus Story:

Vixen's Night Out

Vixen's Night Out

Some nights were just made to be a fox. Nights when the wind was just right, enough to ruffle her hair but not enough to irritate her eyes, when the moon shone bright and clear in the sky, when all of the earth just *sang* with life, it was all Liska could do not to join in.

The day had been what Liska liked to refer to as 'Dragonfly Weather'. A bright, sunny, and warm day that followed several rainy days, and it seemed like the air was swarmed with dragonflies. As night came, there was a slightly brisk hint to the air, which was far more evident to the native Floridians than to Liska. The wind carried the salt of the brackish water from the intracoastal, the spicy-sweet odor of cut grass and decaying leaves, and a hint of drying mud that persisted even above all the people and car scents that prevailed on campus.

It was a week since her last required change and the moon was just shy of full, which probably wasn't helping. Even though the moon actually had nothing to do with a Were's shift, and her lunar phase wasn't full moon anyway, most Weres felt a higher urge to be in animal form during full moon.

The urge could be resisted, of course, and probably should be. There weren't many good places nearby to roam as a fox. Last week, she had spent her fox shift in Ryoko-*Sensei's* backyard. But that didn't feel like it would be enough this time. And spending her fox time in her room was almost never satisfying when this kind of restlessness hit her.

So Liska ignored the urge and tried to focus on her book, a collection of fairy tales. Hopefully reading something for fun would engage her better than trying to study.

It might have worked if she had picked a different book. But fairy tales are full of people being changed into animals, running free in the forests, and the like.

With a sigh, Liska put the book aside. Then she cast a longing glance out the window and made some calculations.

***

Fortunately, Liska was able to avoid anyone who knew Anna Andrews as she made her way to the edge of campus. Or at least, anyone who knew how out of character it was for her to go around in a sundress and flip flops. It was a very common outfit in South Florida, or at least it was when the Floridians weren't going around complaining about how freezing it was while in seventy-degree heat, but not one that she would wear under most circumstances.

No one seemed to take notice as she reached her destination, a dark alcove in a camera blind spot that was close enough to the library, the cafeteria, and one of the main parking lots that any of which *could* have been her destination if someone was trying to use the cameras to track her.

Instead, she slipped deeper into the alcove, to the far end of the dumpster so she was out of view. Liska pulled a bag out of her pocket, unfolded it, and after verifying with her eyes what her ears and nose already told her, that she was alone, she stripped off the dress and shoes, put them in the bag, and hid them behind the dumpster.

A moment later, a small fox trotted to the entrance of the alcove and sniffed the air, delicately. *Play?*

We should stay on campus.

The fox twitched her whiskers at the thought. The campus wasn't a fun place for a fox to play. Too many people, too many cars, not enough prey except lizards, half of which tasted bad, and not enough interesting things to interact with. The other voice would be too nervous. No, not campus.

The smell of salt water tickled her nose, inspiring her. *Sand. Water. Prey. Play?*

The beach?

That was it! *Sand. Dig. Catch crabs. Play in water?*

The other voice seemed conflicted. The fox decided that was good enough.

On quiet paws, she snuck through what was left of the campus, avoiding any of the big, noisy, not-fox people that wandered around. There weren't many, because the humans thought nighttime was for being inside and for sleep. Silly humans.

Then came the first street. She had to cross the street here, because here was the bridge. A big, long one. Long even when she was in person form with bigger steps. Person her walked it sometimes, but she never had as a fox.

The street had cars, and she had to wait until they were gone to cross. It made her impatient, but she waited anyway. They might not see her as a fox, and while she didn't particularly wish to be seen, that was dangerous with cars. But finally, the noisy things were far enough away that she could cross the street and go to the bridge.

Her human memories told her that the beach was about a mile from campus, or a little over one and a half kilometers. This bridge was over twelve hundred feet, or four hundred meters. But that was a much fuzzier concept as a fox. What *she* knew was that the bridge was long enough that she really couldn't see one end from the other.

She was a little over the halfway point, the seam between the two parts of the drawbridge, when the bridge started making very loud sounds, startling the fox. Then scaring her as she realized that her human side was also scared.

They're raising the drawbridge. We have to hurry to the other side. It's not safe to be on the bridge as it's being raised.

A picture formed in her head of portions of the bridge being straight up and down in the air. No, that wouldn't be safe for her at all. Hadn't a woman been killed that way on this bridge a few years ago? That's what they said on campus, anyway.

The fox dashed, watching as the barriers went down to prevent any walkers or cars from going on the bridge. There would be a delay, making sure anyone on the bridge could get to safety before the bridge started to raise. Then the bridge would move slowly. But she didn't know if anyone watched to make sure no one was trapped on the bridge, and even if they did, they weren't likely to see a small fox, especially at night.

The bridge was vibrating under her feet. The fox ran faster.

Into the street! There's a gap on the walkway. That's how the other woman died.

The fox swerved into the empty street, and kept her eyes fixed on the part of the bridge that wasn't moving. She was pretty sure that she was slightly more thrown than running when she reached the part where the bridge stopped moving.

But however it happened, she wasn't hurt, and the bridge was only slightly vibrating under her feet instead of raising her to an unsteady height. The fox slowed her steps and continued on the way to the beach.

As she got closer, a sound attracted her attention. A dog. Someone was walking their dog. And they were coming closer.

The fox dove into a nearby hibiscus shrub and waited. The dog and owner turned the corner a minute later.

Like she had known, hiding in the shrub was not enough to escape the dog's attention. As the dog sniffed, the fox shivered with the need to run, to move.

"No, come on." The owner pulled at the leash. A minute later, they were gone. The little fox waited another moment before leaving and continuing on her way.

When she reached the beach, the first thing she did was plop down in the sand for a few minutes. The world was a dangerous place for a little fox and she wasn't sure she was calm yet.

But the danger was past, and there wasn't any current threat, so it didn't take long for her to want to explore her surroundings.

The beach was deserted, as she expected, since it was closed after sunset. There were other beaches nearby that were open after dark, at least sometimes, but this one wasn't. Not that there was much beyond a sign to deter trespassers. Then again, there wasn't much here in the first place. There was a dock on the end of the beach, but currently there were no boats tied to it. Near the dock were tufts of some kind of sea or beach grass, under the dock was some wood, probably rotten discards from the dock, and some trash that no one had cleaned up. Even the seagulls weren't around.

Probably they were at one of the other beaches, one that got more people and probably more food. Just as well. Seagulls were a little too big and very aggressive for her to want to take on in this form. At least on a night where she just wanted to play.

After a moment, the fox started rolling in the sand. The other voice seemed irritated at this, thinking about getting sand out of fur. But the fox just sent thoughts of a brush. Brushes were good and could get all the sand out easy. The older fox could just brush them! That would be nice.

He's not here.

That was a problem. They would have to have him come along next time. But it would wait for later. Right now, she wanted to dig. Sand was easy to dig in.

The fox spent a while digging holes in the sand. It wasn't solid enough to build tunnels in and for them to stay. Sometimes she chased crabs when she came close. Some she ate, others she let escape. She had just gotten to the point of wondering if she wanted to play in the water, when people entered the beach.

The fox stopped and looked at them. She wasn't sure she liked people watching her. It wouldn't do any harm, though. Or at least, it shouldn't. Most humans didn't care what foxes did. Even if they did watch for a little while, what would it matter?

Still, she moved a little closer to the dock, just in case. It would be easier to hide there if she decided she needed to.

The people, two males, not children, but not full grown either, didn't seem to see her at first, as they set up on some rocks, not too far from the dock.

After a few minutes of watching them sit there and drink, the fox decided they probably weren't a threat and went back to looking for crabs. Or maybe some clams. A snack sounded good right about now.

She had just found a crab when she heard one of them speak. "Hey, what's that?"

Unsurprisingly, he was pointing at her.

"It's just a dog."

Hmph! A dog, indeed. Not very bright, these trespassers. True, she was a pretty good distance and humans didn't see as well in the dark as she did, but the moon was high and bright and she was what humans considered a bright color.

"Are you sure? Doesn't look quite right." The first human said.

"It's a dog." The second human picked up a bottle and threw it in her direction, the bottle shattering when it hit the ground, glass scattering everywhere. "Scat! Get out of here!"

The fox darted under the docks, hiding in the underbrush. The bottle hadn't come too close to hitting her, but it was enough to spook her and anger the other voice inside her head.

I think they need to learn a little lesson. Don't you?

The fox hesitated. Yes, the other voice could handle them easily, especially if they changed back. But the other voice didn't want to change back, not with their clothes far away. No, the other voice wanted *her* to handle things. And she wasn't sure that was a good idea when they were so much bigger, and she thought she smelled a very faint hint of gun powder.

Yes, she could just make out a gleam of a gun in the bag by the first human. A small handgun that the fox was sure her other voice could identify if they got close enough. But she didn't want to get that close.

Maybe it would be better to stay hidden until they left. Even if it looked like they planned to stay awhile as they not just settled into their conversation but actually started to build a fire from wood under the dock and their own rubbish.

A stupid plan, since fires weren't allowed even during the day, let alone at night. Besides, the wood was likely to be waterlogged and rotten. Maybe they wouldn't succeed at all.

But in the end, they did. It took them over an hour, and the fire wasn't very big, but they succeeded in building one.

The fox settled in to wait. They'd leave eventually. Maybe she would just take a nap.

Then they started talking again. She ignored it at first, but her other voice was getting agitated, so she tuned in to listen.

"Are you sure about this?" The first human, the one with the gun in his bag asked. "If this goes wrong, it's ten to twenty. Twenty-five to life, if worst comes to worst."

Twenty-five to life is the jail sentence for murder. There was a pause, probably the other voice trying to pull up random information. *Ten to twenty years is the sentence for armed robbery in Florida.*

"I'm telling you, nothing is going to go wrong. I've *been* to that store, plenty of times. It's owned by this little old Mexican couple. No cameras, no guns, they probably wouldn't even call the police. I'm not even sure they're here legally. They didn't report it when the window got broken a month ago. Go when the wife is running the counter. She'll fold as soon as she sees the gun, and he won't do anything with his wife in danger. We get the money and split."

That is a stupid plan.

Very stupid.

If he had been to the store multiple times, then he might be recognized. People don't always react the way you think they will, especially when you are an amateur thug who thinks everyone will fold at the sight of a gun. Panicky people are dangerous and as likely as not to do the worst possible thing in any situation. And it was entirely possible the couple *had* called the police and these idiots just didn't know it.

The fox let the other voice have a bit more say. They would have to plan this carefully.

***

The other voice seemed pretty sure that these two hadn't actually tried to rob anyone before, or they wouldn't be quite this stupid about it. Maybe getting stopped tonight would help them as well, preventing them from ever going down that path. And if it didn't, well, that was hardly their problem.

The humans were doing part of her job for her, by letting themselves get drunk. Supposedly for courage. It wasn't working. The first human was getting more and more unnerved.

The fire was burning brighter than the fox had expected them to manage. Which might actually work to her advantage.

After she had made some initial preparations, the fox crept closer, staring directly at the first human. He half-turned, saw her eyes reflecting the fire, and screamed.

She ran off while his friend jumped up. "What? What is it? What did you see?"

"These eyes! They were glowing!"

"What? What are you talking about?"

"There was a pair of glowing eyes! That's what I'm talking about!"

The second human huffed in disgust as he went back to sitting on a log. "Sit down. It was probably just that dog. Remember? From earlier?"

"Dogs don't have glowing eyes!"

Then maybe it was a cat!" He rubbed a hand across his face. "Just forget about it."

The first human sat down again, grabbing the bag long enough to pull out another bottle of beer before dropping the bag slightly behind him.

There was silence for a while. Long enough for a small fox to steal the gun from the bag, take it back to the dock, and bury it under a few inches of sand.

"What if it was a ghost?" The first human asked, in a voice like he didn't actually want to be heard.

The second human clearly heard anyway and scoffed. "There's no such thing as ghosts."

Well, you really couldn't ask for a better set-up than that.

She screamed.

Fox mating calls were very unnerving to those who weren't familiar with them. So was the Vixen's Wail.

Both humans jumped. "What was that?" shouted the second human.

"It's a ghost!"

"Ghosts aren't real! But it sounds like a woman being murdered!"

No, that's peacocks.

The humans looked at each other, before seemingly coming to an agreement. Human Two started banking the fire, while Human One packed up the bag, not noticing that she had stolen two of the beer bottles. He *did* notice the missing gun.

"Where's the gun?"

"What? You have it!"

"No, I don't! It's not here!"

Human Two covered Human One's mouth. "Be quiet. If something bad is happening, we don't want to be caught here," he hissed.

Human One pushed him away. "The gun is registered in my dad's name. If it gets found..."

They looked around. The fox screamed again.

"Forget it! Let's just get out of here," the second human insisted. The first human nodded.

The fox knew that humans didn't have the night vision foxes did, but she was still surprised that between the two of them, they managed to trip in at least three of the holes she had dug and slip and fall on the bottles that *some* little fox had *accidentally* left lying on the ground in the shadows.

Then she screamed one more time, just for good measure.

The humans stumbled off the beach, into the parking lot...

And almost directly into a pair of cops that even she was surprised to see.

"Do you gentleman know anything about the reports of a fire on the beach? Or the screaming?" The policewoman asked, sounding like she had a pretty good idea that they did.

"Um, no?" Human One tried.

"Uh huh." The policeman looked no more impressed than his partner. "So you were just, what... trespassing? Drunk and disorderly?" He looked toward the beach. "Looks like littering and vandalism...?"

The two miscreants looked at each other. "Um, yeah. Yeah, we did that," Human Two admitted. "But, um, it sounds like some woman might be in trouble. Shouldn't you be worried about that?"

The fox screamed again, causing all the humans to jump. "Is that the screaming?" The policewoman asked.

"I'll check it out," The policeman offered. "You watch them."

"Don't any of you know a fox when you hear one? Look, over there." The policewoman pointed, as the fox let herself be seen. "City folks," she said with a sigh of not quite disdain.

The little fox decided it was time to go home. Tomorrow, her human self could take care of the gun, and maybe see what happened with the idiots. For now, it was time to go. The police could take care of things from here.

***

Liska yawned as she sat down with her breakfast, joining Todd, Jamal, and Shahara. It had been a long night, but worth it. She felt better than she had in a while.

"Hey, Anna. Bad night?" Todd asked.

"No, just stayed up too late."

"Oh? What kept you up all night?" Shahara asked, teasing smile on her face.

Liska took a drink of water before answering, "Oh, just studying. Nothing all that exciting."

Also Look For:

The Hyde Chronicles: Book One

The Pawn's Play

By H. J. Harding

Violet Peters was ecstatic to get a full scholarship to her dream school, Hyde University, and accepted before she even saw the campus. It wasn't until she got there that she learned the school was stranger than she thought and that she is currently the only human student. Her roommate is a vampire, the librarian is a dragon, and some inhabitants aren't anything she's ever heard of. Trying to learn the truth of a reality she had no idea existed, it takes a little time to realize how unpopular humans are here. A couple near-death experiences later, and Violet is forced to conclude someone wants her gone, no matter what it takes. Caught in a web beyond her understanding, Violet finds herself a pawn to forces out of her control. But even a pawn can checkmate a king.

Also Look For:

Moonlit Memories: Book Two

Nightmare's Revenge

By H. J. Harding

Liska hoped her second semester of college would be quieter than her first. She was wrong. Within her first week it's clear that last semester's problems aren't over and she isn't fully recovered. Then she has to uncover who betrayed a sworn ally to prove her own innocence. Add in an unexpected encounter from the past that complicates her fledgling relationship with Todd, and classes become the least of her concerns.

And then there's Nightmare...

Also Look For:

Those Who Go Do Not Return

By H. J. Harding

The king summoned four people to his elaborate throne room to assign them a quest. Lakara, a scholar who has spent almost her entire life in the palace. Davorin, the best and youngest known necromancer in the land. Sir Jors, a knight who has served for ten years, but who may have been rendered a liability and is on his last chance. Kita, an outsider and thief who is given the choice of going on the quest or being executed. All four are ordered to find the Jewel of Ishni, a gem with no powers of its own but desired by the gods who fought over it.

With no trust and every one of them concealing secrets that could mean death or failure, they must learn to work together, or Death may claim them all.

Also by the Author

Moonlit Memories Series:

Secrets of the Moon Fox

Nightmare's Revenge

Ring of Blood

Hyde Chronicles:

The Pawn's Play

Knightfall

The Bishop's Decoy

Other books:

Those Who Go Do Not Return

Non-Fiction:

Lavender: An Essential Guide